OPERATION PANIC

COLD WAR STORIES OF THE ATOMIC BOMB

EDITED BY

JIMMY J. PACK JR.
& TOM HAZUKA

OPERATION PANIC

COLD WAR STORIES OF THE ATOMIC BOMB

EDITED BY
JIMMY J. PACK JR.
& TOM HAZUKA

Woodhall Press | Norwalk, CT

woodhall press

Woodhall Press, Norwalk, CT 06855
WoodhallPress.com
Copyright © 2024

Cover design: LJ Mucci
Layout artist: LJ Mucci

Library of Congress Cataloging-in-Publication Data available

ISBN 978-1-960456-07-6   (paper: alk paper)
ISBN 978-1-960456-08-3   (electronic)

First Edition
Distributed by Independent Publishers Group
(800) 888-4741

Printed in the United States of America

This book would not be possible without the help of Robert Colombo, Ann Pohl, Emily Pohl-Weary, John Henry Angell, and Earl Terry Kemp in finding the copyright holders of some of the stories. Thank you to Thomas W. Van Osten IV for working on a year-long project with Jimmy J. on Paranoia and the Cold War, and Hudson Saffell for offering Cold War military insight, which were the inspiration for the book. Thank you to Peter Mazzaccaro and Daniel Pulka for proofreading and feedback on the development of the book.

TABLE OF CONTENTS

---⊛---

Crossroads

Warning...

Blast!

Fallout—

Introduction:
The Perpetual Anxiety of the Cold War

Around 2:45 a.m. on August 6th, 1945, a B-29 Superfortress named Enola Gay took off from the air base at North Field, Tinian, in the Marianas Islands. The plane climbed to 9,200 feet and joined two identical bombers over the island of Iwo Jima. The squadron ascended to roughly 31,000 feet and set course for the Japanese mainland—six hours flying time from Tinian.

Japanese radar systems had detected several large groupings of American bombers heading toward major mainland cities during the late evening and early morning of August 5th into the 6th. Alerts were sounded in these cities. In Hiroshima, the all-clear was given just after midnight on the 6th. At around 7:00 a.m., the alert sounded again. Shortly thereafter, the all-clear was given.

Hiroshima had been experiencing its own sense of creeping paranoia. It was one of a handful of major Japanese cities that had been spared incendiary bombing raids like the one in March that destroyed sixteen square miles of central Tokyo, causing massive casualties. The eerie song of the air-raid sirens was a daily occurrence—each time followed by nothing. The everyday back and forth between warning and all-clear wore on the nerves of Hiroshima's citizens. Questions lingered: Why have we been spared? Are the Americans saving something special for Hiroshima? But time passed and life went on. When the siren sounded on August 6th, few people paid much attention to it.

Around 7:00 a.m., 31,000 feet above and not far south of the city, Second Lieutenant Morris R. Jeppson began removing the safety devices from the Super Fortress's payload: "Little Boy," a 9,700-pound bomb, ten feet long and seven feet wide, filled with 140 pounds of uranium-235 that upon fission would be capable of producing a blast equivalent to 16 kilotons of TNT. Jeppson removed three red plugs that resembled car cigarette lighters and replaced them with three green plugs, completing the internal circuitry of the enormous, experimental device. At 8:15, Little Boy was released from the Super Fortress. For fifty-three tense seconds, the only sound the crew of the Enola Gay heard was the roar of the engines. Then the bomb detonated 1,900 feet above the city, sending shock waves that buffeted the plane. The blast destroyed everything within a one-mile radius of the epicenter and caused major destruction four-and-a-half miles outward. Approximately 70% of the buildings in Hiroshima were destroyed. 80,000 people died within seconds.

As the now iconic mushroom cloud rose over Japan, the specter of atomic annihilation spread over the planet. When Nagasaki was bombed three days later, it was clear that the days of conventional combat between world powers might be over and that a new age of unprecedented potential destruction had arrived. The atomic era had dawned, and a heretofore unimaginable level of paranoia began to creep over the world.

One War Ends, Another Begins

When the Empire of Japan surrendered on August 15th, 1945, Americans were jubilant. A long, horrific war had finally ended. To many, it seemed that U.S. ingenuity and technological prowess had won the day and saved thousands of lives and months, even years, of fighting in the Pacific. The Soviet Union, however, was grappling with what to do in the face of a massive new power possessed by their former ally—and now rival. The modest Soviet atomic program was pushed into overdrive. By August of 1949, the USSR possessed its first working atomic weapon, dubbed "Joe-1" by American intelligence. The halcyon years of post-war America were over; the arms race had begun. With both powers possessing atomic weapons, the possibility of atomic war became a terrifying reality, a reality the United States had to be prepared for.

The arms race between the United States and the Soviet Union was one of unprecedented scale and technological innovation. Even in the immediate wake of Hiroshima and Nagasaki, scientists in both countries were dreaming of bigger and better bombs. Physicists knew of a far more powerful force than fission: fusion. If a bomb could be created employing a fusion reaction, the results would be inconceivably more destructive than ever before. Out of this dream, the hydrogen bomb, the world's first thermonuclear weapon, was created by American scientists in 1952. Soviet versions soon followed.

The Atomic Bomb and the End of the World, by W.D. Herrstrom, was printed in 1945, mere months after the dropping of the bombs on Hiroshima and Nagasaki. Herrstrom billed himself as a "World Traveler, News Photographer, Prophetic Analyst." He was also a Reverend who edited a series of publications titled *Bible News Flashes* of which *The Atomic Bomb and the End of the World* was a part. Publications such as these and the preparedness pamphlets offered by the Federal Civil Defense Administration helped fuel paranoia of atomic war.

U.S. and Soviet Union leaders knew that with weapons this powerful any atomic engagement could mean the end of life on earth. Therefore, atomic deterrents needed to be psychological. The arms race became a high-stakes mind-game, as the governments of both nations tried to shift responsibility for atomic destruction onto the other side. Each country claimed it was forced to build up its atomic arsenal to defend against aggression from the other, thus making "the other" the bad guy. With the populace firmly behind the idea of "the other" as a threat, and the only clear defense a build-up of atomic weapons, the arms race escalated quickly.

The United States government sought to assuage the fear of American citizens that atomic weapons were a threat to all life on the planet. On December 1st, 1950, President Harry Truman established the Federal Civil Defense Administration (FCDA), charged with preparing and protecting the American public in the event of a atomic catastrophe. This organization helped create the narrative that it was not atomic weapons that threatened mankind, but the Soviet Union and its insidious Communist ways.

[2]The FCDA was the Cold War precursor to FEMA. It was this organization (which became The Office of Civil Defense Mobilization in 1958, then the Department of Defense's Office of Civil Defense in 1961) that brought us the (in)famous "Duck and Cover" cartoons featuring Bert the Turtle. The Civil Defense structure was a pyramid, with the federal gov- ernment on top, then state governments, local and municipal governments, and finally the average citizen. Each level of the organization was charged with coordinating the ones below it.

President Eisenhower's administration acknowledged a need for a coordinated civil defense program, but it refused, as did much of Congress, to fund a national program. Eisenhower worried that a garrison state would result from a federal government constantly preparing for war. Responsibility fell to the states, who did receive federal money to create their civil defense plans, but this approach created a Potemkin village of fallout shelters and duck

On March 17, 1953, the FCDA took part in an "experiment" during the Annie blast (the first of 11 explosions) as part of Operation Upshot-Knothole. Operation Doorstep measured the effects of an atomic blast on houses, cars, and fallout shelters. For more images from the booklet pictured above, see page 110.

and cover drills that had much of the country convinced that an atomic war with the "commies" was inevitable.

If one blast north of Las Vegas could contaminate milk in New York State, imagine what a blast in the middle of the country could do? Or a blast in New York, Chicago, or Los Angeles? Government officials were fully aware that atomic war would be catastrophic, so much so that analysts coined a new term to measure the destruction: megadeath. One megadeath equals one million deaths. The loss of lives in an atomic conflict would be measured in megadeaths. Millions upon millions of people would die, many of them cooked in their fallout shelters where they had been told they would be safe.

Civil Defense was highly influential in American culture throughout the early Cold War period. It was the Federal Government's mouthpiece to communicate with ordinary citizens and played a critical role in creating a culture of paranoia in the United States. One way this was achieved was by redirecting Americans' fears of atomic weapons to a fear of the Soviet Union, a.k.a. the enemy of freedom, democracy, and American values that was eager to bomb the U.S. into oblivion given half a chance.

The Soviet government painted the United States in similar villainous terms to its citizens. But people just wanted to go about their business unhindered. The real threat was in the mere existence of atomic bombs and their ability to destroy the entire world. In other words, the real danger of the Cold War was not the political differences between the United States and the Soviet Union, but the fact that "The Bomb" existed. Concepts such as Launch on Warning and Mutually Assured Destruction (MAD) made ever clearer the likelihood that should a conflict escalate into atomic war, most of humanity would not survive, and civilization as we knew it would disappear.

Cold War Paranoia and its Literary Influence

The possibility that the earth might be destroyed manifested itself in many facets of popular culture, particularly in science fiction. During the Cold War, science fiction became extremely popular and widely read. Magazines such as *Amazing Stories, IF, Galaxy Science Fiction,* and *Astounding Science Fiction* flourished, their content fueled by an increasingly anxious public seeking diversion from, and answers to, the possibility of atomic annihilation.

The science fiction of the early Cold War deals with the idea of "The Bomb" both directly and indirectly. That is to say, in some stories atomic weapons are central to the plot, whereas in others there is a proxy for the bomb: aliens, natural disasters, mutant creatures created by radiation. Popular magazines such as *The Saturday*

Evening Post and *Collier's* were widely circulated mediums for the type of science fiction that reflected the paranoia of Cold War America. These magazines had a large readership and regularly featured writing that reflected the sentiments of their readers. For example, Philip Wylie's short story "Blunder" in the January 12th, 1946 edition of *Collier's* explores the destruction of the entire planet from a single atomic explosion.

Cold War-era writers often helped perpetuate paranoia, even if they were trying to parody it. Pulp magazines frequently printed stories with themes of paranoia. Douglas Angus's "About Time to Go South," published in *The Magazine of Fantasy and Science Fiction* in 1957, explores what the familiar landscape of America might be like after an atomic exchange. The main characters recall the days of bustling city corners and everyday life that are long gone. The survivors in a post-atomic-war-world suggest that because these highly destructive weapons exist, they will be used; something will trip in the system—the missiles will fly.

Other pulp stories focused on the immediate dangers of atomic warfare. William Tenn's "The Quick and the Bomb," from a 1951 issue of *Suspense*, focuses on the members of the Plunkett family as they practice their drill for an atomic attack. The idea of preparedness corresponds with civil defense as both a method of self-preservation and an ideology. A sturdy, well supplied shelter would keep you alive, and preparedness was the duty of every self-respecting citizen of the United States. The Plunketts are the epitome of this, and of course events do not go as they planned.

Philip K. Dick's "Foster, You're Dead" has a completely opposite take on the U.S.'s civil defense program than Tenn's—if the program is so important, why doesn't the government fund shelters? Dick views civil defense as a capitalist cash-grab for the low-hanging fruit of paranoia—buy a shelter and feel the same comfort as a security blanket, and be equally as "protected" from an atomic war as well.

Ever popular was the idea of aliens as a proxy for Soviets, not only in movies like *Invasion of the Body Snatchers* (based on a series of short stories, "The Body Snatchers," by Jack Finney, published in three parts in *Collier's* magazine, starting on November 26, 1954), but in pulp fiction as well. Theodore L. Thomas' story "Day of Succession," from the August 1959 issue of *Astounding Science Fiction*, deals with the threat of a Soviet invasion that uses aliens as a proxy for hostile Soviet invaders. The story opens in the relatively near future (1979) with a familiar scene: an unidentified object headed fast toward American airspace before making a beeline from Soviet territory.

But of all the stories, the most haunting images come from authors who create a post-atomic war U.S. Cold War era authors like Judith Merril and Carol Amen imagine a world in which the course of human history is irreparably altered—Merril's "That

Only a Mother" delves into the effects of lingering radiation on one particular family, whereas Amen's "Last Testament" asks readers to cope with the effects of a full scale atomic war with the main character, a recently widowed mother, and her three children.

In Fritz Leiber's "A Bad Day for Sales," published in *Galaxy* in 1953, readers are presented with another grisly image of life after an atomic bomb blast. Leiber, like Dick, plays with the trope of American consumerism; his central character is a robot designed to scan potential customers and market appropriate goods to them. It's a startlingly accurate picture of what marketing has become today, however radical and far-fetched it seemed in the fifties.

Operation Panic: Cold War Stories of the Atomic Bomb is divided into three sections: before (Warning…), during (Blast!) and after (Fallout…) an atomic attack. The book explores these familiar topics through an unfamiliar approach: a collection of rare, hard-to-find pieces from publications that no longer exist, which provide insight into people's lives and concerns during roughly the first decade of the Cold War. One of our goals is to give readers a glimpse into the past to understand a fear that defined three+ generations, and to understand the gender/sex roles of the time. Also of note to readers, this fiction was geared toward white suburban America. Demonstrating an inherent bias of the era, Black and other marginalized characters rarely appear in these stories.

At the heart of this book is the reminder that although Americans today rarely see the formerly ubiquitous yellow and black fallout shelter signs bolted to the sides of public buildings anymore, the threat of atomic war is still here.

Federal Civil Defense Insignia

Warning...

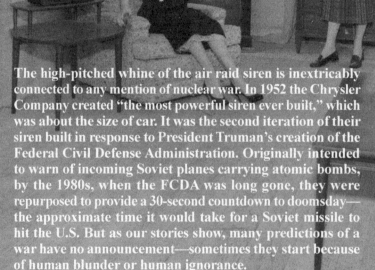

The high-pitched whine of the air raid siren is inextricably connected to any mention of nuclear war. In 1952 the Chrysler Company created "the most powerful siren ever built," which was about the size of car. It was the second iteration of their siren built in response to President Truman's creation of the Federal Civil Defense Administration. Originally intended to warn of incoming Soviet planes carrying atomic bombs, by the 1980s, when the FCDA was long gone, they were repurposed to provide a 30-second countdown to doomsday— the approximate time it would take for a Soviet missile to hit the U.S. But as our stories show, many predictions of a war have no announcement—sometimes they start because of human blunder or human ignorance.

Some Pigs in Sailor Suits
Roger Angell

George Swan came out of the revolving door and walked up the three steps to the lobby. He found himself taking off his hat and then wondering why he had. Going into his college club always made him feel that way; it was like walking into the home of a very rich man. Of course, the club had been built that way; the big leather chairs and heavy drapes would never have to be changed. They would be as much in style ten years from now as they were today, or as they had been fifteen years ago, when Swan had first seen the place. He had never joined the club. When he had graduated and come to work in the city, he couldn't afford it, and later, when he could have afforded it, he discovered that there were very few of his college friends who were, like himself, in the cotton-brokerage business. He liked his old friends but no longer could find much to talk to them about, and he and his wife agreed that it would be a waste for him to join. But he liked going back when someone invited him, if only because the club was the one place in the city that never seemed to change.

At the desk, the attendant told him that Mr. Connors was waiting for him in the bar and he was to go right in. He had started down the hall with his hat in his hand when the attendant called him back to check his hat and briefcase and topcoat at the coatroom by the desk.

In the panelled bar, Swan saw Russell Connors sitting at a round table in a corner with an Army colonel. Connors hadn't changed, either. Swan had seen that the day before, when he had bumped into him on the street and they had made this date for a drink. He was still as thin and red-cheeked as the last time Swan had seen him, five years before. Connors was an executive on a news magazine. Perhaps that was why Swan had agreed to meet him; magazine people were still a little exciting to him. Today Connors was wearing an expensive gray pin-striped suit with a discharge button in the lapel. His shirt collar had rounded points and was pinned under his tie with a gold clasp. His hair was thick and cleanly parted. When he rose and held out his hand, Swan noticed that he wore heavy gold cuff links.

"Hello, Georgie," Connors said, smiling. He shook Swan's hand vigorously. "This is great, simply great. I hope you don't mind my making this a party for three. Jim Lovering here was with me in Washington for a while, and he's just back from Japan and all over the map with a lot of interesting dope. Jim, this is Georgie Swan. We were in college together."

"How do you do," said Swan.

"Glad to know you, George," the Colonel said loudly, shaking his hand. "Any friend of Russ's."

Swan sat down, and Connors beckoned to a waiter. Swan saw that the two men were drinking highballs and ordered the same. He looked at the Colonel. Lovering was tanned and looked young, despite his short gray hair. He had a long nose and flaring nostrils. When he lit a cigarette, Swan let his eyes drop to the wings and the three rows of ribbons over his breast pocket. He didn't recognize any of the decorations.

"Jim has been trying to tell me that I got out of the Air Corps too soon," Connors said, grinning. "He thinks I should have turned into a career man and kept my membership card in the Pentagon Commandos."

"Not at all, Russ," Colonel Lovering said. "I knew none of you P.R.O. boys would stick—no reason for it. You're still in the same line and getting more for it now. Only right. I was just saying that this is the real time now. More doing today than any time I can remember. These next five years will see the biggest change in Air Corps history. Vital times, vital times. And I wouldn't miss a minute of it."

"Jim was just telling me about the bomb damage in Japan, George," Connors said. "I know you'll be interested, even if it isn't right up your alley. I'm not all filled in on it myself."

"Certainly," Swan said. "Go right ahead. I'd like to hear about it." He picked up the drink the waiter had brought and looked over the rim of the glass at the Colonel.

"Well," Lovering said thoughtfully, tapping his cigarette in an ashtray, "I had to tell Russ that this is mostly all off the record. The full report isn't out yet, and I can't even tell you all I know. Not yet. But I'll just have to ask you not to repeat this around. I know you're not a journalist, but you know how it is."

"Oh, certainly," Swan said. "Of course."

The Colonel took two swallows from his glass and quickly put it back on the table. "I was telling Russ about the difference between Japan and the E.T.O. in this business of bomb-damage appraisal. During the war, that is. Those boys in England got all hopped up back in 1943 and 1944 and overestimated their bomb damage. Partly their fault, partly P.R.O.s' fault. Made good reading. Then came the payoff. You remember what happened last spring, Russ."

"Don't I just!" Connors said, shaking his head. "There was a hell of a stink, even in Washington."

"Sure," the Colonel said. "Natural thing. Those ground-forces boys got into Germany and they began to look around. They'd find a target that had been declared wiped out still producing. Not much, maybe, but still turning out steel or oil or what have you. And didn't they yell about it! Y'see, they'd been waiting years for that, just to give the fly boys the business, and they sure poured it on. We heard about it right off, out where we were, on Guam. A lot of the boys with us were from the E.T.O., and they got smart and real careful in a hurry. Now we knew, for instance, that the 29s were raising hell, absolute hell, in Japan. But did we yell about it? No, sir. We went good and easy..."

He was silent as the waiter brought three fresh drinks to the table. Swan discovered that he hadn't finished his. He gulped it and handed the empty glass to the waiter. As the Colonel went on talking, Swan stole a glance at Connors. He was completely absorbed, looking at Lovering's face. Now and then he would nod his head or smile slightly at something Lovering said. Even when he drank, he never took his eyes off the Colonel.

"And Osaka was almost as bad as Kobe," Lovering was saying. "Wasn't much to choose between any of 'em. And every place the same thing happened, we had to revise our figures upward. Now, in Osaka, we'd figured, still goin' easy, on ten square miles burnt out from photos. That's about twenty per cent of the city. But when we got there, it was a good thirty-five per cent—thirty-five per cent, easy. Why, the Japs themselves estimated over fifty per cent, but of course they'd had a lot of personnel losses and they were still a little excited. Thirty-five per cent is closer. But you can bet that it made us all happy, especially the big boys."

"And that campaign took fewer bombers than anything in the E.T.O.," Connors said.

"Sure, but it's not the same thing. Not the same at all. I've always been the first to say it. There never was a good test of all-out bombing against a modern city. Over there in Germany they just had G.P.s and the old incendiaries. That's what they worked with just about all the time."

"G.P.s?" repeated Swan.

"General-purpose bombs," Connors said to him quickly. "High explosive. Go ahead, Jim."

The Colonel finished his drink. "Now, as you know," he said, lighting another cigarette, "we were dealing almost exclusively with M-69s. Fire bombs were right for Japan. Those flimsy houses and slums were all built for us. They were what gave us our percentages. And I'm the first to admit that against German cities or any really modern target, we wouldn't have looked so good. Now, I look at it like this. In the

E.T.O. they had G.P.s. We had the M-69. But if we'd used the G.P.s first, say against a big modern city like Chicago, and then had come in with M-69s, we'd have had a test. That would have been the real business: G.P.s to get the walls and concrete, then the fire to burn out the wreckage. Now, that never happened to a city, so we can't tell. But I claim it would be something to see. Yes, sir, something to see." He slapped the table lightly with the ends of his fingers and sat back in his chair, looking from Connors to Swan.

Connors beckoned to the waiter again, then leaned forward toward Lovering. "But doesn't this atomic deal put that all out of date?" he asked in a low voice.

Again the Colonel paused while the waiter served the drinks. This time Swan had finished his, and he picked up a full glass immediately.

"Naturally, Russ," Lovering said. "At least, that's what we all suspect. And we're going to find out more in July at the Crossroads unless these god-damned agitators put a crimp in it. Now, I shouldn't be telling you this"—he leaned forward across the table—"but I think I've got a good chance to go along on this Crossroads business. In fact, I'll know on Monday. My old boss is in it up to his teeth, and I have a hunch he'll take me on out to Bikini. I want to get in on this Big A stuff. Why, in five years it may be the whole show."

"The Big A?" asked Connors.

"Yeah, that's what I call it," Lovering said.

"Jim, that's damned good," said Connors. "Damned good. The Big A. I like that. Would it be O.K. with you if we used that? It's a new touch—just what we like." He had taken a gold pencil and a little leather notebook from his inside coat pocket.

"Why, sure thing, Russ," Lovering said, smiling. "I didn't think anything about it. It's just what some of the boys call it. Do you really think you'll use it?"

"The Scarlet Letter," Swan said unexpectedly.

There was a pause as the other two men looked at him. "What?" asked the Colonel finally.

"The Scarlet Letter," Swan repeated. "The Scarlet Letter was a Big A."

"What is this, some gag?" asked the Colonel, smiling. "Something from college?"

"That's right," Connors said quickly, looking at Swan. "Just something from college." Swan thought he saw Connors frown at him and shake his head slightly as he put his pencil away. Swan's tongue felt dry. He looked at his glass and then took a big swallow of liquor.

"I just spent two weeks in New Mexico with those kids," he heard Lovering say, "and I've never seen anything like it. Those boys are fighting for the privilege of flying that plane with the bomb just like kids fighting to make the first team in college. It does your heart good. That's what I mean about vital times. I can't remember ever seeing morale so high. Now, you hear all these officers bitching about losing a big army. Not me. I say let's lose 'em. Let's separate the men from the boys. Get the grousers and the malcontents back to their wives, if that's what they want so damned much. We don't want 'em. I'll just stick with those men I saw in New Mexico. They're making the future and they know it. They're happy about it."

"What about those people on Bikini?" Swan asked. "How's their morale?"

"Who, the scientists?"

"No, the natives. I saw a picture of them getting ready to move, and they didn't look so happy."

"Oh, hell," Lovering said in a relieved tone. "You mean the gooks. Well, I wouldn't worry about them. I've seen them, millions of them, and I've seen their islands. Why, the Marshalls are just crawling with lousy islands like that, all alike. Those gooks are just being taken off one and put on another. It'll give them something to talk about, and in six weeks they'll forget all about it. Don't worry about the gooks; they're not worried. I'll tell you who is jumpy, though. I'll tell you the really nervous boys." He was grinning now. "That's the Navy. Those little boys in blue are just scared breathless they're all going to be out of jobs. They're busy as a cat on a tin roof, trying to scratch up some excuse for themselves if this test does what we think it will to their ships. Christ, I have to laugh. After the way those boys carried on about winning the war out there—singlehanded, too."

"I understand they're going to dress the pigs in sailor suits," said Swan. He put his empty glass down on the table, conscious of the eyes of the other two men on him.

"What?" said Connors.

"In the test—that test," Swan said, looking at the table. "All those pigs. I read about it."

"Oh," said Lovering, "I know what he means. You mean flashproof clothing, like the sailors wear, don't you?" he asked loudly, as if Swan were deaf.

"And goats in the turrets," Swan said. He was feeling a little drunk, and he tried to concentrate on Lovering's face. "Go ahead," he said. "Tell about those pigs."

"Well, you're right about those pigs and goats," Lovering said as Connors waved to the waiter again. "The medics and the scientists want wounded animals, not dead ones. They want to test victims. They got pigs and goats because they're big, like men. And pigs have a skin like human skin. Some of the pigs will wear flashproof clothing, like Navy gunners. They've got rats, too—thousands of 'em. I don't know too much about that, though—not my line. This show is more for the medics and the Navy. Now, if they were testing a city, I'd have been in on it from the start. That's one thing that was too bad about Hiroshima and Nagasaki. With the war still on, we couldn't do much but drop the things. A war's a bad place for a really scientific test. Can't get in quick enough to check on immediate results. Photos, sure, but what can you tell from photos? By the time you get in, the casualties are gone, personnel replaced, streets policed up. Nothing to do but look at what's left and make a guess at your effectiveness. No, I say the Big A was never really tested against a city—scientifically tested. And, as I said, those Jap cities are no real criterion. I saw 'em; I know."

"That's true, Jim, very true," Connors said. "I'd never realized that, but I'm sure you're right."

"No doubt about it," Lovering said, picking up the fresh drink the waiter had just brought.

"Now, Jim," Connors began, leaning forward, "this is presumptuous and don't feel that you have to answer. But just what do you believe would happen in a big city like this? Off the record, of course."

"Well, now," the Colonel said, and then paused. "Well, I think that's a fair question, Russ. Something I've been considering, too. Matter of fact, I looked at the city with that in mind yesterday in the taxi when I came from the terminal. But even with this old Model T bomb they're using at Crossroads it's hard to say. You have lots of imponderables, new factors: skyscrapers, subways, all permanent buildings, and the like. But I think these civilian extremists are way off in one thing, and that's blast damage. From all I know, it would be much less, with this old bomb, than they estimate. Sure, you'd lose walls, plenty of small buildings in residential districts, but all replaceable stuff. Maybe a few big buildings, but not half what they figure. Of course, your big losses would be from the heat—personnel losses."

"What?" said Swan.

"I say it's the heat that'll be most effective, not blast," Lovering said, "So your main losses would be personnel, not construction."

"You mean people?" Swan asked in a loud, angry voice.

"Yeah," said the Colonel, puzzled. "People—personnel. Nothing irreplaceable. Depend mostly on the time of day for your casualty figures, of course. But your permanent features—buildings, streets—would take it better than most people imagine."

"You've got it down pretty fine, haven't you?" Swan said after a moment. "I'll bet you know the percentages already, don't you? They're all right in your head."

"How do you mean?" asked the Colonel. "I don't get you. As I said, it's just my estimate. We don't know for sure. We're just working with pigs and battleships now. Not cities. Does that answer your question?"

But Swan, looking angrily at the Colonel, didn't reply. Finally, it was Connors who spoke. He was looking up at the high ceiling of the panelled bar, his drink held neatly away from his crossed legs and well-pressed trousers. "It would be something to see, though, wouldn't it?" he said musingly. "A big place like this, I mean. A whole city, all built up like this."

"Hell, yes," said the Colonel, smiling. "It'll be something to see, all right."

The Federal Civil Defense Administration's Operation Cue exhibit with different types of homes and shelters about to be exposed to atomic blasts. (Photo United States Archives.)

End of the Race
Albert Bermel

At that time the nations known as America and Russia had set off 2,500 nuclear explosions, pulverized every small island in the Pacific, Arctic and Indian Oceans, blown out of the earth lumps of great magnitude and little mineralogical value, and saturated the enclosing atmosphere and stratosphere with new elements, from Strontium-90 to Neptunium-237. It was then that the American Secretary of State and the Russian Foreign Minister pointed out to their respective leaders that the "tests," as these detonations were popularly called, had not been successful. "By not successful," the Secretary of State added, "I mean that we have failed to widen the gap."

"By not successful," the Foreign Minister elaborated, "I mean that we have failed to widen the gap."

The leaders of both nations immediately called for a conference and met near a beautiful lake in an intermediate country. Warmed by their consultations with eighty-proof bourbon and one-hundred-ten-proof vodka, they agreed that they would neither widen the gap nor narrow it, but simply eliminate gaps once and for all. The Russian leader told the story of a Ukrainian peasant who loved to eat bacon, "but he was so fond of his pig that he could not bring himself to kill it. He therefore swapped pigs with his neighbor." The American leader replied: "We must not hesitate to make sacrifices and, as our scientists have repeatedly stated, we must not be afraid to think about the unthinkable."

The conversation continued in this vein for forty-five minutes. As a result, the leaders drew up the outline for a new treaty: they would each drop one medium-sized hydrogen bomb—with a 150-megaton yield—onto the other's home territory, or over it, whichever proved the more convenient. This co-operative action would have two advantages or, as the American leader expressed it, two consumer benefits. Firstly, the impact of the explosions could be tested, not on thin air alone but also on people. Secondly, the two countries would be able to try out their civil defense programs under genuine rather than simulated conditions.

The American leader said, "This ought to deter certain of our citizens from sitting down in Times Square during drill time." The Russian leader answered, "We allow nobody to sit down in Red Square at any time." The two men then shook hands, paid handsome tribute to the country in which they had convened as a bastion of international understanding, issued a cheerful communique which the news services somehow misinterpreted and flew away, the American leader to his yacht, the Russian leader to his dacha.

And it was then that the disagreements began.

Over Aquavita-flavored tea (*en verre*) and highballs à la Philadelphia, the Russian Foreign Minister and the American Secretary of State (with their Ambassadors to the United Nations in attendance) sat for twelve hours at an oval table inlaid with Mollweide's projection of the world in five colors, to implement the details of the treaty by selecting a Russian and an American city as targets. The principal difficulty was that the cities must be equal in population and wealth although, as the Foreign Minister observed, "We should be prepared to give or take a few citizens in exchange for a few hundred roubles."

There followed a number of fruitless comparisons between San Francisco and Kiev, Nijny-Novgorod and Detroit, Portland (Me.) and Archangel. The four men bent long over the Mollweide projection and eventually arrived at a temporary compromise, London and Warsaw. Then they parted for the night and their hotels in order to telephone the respective shores of Florida and the Black Sea.

The next morning they came together again with firm instructions from home to abandon the temporary compromise. Overnight, the Presidential yacht had bidden its second-in-command to "stay within Soviet boundaries but West of the Urals if humanly possible" and not to "sell America's Polish vote down the Vistula." The Chairman's dacha, on the other hand, had begun his discourse with a folk tale about a canny peasant from the Ukraine who had succeeded in exchanging a sparrow (Warsaw? London?) for a duck (London? Warsaw?), but the duck now had to be fed, whereas the sparrow had been capable of finding its own food and...

On the word "and" the Foreign Minister had fallen asleep with the receiver at his ear. He had awakened thirty-five minutes later, just in time to learn that the destruction of Warsaw would irrevocably lead to uprisings in Prague, Tirana, Sofia, Bucharest and God help the Red Army—Budapest. The message ended: "Did nobody think of East and West Berlin? Alternatively, the people of the Soviet Union would reluctantly have relinquished Peking for London, except that *Das Kapital* was written in the British Museum, and the People's Democracy of China almost certainly has its own atomic firecrackers and might retaliate."

After reshaping these communications in diplomatic terminology, the Foreign Minister and the Secretary of State again took up their bargaining.

To their surprise, and almost grudgingly, they came to terms within minutes. The American bomb would be dropped over Voronezh which, as the Secretary of State confided to his Ambassador, gave promising possibilities of fallout on Rostov, Dnepropetrovsk, Kursk, Kharkov and Moscow. The Ambassador studied Mollweide and saw that the Secretary was right. For Voronezh and its bonuses, the Secretary of State was more than willing to concede Columbus, Ohio, which, he explained, had long been considered a "test city" in a less conclusive sense by the American advertising community, as well as by several motivational research organizations. So Voronezh-Columbus it was, and in good time for lunch. The two Ambassadors to the United Nations gratefully fastened their briefcases and talked about an afternoon swim in the neighboring lake.

But during the caviar *aux trufles* the Foreign Minister looked thoughtful, and halfway through the *wurst piernontaise* he spoke a vehement *nyet* and called an afternoon session.

Sadly the Ambassadors reopened their briefcases at two p.m. The Foreign Minister now claimed—although he would not produce census figures to prove it — that the population of Voronezh had swollen considerably under the latest ten-year industrial plan, and that Baltimore would be more nearly equivalent than Columbus.

The Secretary of State could not accept this demand, in view of the proximity of Baltimore to New York. (The American Ambassador was momentarily surprised that his colleague had overlooked Washington, which was much closer). The Secretary then offered, in quick but unsuccessful succession: Atlanta, Little Rock (which the Foreign Minister rejected out of hand), New Orleans and Butte.

The conference thereupon "deadlocked," as most of the press reported. (By means of judicious leaks from two Northern senators and one Russian general, the corps of correspondents had been led to believe that the conference was concerned with the exchange of American alfalfa for Russian millet.)

That evening at a jazz concert in the Russian embassy the Foreign Minister was urged by his counterpart to relent, but in vain. The Secretary of State left early and lay inert on his hotel bed for over an hour, watching the pendulum of a cuckoo clock and wondering whether Baltimore and New York were worth the effort.

Top-secret telephone messages went out that night to Biscayne Bay and the Crimean waters, and were meticulously tapped by two espionage organizations, the KGB and the CIA. The following morning the American and Russian leaders returned almost simultaneously on the same airstrip and paid immediate tribute to their host, this tiny country from which the spirit of international good will irradiated the globe. Within an hour they had displayed the decisiveness for which both were famous, and had settled—that is, undeadlocked—the conference with a new agreement of breathtaking simplicity.

Russia would drop its own bomb on Moscow… and America would drop its own bomb on New York City.

Thus, thanks to an astute combination of statesmanship and generosity, the long-feared Third World War never came to pass.

THE EFFECT OF ONE 20 KILOTON ATOMIC BOMB ON OUR POPULATION

Sample Cities	Public Uneducated in Civil Defense No Civil Defense Program	An Educated Public with a Coordinated Civil Defense Program
	Number of Persons (1) *Killed and Injured*	*Number of Persons* (2) *Saved from being Killed and Injured*
BOSTON	152,000	78,000
NEW YORK	288,000	142,000
ATLANTA	84,000	44,000
CLEVELAND	112,000	56,000
CHICAGO	156,000	76,000
DENVER	64,000	33,000
DALLAS	132,000	64,000
SAN FRANCISCO	152,000	77,000
SEATTLE	60,000	32,000

(1) *Estimated casualties resulting from one 20 kiloton atomic bomb exploded in the air during daytime without warning.*

(2) *Based on assumption that casualties would be reduced by approximately one-half.*

The Federal Civil Defense Administration's comparison of estimated casualties of a full scale atomic war. These numbers are all theoretical, based on the results of the bombing of Hiroshima and Nagasaki, as well as the few atomic bomb tests that took place in the early 1950s.

MODERN VOICE OF
Independence!

CHRYSLER AIR RAID SIREN
sounds loudest warning you've ever heard!

First announcement that Americans would willingly fight for freedom came with the ringing of the Liberty Bell atop Independence Hall, 176 years ago.

Today, as more and more cities and towns observe Civil Defense precautions, American determination to defend that freedom sounds forth regularly in the mighty voice of Chrysler Air Raid Sirens.

Thanks to the 180 horsepower and unusual operating characteristics of the great new Chrysler Industrial V-8 Engine, sound engineers now have made available the loudest and most practical siren ever devised for civil defense purposes.

At 100 feet from its throat, the Chrysler Siren delivers 138 decibels of sound. Under normal conditions, its shrill voice carries *four miles*, thus making it possible to warn all persons in an approximate circular area, eight miles in diameter. Because of the great power of Chrysler Sirens, complete coverage of any desired area can be accomplished with fewer sirens, and at lower cost.

By ingenious utilities' circuits, defense organizations can operate a system of Chrysler Sirens by remote control from a central control station. When desired, the sirens can also be operated manually at the site.

Since each Chrysler Siren is individually powered, it operates independently of central power systems, an obvious advantage in case of attack. For mobility, Chrysler sirens can be mounted on trucks or boats.

To secure complete information, specifications and availability for your city, write Siren Layout Service, *Industrial Engine Division, Chrysler Corporation, Trenton, Michigan.*

 Civil Defense is a common need, shared by all. Join the Civil Defense group in your area.

CHRYSLER
AIR RAID SIREN

Magazine ad for Chrysler air raid siren, 1950s.

Foster, You're Dead
Philip K. Dick

School was agony, as always. Only today it was worse. Mike Foster finished weaving his two watertight baskets and sat rigid, while all around him the other children worked. Outside the concrete-and-steel building the late-afternoon sun shone cool. The hills sparkled green and brown in the crisp autumn air. In the overhead sky a few NATS circled lazily above the town.

The vast, ominous shape of Mrs. Cummings, the teacher, silently approached his desk. "Foster, are you finished?"

"Yes ma'am," he answered eagerly. He pushed the baskets up. "Can I leave now?"

Mrs. Cummings examined the baskets critically. "What about your trap-making?" she demanded.

He fumbled in his desk and brought out his intricate small-animal trap. "All finished, Mrs. Cummings. And my knife, it's done, too." He showed her the razor-edged blade of his knife, glittering metal he had shaped from a discarded gasoline drum. She picked up the knife and ran her expert finger doubtfully along the blade.

"Not strong enough," she stated. "You've oversharpened it. It'll lose its edge the first time you use it. Go down to the main weapons-lab and examine the knives they've got there. Then hone it back some and get a thicker blade."

"Mrs. Cummings," Mike Foster pleaded, "could I fix it tomorrow? Could I not fix it right now, please?"

Everybody in the classroom was watching with interest. Mike Foster flushed; he hated to be singled out and made conspicuous, but he had to get away. He couldn't stay in school one minute more.

Inexorable, Mrs. Cummings rumbled, "Tomorrow is digging day. You won't have time to work on your knife."

"I will," he assured her quickly. "After the digging."

"No, you're not too good at digging." The old woman was measuring the boy's spindly arms and legs. "I think you better get your knife finished today. And spend all day tomorrow down at the field."

"What's the use of digging?" Mike Foster demanded, in despair.

"Everybody has to know how to dig," Mrs. Cummings answered patiently. Children were snickering on all sides; she shushed them with a hostile glare. "You all know the

20

importance of digging. When the war begins the whole surface will be littered with debris and rubble. If we hope to survive we'll have to dig down, won't we? Have any of you ever watched a gopher digging around the roots of plants? The gopher knows he'll find something valuable down there under the surface of the ground. We're all going to be little brown gophers. We'll all have to learn to dig down in the rubble and find the good things, because that's where they'll be."

Mike Foster sat miserably plucking his knife, as Mrs. Cummings moved away from his desk and up the aisle. A few children grinned contemptuously at him, but nothing penetrated his haze of wretchedness. Digging wouldn't do him any good. When the bombs came he'd be killed instantly. All the vaccination shots up and down his arms, on his thighs and buttocks, would be of no use. He had wasted his allowance money: Mike Foster wouldn't be alive to catch any of the bacterial plagues. Not unless—

He sprang up and followed Mrs. Cummings to her desk. In an agony of desperation he blurted, "Please, I have to leave. I have to do something."

Mrs. Cummings' tired lips twisted angrily. But the boy's fearful eyes stopped her. "What's wrong?" she demanded. "Don't you feel well?"

The boy stood frozen, unable to answer her. Pleased by the tableau, the class murmured and giggled until Mrs. Cummings rapped angrily on her desk with a writer. "Be quiet," she snapped. Her voice softened a shade. "Michael, if you're not functioning properly, go downstairs to the psych clinic. There's no point trying to work when your reactions are conflicted. Miss Groves will be glad to optimum you."

"No," Foster said.

"Then what is it?"

The class stirred. Voices answered for Foster; his tongue was stuck with misery and humiliation. "His father's an anti-P," the voices explained. "They don't have a shelter and he isn't registered in the Civic Defense. His father hasn't even contributed to the NATS. They haven't done anything."

Mrs. Cummings gazed up in amazement at the mute boy. "You don't have a shelter?" He shook his head.

A strange feeling filled the woman. "But—" She had started to say, *but you'll die up here*. She changed it to, "But where'll you go?"

"Nowhere," the mild voices answered for him. "Everybody else'll be down in their shelters and he'll be up here. He even doesn't have a permit to the school shelter."

Mrs. Cummings was shocked. In her dull, scholastic way she had assumed every child in the school had a permit to the elaborate subsurface chambers under the building.

But of course not. Only children whose parents were part of CD, who contributed to arming the community. And if Foster's father was an anti-P...

"He's afraid to sit here," the voices chimed calmly. "He's afraid it'll come while he's sitting here, and everybody else will be safe down in the shelter."

He wandered slowly along, hands deep in his pockets, kicking at dark stones on the sidewalk. The sun was setting. Snub-nosed commute rockets were unloading tired people, glad to be home from the factory strip a hundred miles to the west. On the distant hills something flashed: a radar tower revolving silently in the evening gloom. The circling NATS had increased in number. The twilight hours were the most dangerous; visual observers couldn't spot high-speed missiles coming in close to the ground. Assuming the missiles came.

A mechanical newsmachine shouted at him excitedly as he passed. War, death, amazing new weapons developed at home and abroad. He hunched his shoulders and continued on, past the little concrete shells that served as houses, each exactly alike, sturdy reinforced pillboxes. Ahead of him bright neon signs glowed in the settling gloom: the business district, alive with traffic and milling people.

Half a block from the bright cluster of neons he halted. To his right was a public shelter, a dark tunnel-like entrance with a mechanical turnstile glowing dully. Fifty cents admission. If he was here, on the street, and he had fifty cents, he'd be all right. He had pushed down into public shelters many times, during the practice raids. But other times, hideous, nightmare times that never left his mind, he hadn't had the fifty cents. He had stood mute and terrified, while people pushed excitedly past him; and the shrill shrieks of the sirens thundered everywhere.

He continued slowly, until he came to the brightest blotch of light, the great, gleaming showrooms of General Electronics, two blocks long, illuminated on all sides, a vast square of pure color and radiation. He halted and examined for the millionth time the fascinating shapes, the display that always drew him to a hypnotized stop whenever he passed.

In the center of the vast room was a single object. An elaborate, pulsing blob of machinery and support struts, beams and walls and sealed locks. All spotlights were turned on it; huge signs announced its hundred-and-one advantages—as if there could be any doubt.

earn your **HOME**
PREPAREDNESS
AWARD

obtain
information
from your local

CIVIL DEFENSE

Poster promoting Civil Defense Home Preparedness from the U.S. Government Priting Office, 1959.

THE NEW 1972 BOMB-PROOF RADIATION-SEALED SUBSURFACE SHEL-
TER IS HERE!

Check these star-studded features:

* automatic descent-lift—jam-proof, self-powered, e-z locking
* triple-layer hull guaranteed to withstand 5g pressure without buckling
* A-powered heating and refrigeration system—self-servicing air-purification network
* three decontamination stages for food and water
* four hygienic stages for pre-burn exposure
* complete anti-biotic processing
* e-z payment plan

He gazed at the shelter a long time. It was mostly a big tank, with a neck at one end that was the descent tube, and an emergency escape-hatch at the other. It was completely self-contained; a miniature world that supplied its own light, heat, air, water, medicines, and almost inexhaustible food. When fully stocked there were visual and audio tapes, entertainment, beds, chairs, vidscreen, everything that made up the above-surface home. It was, actually, a home below the ground. Nothing was missing that might be needed or enjoyed. A family would be safe, even comfortable, during the most severe H-bomb and bacterial-spray attack.

It cost twenty thousand dollars.

While he was gazing silently at the massive display, one of the salesmen stepped out onto the dark sidewalk, on his way to the cafeteria. "Hi, sonny," he said automatically, as he passed Mike Foster. "Not bad, is it?"

"Can I go inside?" Foster asked quickly. "Can I go down in it?"

The salesman stopped, as he recognized the boy. "You're that kid," he said slowly, "that damn kid who's always pestering us."

"I'd like to go down in it. Just for a couple minutes. I won't bust anything—I promise. I won't even touch anything."

The salesman was young and blond, a good-looking man in his early twenties. He hesitated, his reactions divided. The kid was a pest. But he had a family, and that meant a reasonable prospect. Business was bad; it was late September and the seasonal slump was still on. There was no profit in telling the boy to go peddle his newstapes; but on the other hand it was bad business encouraging small fry to crawl around the merchandise. They wasted time; they broke things; they pilfered small stuff when nobody was looking.

"No dice," the salesman said. "Look, send your old man down here. Has he seen what we've got?"

"Yes," Mike Foster said tightly.

"What's holding him back?" The salesman waved expansively up at the great gleaming display. "We'll give him a good trade-in on his old one, allowing for depreciation and obsolescence. What model has he got?"

"We don't have any," Mike Foster said.

The salesman blinked. "Come again?"

"My father says it's a waste of money. He says they're trying to scare people into buying things they don't need. He says—"

"Your father's an anti-P?"

"Yes," Mike Foster answered unhappily.

The salesman let out his breath. "Okay, kid. Sorry we can't do business. It's not your fault." He lingered. "What the hell's wrong with him? Does he put in on the NATS?"

"No."

The salesman swore under his breath. A coaster, sliding along, safe because the rest of the community was putting up thirty per cent of its income to keep a constant-defense system going. There were always a few of them, in every town. "How's your mother feel?" the salesman demanded. "She go along with him?"

"She says—" Mike Foster broke off. "Couldn't I go down in it for a little while? I won't bust anything. Just once."

"How'd we ever sell it if we let kids run through it? We're not marking it down as a demonstration model—we've got roped into that too often." The salesman's curiosity was aroused. "How's a guy get to be an anti-P? He always feel this way, or did he get stung with something?"

"He says they sold people as many cars and washing machines and television sets as they could use. He says NATS and bomb shelters aren't good for anything, so people never get all they can use. He says factories can keep turning out guns and gas masks forever, and as long as people are afraid they'll keep paying for them because they think if they don't they might get killed, and maybe a man gets tired of paying for a new car every year and stops, but he's never going to stop buying shelters to protect his children."

"You believe that?" the salesman asked.

"I wish we had that shelter," Mike Foster answered. "If we had a shelter like that I'd go down and sleep in it every night. It'd be there when we needed it."

"Maybe there won't be a war," the salesman said. He sensed the boy's misery and fear, and he grinned good-naturedly down at him. "Don't worry all the time. You probably watch too many vidtapes—get out and play, for a change."

"Nobody's safe on the surface," Mike Foster said. "We have to be down below. And there's no place I can go."

"Send your old man around," the salesman muttered uneasily. "Maybe we can talk him into it. We've got a lot of time-payment plans. Tell him to ask for Bill O'Neill. Okay?"

Mike Foster wandered away, down the black evening street. He knew he was supposed to be home, but his feet dragged and his body was heavy and dull. His fatigue made him remember what the athletic coach had said the day before, during exercises. They were practicing breath suspension, holding a lungful of air and running. He hadn't done well; the others were still red-faced and racing when he halted, expelled his air, and stood gasping frantically for breath.

"Foster," the coach said angrily, "you're dead. You know that? If this had been a gas attack—" He shook his head wearily. "Go over there and practice by yourself. You've got to do better, if you expect to survive."

But he didn't expect to survive.

When he stepped up on the porch of his home, he found the living-room lights already on. He could hear his father's voice, and more faintly his mother's from the kitchen. He closed the door after him and began unpeeling his coat.

"Is that you?" his father demanded. Bob Foster sat sprawled out in his chair, his lap full of tapes and report sheets from his retail furniture store. "Where have you been? Dinner's been ready half an hour." He had taken off his coat and rolled up his sleeves. His arms were pale and thin, but muscular. He was tired; his eyes were large and dark, his hair thinning. Restlessly, he moved the tapes around, from one stack to another.

"I'm sorry," Mike Foster said.

His father examined his pocket watch; he was surely the only man who still carried a watch. "Go wash your hands. What have you been doing?" He scrutinized his son. "You look odd. Do you feel all right?"

"I was down town," Mike Foster said.

"What were you doing?"

"Looking at the shelters."

Wordless, his father grabbed up a handful of reports and stuffed them into a folder. His thin lips set; hard lines wrinkled his forehead. He snorted furiously as tapes spilled everywhere; he bent stiffly to pick them up. Mike Foster made no move to help him.

He crossed to the closet and gave his coat to the hanger. When he turned away his mother was directing the table of food into the dining room.

They ate without speaking, intent on their food and not looking at each other. Finally his father said, "What'd you see? Same old dogs, I. suppose."

"There's the new '72 models," Mike Foster answered.

"They're the same as the '71 models." His father threw down his fork savagely; the table caught and absorbed it. "A few new gadgets, some more chrome. That's all." Suddenly he was facing his son defiantly. "Right?"

Mike Foster toyed wretchedly with his creamed chicken. "The new ones have a jam-proof descent lift. You can't get stuck half-way down. All you have to do is get in it, and it does the rest."

"There'll be one next year that'll pick you up and carry you down. This one'll be obsolete as soon as people buy it. That's what they want—they want you to keep buying. They keep putting out new ones as fast as they can. This isn't 1972, it's still 1971. What's that thing doing out already? Can't they wait?"

Mike Foster didn't answer. He had heard it all before, many times. There was never anything new, only chrome and gadgets; yet the old ones became obsolete, anyhow. His father's argument was loud, impassioned, almost frenzied, but it made no sense. "Let's get an old one, then," he blurted out. "I don't care, any one'll do. Even a second-hand one."

"No, you want the new one. Shiny and glittery to impress the neighbors. Lots of dials and knobs and machinery. How much do they want for it?"

"Twenty thousand dollars."

His father let his breath out. "Just like that."

"They have easy time-payment plans."

"Sure. You pay for it the rest of your life. Interest, carrying charges, and how long is it guaranteed for?"

"Three months."

"What happens when it breaks down? It'll stop purifying and decontaminating. It'll fall apart as soon as the three months are over."

Mike Foster shook his head. "No. It's big and sturdy."

His father flushed. He was a small man, slender and light, brittle-boned. He thought suddenly of his lifetime of lost battles, struggling up the hard way, carefully collecting and holding onto something, a job, money, his retail store, bookkeeper to manager, finally owner. "They're scaring us to keep the wheels going," he yelled desperately at his wife and son. "They don't want another depression."

"Bob," his wife said, slowly and quietly, "you have to stop this. I can't stand any more."

Bob Foster blinked. "What're you talking about?" he muttered. "I'm tired. These god-damn taxes. It isn't possible for a little store to keep open, not with the big chains. There ought to be a law." His voice trailed off. "I guess I'm through eating." He pushed away from the table and got to his feet. "I'm going to lie down on the couch and take a nap."

His wife's thin face blazed. "You have to get one! I can't stand the way they talk about us. All the neighbors and the merchants, everybody who knows. I can't go anywhere or do anything without hearing about it. Ever since that day they put up the flag. Anti-P. The last in the whole town. Those things circling around up there, and everybody paying for them but us."

"No," Bob Foster said. "I can't get one."

"Why not?"

"Because," he answered simply, "I can't afford it."

There was silence.

"You've put everything in that store," Ruth said finally. "And it's failing, anyhow. You're just like a packrat, hoarding everything down at that ratty little hole-in-the-wall. Nobody wants wood furniture, any more. You're a relic—a curiosity." She slammed at the table and it leaped wildly to gather the empty dishes, like a startled animal. It dashed furiously from the room and back into the kitchen, the dishes churning in its wash-tank as it raced.

Bob Foster sighed wearily. "Let's not fight. I'll be in the living room. Let me take a nap for an hour or so. Maybe we can talk about it later."

"Always later," Ruth said bitterly.

Her husband disappeared into the living room, a small, hunched-over figure, hair scraggly and gray, shoulder blades like broken wings.

Mike got to his feet. "I'll go study my homework," he said. He followed after his father, a strange look on his face.

The living room was quiet; the vidset was off and the lamp was down low. Ruth was in the kitchen setting the controls on the stove for the next month's meals. Bob Foster lay stretched out on the couch, his shoes off, his head on a pillow. His face was gray with fatigue. Mike hesitated for a moment and then said, "Can I ask you something?"

His father grunted and stirred, opened his eyes. "What?"

Mike sat down facing him. "Tell me again how you gave advice to the President."

His father pulled himself up. "I didn't give any advice to the President. I just talked to him."

"Tell me about it."

"I've told you a million times. Every once in a while, since you were a baby. You were with me." His voice softened, as he remembered. "You were just a toddler—we had to carry you."

"What did he look like?"

"Well," his father began, slipping into a routine he had worked out and petrified over the years, "he looked about like he does in the vidscreen, Smaller, though."

"Why was he here?" Mike demanded avidly, although he knew every detail. The President was his hero, the man he most admired in all the world. "Why'd he come all the way out here to our town?"

"He was on a tour." Bitterness crept into his father's voice. "He happened to be passing through."

"What kind of a tour?"

"Visiting towns all over the country." The harshness increased. "Seeing how we were getting along. Seeing if we had bought enough NATS and bomb shelters and plague shots and gas masks and radar networks to repel attack. The General Electronics Corporation was just beginning to put up its big showrooms and displays—everything bright and glittering and expensive. The first defense equipment available for home purchase." His lips twisted. "All on easy payment plans. Ads, posters, searchlights, free gardenias and dishes for the ladies."

Mike Foster's breath panted in his throat. "That was the day we got our Preparedness Flag," he said hungrily. "That was the day he came to give us our flag. And they ran it up on the flagpole in the middle of the town, and everybody was there yelling and cheering."

"You remember that?"

"I—think so. I remember people and sounds. And it was hot. It was June, wasn't it?"

"June 10, 1965. Quite an occasion. Not many towns had the big green flag, then. People were still buying cars and TV sets. They hadn't discovered those days were over. TV sets and cars are good for something—you can only manufacture and sell so many of them."

"He gave you the flag, didn't he?"

"Well, he gave it to all us merchants. The Chamber of Commerce had it arranged. Competition between towns, see who can buy the most the soonest. Improve our town and at the same time stimulate business. Of course, the way they put it, the idea was

29

if we had to buy our gas masks and bomb shelters we'd take better care of them. As if we ever damaged telephones and sidewalks. Or highways, because the whole state provided them. Or armies. Haven't there always been armies? Hasn't the government always organized its people for defense? I guess defense costs too much. I guess they save a lot of money, cut down the national debt by this."

"Tell me what he said," Mike Foster whispered.

His father fumbled for his pipe and lit it with trembling hands. "He said, *'Here's your flag, boys. You've done a good job.'* Bob Foster choked, as acrid pipe fumes guzzled up. "He was red-faced, sunburned, not embarrassed. Perspiring and grinning. He knew how to handle himself. He knew a lot of first names. Told a funny joke."

The boy's eyes were wide with awe. "He came all the way out here, and you talked to him."

"Yeah," his father said. "I talked to him. They were all yelling and cheering. The flag was going up, the big green Preparedness Flag."

"You said—"

"I said to him, 'is that all you brought us? A strip of green cloth?'" Bob Foster dragged tensely on his pipe. "That was when I became an anti-P. Only I didn't know it at the time. All I knew was we were on our own, except for a strip of green cloth. We should have been a country, a whole nation, one hundred and seventy million people working together to defend ourselves. And instead, we're a lot of separate little towns, little walled forts. Sliding and slipping back to the Middle Ages. Raising our separate armies—"

"Will the President ever come back?" Mike asked.

"I doubt it. He was—just passing through."

"If he comes back," Mike whispered, tense and not daring to hope, "can we go see him? Can we *look* at him?"

Bob Foster pulled himself up to a sitting position. His bony arms were bare and white; his lean face was drab with weariness. And resignation. "How much was that damn thing you saw?" he demanded hoarsely. "That bomb shelter?"

Mike's heart stopped beating. "Twenty thousand dollars."

"This is Thursday. I'll go down with you and your mother next Saturday." Bob Foster knocked out his smoldering, half-lit pipe. "I'll get it on the easy-payment plan. The fall buying season is coming up, soon. I usually do good—people buy wood furniture for Christmas gifts." He got up abruptly from the couch. "Is it a deal?"

Mike couldn't answer; he could only nod.

A number of firms have entered the home shelter field. As in any new commercial activity there are abuses. Advertising claims may be misleading; designs and products may be inadequate. Your State and Federal governments will do what they properly can to minimize these abuses, but the most effective discouragement to those taking advantage of the rising interest in home shelters is your caution and shrewdness. You will have the cooperation of the Better Business Bureau, your local Civil Defense director, and of your local, State, and Federal government officials concerned with such matters.

Trade associations that are interested in the shelter construction business have offered their cooperation in making home shelter plans available to the public and in working with others to maintain a high level of business practice. Several of these are listed on the last page of this booklet.

In the event of a nuclear attack, be prepared to live in a shelter as long as two weeks, coming out for short trips only if necessary. Fallout would be most dangerous in the first two days

This prefab backyard shelter for four can be bought for under $150. The price includes the corrugated steel-pipe unit (4-foot diameter), entry and air vent pipes.

Page 22 of the booklet, *Fallout Protection: What To Know And Do About Nuclear Attack*, published by the Departmet Of Defense, Office Of Civil Defense, December, 1961.

"Fine," his father said, with desperate cheerfulness. "Now you won't have to go down and look at it in the window."

The shelter was installed—at an additional two hundred dollars—by a fast-working team of laborers in brown coats with the words GENERAL ELECTRONICS stitched across their backs. The back yard was quickly restored, dirt and shrubs spaded in place, the surface smoothed over, and the bill respectfully slipped under the front door. The lumbering delivery truck, now empty, clattered off down the street and the neighborhood was again silent.

Mike Foster stood with his mother and a small group of admiring neighbors on the back porch of the house. "Well," Mrs. Carlyle said finally, "now you've got a shelter. The best there is."

"That's right," Ruth Foster agreed. She was conscious of the people around her; it had been some time since so many had shown up at once. Grim satisfaction filled her gaunt frame, almost resentment. "It certainly makes a difference," she said harshly.

"Yes," Mr. Douglas from down the street agreed. "Now you have someplace to go." He had picked up the thick book of instructions the laborers had left. "It says here you can stock it for a whole year. Live down there twelve months without coming up once." He shook his head admiringly. "Mine's an old '69 model. Good for only six months. I guess maybe—"

"It's still good enough for us," his wife cut in, but there was a longing wistfulness in her voice. "Can we go down and peek at it, Ruth? It's all ready, isn't it?"

Mike made a strangled noise and moved jerkily forward. His mother smiled understandingly. "He has to go down there first. He gets first look at it—it's really for him, you know."

Their arms folded against the chill September wind, the group of men and women stood waiting and watching, as the boy approached the neck of the shelter and halted a few steps in front of it.

He entered the shelter carefully, almost afraid to touch anything. The neck was big for him; it was built to admit a full grown man. As soon as his weight was on the descent lift it dropped beneath him. With a breathless whoosh it plummeted down the pitch-black tube to the body of the shelter. The lift slammed hard against its shock-absorbers and the boy stumbled from it. The lift shot back to the surface, simultaneously sealing off the subsurface shelter, an impassable steel and plastic cork in the narrow neck.

Lights had come on around him automatically. The shelter was bare and empty; no supplies had yet been carried down. It smelled of varnish and motor grease: below him the generators were throbbing dully. His presence activated the purifying and decontamination systems; on the blank concrete wall meters and dials moved into sudden activity.

He sat down on the floor, knees drawn up, face solemn, eyes wide. There was no sound but the generators; the world above was completely cut off. He was in a little self-contained cosmos: everything needed was here—or would be here, soon. Food, water, air, things to do. Nothing else was wanted. He could reach out and touch—whatever he needed. He could stay here forever, through all time, without stirring. Complete and entire. Not lacking, not fearing, with only the sound of the generators purring below him. and the sheer, ascetic walls around and above him on all sides, faintly warm, completely friendly, like a living container.

Suddenly he shouted, a loud jubilant shout that echoed and bounced from wall to wall. He was deafened by the reverberation. He shut his eyes tight and clenched his fists. Joy filled him. He shouted again—and let the roar of sound lap over him, his own voice reinforced by the near walls, close and hard and incredibly powerful.

The kids in school knew even before he showed up, the next morning. They greeted him as he approached, all of them grinning and nudging each other. "Is it true your folks got a new General Electronics Model S-72ft?" Earl Peters demanded.

"That's right," Mike answered. His heart swelled with a peaceful confidence he had never known. "Drop around," he said, as casually as he could. "I'll show it to you."

He passed on, conscious of their envious faces.

"Well, Mike," Mrs. Cummings said, as he was leaving the classroom at the end of the day. "How does it feel?"

He halted by her desk, shy and full of quiet pride. "It feels good," he admitted.

"Is your father contributing to the NATS?"

"Yes."

"And you've got a permit for our school shelter?"

He happily showed her the small blue seal clamped around his wrist. "He mailed a check to the city for everything. He said, 'as long as I've gone this far I might as well go the rest of the way.'"

"Now you have everything everybody else has." The elderly woman smiled across at him. "I'm glad of that. You're now a pro-P, except there's no such term. You're just—like everyone else."

The next day the newsmachines shrilled out the news. The first revelation of the new Soviet bore-pellets.

Bob Foster stood in the middle of the living room, the newstape in his hands, his thin face flushed with fury and despair. "God damn it, it's a plot!" His voice rose in baffled frenzy, "We just bought the thing and now look. *Look!*" He shoved the tape at his wife. "You see? I told you!"

"I've seen it," Ruth said wildly. "I suppose you think the whole world was just waiting with you in mind. They're always improving weapons, Bob. Last week it was those grain-impregnation flakes. This week it's bore-pellets. You don't expect them to stop the wheels of progress because you finally broke down and bought a shelter, do you?"

The man and woman faced each other. "What the hell are we going to do?" Bob Foster asked quietly.

Ruth paced back into the kitchen. "I heard they were going to turn out adaptors."

"Adaptors! What do you mean?"

"So people won't have to buy new shelters. There was a commercial on the vid-screen. They're going to put some kind of metal grill on the market, as soon as the government approves it. They spread it over the ground and it intercepts the bore-pellets. It screens them, makes them explode on the surface, so they can't burrow down to the shelter."

"How much?"

"They didn't say."

Mike Foster sat crouched on the sofa, listening. He had heard the news at school. They were taking their test on berry-identification, examining encased samples of wild berries to distinguish the harmless ones from the toxic, when the bell had announced a general assembly. The principal read them the news about the bore-pellets and then gave a routine lecture on emergency treatment of a new variant of typhus, recently developed.

His parents were still arguing. "We'll have to get one," Ruth Foster said calmly. "Otherwise it won't make any difference whether we've got a shelter or not. The bore-pellets were specifically designed to penetrate the surface and seek out warmth. As soon as the Russians have them in production—"

"I'll get one," Bob Foster said. "I'll get an anti-pellet grill and whatever else they have. buy everything they put on the market. Never stop buying."

"It's not as bad as that."

"You know, this game has one real advantage over selling people cars and TV sets. With something like this we have to buy. It isn't a luxury, something big and flashy to impress the neighbors, something we could do without. If we don't buy this we die. They always said the way to sell something was create anxiety in people. Create a sense of insecurity—tell them they smell bad or look funny. But this makes a joke out of deodorant and hair oil. You can't escape this. If you don't buy, *they'll kill you*. The perfect sales-pitch. Buy or die—new slogan. Have a shiny new General Electronics H-bomb shelter in your back yard or be slaughtered."

"Stop talking like that!" Ruth snapped.

Bob Foster threw himself down at the kitchen table. "All right. I give up. Go along with it."

"You'll get one? I think they'll be on the market by Christinas."

"Oh, yes," Foster said. "They'll be out by Christmas." There was a strange look on his face. "I'll buy one of the damn things for Christmas, and so will everybody else."

The GEC grill-screen adaptors were a sensation.

Mike Foster walked slowly along the crowd-packed December street, through the late-afternoon twilight. Adaptors glittered in every store window. All shapes and sizes, for every kind of shelter. All prices, for every pocket-book. The crowds of people were gay and excited, typical Christmas crowds, shoving good-naturedly, loaded down with packages and heavy overcoats. The air was white with gusts of sweeping snow. Cars nosed cautiously along the jammed streets. Lights and neon displays, immense glowing store windows gleamed on all sides.

His own house was dark and silent. His parents weren't home yet. Both of them were down at the store working; business had been bad and his mother was taking the place of one of the clerks. Mike held his hand up to the code-key, and the front door let him in. The automatic furnace had kept the house warm and pleasant. He removed his coat and put away his school books.

He didn't stay in the house long. His heart pounding with excitement, he felt his way out the back door and started onto the back porch.

He forced himself to stop, turn around, and re-enter the house. It was better if he didn't hurry things. He had worked out every moment of the process, from the first instant he saw the low hinge of the neck reared up hard and firm against the evening sky. He had made a fine art of it; there was no wasted motion. His procedure had been shaped, molded until it was a beautiful thing. The first overwhelming sense of *presence* as the neck of the shelter came around him. Then the blood-freezing rush of air as the descent-lift hurtled down all the way to the bottom.

And the grandeur of the shelter itself.

Every afternoon, as soon as he was home, he made his way down into it, below the surface, concealed and protected in its steel silence, as he had done since the first day. Now the chamber was full, not empty. Filled with endless cans of food, pillows, books, vidtapes, audio-tapes, prints on the walls, bright fabrics, textures and colors, even vases of flowers. The shelter was his place, where he crouched curled up, surrounded by everything he needed.

Delaying things as long as possible, he hurried back through the house and rummaged in the audio-tape file. He'd sit down in the shelter until dinner, listening to *The Wind in the Willows*. His parents knew where to find him; he was always down there. Two hours of uninterrupted happiness, alone by himself in the shelter. And then when dinner was over he would hurry back down, to stay until time for bed. Sometimes late at night, when his parents were sound asleep, he got quietly up and made his way outside, to the shelter-neck, and down into its silent depths. To hide until morning.

He found the audio-tape and hurried through the house, out onto the back porch and into the yard. The sky was a bleak gray, shot with streamers of ugly black clouds. The lights of the town were coming on here and there. The yard was cold and hostile. He made his way uncertainly down the steps—and froze.

A vast yawning cavity loomed. A gaping mouth, vacant and toothless, fixed open to the night sky. There was nothing else. The shelter was gone.

He stood for an endless time, the tape clutched in one hand, the other hand on the porch railing. Night came on; the dead hole dissolved in darkness. The whole world gradually collapsed into silence and abysmal gloom. Weak stars came out; lights in nearby houses came on fitfully, cold and faint. The boy saw nothing. He stood unmoving, his body rigid as stone, still facing the great pit where the shelter had been.

Then his father was standing beside him. "How long have you been here?" his father was saying. "How long, Mike? Answer me!"

With a violent effort Mike managed to drag himself back. "You're home early," he muttered.

"I left the store early on purpose. I wanted to be here when you—got home."

"It's gone."

"Yes." His father's voice was cold, without emotion. "The shelter's gone. I'm sorry, Mike. I called them and told them to take it back."

"Why?"

"I couldn't pay for it. Not this Christmas, with those grills everyone's getting. I can't compete with them." He broke off and then continued wretchedly, "They were damn decent. They gave me back half the money I put in." His voice twisted ironically.

"I knew if I made a deal with them before Christmas I'd come out better. They can re-sell it to somebody else."

Mike said nothing.

"Try to understand," his father went on harshly. "I had to throw what capital I could scrape together into the store. I have to keep it running. It was either give up the shelter or the store. And if I gave up the store—"

"Then we wouldn't have anything."

His father caught hold of his arm. "Then we'd have to give up the shelter, too." His thin, strong fingers dug in spasmodically. "You're growing up—you're old enough to understand. We'll get one later, maybe not the biggest, the most expensive, but something. It was a mistake, Mike. I couldn't swing it, not with the god-damn adaptor-things to buck. I'm keeping up the NAT payments, though. And your school tab. I'm keeping that going. This isn't a matter of principle," he finished desperately. "I can't help it. Do you understand, Mike? *I had to do it.*"

Mike pulled away.

"Where are you going?" His father hurried after him. "Come back here!" He grabbed for his son frantically, but in the gloom he stumbled and fell. Stars blinded him as his head smashed into the edge of the house; he pulled himself up painfully and groped for some support.

When he could see again, the yard was empty. His son was gone.

"Mike!" he yelled. "Where are you?"

There was no answer. The night wind blew clouds of snow around him, a thin bitter gust of chilled air. Wind and darkness, nothing else.

Bill O'Neill wearily examined the clock on the wall. It was nine-thirty: he could finally close the doors and lock up the big dazzling store. Push the milling, murmuring throngs of people outside and on their way home.

"Thank God," he breathed, as he held the door open for the last old lady, loaded down with packages and presents. He threw the code-bolt in place and pulled down the shade. "What a mob. I never saw so many people."

"All done," Al Conners said, from the cash register. "I'll count the money—you go around and check everything. Make sure we got all of them out."

O'Neill pushed his blond hair back and loosened his tie. He lit a cigarette gratefully, then moved around the store, checking light switches, turning off the massive GEC displays and appliances. Finally he approached the huge bomb shelter that took up the center of the floor.

He climbed the ladder to the neck and stepped onto the lift. The lift dropped with a whoosh and a second later he stepped out in the cave-like interior of the shelter.

In one corner Mike Foster sat curled up in a tight heap, his knees drawn up against his chin, his skinny arms wrapped around his ankles. His face was pushed down; only his ragged brown hair showed. He didn't move as the salesman approached him, astounded.

"Jesus!" O'Neill exclaimed. "It's that kid."

Mike said nothing. He hugged his legs tighter and buried his head as far down as possible.

"What the hell are you doing down here?" O'Neill demanded, surprised and angry. His outrage increased. "I thought your folks got one of these." Then he remembered. "That's right. We had to repossess it."

Al Conners appeared from the descent-lift. "What's holding you up? Let's get out of here and—" He saw Mike and broke off. "What's he doing down here? Get him out and let's go."

"Come on, kid," O'Neill said gently. "Time to go home."

Mike didn't move.

The two men looked at each other. "I guess we're going to have to drag him out," Conners said grimly. He took off his coat and tossed it over a decontamination-fixture. "Come on. Let's get it over with."

It took both of them. The boy fought desperately, without sound, clawing and struggling and tearing at them with his fingernails, kicking them, slashing at them, biting them when they grabbed him. They half-dragged, half-carried him to the descent-lift and pushed him into it long enough to activate the mechanism. O'Neill rode up with him; Conners came immediately after. Grimly, efficiently, they bundled the boy to the front door, threw him out, and locked the bolts after him.

"Wow," Conners gasped, sinking down against the counter. His sleeve was torn and his cheek was cut and gashed. His glasses hung from one ear; his hair was rumpled and he was exhausted. "Think we ought to call the cops? There's something wrong with that kid."

O'Neill stood by the door, panting for breath and gazing out into the darkness. He could see the boy sitting on the pavement. "He's still out there," he muttered. People pushed by the boy on both sides. Finally one of them stopped and got him up. The boy struggled away, and then disappeared into the darkness. The larger figure picked up its packages, hesitated a moment, and then went on. O'Neill turned away. "What a hell of a thing." He wiped his face with his handkerchief. "He sure put up a fight."

"What was the matter with him? He never said anything, not a god-damn word."

"Christmas is a hell of a time to repossess something," O'Neill said. He reached shakily for his coat. "It's too bad. I wish they could have kept it."

Conners shrugged. "No tickie, no laundly."

"Why the hell can't we give them a deal? Maybe—" O'Neill struggled to get the word out. "Maybe sell the shelter wholesale, to people like that."

Conners glared at him angrily. "Wholesale? And then everybody wants it wholesale. It wouldn't be fair—and how long would we stay in business? How long would GEC last that way?"

"I guess not very long," O'Neill admitted moodily.

"Use your head." Conners laughed sharply. "What you need is a good stiff drink. Come on in the back closet—I've got a fifth of Haig and Haig in a drawer back there. A little something to warm you up, before you go home. That's what you need."

Mike Foster wandered aimlessly along the dark street, among the crowds of shoppers hurrying home. He saw nothing; people pushed against him but he was unaware of them. Lights, laughing people, the honking of car horns, the clang of signals. He was blank, his mind empty and dead. He walked automatically, without consciousness or feeling.

To his right a garish neon sign winked and glowed in the deepening night shadows. A huge sign, bright and colorful.

PEACE ON EARTH GOOD WILL TO MEN
PUBLIC SHELTER ADMISSION 50c

Day of Succession
Theodore Thomas

General Paul T. Tredway was an arrogant man with the unforgivable gift of being always right. When the object came out of the sky in the late spring of 1979, it was General Tredway who made all of the decisions concerning it. Sweeping in over the northern tip of Greenland, coming on a dead line from the Yamal Peninsula, the object alerted every warning unit from the Dew Line to the radar operator at the Philadelphia National Airport. Based on the earliest reports, General Tredway concluded that the object was acting in an anomalous fashion; its altitude was too low too long. Accordingly, acting with a colossal confidence, he called off the manned interceptor units and forbade the launching of interceptor missiles. The object came in low over the Pocono Mountains and crashed in southeastern Pennsylvania two miles due west of Terre Hill.

The object still glowed a dull red, and the fire of the smashed house still smoldered when General Tredway arrived with the troops. He threw a cordon around it, and made a swift investigation. The object: fifty feet long, thirty feet in diameter, football-shaped, metallic, too hot to inspect closely. Visualizing immediately what had to be done, the general set up a Command Headquarters and began ordering the items he needed. With no wasted word or motion he built toward the finished plan as he saw it.

Scientists arrived at the same time as the asbestos clothing needed for them to get close. Tanks and other materiel flowed toward the impact site. Radios and oscillators scanned all frequencies seeking—what? No man there knew what to expect, but no man cared. General Tredway was on the ground personally, and no one had time for anything but his job. The gunners sat with eyes glued to sights, mindful of the firing pattern in which they had been instructed. Handlers poised over their ammunition. Drivers waited with hands on the wheel, motors idling. Behind this ring of steel a more permanent bulwark sprang up. Spotted back further were the technical shacks for housing the scientific equipment. Behind the shacks the reporters gathered, held firmly in check by armed troops. The site itself was a strange mixture of taut men in frozen immobility, and casual men in bustling activity.

In an hour the fact emerged which General Tredway had suspected all along: the object was not of Earthly origin. The alloy of which it was made was a known high-temperature alloy, but no technology on Earth could cast it in seamless form in that size and shape. Mass determinations and ultrasonic probes showed that the object was hollow but was crammed inside with a material different from the shell. It was then that General Tredway completely reorganized his fire power, and mapped out a plan of action that widened the eyes of those who were to carry it out.

On the general's instructions, everything said at the site was said into radio transmitters and thus recorded a safe fifty miles away. And it was the broadcasting of the general's latest plan of action that brought in the first waves of mild protest. But the general went ahead.

The object had lost its dull hot glow when the first indications of activity inside could be heard. General Tredway immediately removed all personnel to positions of safety outside the ring of steel. The ring itself buttoned up; when a circle of men fire toward a common center, someone can get hurt.

With the sound of tearing, protesting metal, a three foot circle appeared at the top of the object, and the circle began to turn. As it turned it began to lift away from the main body of the object, and soon screw threads could be seen. The hatch rose silently, looking like a bung being unscrewed from a barrel. The time came when there was a gentle click, and the hatch dropped back a fraction of an inch; the last thread had become disengaged. There was a pause. The heavy silence was broken by a throbbing sound from the object that continued for forty-five seconds and then stopped. Then, without further sound, the hatch began to lift back on its northernmost rim.

In casual tones, as if he were speaking in a classroom, General Tredway ordered the northern, northeastern, and northwestern regions of the ring into complete cover. The hatch lifted until finally its underside could be seen; it was colored a dull, non-reflecting black. Higher the hatch lifted, and immediately following it was a bulbous mass that looked like a half-opened rose blossom. Deep within the mass there glowed a soft violet light, clearly apparent to the eye even in the sharp Pennsylvania sunshine.

The machine gun bullets struck the mass first, and the tracers could be seen glancing off. But an instant later the shaped charges in the rockets struck the mass and shattered it. The 105's, the 101 rifles, the rocket launchers, poured a hail of steel onto the canted hatch, ricocheting much of the steel into the interior of the object. Delay-timed high-explosive shells went inside and detonated.

A flame tank left the ring of steel and lumbered forward, followed by two armored trucks. At twenty-five yards a thin stream of fire leaped from the nozzle of the tank and splashed off the hatch in a Niagara of flame. A slight correction, and the Niagara poured down into the opening. The tank moved in close, and the guns fell suddenly silent. Left in the air was a high-pitched shrieking wail, abruptly cut off.

Flames leaped from the opening, so the tank turned off its igniter and simply shot fuel into the object. Asbestos-clad men jumped from the trucks and fed a metal hose through the opening and forced it deep into the object. The compressors started, and a blast of high-pressure air passed through the hose, insuring complete combustion of everything inside. For three minutes the men fed fuel and air to the interior of the object, paying in the metal hose as the end fused off. Flames shot skyward with the roar of a blast furnace. The heat was so great that the men at work were saved only by the constant streams of water that played on them. Then it was over.

General Tredway placed the burned-out cinder in charge of the scientists, and then regrouped his men for resupply and criticism. These were in progress when the report of the second object came in.

The trackers were waiting for it. General Tredway had reasoned that when one object arrived, another might follow, and so he had ordered the trackers to look for it. It hit twenty-five miles west of the first one, near Florin. General Tredway and his men were on their way even before impact. They arrived twenty minutes after it hit.

The preparations were the same, only more streamlined now. The soldiers and the scientists moved more surely, with less wasted motion than before. But as the cooling period progressed, the waves of protest came out of Washington and reached toward General Tredway. "Terrible." "First contact..." "Exterminating them like vermin..." "Peaceful relationship..." "...military mind." The protests took on an official character just before the hatch on the second object opened. An actual countermanding of General Tredway's authority came through just as the rockets opened fire on the half-opened rose blossom. The burning-out proceeded on schedule. Before it was complete, General Tredway climbed into a helicopter to fly the hundred miles to Washington, D. C. In half an hour he was there.

It is one of the circumstances of a democracy that in an emergency half a dozen men can speak for the entire country. General Tredway stalked into a White House conference room where waited the President, the Vice President, the Speaker of the House, the President pro tempore of the Senate, the House minority leader, and a cabinet member. No sooner had he entered when the storm broke.

"Sit down, general, and explain to us if you can the meaning of your reprehensible conduct."

"What are you trying to do, make butchers of us all?"

"You didn't give those...those persons a chance."

"Here we had a chance to learn something, to learn a lot, and you killed them and destroyed their equipment."

General Tredway sat immobile until the hot flood of words subsided. Then he said, "Do any of you gentlemen have any evidence that their intentions were peaceable? Any evidence at all?"

There was silence for a moment as they stared at him. The President said, "What evidence have you got they meant harm? You killed them before there was any evidence of anything."

General Tredway shook his head, and a familiar supercilious tone crept unbidden into his voice. They were the ones who landed on our planet. It was incumbent on them to find a way to convince us of their friendliness. Instead they landed with no warning at all, and with a complete disregard of human life. The first missile shattered a house, killed a man. There is ample evidence of their hostility," and he could not help adding, "if you care to look for it."

The President flushed and snapped, "That's not the way I see it. You could have kept them covered; you had enough firepower there to cover an army. If they made any hostile, move, that would have been time enough for you to have opened up on them."

The House Speaker leaned forward and plunked a sheaf of telegrams on the table. He tapped the pile with a forefinger and said, "These are some of thousands that have come in. I picked out the ones from some of our outstanding citizens—educators, scientists, statesmen. All of them agree that this is a foolhardy thing you have done. You've destroyed a mighty source of knowledge for the human race."

"None of them is a soldier," said the general. "I would not expect them to know anything about attack and defense."

The Speaker nodded and drew one more telegram from an inner pocket. General Tredway, seeing what was coming, had to admire his tactics; this man was not Speaker for nothing. "Here," said the Speaker, "is a reply to my telegram. It is from the Joint Chiefs. Care to read it?"

They all stared at the general, and he shook his head coldly. "No. I take it that they do not understand the problem either."

"Now just a min…" A colonel entered the room and whispered softly to the President. The President pushed his chair back, but he did not get up. Nodding he said, "Good. Have Barnes take over. And see that he holds his fire until something happens. Hear? Make certain of that. I'll not tolerate any more of this unnecessary slaughter." The colonel left.

The President turned and noted the understanding in the faces of the men at the table. He nodded and said, "Yes, another one. And this time we'll do it right. I only hope the other two haven't got word to the third one that we're a bunch of killers."

"There could be no communication of any kind emanating from the first two," said General Tredway. "I watched for that."

"Yes. Well, it's the only thing you did right. I want you to watch to see the proper way to handle this."

In the intervening hours General Tredway tried to persuade the others to adopt his point of view. He succeeded only in infuriating them. When the time came for the third object to open, the group of men were trembling in anger. They gathered around the television screen to watch General Barnes' handling of the situation.

General Tredway stood to the rear of the others, watching the hatch unscrew. General Barnes was using the same formation as that developed by General Tredway; the ring of steel was as tight as ever.

The familiar black at the bottom of the hatch came into view, followed closely by the top of the gleaming rose blossom. General Tredway snapped his fingers, the sound cracking loud in the still room. The men close to the set jumped and looked back at Tredway in annoyance. It was plain that the general had announced in his own way the proper moment to fire. Their eyes had hardly got back to the screen when it happened.

A thin beam of delicate violet light danced from the heart of the rose to the front of the steel ring. The beam rotated like a lighthouse beacon, only far far faster. Whatever it touched it sliced. Through tanks and trucks and guns and men it sliced, over and over again as the swift circular path of the beam spun in ever-widening circles. Explosions rocked the site as high explosives detonated under the touch of the beam. The hatch of the object itself, neatly cut near the bottom, rolled ponderously down the side of the object to the ground. The beam bit into the ground and left seething ribbons of slag. In three seconds the area was a mass of fused metal and molten rock and minced bodies and flame and smoke and thunder, in another two seconds the beam reached the television cameras, and the screen went blank.

The men near the screen stared speechless. At that moment the colonel returned and announced softly that a fourth object was on its way, and that its probable impact point was two miles due east of Harrisburg.

The group turned as one man to General Tredway, but he paid no attention. He was pacing back and forth, pulling at his lower lip, frowning in concentration. "General," said the President. "I… I guess you had the right idea. These things are monsters. Will you handle this next one?'

General Tredway stopped and said, "Yes, but I had better explain what is now involved. I want every vehicle that can move to converge on the fourth object; the one that is now loose will attempt to protect it. I want every plane and copter that can fly to launch a continuing attack on it. I want every available missile zeroed in and launched at it immediately. I want every fusion and fission bomb we've got directed at the fourth object by means of artillery, missiles, and planes; one of them might get through. I want a request made to Canada, Brazil, Great Britain, France, Germany, Russia, and Italy to launch fusion-headed missiles at the site of the fourth object immediately. In this way we might have a chance to stop them. Let us proceed."

The President stared at him and said, "Have you gone crazy? I will give no such orders. What you ask for will destroy our middle eastern seaboard."

The general nodded. "Yes, everything from Richmond to Pittsburgh to Syracuse, I think, possibly more. Fallout will cover a wider area. There's no help for it."

"You're insane. I will do no such thing."

The Speaker stepped forward and said, "Mr. President, I think you should reconsider this. You saw what that thing could do; think of two of them loose. I am very much afraid the general may be right."

"Don't be ridiculous."

The Vice President stepped to the President's side and said, "I agree with the President. I never heard of such an absurd suggestion."

The moment froze into silence. The general stared at the three men. Then, moving slowly and deliberately, he undid his holster flap and pulled out his pistol. He snapped the slide back and fired once at point-blank range, shifted the gun, and fired again. He walked over to the table and carefully placed the gun on it. Then he turned to the Speaker and said, "Mr. President, there is very little time. Will you give the necessary orders?"

Generation of Noah
William Tenn

That was the day Plunkett heard his wife screaming guardedly to their youngest boy.

He let the door of the laying house slam behind him, forgetful of the nervously feeding hens. She had, he realized, cupped her hands over her mouth so that only the boy would hear.

"Saul! You, Saul! Come back, come right back this instant. Do you want your father to catch you out there on the road? Saul!"

The last shriek was higher and clearer, as if she had despaired of attracting the boy's attention without at the same time warning the man.

Poor Ann!

Gently, rapidly, Plunkett shh'ed his way through the bustling and hungry hens to the side door. He came out facing the brooder run and broke into a heavy, unathletic trot.

They have the responsibility after Ann and me, Plunkett told himself. Let them watch and learn again. He heard the other children clatter out of the feed house. Good!

"Saul!" his wife's voice shrilled unhappily. "Saul, your father's coming!"

Ann came out of the front door and paused. "Elliot," she called at his back as he leaped over the flush well-cover. "Please. I don't feel well."

A difficult pregnancy, of course, and in her sixth month. But that had nothing to do with Saul. Saul knew better.

At the last frozen furrow of the truck garden Plunkett gave himself a moment to gather the necessary air for his lungs. Years ago, when Von Rundstedt's Tigers roared through the Bulge, he would have been able to dig a fox-hole after such a run. Now, he was just winded. Just showed you: such a short distance from the far end of the middle chicken house to the far end of the vegetable garden—merely crossing four acres—and he was winded. And consider the practice he'd had.

He could just about see the boy idly lifting a stick to throw for the dog's pleasure. Saul was in the further ditch, well past the white line his father had painted across the road.

"Elliot," his wife began again. "He's only six years old. He—" Plunkett drew his jaws apart and let breath out in a bellyful of sound. "Saul! Saul Plunkett!" he bellowed. "Start running!"

He knew his voice had carried. He clicked the button on his stopwatch and threw his right arm up, pumping his clenched fist.

The boy had heard the yell. He turned, and, at the sight of the moving arm that meant the stopwatch had started, he dropped the stick. But, for the fearful moment, he was too startled to move.

Eight seconds. He lifted his lids slightly. Saul had begun to run. But he hadn't picked up speed, and Rusty skipping playfully between his legs threw him off his stride.

Ann had crossed the garden laboriously and stood at his side, alternately staring over his jutting elbow at the watch and smiling hesitantly sidewise at his face. She shouldn't have come out in her thin house-dress in November. But it was good for Ann. Plunkett kept his eyes stolidly on the unemotional second hand.

One minute forty.

He could hear the dog's joyful barks coming closer, but as yet there was no echo of sneakers slapping the highway. Two minutes. He wouldn't make it.

The old bitter thoughts came crowding back to Plunkett. A father timing his six-year-old son's speed with the best watch he could afford. This, then, was the scientific way to raise children in Earth's most enlightened era. Well, it was scientific... in keeping with the very latest discoveries. ...

Two and a half minutes. Rusty's barks didn't sound so very far off. Plunkett could hear the desperate pad-pad-pad of the boy's feet. He might make it at that. If only he could!

"Hurry, Saul," his mother breathed. "You can make it."

Plunkett looked up in time to see his son pound past, his jeans already darkened with perspiration. "Why doesn't he breathe like I told him?" he muttered. "He'll be out of breath in no time."

Halfway to the house, a furrow caught at Saul's toes. As he sprawled, Ann gasped. "You can't count that, Elliot. He tripped."

"Of course he tripped. He should count on tripping."

"Get up, Saulie," Herbie, his older brother, screamed from the garage where he stood with Louise Dawkins, the pail of eggs still between them. "Get up and run! This corner here! You can make it!"

The boy weaved to his feet, and threw his body forward again. Plunkett could hear him sobbing. He reached the cellar steps—and literally plunged down.

Plunkett pressed the stopwatch and the second hand halted. Three minutes thirteen seconds.

He held the watch up for his wife to see. "Thirteen seconds, Ann."

Her face wrinkled.

He walked to the house. Saul crawled back up the steps, fragments of unrecovered breath rattling in his chest. He kept his eyes on his father.

"Come here, Saul. Come right here. Look at the watch. Now, what do you see?"

The boy stared intently at the watch. His lips began twisting; startled tears writhed down his stained face. "More—more than three m-minutes, poppa?"

"More than three minutes, Saul. Now, Saul—don't cry son; it isn't any use—Saul, what would have happened when you got to the steps?"

A small voice, pitifully trying to cover its cracks: "The big doors would be shut."

"The big doors would be shut. You would be locked outside. Then what would have happened to you? Stop crying. Answer me!"

"Then, when the bombs fell, I'd—I'd have no place to hide. I'd burn like the head of a match. An'—an' the only thing left of me would be a dark spot on the ground, shaped like my shadow. An'—an'—"

"And the radioactive dust," his father helped with the catechism.

"Elliot—" Ann sobbed behind him, "I don't—"

"Please, Ann! And the radioactive dust, son?"

"An' if it was ra-di-o-ac-tive dust 'stead of atom bombs, my skin would come right off my body, an' my lungs would burn up inside me—please, poppa, I won't do it again!"

"And your eyes? What would happen to your eyes?"

A chubby brown fist dug into one of the eyes. "An' my eyes would fall out, an' my teeth would fall out, and I'd feel such terrible terrible pain—"

"All over you and inside you. That's what would happen if you got to the cellar too late when the alarm went off, if you got locked out. At the end of three minutes, we pull the levers, and no matter who's outside—no matter who—all four corner doors swing shut and the cellar will be sealed. You understand that, Saul?"

The two Dawkins children were listening with white faces and dry lips. Their parents had brought them from the city and begged Elliot Plunkett as he remembered old friends to give their children the same protection as his. Well, they were getting it. This was the way to get it.

"Yes, I understand it, poppa. I won't ever do it again. Never again."

"I hope you won't. Now, start for the barn, Saul. Go ahead." Plunkett slid his heavy leather belt from its loops.

"Elliot! Don't you think he understands the horrible thing? A beating won't make it any clearer."

He paused behind the weeping boy trudging to the barn. "It won't make it any clearer, but it will teach him the lesson another way. All seven of us are going to be in that cellar three minutes after the alarm, if I have to wear this strap clear down to the buckle!"

When Plunkett later clumped into the kitchen with his heavy farm boots, he stopped and sighed.

Ann was feeding Dinah. With her eyes on the baby, she asked, "No supper for him, Elliot?"

"No supper." He sighed again. "It does take it out of a man."

"Especially you. Not many men would become a farmer at thirty-five. Not many men would sink every last penny into an underground fort and powerhouse, just for insurance. But you're right."

"I only wish," he said restlessly, "that I could work out some way of getting Nancy's heifer into the cellar. And if eggs stay high one more month I can build the tunnel to the generator. Then, there's the well. Only one well, even if it's enclosed—"

"And when we came out here seven years ago—" She rose to him at last and rubbed her lips gently against his thick blue shirt. "We only had a piece of ground. Now, we have three chicken houses, a thousand broilers, and I can't keep track of how many layers and breeders."

She stopped as his body tightened and he gripped her shoulders.

"Ann, Ann! If you think like that, you'll act like that! How can I expect the children to—Ann, what we have—all we have—is a five room cellar, concrete-lined, which we can seal in a few seconds, an enclosed well from a fairly deep underground stream, a windmill generator for power and a sunken oil-burner-driven generator for emergencies. We have supplies to carry us through, geiger counters to detect radiation and lead-lined suits to move about in—afterwards. I've told you again and again that these things are our lifeboat, and the farm is just a sinking ship."

"Of course, darling." Plunkett's teeth ground together, then parted helplessly as his wife went back to feeding Dinah, the baby.

"You're perfectly right. Swallow now, Dinah. Why, that last bulletin from the Survivors Club would make anybody think."

He had been quoting from the October Survivor, and Ann had recognized it. Well? At least they were doing something—seeking out nooks and feverishly building crannies—pooling their various ingenuities in an attempt to haul themselves and their families through the military years of the Atomic Age.

The familiar green cover of the mimeographed magazine was very noticeable on. the kitchen table. He flipped the sheets to the thumb-smudged article on page five and shook his head.

"Imagine!" he said loudly. "The poor fools agreeing with the government again on the safety factor. Six minutes! How can they—an organization like the Survivors Club making that their official opinion! Why freeze, freeze alone...."

"They're ridiculous," Ann murmured, scraping the bottom of the bowl.

"All right, we have automatic detectors. But human beings still have to look at the radar scope, or we'd be diving underground every time there's a meteor shower."

He strode along a huge table, beating a fist rhythmically into one hand. "They won't be so sure, at first. Who wants to risk his rank by giving the nationwide signal that makes everyone in the country pull ground over his head, that makes our own projectile sites set to buzz? Finally, they are certain: they freeze for a moment. Meanwhile, the rockets are zooming down—how fast, we don't know. The men un-freeze, they trip each other up, they tangle frantically. Then, they press the button; then, the nationwide signal starts our radio alarms."

Plunkett turned to his wife, spread earnest, quivering arms. "And then, Ann, we freeze when we hear it! At last, we start for the cellar. Who knows, who can dare to say, how much has been cut off the margin of safety by that time? No, if they claim that six minutes is the safety factor, we'll give half of it to the alarm system. Three minutes for us."

One more spoonful," Ann urged Dinah. "Just one more. Down it goes!"

Josephine Dawkins and Herbie were cleaning the feed trolley in the shed at the near end of the chicken house.

"All done, pop," the boy grinned at his father. "And the eggs taken care of. When does Mr. Whiting pick 'em up?"

"Nine o'clock. Did you finish feeding the hens in the last house?"

"I said all done, didn't I?" Herbie asked with adolescent impatience. "When I say a thing, I mean it."

"Good. You kids better get at your books. Hey, stop that! Education will be very important, afterwards. You never know what will be useful. And maybe only your mother and I to teach you."

"Gee," Herbie nodded at Josephine. "Think of that."

She pulled at her jumper where it was very tight over newly swelling breasts and patted her blonde braided hair. "What about my mother and father, Mr. Plunkett? Won't they be—be—"

"Naw!" Herbie laughed the loud, country laugh he'd been practicing lately. "They're dead-enders. They won't pull through. They live in the City, don't they? They'll just be some—"

"Herbie!"

"—some foam on a mushroom-shaped cloud," he finished, utterly entranced by the image. "Gosh, I'm sorry," he said, as he looked from his angry father to the quivering girl. He went on in a studiously reasonable voice. "But it's the truth, anyway. That's why they sent you and Lester here. I guess I'll marry you afterwards. And you ought to get in the habit of calling him pop. Because that's the way it'll be."

Josephine squeezed her eyes shut, kicked the shed door open, and ran out. "I hate you, Herbie Plunkett," she wept. "You're a beast!"

Herbie grimaced at his father—*women, women, women!*—and ran after her. "Hey, Jo! Listen!"

The trouble was, Plunkett thought worriedly as he carried the emergency bulbs for the hydroponic garden into the cellar—the trouble was that Herbie had learned through constant reiteration the one thing; survival came before all else, and amenities were merely amenities.

Strength and self-sufficiency—Plunkett had worked out the virtues his children needed years ago, sitting in air-conditioned offices and totting corporation balances with one eye always on the calendar.

"Still," Plunkett muttered, "still—Herbie shouldn't—" He shook his head.

He inspected the incubators near the long steaming tables of the hydroponic garden. A tray about ready to hatch. They'd have to start assembling eggs to replace it in the morning. He paused in the third room, filled a gap in the bookshelves.

"Hope Josephine steadies the boy in his schoolwork. If he fails that next exam, they'll make me send him to town regularly. Now *there's* an aspect of survival I can hit Herbie with."

He realized he'd been talking to himself, a habit he'd been combating futilely for more than a month. Stuffy talk, too. He was becoming like those people who left tracts on trolley cars.

"Have to start watching myself," he commented. "Dammit, again!"

The telephone clattered upstairs. He heard Ann walk across to it, that serene, unhurried walk all pregnant women seem to have.

"Elliot! Nat Medarie."

"Tell him I'm coming, Ann." He swung the vault-like door carefully shut behind him, looked at it for a moment, and started up the high stone steps.

"Hello, Nat. What's new?"

"Hi, Plunk. Just got a postcard from Fitzgerald. Remember him? The abandoned silver mine in Montana? Yeah. He says we've got to go on the basis that lithium and hydrogen bombs will be used."

Plunkett leaned against the wall with his elbow. He cradled the receiver, on his right shoulder so he could light a cigarette. "Fitzgerald can be wrong sometimes."

"Uhm. I don't know. But you know what a lithium bomb means, don't you?"

"It means," Plunkett said, staring through the wall of the house and into a boiling Earth, "that a chain reaction may be set off in the atmosphere if enough of them are used. Maybe if only one—"

"Oh, can it," Medarie interrupted. "That gets us nowhere. That way nobody gets through, and we might as well start shuttling from church to bar-room like my brother-in-law in Chicago is doing right now. Fred, I used to say to him——No, listen Plunk: it means I was right. You didn't dig deep enough."

"*Deep* enough! I'm as far down as I want to go. If I don't have enough layers of lead and concrete to shield me—well, if they can crack my shell, then you won't be able to walk on the surface before you die of thirst, Nat. No—I sunk my dough in power supply. Once that fails, you'll find yourself putting the used air back into your empty oxygen tanks by hand!"

The other man chuckled. "All right. I *hope* I see you around."

"And I hope I see…" Plunkett twisted around to face the front window as an old station wagon bumped over the ruts in his driveway. "Say, Nat, what do you know? Charlie Whiting just drove up. Isn't this Sunday?"

"Yeah. He hit my place early, too. Some sort of political meeting in town and he wants to make it. It's not enough that the striped-pants brigade are practically glaring into each other's eyebrows this time. A couple of local philosophers are impatient with the slow pace at which their extinction is approaching, and they're getting together to see if they can't hurry it up some."

"Don't be bitter," Plunkett smiled.

"Here's praying at you. Regards to Ann, Plunk."

Plunkett cradled the receiver and ambled downstairs. Outside, he watched Charlie Whiting pull the door of the station wagon open on its one desperate hinge.

"Eggs stowed, Mr. Plunkett," Charlie said. "Receipt signed. Here. You'll get a check Wednesday."

"Thanks, Charlie. Hey, you kids get back to your books. Go on, Herbie. You're having an English quiz tonight. Eggs still going up, Charlie?"

"Up she goes." The old man slid onto the cracked leather seat and pulled the door shut deftly. He bent his arm on the open window. "Heh. And every time she does I make a little more off you survivor fellas who are too scairt to carry 'em into town yourself."

"Well, you're entitled to it," Plunkett said, uncomfortably. "What about this meeting in town?"

"Bunch of folks goin' to discuss the conference. I say we pull out. I say we walk right out of the dern thing. This country never won a conference yet. A million conferences the last few years and everyone knows what's gonna happen sooner or later. Heh. They're just wastin' time. Hit 'em first, I say."

"Maybe we will. Maybe they will. Or—maybe, Charlie—a couple of different nations will get what looks like a good idea at the same time."

Charlie Whiting shoved his foot down and ground the starter. "You don't make sense. If we hit 'em first how can they do the same to us? Hit 'em first—hard enough— and they'll never recover in time to hit us back. That's what I say. But you survivor fellas—" he shook his white head angrily as the car shot away.

"Hey!" he yelled, turning into the road. "Hey, look!"

Plunkett looked over his shoulder. Charlie Whiting was gesturing at him with his left hand, the forefinger pointing out and the thumb up straight.

"Look, Mr. Plunkett," the old man called. "Boom! Boom! Boom!" He cackled hysterically and writhed over the steering wheel.

Rusty scuttled around the side of the house, and after him, yipping frantically in ancient canine tradition.

Plunkett watched the receding car until it swept around the curve two miles away. He stared at the small dog returning proudly.

Poor Whiting. Poor everybody, for that matter, who had a normal distrust of crackpots.

How could you permit a greedy old codger like Whiting to buy your produce, just so you and your family wouldn't have to risk trips into town?

Well, it was a matter of having decided years ago that the world was too full of people who were convinced that they were faster on the draw than anyone else—and the other fellow was bluffing anyway. People who believed that two small boys could pile up snowballs across the street from each other and go home without having used them, people who discussed the merits of concrete fences as opposed to wire guardrails while their automobile skidded over the cliff. People who were righteous. People who were apathetic.

It was the last group, Plunkett remembered, who had made him stop buttonholing his fellows, at last. You got tired of standing around in a hair shirt and pointing ominously at the heavens. You got to the point where you wished the human race well but you wanted to pull you and yours out of the way of its tantrums. Survival for the individual and his family, you thought

Clang-ng-ng-ng-ng!

Plunkett pressed the stud on his stopwatch. Funny. There was no practice alarm scheduled for today. All the kids were out of the house, except for Saul—and he wouldn't dare to leave his room, let alone tamper with the alarm. Unless, perhaps, Ann—

He walked inside the kitchen. Ann was running toward the door, carrying Dinah. Her face was oddly unfamiliar. "Saulie!" she screamed. "Saulie! Hurry up, Saulie!"

"I'm, coming, momma," the boy yelled as he clattered down the stairs. "I'm coming as fast as I can! I'll make it!"

Plunkett understood. He put a heavy hand on the wall, under the dinner-plate clock.

He watched his wife struggle down the steps into the cellar. Saul ran past him and out of the door, arms flailing. "I'll make it, poppa! I'll make it!"

Plunkett felt his stomach move. He swallowed with great care. "Don't hurry, son," he whispered. "It's only judgment day."

He straightened out and looked at his watch, noticing that his hand on the wall had left its moist outline behind. One minute, twelve seconds. Not bad. Not bad at all. He'd figured on three.

Clang-ng-ng-ng-ng!

He started to shake himself and began a shudder that he couldn't control. What was the matter? He knew what he had to do. He had to unpack the portable lathe that was still in the barn....

"Elliot!" his wife called.

He found himself sliding down the steps on feet that somehow wouldn't lift when he wanted them to. He stumbled through the open cellar door. Frightened faces dotted the room in an unrecognizable jumble.

"We all here?" he croaked.

"All here, poppa," Saul said from his position near the aeration machinery. "Lester and Herbie are in the far room, by the other switch. Why is Josephine crying? Lester isn't crying. I'm not crying, either."

Plunkett nodded vaguely at the slim, sobbing girl and put his hand on the lever protruding from the concrete wall. He glanced at his watch again. Two minutes, ten seconds. Not bad.

"Mr. Plunkett!" Lester Dawkins sped in from the corridor. "Mr. Plunkett! Herbie ran out of the other door to get Rusty. I told him—"

Two minutes, twenty seconds, Plunkett realized as he leaped to the top of the steps. Herbie was running across the vegetable garden, snapping his fingers behind him to lure Rusty on. When he saw his father, his mouth stiffened with shock. He broke stride for a moment, and the dog charged joyously between his legs. Herbie fell.

Plunkett stepped forward. *Two minutes, forty seconds.* Herbie jerked himself to his feet, put his head down—and ran.

Was that dim thump a distant explosion? There — another one! Like a giant belching. Who had started it? And did it matter—now?

Three minutes. Rusty scampered down the cellar steps, his head back, his tail flickering from side to side. Herbie panted up. Plunkett grabbed him by the collar and jumped.

And as he jumped he saw—far to the south—the umbrellas opening their agony upon the land. Rows upon swirling rows of them….

He tossed the boy ahead when he landed. *Three minutes, five seconds.* He threw the switch, and, without waiting for the door to close and seal, darted into the corridor. That took care of two doors; the other switch controlled the remaining entrances. He reached it. He pulled it. He looked at his watch. *Three minutes, twenty seconds.* "The bombs," blubbered Josephine. "The bombs!"

Ann was scrabbling Herbie to her in the main room, feeling his arm caressing his hair, pulling him in for a wild hug and crying out yet again, "Herbie! Herbie! Herbie!"

"I know you're gonna lick me pop. I—I just want you to know that I think you ought to."

"I'm not going to lick you, son."

"You're not ? But gee, I deserve a licking. I deserve the worst—"

"You may," Plunkett said, gasping at the wall of clicking geigers. "*You may deserve a beating,*" he yelled, so loudly that they all whirled to face him, "but I won't punish you, not only for now, but forever! And as I with you," he screamed, "so you, with yours! Understand?"

"Yes," they replied in a weeping, ragged chorus. "We understand!"

"Swear!" Swear that you and your children and your children's chilldren will never punish another human being—no matter what the provocation."

"We swear!" they bawled at him. "We swear!"

Then they all sat down.

To wait.

0.053 SEC.
N

100 METERS

AEC-55-529

AEC-55-5294
Los Alamos, New Mexico...The fireball of the Trinity explosion, .053 seconds after detonation, as it shook the desert near the town of San Antonio, New Mexico, on July 16, 1945. This first atomic device, developed and built by the university of California's Los Alamos Scientific Laboratory in New Mexico, had a yield equivalent to about 20 kilotons (20,000 tons) of TNT. Credit Los Alamos Scientific Laboratory

Photograph and orignal caption of the Trinity explosion, 1945.
(Photo United States Archives.)

Blast!

On July 25th, Bikini Atoll experienced the fourth nuclear weapon ever detonated, Shot Baker, which turned the peaceful waters of the Bikini lagoon into the largest radioactive soup on the planet. Sealife was irradiated, and fallout particles covered what remained afloat of the 95 ships first anchored in the lagoon, some with their decks holding caged sheep, goats, pigs, and rats. In less than an hour patrol boats carrying men to recover instruments were sent to the ships. Salvage crews were working underneath the water two hours later. All told the U.S. Government exposed 15,000 sailors to the after effects of nuclear weapons, shortening their lifespans based on the amounts of exposure to radioactive material. The blasts of Operation Crossroads were all bigger than expected, and as the Cold War progressed, mushroom clouds became larger, and fallout more and more of a problem. The blast always sets off a different series of problems for mankind in our stories, not all with predictable results.

The Blast
Stuart Cloete

I am writing this because today I saw two girls. It was very odd after twenty years. I do not know if anyone—the word anyone looks funny—will ever find this, or be able to read it, or even if it will last, because it is written in pencil. Naturally there is no ink. It all dried up long ago, but there are plenty of pencils, thousands of them, pencils by the hundred thousand gross—all the best kinds, just for the picking up.

It's difficult to know where to begin. It all happened so long ago that some of the details are fogged and I'm even doubtful of the chronology. The big thing, of course, the real beginning, was the bombing of Hiroshima and Nagasaki—the atomic bomb and the bungling that followed it after the war: fear of Russia, fear of free enterprise, fear of Communism, of Fascism—fear, in fact. I remember one thing in '46, and that was a senator from Florida saying that we should destroy every facility we possessed capable of producing only destructive forms of atomic energy. This made a great impression on me, just as Roosevelt's saying, "All we have to fear is fear itself," had done. But, of course, we did not pay any more attention to this senator than we had to the late President. We entered into a kind of armament race. Strength was the thing, power politics; and atoms were power. The common man didn't really believe in it, but what could he do? When had he ever been able to prevent wars? All he did was fight them. Anyway, there was no war. There was only a state of fear. There were only rumors—stories that Russia and Spain were only a year behind us in the race for atomic production.

These two countries were, of course, at opposite ideological poles and were a constant threat not only to each other, but to the world. Then there was the rumor that no one believed, but which nevertheless had the psychological effect of adding to the general fear and uncertainty of mankind. It was that a group of Germans in South America had discovered new fissionable material and that the process of refining it was so simple that bombs could be made in any garage—or if not quite in a garage, in almost any small machine shop. This, if it were true, naturally would render the inspection measures discussed by the United Nations completely ineffective because, quite obviously, all small plants all over the world could not be kept under supervision. This rumor appeared, if I remember correctly, in the late spring of '47 after the U.N. had met at Lake Success.

Then in the summer of '47 came a new rumor—only it was a little more than a rumor because the same story came from several accredited sources—that the new bombs were minuscule, no bigger than a fountain pen, and could be taken anywhere and planted with impunity. This probably was untrue, but certainly the underlying principle was true. Bombs were being made that were both smaller and more powerful. We had been making them ourselves, ever since the very first ones we'd used in the New Mexico test and in Japan, but this information was kept from the people. Things of the greatest moment to the public were seldom made public, and the man in the street, misled by the silence of the Army and Navy and the scientists they muzzled, had no inkling of the improvements which had been effected or of the fact that the State Department was aware that the experiments in heavy water, begun during the war by the Germans, were being continued in this hemisphere. We knew that there were many Germans in South America. We knew that many war criminals had escaped there, by various subterfuges and in various disguises. We knew that young Norwegian Nazis had been invited over as colonists. We knew that Russia was courting the all but openly Fascist southern republics—and knowing all this we discounted it all.

What happened next is history. I never bothered writing about it till today, because, thinking myself the only survivor, I could see little point in recording the events of the last twenty years. It is, I think, the year 1967 now; and the month—I am less certain of the months—is probably May. I deduce this from the flowering shrubs, the state of the foliage, and the fact that most of the young birds have flown from their nests.

Perhaps, too, I have avoided writing, though writing comes easily to me (it used to be my profession; I was a novelist), because of the terror of those days, which I wish to forget if possible. Even now, though the pain has been softened slightly by the passage of time, it will be difficult for me to write of the death of my wife, who, having survived the first blasts and succeeded in living with me almost a year, finally died in my arms, of the Red Death, as it came to be called.

None of this, of course, is the true reason for having either not written before or for writing now. The real reason is that previously there was no one to write for; but now there is, because I have seen people. People are an audience, and some old reflex in me has been activated.

That was the way I used to be, as full of ideas as an oyster is full of meat (or fish, I suppose it is). But anyway, once I had an idea, I had to write it to make room for new ideas.

I thought I was over it all. Just as I had thought I was over women—girls. But I see that I have deceived myself and that this manuscript, this record, may be of some historic value. That is the true reason for this work that I am writing in a mixture of hope and fear. I am filling in time till something happens. Till what happens? That is what I want to know. But something must happen....

At the time of the blast—before it, that is—I was well known as the author of several South African novels. I am of South African descent and, at that time, still had a farm in the Transvaal. I suppose I have it still—even now. This is probably what saved my life, for in the beginning, though there were others who came through the plague, most people were apparently unable to stand the conditions of life when all meat had to be hunted and savage animals roamed through the piled canyons of what had been the greatest city in the world. Of course, there were great quantities of canned goods, but fresh meat, fuel and water were difficult to obtain for those who were unaccustomed to dealing with life in the raw.

I had better go back to the day of the blast. The explosion took place on the 5th of October, 1947. That date is engraved on my mind. It was what might be called the last real date in history. I was in the interesting position of having survived history, of being history itself—a kind of lonely Adam in a jungle where terror stalked by day and night.

The Adam idea is now suddenly particularly apt because of the Eves that I have seen. I wonder what Adam would have done with two Eves. Anyway, I am glad I have hidden from them, because if they have survived, others must have. It has always seemed possible to me that in remote parts of the world some groups of those people we used to call savages might have survived, saved by their isolation from the diseases set up by radioactivity and immune or partially immune, because of their diet and the lives they led, to the Red Death which spread over the North. I have evidently been right, for the two girls—they are in their early twenties from the look of them—could not have raised themselves; which again brings up the question: Are those with them friends or enemies, and what is my position? Do I wish to be a friend to these strangers after twenty years alone? That remains to be seen. The thing to do now is to continue my narrative and to describe what was certainly the end of our civilization and might have been the end of mankind—though of course man might have reappeared again by a process of natural selection in a few million years; unless this time the new animals, such as the giant wolves that stand as high as a horse, and the immense brown and white minks that attack cattle and suck their blood in a few minutes, and the many other strange beasts and birds should prove to be too much for such primitive types of man as might arise. This, at any rate, had been my opinion until I saw the two girls. It is now subject to modification.

That I have succeeded in my fight against such wild beasts as I have described is due to my possession of modern weapons. These animals, however, are quite natural—phenomena that science once predicted might arise through the effect of atomic fission on the genes and chromosomes of the embryos extant at the time of the explosion. Or at least that is the way I remember it, though at the time—that is, before it happened—I did not pay much attention to the details about the atom in the magazines and papers, because I had no inclinations toward nuclear physics, being engaged at the time in writing a play about some veterans who sought to escape reality on a desert island.

It is interesting to me to see how I keep evading the issue, how I keep side-tracking myself in a kind of escape mechanism. Evidently I do not want to write about that time, about the terror of those days and the horror that followed them.

The center of the blast was said to have been Gramercy Park, probably the Players Club. It was estimated that three hundred thousand people were killed. To physicists, a human being is an object as full of holes as a Swiss cheese and held together only by some subtle balance of electrical forces which I have never understood or even really believed in. It is hard to believe that a beautiful woman held warm and soft in your arms has no reality, or that a dog or a horse is merely a combination of chemicals which react upon one another and produce the illusion which we—illusions ourselves—call dogs and horses. Anyway, the scientists who discovered all this have gone. Never have men been more unjustly hoisted with their own petard.

The scientists were for the most part against millitary control of the bomb, and almost joined the church, in a strange remarriage of opposing forces, against its use. The power of this nuclear force had proved strong enough to weld the breach which had separated God and Science during the last century. No longer did a man have to choose between them: If he believed in Science, he had to believe in God. But there were too few believers in either—in God or in Science—or in anything. Ours was a time of cynical disbelief.

I note here that I have written about holding a beautiful woman in my arms. This is a disturbing thought. It is so new. Women belong to the past.

But to return to my story—

Another half-million people were wounded by flying debris or burned in varying degrees. A tiny blister, however, proved as bad as a serious burn: There was no case of recovery from a burn of any size. The patient simply appeared to dissolve slowly from the nucleus of the wound. The deaths were extremely painful, and since there were neither sufficient hospital facilities nor enough drugs of any kind to stifle pain, thousands committed suicide, while others were killed by their friends in mercy killings.

All public services broke down, including fire and police, keymen having been killed, water mains destroyed, telephone and telegraph communication ruined beyond repair. Our technological back was broken; our civilization writhed like a wounded snake, unable to advance and incapable of retreat. We were too complex to return to simplicity; and only then, when it was too late, did it become apparent to the man in the street on what a fragile base his life had rested and how tenuous had been his hold upon existence. "One world or no world," our greatest men had said, but no one had believed them. Having refused one world, we now had no world, and each man reacted according to his nature. Some, as I say, committed suicide, not merely because they were wounded or burned but because they were terrified. They bolted like animals, leaping from the housetops of the vast circle of buildings that surrounded the empty center of devastation. Some prayed, some cursed, some raped and murdered, their lusts liberated in final orgy. The police tried in certain parts to keep order, and shot looters and assassins till their ammunition gave out, when they were lynched by police-hating mobs. All the jewelry stores were broken into, and rings and ornaments were scattered everywhere. But now, of course, diamonds and gold were useless.

The odd thing was how quickly moral disintegration set in. Within an hour of the blast, there were shots and screams in the streets. The human wolves of the underworld found themselves free to do their will and were quick to seize the opportunity, evidently not realizing that they had in this hour become obsolete. For the things they liked—cars, jewels, furs, money, clothes—had actually ceased to exist, in principle, though they were all there, to be had for the taking. For forty-eight hours, there was madness and murder, screams, shots and shouts; the parading of loose women in stolen ermine cloaks, mink coats, stone marten stoles, with diamond tiaras on their bleached-blond hair. For forty-eight hours, cars roared through the streets and tommy guns spat from the cars. Then the gasoline began to give out in the filling stations, and the ammunition began to give out for the tommy guns as it had earlier for the police, and there was no one to hold up. Gangsters could go into any store and take anything. Their women dripped with jewels, their cars were stacked with valuable furs and piled with cases of Scotch and gin and rye. They had eaten their fill of steak cooked by trembling chefs at the point of a gun. But now there were neither steaks nor chefs left, and there was no water to wash the grime from their faces and the blood from their hands. And then, as suddenly as their reign of terror had begun, it ended in terror on their part. Here was a new world that they could not understand, where all that they had ever wanted was theirs and they were carrying it off. But to where, and for what? In this world they were the suckers, and, like wild animals betrayed by this new environment, they turned upon one another in a kind of gang war of extinction. Enemies of society, finding no society, they could logically do little else.

This, of course, is all somewhat academically stated, the drama having lost its sharp cutting edge with the passing years. But there are incidents, vignettes that still stand out, separated from the general mass of somewhat amorphous memory and theory and rationalization, like the red-capped figure to be found in almost every Corot landscape. There was the girl who ran into Grand Central Station pursued by two men, whom I shot. It was as simple as that. I was going out to get canned goods from the basement of a ruined store and had a rifle in my hand. I knew the girl by sight; she was a dancer in a nearby musical show. She smiled at me and said thank you as if I had opened a door for her. And I, regretting the expenditure of my two shells, wondered if it had been worthwhile. The shots on my part, and the smile on the girl's, belonged to the other, finished world. They were out of their context here. But it was interesting or it appears to have been so now, to watch the changing forms of action; to watch readjustment and adaptation in this strange period where aeons overlapped as the first terrible waves of the future beat against the fragile mosaic of our civilization.

In a book published a year or so before it happened, a number of scientists had predicted what might occur, and one of them had explained what would take place if an atomic bomb were dropped in Gramercy Park. The fact that the explosion actually did take place in Gramercy Park could have been a matter of coincidence, or luck, or it might have been suggested by the chapter in question. The depositor of the bomb may have said, "Well, if they want it there, let them have it there." He may even have had a kind of perverted sense of humor, like the guards at Buchenwald who gave towels to those of their victims who were about to be gassed, telling them the Murder House was for baths; or again, with that tidy Nazi mind, he may have wished to make fact conform to fiction. God knows this has happened often enough before with Jules Verne, Conan Doyle, H. G. Wells, and an endless series of "astounding stories" all based on scientific possibilities. The point, however, is that the explosion did not operate quite as was expected, because, for some unknown reason, the blast did not fade out and get weaker and weaker as the distance from its center increased. Instead, it ended as if it were cut off by an invisible wall.

The best way to describe it would be to imagine the force of the blast as something tied to a string that was being swung round and round. Everything within the area covered by the string was destroyed, and everything only a few yards beyond it was left, with the exception of such minor damage as some broken windows, intact. The blast at that point appeared to take an upward direction, so that in the area beyond the destroyed center there was no further destruction except that due to fires caused by the falling debris. This destruction was somewhat haphazard, certain buildings escaped all damage while whole areas were completely gutted.

After the original reign of disorder and mayhem, the city started to reorganize itself. Emergency repairs were effected to water supplies, and local authorities were linked by provisional army field telephones. Citizens formed themselves into troops of vigilantes, and though there was some street fighting between different groups which took each other for bandit bands, order was in some degree restored. But there was no sense of security or continuity, for if there is no reason to expect tomorrow to dawn, today loses its validity. Were more bombs going to go off? What was going to happen about food, or work, or money?

People began to evacuate the city in cars, on foot, on bicycles. They left the island of Manhattan, endless black caterpillars of humanity creeping over every bridge, appearing from under the ground in every tunnel. They were migrating like lemmings. Driven by fear, they were going into the unknown where they would inevitably die.

They swarmed over the land like locusts, devastating it, marching till they were halfway to Canada. Some even reached the Canadian border, where they met Canadians marching down from Montreal and Toronto. What had taken place in New York was not an isolated phenomenon. Every big city in North America had suffered the same experience. No city except Washington was completely destroyed, but the population of all had been panicked, and the cumulative effect of these multiple bombings was much more serious than the total destruction of any single city, because all the urban populations fled to the country—which they destroyed; to the small towns and villages where, when once what was happening was understood, the villagers defended themselves with guns and even pitchforks, ex-soldiers fighting from tractors as if they were tanks. It was civil war, mass suicide. Millions starved, hundreds of thousands were killed. And North America as a power, as a civilization, ceased to exist. But as if even this were not enough, disaster was piled upon disaster, and the sickness hit us. First came diseases that were caused, it was said, by radioactivity. Then came the Red Death. The Red Death appears to have been general all over the civilized world.

The news of the period, naturally, was garbled; but there was some news. A few radio hams were able to receive messages. Ships at sea relayed frantic, and conflicting reports. Naturally, within hours of the disaster, our air fleets set out for Europe and in a series of retaliatory raids blotted out many centers of military and industrial strength. Every big town in England had been blown up at the same time that ours were: London, Manchester, Birmingham, Liverpool, all had ceased to exist. But fortunately the United States, anticipating the possibility of such an attack, had the foresight to be ready for it and had several fleets of immense bombers, complete with atomic bombs and personnel hidden in secret underground hangars not only in vast deserts of the Southwest, but in the depths of the Louisiana swamps and in the great isolated plains of the Northwest. These fleets were manned by men who had signed articles that subjected them to punishments of the greatest severity should any information about their work leak out. Even anticipating the destruction of central authority, the commanding officers of these areas had sealed instructions that they were to open if communication broke down.

When the attack came, the wings of retaliation were soon in the air and within hours of the first blast our world was gone. There was never in anyone's mind, apparently, the idea that any country other than Russia could have been responsible for the attack upon us. Ever since the end of the great Thirty Years War—which raged openly or secretly from 1914 through 1945—we had been barraged with stories of the Russian menace. It was an improved model of the old "yellow peril" danger.

What was forgotten was that Germany was our enemy—the enemy of Russia and America and England—and that nothing would please Germany better than the mutual destruction of the U.S.S.R. and the Western democracies. The Germans hoped this would happen and, in my opinion, engineered it—perhaps even by setting off the explosion in America, knowing that we, in our fear and bewilderment, would attack Russia in a retaliatory reflex. What the Germans did not foresee (or perhaps they did not care) was that such a war would extinguish them with the rest of mechanized mankind. Or again they—the Germans—may have had such confidence in their Spenglerian myth that they assumed their blond beasts could survive any terror.

And so, perhaps, they could have—until the plague came along. Then they died along with others, as far as one can make out.

The Red Death was a contagious fever with an incubation period of seven days. The first symptom was a high color which gave the appearance of great health. With this went high spirits, a mad gaiety which made the victims dance and sing, even in the streets, so that we ran from people we saw singing or dancing, as if they were the plague, which indeed they were. They next fell into a coma from which they awakened with their skins scarlet in color, in a state of berserk fury, with the strength of maniacs—attacking anyone they saw, striking at them, scratching and biting like mad dogs. Then, their energy exhausted, they fell to the ground and died in a few hours, fully conscious of what was going on around them. I believe direct contact was the commonest cause of infection, though there must have been others: through dust in the air or, perhaps, the contamination of water. Escape was virtually impossible; the disease seemed in the end to have struck down everyone.

This, then, is the approximate sequence of events: the explosion; the reign of terror; the exodus; the temporary reorganization; the civil war between escaping city people and the rural population, which finally turned into a States' War as refugees were stopped at the state lines; the illnesses that we called radioactive; and, finally, the pestilence that till today I thought had killed every living human being in the Western Hemisphere with the exception of myself and perhaps some Indians in the forests of the upper Amazon or Orinoco. Some of the last news that we got through was that the same disease had broken out in both Buenos Aires and Rio. This makes me think now, looking back on it, that the bacteriological war the attackers planned for us got completely out of control.

What happened in the Far East, in Australia and Asia, I have no idea. We never heard anything from there, and perhaps they, too, survived. Perhaps a new empire of Orientals arose. I doubt it, though, because I feel that they would surely have established some kind of communication with the East coast of the United States. I think it is safe to assume that sickness and death overtook everyone in the Far East as well, except for isolated tribesmen and perhaps the inhabitants of such a remote place as Lhasa, the sacred city of Tibet. It would be interesting if Lhasa alone were left as the last center of learning, since it was probably the first.

At one time some of us considered it possible that Hitler, whose death had never been actually proved, had had the bombs placed and had followed them with bacteriological warfare in his mad plan of revenge. But when we found the disease had reached Europe, where the population, weakened by famine, would certainly not have been able to resist a sickness which had struck us here, where we were in our full strength, and exterminated us, this idea seemed less likely, though Hitler had said that if he fell, the world would fall with him.

It is here that the theory of something having gone wrong comes in and the possibility of a certain poetic justice enters the picture. And I for one return to the theory that the

Germans, acting as agents provocateurs, incited the military titans of the world against one another, and then, having started the war, found themselves ground between the upper and the nether millstones of the Lord God, Who is not lightly mocked.

The two girls I had seen were standing on a small hill on the corner of Fifth Avenue and 23d Street. I saw them clearly silhouetted against the sky line. They had long spears in their hands and were leading horses. One horse was a bay and the other a chestnut. The girls were staring north, shading their eyes with their hands, while the horses cropped the grass beside them. Both girls were blond. Their hair was knotted on their necks and they wore what looked like buckskin shirts and trousers. I had trouble with the dogs, Vixen and Bodo; the girls were upwind and the dogs had never smelled a woman before—or any other human being but me, for that matter—and they probably thought of me as one of themselves, since I had bred them and their parents before them and they were never separated from me, even sleeping on the same heap of skins in the cave I had constructed in the ruins of the Chelsea Hotel. It has always seemed to me that the great secret of training and handling animals is identification with them; and my years alone with them have fully confirmed this belief.

Having described the girls, I suppose I had better describe myself, for if, as it now seems, there may be other people in the world, I and my kind are certainly all but extinct.

I was born in Paris in 1897, just in time to serve in the first World War. I was severely wounded and went to live in South Africa, where I farmed cattle for ten years. I then took to writing, returned to England and came from there to the United States, where I remained, apart from a few trips to England, France and the Bahamas, till the second World War, when I married a charming American girl, an artist, and continued writing while I waited for the war to end. My age and disabilities prevented my doing anything more active. Among others, I wrote and talked of the dangers of our Anglo-American retention of the bomb secret, maintaining that manufacture should cease and control be given to the United Nations. I also said that our civilization, as we knew it, was finished; and that as others were saying and writing at the same time the future presented only two alternatives: the liberation of man through atomic power or the destruction of our civilization, either by great nations in an undeclared war, which was what we feared, or by—and this was more or less in the realm of "astounding fiction" stories—atomic bandits or nihilists.

My wife and I lived in a small studio penthouse on the eleventh floor of the Whitby Apartments on West 45th Street, opposite the Martin Beck Theater. I was over there yesterday and it is still almost intact, having been extremely well constructed sometime in the twenties. As a matter of fact, I shot a mountain lion that my dogs had driven into a basement apartment which had, when we lived there, been occupied by a drummer. Hunting big game in old apartment houses is the most dangerous form of shooting there is and makes any African safari look like child's play, because the animals are likely to attack from the immediate flank—that is, from any apartment—as you move down a passage. Hunting under such conditions would be quite impossible without dogs that first investigate the building and bay up the den of any animal that is lurking there. The losses in dogs are heavy; but I am continually breeding new ones—huge animals of mixed Saint Bernard, Newfoundland, great Dane, Irish wolf-hound, bloodhound, mastiff, police dog and Husky blood—which generation by generation become larger, fiercer, and better hunters by the Darwinian process of survival of the fittest. The feral dogs—the wild stock that has survived and bred itself by mongrelization—are not much bigger than jackals or coyotes, but are of a broken color. The wild cattle, too, are often strangely colored—red and black, or brindle and white—and in many other animals the pigmentation has been changed, with the result that most animals are now pintos or piebald rather than red or brown as they used to be, while albinos have been almost completely bred out among both cats and poultry that have gone wild.

When I am out for a stroll, as I was today, I usually take only a couple of well-trained dogs as guards to inform me of any danger that I do not see myself, which was lucky for the girls and their horses. For had I been hunting with my pack, as I do every second day or so, the girls would undoubtedly have been torn to pieces, since this is my way of feeding my dogs. They are trained to pull down any living thing and, having done so, to break it up as English hounds did a fox. Of course, when hunting the mutations such as the giant wolf and mink and a kind of wild ox that resembles the extinct European aurochs, I use a rifle—a 450 express that I selected at Abercrombie and Fitch—which has immense striking power. The dogs, instead of attacking game that is too big for them, merely bring it to bay and hold it till I come and then, as I fire, run in upon it. It is impossible for anyone who has not seen them to imagine the strength of these dogs, standing over thirty inches at the shoulder, or, for that matter, to visualize the animals against which they are pitted.

From my point of view, there is a certain interest in the change in my own character because, when I first went to Africa as a young man, I was an ardent hunter. Then, at the age of thirty-five, I gave up shooting altogether. Now I, like my dogs, have reverted atavistically, and hunting is my only pleasure. My mind is less disciplined than it was when I used to write for the magazines—for the *Saturday Evening Post* and *Collier's* and *Cosmopolitan*. It drifts along strange paths. I can imagine what an editor would say about this manuscript, but where are the editors now? Dogs and hunting have become my passion. For at least ten years, I have done no thinking beyond following the spoor of a gigantic bear or looking for the sign of a moose. So the shock of seeing people again has disturbed my mind and, like one of my own dogs grubbing for a buried bone, I dig among my memories seeking for incidents and examples that will elucidate or explain what has happened. This is not a story. It has no plot. It is a testament, a form of history, a literary curiosity written for myself as a form of justification, as a debt that I, the last man of the past, must owe to an unborn future.

My narrative must drift back and forth to catch memories that are like butterflies as they flick through my mind, for I am an old man and cannot be certain that they will ever return. So I use what used to be called the technique of the throwback, or flashback. I editorialize. I evade issues. I return to them. How, for instance, can I write about the death of my wife? I can't. But the description of her death will be there, threaded like every twentieth bead on the string of my life. I cannot coldly discuss killing and eating Annie, my pet dog. Nevertheless, I did kill and eat her. I also killed many other pet dogs for people who at first reviled me and then, finding they had no means of feeding them, begged me to do what they could not do themselves.

We also ate Edward, the kinkajou we had had for four years, in a stew. There was no food for pet animals, and it was necessary to dispose of them all. I have never had a nicer pet than a kinkajou, a South American animal resembling, though not connected with, a lemur. It has a long prehensile tail, a soft fur, and charming snuggly habits. It is about the size of a cat and is more or less nocturnal. We never took to cannibalism, though both cannibalism and infanticide were widely practiced and probably, under such conditions, to be condoned. Morality can exist only in a social framework. Once the framework has gone, there can be no morality and, for that matter, no immorality. I, for instance, alone in the world, cannot be immoral. There is no subject for immorality and no one to declare any act to be immoral. A man alone cannot be good or bad. He cannot steal, fight, lie or murder.

Now I return to animals because it is among animals that the last twenty years of my life have been lived. There were, as I have said, several animal mutations: the giant wolf, the great mink and the aurochs. In addition to these, there was an immense increase in the wild animals indigenous to New York State, such as the timber wolf, beaver, black bear, lynx, mountain lion, deer, moose and bobcat. There were even some bison and caribou. There were, of course, packs of wild dogs descended from such domestic dogs as survived, and feral cats which looked like big tabbies. There were also many game birds: pheasant, ptarmigan, grouse, and a new kind of American jungle fowl which evolved from ordinary poultry. There were a great number of wild goats in the ruins of New York City. They came from the few domestic goats that were here at the time of the disaster. There were also some ibex, white Rocky Mountain goats, mouflon and other wild sheep, and a herd of Shetland ponies, descendants of those which escaped from the Central Park Zoo. Some lunatic, very shortly after the explosion, had thrown open every cage in the zoo, and since no one had time to deal with the liberated animals, a number of them survived and became acclimated. Now there are tigers in New York, which, in their long winter coats, resemble the great tigers of Manchuria. There are also leopards, jaguars and a wide variety of buck and antelope which, despite the severity of the winters, have managed to survive. As happened elsewhere where their ranges overlapped, the lions were soon exterminated by the tigers. There is at least one herd of zebra and another of donkeys. Occasionally they hybridize. There are no horses, and the two that I saw today are the first I have seen for twenty years. Grizzly bears have spread from the West and are very large—even bigger, I should say, than the Kodiak bears. I have seen marks where they sharpened their claws against a tree in Central Park more than twenty feet from the ground. There are several families of polar bears living along both the Hudson and East rivers. There is a great colony of seals at Ellis Island. This gives a picture of the fauna of Manhattan Island and the vicinity today.

The great bald eagle now nests in the abandoned cliffs of every skyscraper. There are pigeons by the millions; and ducks, wild geese and swans in all the ponds and rivers. Buzzards and kites circle everywhere. House mice are almost extinct, since they are dependent on man.

Many of the larger carnivora live in the drains, which is probably how those from more tropical countries survived their first winter. It is of course for the same reason that I live in a cave, where the temperature is more or less stable, rather than in an apartment, of which there is certainly no shortage. It occurred to me when I moved in here that, after all, a cave was man's natural habitat, and that a house was only an artificial cave. A cave is a space in a rock, a house is a rock constructed around a space.

At least one more thing is necessary to supply a picture of this area as it is now. New York was always famous for its skyline. This skyline is now vastly changed. There are a number of large buildings—blocks of flats, hospitals and hotels—more or less intact. Rockefeller Center stands; so does the pinnacle of the Empire State Building, an eagles' aerie now. The Chrysler Building stands, but its pinnacle hangs

70

from it at an angle, like the Virgin from the church at Albert in the first World War. I should note here that though some of the larger structures stand almost intact, many others, particularly department stores having fewer interior walls, have crumpled into great rounded hillocks, each of which contains a thousand Aladdin caves. Most of the old brownstone houses have fallen down, and, of course, the bomb blast area is completely bare and almost as flat as a polo field. A curious thing, however, has occurred. The debris that landed on the housetops, combined with the guano from the countless birds that took to roosting on them, has formed a soil so fertile that trees and shrubs cover the flat tops of higher buildings. Countless sea gulls, herring gulls, kittiwakes, and great blackbacked gulls nest on the ledges and in this scrubby vegetation; while on the ridges of the lower-level, collapsed houses there is a thick layer of excellent grass growing on the newly formed topsoil. It is my opinion that, though at first much of the debris and the land exposed to the explosion was radioactive (indeed, some of it glowed at night and we took precautions to avoid such areas), the soil and dirt later became almost incredibly fertile, so that no matter how much it is grazed down, this grass carpet now appears to be indestructible. This fertility accounts for the amount of game, the several thousand head, that is to be found here.

The Washington Bridge is intact and so is the Brooklyn Bridge, these two being the main migration routes for those animals which leave or come to the island of Manhattan. The polar bears, moose and caribou seem to prefer swimming, as do the tigers in the summer months. But most animals use the bridges, and very good sport is often to be had near them.

As there have been animal mutations, so there have also been mutations among the plants. There are some great ferns as big as trees, and there is a new elm which creeps along the ground, one tree covering as much as an acre. Everything grows with great rapidity; and if it were not for the goats that prefer young trees and tree shoots to grass, the place would soon revert to forest. However, a natural balance seems, after the first few years, to have set in. There are enough goats to keep down the trees and enough herbivorous animals to graze the grass till it is like a thick lawn, and enough carnivorous animals to keep the grazing animals from completely destroying the herbage.

The scene from a hilltop or a ruin is of strange and almost incredible beauty. The game is so thick that it is reminiscent of the Sabi game reserve in the Transvaal. Standing out above the rolling greensward that covers the fallen buildings, great towers of masonry rise like ancient forts. Everywhere there are small woods, clumps of trees, and little streams and rivers. There are large numbers of flowers, many of them completely new, at least new as wild flowers. Varieties of roses which usually had to be budded now grow wild, as do gladioli, dahlias, tulips and every other kind of bulb. Hyacinths, daffodils and crocuses cover large patches in solid mats of color; they lie like scatter rugs on the green floor of the city; and nothing more beautiful could be imagined than coming across a great striped Bengal tiger asleep on a carpet of purple crocuses in the first warm afternoon of early spring, or seeing a red and white wild ox standing belly-deep in orange gladioli. There are ferns and mosses to be found wherever water drips or runs among the rocky gullies. And in no place are they more beautiful than in the natural grotto in front of the Chelsea Hotel, where a clear spring bubbles up and falls with a delightful splash into the small lake made by the subsidence of the ground in 23d Street. It is in this lake that I keep the black bass, rainbow trout and carp that I catch when I need a change of diet. They have become adapted to this way of life and are very little different from their ancestors.

I must say that after the hardships we underwent in the beginning while we were learning to adjust ourselves, I now live very well. I have fresh meat and fish, wine and whisky when I want it, and plenty of canned food of all kinds. I still miss bread and potatoes, but I have become accustomed to bottled spaghetti, and only occasionally dream about French fried potatoes or a loaf of good fresh bread.

I have often thought about the question of luck—of my good luck in being left alive, for instance. But are we really sure about what is good luck and what is bad? Why was I chosen to be spared out of so many millions? Why was I so blessed, so lucky? What had I done to deserve so unique a reward as life?

Or, on the other hand, why was I so damned as to be made to survive, to live alone in a world of death and putrescence—made to revert atavistically to a subhuman existence? What had I done to deserve a lonely hell like this, when all other men—as I had supposed until today—were killed quickly and mercifully, or at least relatively quickly and mercifully? Now that it is all over, and my adjustments are made—now that I have gotten over my loneliness and overcompensated to the point where, having seen two fellow human beings, I hide like an animal—I go over it all again in my mind.

It was naturally a great shock for a modern man to be thrust back into pre-history, and to see how, having misused our means, we had lost our ends, which should have been, not the search for a life of more and more comfort and the possession of more and more things, but the integration of the personality—man becoming man at last. I had visualized in the last years of our era a new type of co-operative, nonpredatory man living at peace with his fellows in a world of plenty made possible by modern technology. This aim of man, as I saw it, was unemployment—was goods and services without work as such, or with very little work. Man would have employed his newly acquired leisure time in study, in the arts and crafts, and in the enjoyment of amenities rather than amusements.

Nothing, of course, could be easier than this philosophizing when it was all over, than being wise after the event, and shouting "I told you so" to the echoing hills. Never was a horse more stolen, or a stable so destroyed. There was not even a door left to lock. Still, there were some prophets, wise before the event, who cried havoc. Why had they not been heeded? What was the matter with mankind that, having reached the end of its tether, it refused to face the fact and change before it was too late? Had men weighted themselves down with a way of life, with a system that corresponded to the armor of the prehistoric reptiles and, like them, unable to change, been forced by the very extent of its development into self-destruction?

Looking back, I see I have written that I had not thought seriously about anything for ten years. This is approximately correct. Obviously, in the first rush of events and difficulties of adjustment there was little time for thought; it was hard enough just to stay alive. But about five years after the disaster, for a period of several years, I thought and read a great deal. I still have a very fine library that I collected at that time, and sometimes on a sunny day I sit and read in the grotto with my gun and dogs beside me. But I read mainly poetry now, stuff with a ringing meter, that I learned as a child: Tennyson, Macaulay's *Lays of Ancient Rome*, Kipling, Swinburne, and Hood. It is what critics used to call the best bad poetry. I think that unconsciously I have gone back to it so as to keep the song of words and the power of simile functioning in a mind that was becoming atrophied from disuse. For I had stopped thinking in words and was only feeling things, like an animal. I had even stopped speaking to my dogs, and controlled them by gestures and sounds: *sah* to attack, *ah* to check them, *hi-lorst* to hunt, *er* to warn, *hup* to jump. So, to regain the use of my tongue and vocal cords, I went back to the poems of my school days, taking an almost childish pleasure in watching the development of my own defense mechasnisms, laughing wryly at the devices of a so-called cultured mind as it strove to fight madness alone in lovely wilderness.

Perhaps in a way these neoclinical symptoms, tricks, alibis, and fantasies are the most important part of this narrative, since disaster is unconstructive, and even the very greatest can be imagined by multiplying the smallest to the required degree. The real fight was not, as might be imagined, with wild beasts. Indeed, as must by now have become apparent, this war with the wild game was both my way of living and my pleasure. No, the real fight was with loneliness and boredom. Alcoholism was a way out, and for a while I tried it, reeling drunk and singing through the ruined, empty streets, through the reek of putrescence. I tried it till I fell and came to with a pack of starving mongrels sniffing and growling round me as I lay in the gutter. Another few minutes—if I had taken one more drink and had been just that much drunker—and the boldest of the dogs would have been at my throat. But alcohol was a great temptation. There were so many wonderful wines to be found: Château Ausone, Château Climents, Bel-Air-Marignants, Chambertin, Nuits Saint-Georges; Burgundy, claret, port, Rhine wines by the cellarful; and it took time for me to learn to drink with moderation, as I do now.

At one time I contemplated suicide, and here, oddly enough, I discovered a great truth: A man alone, unless he is in great pain, does not commit suicide if he still has the means of living. Suicide is an act, when it is not done in a panic of fear which is a more or less unconscious running away, that is committed in order to impress, astonish, and dismay those who cause it. It is committed as a final act of annoyance, a kind of blackmail by which the dead hope to make the living pay. Either this, or it is a way for someone who has never been important in life to become important in death. Thus it was impossible for me, once I had made these discoveries, to kill myself.

It was about this time, and probably a part of the same mechanism—the opposite side of the same psychological penny—that I decided to collect and breed a pack of dogs as a distraction and as a means of hunting. There were a number of large dogs roaming about, some of which showed a tendency to follow me. I shot game for them, and even shot other dogs for them to eat. Some dogs had gone completely savage and, having lived on cadavers, were much more dangerous than any wild animal, for it is the half-wild animal which has lost its fear of man that is the most likely to attack him. There were some terrific fights between my dogs and these wild dogs, but by degrees the larger of the wild dogs died off and were replaced by the smaller coyotelike animal which skulks in the scrub and ruins today.

But I must go back to the disaster, and to the events, as far as I can remember them, that preceded it.

In the summer of 1946 there were bomb tests at Bikini, a coral atoll in the Pacific. A great fleet was assembled there and bombed. A man called, if I remember, something like Truelove was President of the United States at that time. He was the last President; an Englishman by the name of Washington was the first. This Truelove was a good man but no more up to the times in which we lived then than any other statesman. We had concentrated on making Time, on saving Time, and then the Time we had saved turned on us and destroyed us, along with, and in spite of, all our little statesmen.

The funny thing to me, as I look back at it, is that the atom, the smallest thing in the world, should turn out to be the biggest thing in the world.

Everything went wrong about that time. It was, if one had been clever enough to see it, the beginning of the end. There was fear on every face—fear and anger. There was no kindness anywhere, because fear and kindness cannot live together. All over the world people were hungry, and their anger, born of fear, became fury. I saw it only in New York, and there I withdrew myself, seeing fewer and fewer people and losing myself in the ivory tower of my storytelling, a trick that I had taught myself when I first found it necessary to escape from life—a trick at which, as life became progressively worse, I became progressively better, able to live more and more within my dreams, to love women I created in my mind, to ride horses that I bred in my brain, to gallop in the company of beauty through the wild meadows of desire. I disdained the films that were the national pastime; my dreams and inventions were better to me than anything Hollywood could do; besides, Hollywood was realistic compared to me, and without the thousand subtleties that I needed as a defense against a future that came nearer every day, stepping silently on synthetic rubber-soled feet, a giant who carried death in his hand—a giant only a few artists, some columnists, and a senator or two seemed to know about.

This idea of mine must have come from the time I encountered a battalion marching down Eighth Avenue on rubber-soled boots. In a terrifying silence, a thousand-odd young men, armed to the teeth, moved unheard through a city. That was the way the future was coming, and there was no one to stop it. Only a few men were crying in the wilderness; others, like me (I had given up trying to warn people) were hiding, knowing it was coming but pretending it would be all right, pretending that it would never be twelve o'clock—thinking, if it could be called thinking, that because we had replaced God with the Horatio Alger and Cinderella myths, everything must work out all right in the end.

One sign of the times was these atom tests. We moved a lot of natives out of this atoll—this pink, palm-frilled ring of coral that enclosed a blue lagoon—so that we could play our prelude to the great death game there; but at that same time, when land was wanted for a Palace of Peace no one would give it. The real estate was too valuable—and who wanted a society of all nations in his vicinity? All nations meant all color, all religions; and no one seemed to understand, or even care, that there is a man who is not a hundred per cent human. It seemed that no one cared, no one stopped to think. No one but a man named Rockefeller.

But to get back to the experiment. There were stories about it, the best being that some goats on the battleship had survived the blast. There are goats in New York City today. I can see goats any time I go out, and I hardly ever shoot one because their taste is too rank even for the dogs. But where are the people?

There has to be this background of politics, a rough description of the work as I remember it in its final flowering not merely to give a picture of those feverish times, but, for my own sake, to drive my mind back into the unaccustomed paths and recapture past mood by trick and stratagem.

In those days, there was a world famine. Men had increased tremendously in numbers despite wars and disasters and the safety margin of nutrition was gone. This margin had never been very wide, and a world drought, combined with the effects of war, had closed the gap. And those who talked of a continually rising standard in American terms of eating were, whether they knew it or not, talking also in terms of reduced population, for the billions who were on earth then had to live on grain rather than meat except such meat as could be grass-fed. Here is another odd paradox, for now in this savage world of animals it is grain that is the luxury—grain and fat, because most animals do not carry fat, except a little around the kidneys, and I get most of mine from bears and porcupines. I melt it down and save it in airtight jars.

But I was trying to describe those times—the hate and fear and the little love. There was not even much love between men and women. There was marriage, of course, but only three marriages in five lasted. Some children got out of hand at the age of three or four and became unmanageable—the world fear having infected their infant minds. Other children, older ones, became criminals.

It is easy now, so long after the event, to be wise and see that probably we should never have employed the bomb at all—not even on Japan. Instead, we should have brought Japanese observers under safe conduct from Ireland or other neutral countries to witness the first trials in the New Mexican desert and then said, "Give up or we will do this to you." How else could we expect the confidence of the world? We said: "We will never use the bomb. You can be sure of that." And the world answered: "But you have used it twice and you are still experimenting with it." To which we had no reply.

But perhaps not even this would have saved us, because it appears now that we suffered, not from those we feared most, but from our late enemies, whom we thought we had utterly crushed—though why we should have been so certain that our victory was permanent is now beyond me. Since we knew the furious hatred of Hitler, and since we had seen the effects of Goering's cleverly contrived martyrdom, it is astonishing that we did not put two and two together and perceive that the followers of Nazism were preparing to wreck what they could not conquer. And here is another paradox: The Nazis, having now destroyed the civilization of the West, including their own, have spared only those primitive cultures which have always existed in the "backward" sections of "unenlightened" continents—peoples whom they once ridiculed as "colored." For now that Indians appear to have survived here, I am sure that they have survived in South America, that Eskimos have survived in the North and that Chinese and Russians of the more primitive types are still living as they did five thousand years ago. It is, however, curious that the two girls I saw were blond. I have no recollection of fair Indians. There is, of course, the possibility that their hair was dyed.

But this is all surmise and, having described the times of President Truelove and the general feeling in the air before the blast, I must tell something of my own personal life. This brings me to my home, and my wife, and the life we led together before it ended, and its end—a difficult and painful thing to do, but one which must be done as a duty, for this phase, too, is coming to an end. I feel it in my bones and heart. Even the dogs feel it: At this moment Bodo, who was sitting with his head on my knee, has gone toward the door and stands there growling, with his hackles erect and his tail stiff. Vixen, more dangerous but more restrained than he, is backing him silently; her eyes are on him and on the door. My hand is on the rifle at my side. I lay it across my knees and watch the dogs.

The dogs that have been growling by the door have quieted down and come back to me. Whatever had been outside has gone and I have relaxed. I can now go on with my narrative again, continuing where I had left off.

My wife, Mildred, was an American, a very small and beautiful woman who hailed from the swamps of New Jersey that are now inhabited by every kind of savage creature. She was an artist, and our small and unpretentious apartment in the Whitby Apartments was decorated with her work. She painted and I wrote, and we amused ourselves with our pets: a miniature pinscher called Annie; a kinkajou called Edward, which was a female but did not know it; a South American bugle bird or troupial, called Sam; a golden hamster by the name of Stompie; and some sixty-odd tropical fish of various species whose names still come to me without difficulty: zebras, platties, angels, neons, moons, swordtails, clowns, guppies, gouramis, Siamese fighting fish, miniature catfish, and many others. The fish lived amid water plants in a large tank which, when lighted by a fluorescent light, looked like fairyland. My wife, who was filled with imaginations and fantasies, always said how wonderful it would be if we could only be very small (and able to breathe under water) and therefore able to walk about in so lovely a garden, sitting on the rocks and strolling over the silver sand which covered the bottom.

We had three rooms in the apartment: a studio sitting room, a bedroom, and a small study. There were, in addition, a kitchen, a bathroom, several large closets, and a terrace garden with plants and trees in pots and boxes, chairs, swings, and a striped awning which could be lowered or pulled up by means of ropes. The apartment was, in fact, an ordinary small New York penthouse in the theatrical district, chosen for a combination of privacy, economy and delight in the situation—this being in what was known as Times Square and corresponding in this city to the grand boulevards of my native Paris. This was Metropolis, Sodom and Gomorrah, Byzantium—the art and amusement center of the world, since the Old World capitals had ceased to function. In Times Square then, and around us each time we took the air to buy a pack of cigarettes or a bottle of beer, were the cream of the world's artists, actors, playwriters, musicians, dancers, singers, prize fighters, cowboys. There were also pimps, gamblers and prostitutes—and their prey: the curious and the rich who sought on the West Side those diversions which the West Side sought on the East. The strange woman or strange eating place, even within the bounds of a city, always seemed better than the local product. This, then, was the atmosphere in which we lived.

I was shaving. I had been ill, and to interest myself had grown a beard which each day I marked out like a tennis court, shaving up to the soap mark. The immense white beard which now sweeps my belt buckle was thus simply born. My wife was in the kitchen washing up the things which would be needed for breakfast, and which in a more meticulous household would have been washed the previous night (when we had made tea on coming in from the theater). It was fortunate that she had left the dishes until morning; if she had not, she would have been in the bedroom and exposed to the direct rays of the blinding flash of the explosion. It is hard to recall with exactness what I felt, or heard, or to differentiate between what I have reconstructed and my actual memory. My first conscious act was to run from the bathroom to meet Mildred running toward me from the kitchen. She was followed by the dog, which jumped into my arms. With one arm around my wife, and carrying the dog, I went toward the bedroom. I do not think we spoke. I do not think we even said: "What was that?" It was obvious that something had taken place that was beyond both question or explanation.

I cannot even remember if the sound—an incredible, dull, slow explosion, if such a thing is possible to imagine, like the bursting of a shell which takes minutes instead of seconds to explode—or the unearthly light came first, or if they came together as lightning and thunder come when they strike nearby.

It seems almost certain to me now that we both knew what it was. That it was it—the atomic bomb, the "new god" that we had talked about for so long and whose name, like that of older gods, we feared to mention, calling it it. Saying: It can't happen here; it can't happen to us. Saying: It is not so dangerous as has been supposed because the Navy tests at Bikini have proved that it is not fatal to every living thing. Few of us realizing that the officers of the Navy were unlikely to render themselves obsolete by any experiment over which they had full control.

We might have guessed this, when a year later certain admirals regretted the fact that the bomb had ever been used, saying that it had not been necessary and that the war would have been won without it almost as quickly. Did these gentlemen regret the hundreds of thousands of unnecessary dead, or the fact that the bomb and its implications had jeopardized their professional security? What were a hundred thousand kimono-clad dead compared to the loss of their authority? Or am I cynical? Or again, is it possible for a man in my position to be cynical?

I do not know what I felt when it happened. Fear certainly, then perhaps an odd kind of relief. *It* had happened, and we were still alive. This was the worst that could happen—that was what we thought, then. In a way, it was like walking through a barrage. A thing that seemed impossible had taken place; we had passed through a wall of death and fire. We had survived. In us then, consciously or not, was the terrible selfish joy of the survivor. Only the dog had more sense. She trembled so much that when I put her down she could not stand but fell on her side. And the kinkajou in the kitchen was uttering loud screams.

The glass from the bedroom windows was on the floor and window sill. Since some of it still stuck to the frames, it was obvious that it had not been smashed the way glass is usually broken by an explosion, but that it had been bent, like a plastic, by inward pressure and then had fallen, instead of being blown into the room. Thus all laws of physics were shattered; everything that I had learned of what, at school, we had called "heat, light, and sound" was now reversed. We and all mankind were dwelling in a vacuum universe where even Einstein must find himself a child spending his first day in a cosmic kindergarten. But this thought did not come then, as I stood with my wife in my arms, as she clung like a small bird to the only safety that she knew. We stared, not out—for we dared not—but at the familiarity of our bedroom which was bathed in an unearthly light. Only a true artist would know what I mean when I say it was a *cold* rose. Only he would know that this is not an impossibility—for by the rules all reds and pinks are warm, and it is the blues that are cold. Only he would know—and it makes me laugh as I write, for there is not an artist left alive today, not a damned soul who can understand this message from the damned. I write alone—the last of my time and race—and describe the finer points of color for people who no longer exist.

My wife's dressing table was intact, its mirror unshattered, her comb, brushes and other accessories as they had always been in that woman's disorder, that asymmetry which always appalls a man. There was a lipstick lying open. There was a scattering of powder. A cut-glass perfume bottle was unstoppered. It occurred to me to ask her how she expected the perfume to retain its strength if she did not put the stopper back—a thing I had done a hundred times, to no effect. And I smiled inside my mind at the thought and turned my eyes to the bed. There we had lain. There were the marks of our lying. The sheets crumpled, the bed no doubt still warm; and this had happened. This had taken place. Still looking, my eyes moved to the bird cage. At night we brought Sam into the bedroom so that his chuckling and calling would wake us slowly in the morning, (That was one advantage of my profession; I was no servant to time or to the shattering effect of an alarm clock. As it is to every man, my belly was no master, but I could choose my time to make the wherewithal to fill it, and use, if I so desired, a bird to wake me.) At the bottom of the cage my bird lay dead, a crumpled ball of black and yellow.

Apart from the curious cold pink glow in the room, there was a smell of hot iron. Mixed with this smell was a faint odor of ozone, a sort of seashore smell. There also a feeling of warmth—not heat, just warmth, like that felt from the shortwave diathermy treatment that doctors used to give sometimes for a strained back. I had the feeling of being enveloped in a blanket of powerful, almost palpitating warmth. I remember thinking: Are these the fatal radioactive waves that we read about? A writer whose name I cannot recall had written a magnificent description of the bombing of Hiroshima in a magazine called *The New Yorker*, which, though it was a magazine of sophisticated humor, devoted a whole issue to his report. His description gave us a standard of comparison. It is odd how it all comes back, how details of the story, but not the name of the man who wrote it, spring into my mind.

WHAT IS CONELRAD?

The system is officially entitled "Plan for CONtrol of ELectromagnetic RADiation"—CONELRAD for short . . . It is a system devised by the broadcasting industry and the Government, working together to bring you official information and civil defense instruction in times of emergency.

WHY DO WE NEED CONELRAD?

Without it, enemy bombers could tune their direction finders to a station broadcasting in a target city and "beam" right in to their targets. To prevent this from happening in World War II, all stations went off the air—just when life-saving civil defense information and instructions were vitally important to the people under attack. CONELRAD stations CAN continue to operate, even under actual attack conditions, and still deny enemy bombers this navigational aid!

HOW DOES CONELRAD WORK?

When CONELRAD goes into operation, ALL stations first sign off the air with a standard alert announcement. The stations of the CONELRAD system then reduce power and change their broadcasting frequency to 640 or 1240 kilocycles. Then they *return* to the air.

CONELRAD stations in each city join in a "cluster" of three or more stations. These "cluster" stations broadcast a common program. One station in a "cluster" is on the air for only a few seconds. Then another cluster station picks up the *same* program as the other station leaves off.

You will hear a CONTINUOUS program without interruption, although the volume may vary as the program is "switched" from a station near you to one at a more distant point. However, by turning the volume up until you can plainly hear the weakest station, you should always receive a continuous and uninterrupted program.

The effect of this "switching" on a bomber direction finder is to make it swing erratically, so that it cannot "fix" or "home" on a single station.

With many CONELRAD stations in operation, all on 640 or 1240 kilocycles, this completely confuses the "homing" capability of the finder. Many tests conducted by our own Air Force have proved that the CONELRAD system eliminates broadcasting as a navigational aid.

IF YOU ARE LISTENING TO ANY RADIO OR TELEVISION SET WHEN THE ALERT SOUNDS, YOU WILL HEAR A MESSAGE LIKE THIS:

"We interrupt our normal program to cooperate in security and civil defense measures as requested by the United States Government . . . This is a CONELRAD radio alert . . . Listen carefully: This station is now leaving the air. During the CONELRAD alert there will be no FM or TV programs. The only program on the air will be on your standard radio at 640 or 1240 kilocycles, beginning after a short period of silence. Be patient. Tune the dial of your standard radio receiver to 640 or 1240."

If you are NOT listening to a radio or TV set when this announcement is made, you will know the CONELRAD system has gone into operation when you hear the civil defense sirens or attack warning signals . . . Tune your AM (Standard) radio immediately to the proper dial setting—640 or 1240—and listen for the official broadcast.

REMEMBER: When an alert sounds,
   ALL NORMAL BROADCASTING WILL CEASE.

After a short period of silence, CONELRAD stations will return to the air at 640 or 1240 kilocycles on your standard AM radio. This off-the-air period is due to necessary broadcasting-equipment changes. It will vary for different areas. Contact your local civil defense director for the approximate time lapse in your area.

CONELRAD, an acronym for CONtrol of ELectromagnetic RADiation, was developed in 1951 as a way for all radio braodcasts in the United States to safely transmit information. The Truman administration wanted to ensure that the public could still be informed without compromising the safety of Americans who could possibly be bombed by enemy bombers that used radio stations as a way of organizing attacks on cities. Car, home, and transistor radios throughout the 1950s and early 60s were marked with triangles denoting the 640 and 1240 radio stations that would be used to deliver information from the federal government and local Civil Defense authorities. By 1963, after the development of Intercontinental Ballistic Missles (ICBMs) made the likelihood of bomber attack slim, CONELRAD was phased into the Emergency Broadcast System, now known as the Emergency Alert System since 1997. (Pamphlet from the FCDA.)

We now dared to look out of the window. The McGraw-Hill Building was still standing, and so was the Holland Hotel, but beyond them there was only an incandescent orange redness against which they were blackly silhouetted. This redness was the center of what can only be described as a frightful, cream-colored, cauliflower shaped cloud. Branches of white and butter-yellow broccoli seemed to grey writhing out from this center in mushroom layers. The whole thing was vegetablelike, a vivid, livid, mushroom-cauliflower-broccoli that formed great branches which grew, changing into white trees growing out of the scarlet, central heart, against a background of thick brown smoke. Everything writhed and churned, the branches becoming intricate tendrils of marblelike delicacy—orange-pink, scarlet, amber-yellow citron; and then the veins thickened into arms so that the vegetable simile failed and one thought of the writhing arms of an octopus.

An octopus is what it was—an octopus that was throttling all that we knew and loved. It was incredible to stand there watching the end of the world. Each man who watched was a modern Nero—for it was we who had set this thing going, who had by our apathy set this final blaze, and fiddled while the preparations for it had been made. All this naturally easily now. I cannot describe fully what I felt then. What we felt was without precedent, and the most we could hope for was the strength to disguise our fear and, by so doing, prevent the personal panic which would be fatal.

Having watched this tree of death grow, having seen it mount into the firmament, break into two parts and drift in majesty toward the west, we turned our attention to our home, which we knew already to be shattered, cracked like a mended cup which seems, as it is dropped for the last time, to retain its shape for an instant so that a memory of it can be fixed before it breaks into tiny shards.

Now we looked for signs. Now I wished that I had not forgotten how to pray, and thought: If more had prayed, this would not have happened. God is not lightly mocked, and this was the answer of a God mocked.

Meanwhile, other things had happened, as we found out when we looked around more carefully. The kinkajou had stopped screaming and had gone to sleep. This was her answer to all problems and corresponded to our method of anesthesia by means of drink, drugs, or women. But some of the tropical fish were dead, floating with their white bellies in the air; and the plants which filled the big studio window had their leaves browned on the edges. Why only the edges? Why had only some of the fish died? I forget which now, but all of two or three varieties were dead while the others swam at ease, seeking food in the corners of the tank. We picked out the dead fish to feed to Edward when she woke, as was our habit. We scattered some food in the feed ring and watched the multicolored fish cluster near the surface to eat. I said, "Put on the kettle and we'll have some tea"; a cup of tea being my answer to any crisis—tea and aspirin.

Then suddenly I felt weak. I saw how we were going through the motions of life: feeding the animals, making tea. Mildred must have felt the same, because she said from the kitchen, "The gas is all right."

I said, "And the water?" though I had heard her fill the kettle and knew that the water was still running.

"The water's all right, too," she said.

It won't be for long, I thought; and got up and put the plug into the bath and filled it. That would give us fifty gallons or so—enough for a few days anyway. I was trying to bridge the gap between a technological past of half an hour ago and the future, trying to think what would work and what wouldn't, and making decisions that seemed very wise at the time—conditioned reflexes to disaster brought out of the past from African droughts, from memories of the last war, from stories and letters I had had about London in the blitz. The next minute I was being violently sick. Lucky I'm in here, I thought. If one had to be sick it was a good thing to be in the place where it was easiest to be sick. It all comes back to me very clearly as I relive that day. Again I hear my wife's voice saying, "Are you all right?" And my answer: "Yes, I'm all right." The persistence of those words. Was the gas *all right*? Was the water? Were we?

And now I became aware of the smoke and the smell. Smoke was coming in through the shattered window of the bedroom. Fires must have broken out everywhere, I thought. Probably the destruction of the explosion, though it must have caused the fires, had banked them, as it were, with falling buildings, and only now were they breaking out with real severity. I heard a great crash as something fell on the flat roof and, looking out, saw it was a big wooden beam; more things fell, half bricks, tiles, dust, something that looked as if it had once been a man. I must get that away—overboard—before Mildred saw it.

I did later, when things had stopped falling, and wondered as I handled the broken body if it was radioactive. I wondered how things had stayed in the air so long. Or was it not long; had it all happened so fast, in minutes—and what did it matter, anyway? I thought of what we had done, of filling the bath and the kettle, and decided that the debris falling on the roof was the result of a later explosion. There would no doubt be many of them. The kettle—it was one of those with a whistle on it—began to whistle.

I said, "It's boiling."

Mildred said, "Yes."

I said, "Let's make the tea. We'll feel better when we've had tea."

Mildred said, "Yes," and we went into the kitchen together with the dog between us, right on our heels so that when we stopped, she bumped into us. The very act of making tea was calming. I carried the tray into the sitting room.

Things still kept falling, and the air was filled with papers that rose sailing like kites on the currents between the high buildings. It was very dark and there was no light when I tried to turn on the table lamp. Neither of us said anything. The wind continued to rise, assuming almost whirlwind proportions. I began to be aware of the noise of sirens. Fire engines and ambulances and police cars were evidently out on the streets. We both said, "Listen to the fire engines." Then there was a shot and Mildred said, "Is that a shot?" and I said, "Yes." There were to be plenty more later. Then we heard a scream. The paralysis of fear was now changing to hysteria. Terrified people were rushing out to escape from themselves, to see, to do, to find out. We'd have to go out ourselves sometime—but not yet.

We had a second cup of tea. I was surprised how very calm I seemed; my hand hardly trembled. That amused me, not because it showed my lack of fear but because it showed my ability to control most of it. Probably the only people who were not frightened at that moment were lunatics, to whom this must all have seemed very logical and predestined. Perhaps that is why I was not more frightened, having been classified, because I had expected something of this kind to happen, as a lunatic. I was, in a way, psychologically prepared for the end of the world, but there was little satisfaction in being able to say, "I told you so," and, at the moment, no one to whom I could say it except my wife, who always believed everything I said and thought me an altogether remarkable man, thus tempering the value of her criticism with the balmy breeze of her charm.

I went into the bedroom to try the telephone. The room was very smoky but not so bad as it might have been, for the wind had changed again. I did not know whom I was going to call. It was just that I wanted to see if the telephone worked. I had always hated the telephone—the network of copper threads that tied all civilized mankind together in a web of misunderstanding. If there had been no telephones and no airplanes and no electricity, there would have been no atomic bomb. I held the receiver to my ear. It was dead. No phone. That, after all, was not surprising after the failure of the electric light. But as the discovery of the telephone had been hailed as a great advance of our civilization, its end—for there was no doubt in my mind that it had ended—was a definite sign that our civilization was disintegrating. We were cut off from the world.

I went to look in the kitchen to see what we had to eat. There was quite a lot of stuff: cans of baked beans, boned chicken, soups, glass jars of tongue.

There were other factors that were to the good. Once the first shock had worn off, I began to consider the possibilities of life as well as I was able—began to look and see if there was anything to reconstruct with. As I say, there was a fair amount of canned food in the kitchen and there were, in addition, about ten large parcels of food that we had wrapped and were going to send to friends in England and France. It was remarkable how distant England and France seemed and how little our dearest friends now mattered. I was grateful to them for my own good impulse that had made me buy the food, and delighted with the habit of procrastination which had prevented my sending it to them. Another good thing, though I did not realize it fully at the time, was that I had a thousand rounds of .22 ammunition for the Mauser, because we had been intending to go on a holiday and I had meant to do some target shooting. I must have thought of this, though subconsciously, because my next move was to go and see the manager of the hotel, a great deer hunter who lived in the adjoining penthouse, and ask him if he would let me have one of his heavier rifles and some ammunition. I was already aware that there would be a necessity for weapons, that civilization in terms of protection had broken down and that it must be every man for himself, or men banded together for themselves as units, or tribes, against other men similarly banded.

I obtained a rifle and fifty rounds of 303 ammunition without much difficulty —the manager had more guns than he could use—in exchange for a case of whisky that I had just bought. We talked around the subject of the bomb and our predicament, more or less ignoring it, which was fantastic, since the air was filled with smoke. Like me, he must have had the feeling that this was the end of everything. Actually, of course, there was nothing to say. And to talk would probably only have torn the last shreds of self-control from our naked fear. We got no further than saying it was terrible that neither of us had been out, that we had better be careful, and that it would probably be all right. We parted with expressions of mutual trust, promises of mutual aid, and a handshake—though our doors were no more than six feet apart.

My wife fixed some food. We had meat in the icebox, which by this time had stopped working; we had potatoes and soup. Surprisingly, the gas was still on: our supply had evidently been unaffected. And we had water; it was still running, probably from the reserve tank on the roof above us, and we did not have to use the reserve in the bath. We gave the kinkajou the dead fish from the tank and a banana, the last and a bit of bread, and Annie had our leavings. The day passed somehow. I forget how. Night came—a night like those of the blackouts of the war but without air-raid wardens or police. The streets were dark and lighted only by the light reflected down from the low ceiling of cloud and smoke which was illuminated by those parts of the city that were still burning. It was a night filled with strange happenings—screams, cries. shouts, shots, the noise of doors being forced; a night of black horror edged by the glare of the buildings that still burned to the south of us. The McGraw-Hill Building still stood out like a great black pinnacle against the glow of the sky. There was still the sound of sirens as fire engines and police tried to keep some semblance of order, but it was all sporadic. There was no sleep for us, but we lay down with the dog between us and tried to rest. I had the deer rifle loaded beside me, and I had a Gurkha kukri in its sheath under my pillow; I had sharpened it till it was like a razor. 1 have it still, having carried it since that day. I say we did not sleep, but we must have dozed off, for at dawn we were wakened by a sound truck.

An impersonal voice was giving out the news. It made me think of the town crier who had in the old days brought the news of war, of victory or disaster. It appeared that Washington was completely obliterated and that, since the federal government no longer existed, New York and all the other states were on their own. Governor Dewey advised calm and patience. He said he would undertake to keep order and restore vital utilities. People were advised to stay where they were and wait and not rush off to the country. This news, of course, succeeded in achieving the purpose opposite to that desired and stampeded everyone, so that later in the day there was a veritable exodus of such cars as had gas in their tanks. The rest of the news was that, bad as things were, there was no cause for panic or alarm and, though the casualties in New York City were estimated to be more than seven hundred thousand, the fires were under control and we should remain calm.

The voice went on and on. Detroit, Chicago, Philadelphia, Boston and every other major city had been severely damaged. But everything would be all right; this foolish catch phrase was reiterated and we were again advised to remain calm, stay at home if possible, until normalcy was restored. How this was to be done with seven hundred thousand casualties and a quarter of Manhattan destroyed was not revealed. Nor, at this time, was any explanation given of the disaster, or excuse offered for the negligence which had occasioned it. An event less disastrous in a country less civilized might easily have sent the populace roaring off to Albany to hang their masters as scapegoats, since there was no one in Washington left alive to blame. Disaster demands its scapegoats, but things were now so bad that it did not seem worthwhile hanging anyone.

There were a great number of suicides. Within an hour of the blast, we saw one woman throw her child out of a high window in the Lincoln Hotel, stand naked for an instant on the parapet and then follow her child in a head-first dive. Most suicides, however, were on the fashionable upper East Side—the working poor being more able to stand disaster: Having so little, they had little to lose. Café society, the least stable element, was the hardest hit.

Forced by curiosity and the knowledge that the longer we waited, the harder it would be to go out, we made our way down the stairs from our eleventh-floor apartment to the street. I had often called dwellers in apartment houses "troglodytes," and I remember thinking how right I had been as we climbed down the concrete stairs and crossed the paved passages that divided one flight from the next, pausing to rest and to listen to the strange sounds we heard. There was some drunken singing, the sound of quarrels, a hysterical woman blaming her husband for what had happened and asking him why he did not do something about it. He did. He struck her; she fell down and got up screaming she'd "have the law on him for that"; at which he laughed and she burst out crying loudly because now there was no law. On another floor, people were having a prayer meeting and singing hymns. There was no one in the office, and the lobby was deserted.

We went into the street and found it empty. It was rather like a Sunday afternoon with everyone away, or a Saturday —a weekend—because a car was being loaded with things from a house almost opposite the hotel entrance. I had with me a heavy blackthorn stick that I always carry on account of the lameness caused by an old wound, and since we had money with us, we thought we might as well go up to the corner and see if we could buy more food. Obviously, money was no good any more, but there was the possibility the grocer would not have come to that conclusion yet; he might not have had the sense to load up his stock and take it home with him. This guess proved to be right, and we were able to buy fifty dollars' worth of canned goods: sardines, herring, salmon, tuna fish, and potted meat. We obtained a gunny sack and staggered back with our wealth—for that is what it was at the new rate of exchange. America was about to take over from starving and liberated Europe, where a cake of soap or a bar of chocolate was the price of what had once been called a woman's honor. What I had bought with fifty dollars would, the previous day, have cost about twelve dollars, and five years before that about five dollars.

Carrying a sack of groceries up eleven floors is not an easy job for a lame man who has led a sedentary life for ten years. Now, though I am seventy, I could carry double that amount without a pause or even any loss of breath, but I am much stronger than I was then, the vicissitudes I have passed through having tempered and strengthened my muscles. Though I am amazed at my own agility and powers, I sometimes think that the presence of so much radioactivity in the soil of the vicinity may have something to do with it. Once one has acquired some kind of immunity to its dangers, one can perhaps benefit from its virtues.

But, as I was saying, we were confronted with the problem of getting this sack upstairs. I managed it eventually carrying it on my back. For a change, I would try dragging it, and Mildred would pull on one corner like a willing but ineffective ant. We were, however delighted by our prize and very glad to get home with it safely. There had been one or two disquieting incidents: A pawnbroker's on Eighth Avenue had been broken into; cheap rings and trinkets were scattered on the pavement, and a smashed safe lay on the doorstep, The three golden balls of the pawnbroker's sign lay beside it, a curious end for this heraldic symbol of the Medici. It's funny how pleased I am to remember an irrelevant detail like that. There was the body of a man—his head had been bashed in—lying in the gutter on the corner of 45th Street, opposite a liquor store which had been raided and was completely empty. And, as we were getting our stuff in the grocery store, a girl ran screaming past us pursued by a gang of young hooligans. I judged from the noise that followed that they must have pulled her down in the next block. It was this incident which decided me to cut off Mildred's hair (she wore it long, more than shoulder length) and make her dress in dungarees. With short hair, dungarees, and a dirty face, she would pass for a youngish, rather queer-looking boy, but everyone looked queer now and she would certainly be safer.

We lay low for a few days. This was the time that the sediment of the underworld rose to the surface and took over. The streets were the scene of unrestricted pillage, murder and fights between rival gangs. From our roof we saw some amazing sights. But by degrees, in a matter of four or five days, things improved. My friend the manager told me that he had heard that the city was full of wounded and crazed people. He asked if I had seen any and I said no. He said they were flooding up Lexington and Park avenues. He told me more of the exodus, of how the routes out of the city were packed with refugees in cars and on foot. The police were making no effort to control them, since control was impossible. But what could they have done, anyway? Given tickets? Made arrests? Broken cars were jamming the roads. People were being run down and robbed, girls abducted; other people were jumping off bridges and out of windows. But still they were moving outward like the spokes running from the shattered hub of a wheel. He asked me what I was going to do. I said I was going to stay. He asked me what I thought he should do, and I advised him to stay, too. I told him that in my opinion the people who were running off into the country were making a great mistake, but that the more of them that went, the better it would be for us.

Though my memory of the sequence of events that followed is somewhat confused, certain incidents stand out very clearly, the first among them being the destruction of our pets. The fish went first, since they could not live without the light in the tank. But then they did not count as pets; they were merely a decoration and an interest—no more than that. The kinkajou was different. She was very affectionate and never bit hard enough to draw blood. Looking back on it, it seems funny now; but I had been away from farming for fifteen years or so and had gotten out of the habit of killing things. It was only with the greatest difficulty that, holding her in the crook of my left arm, I made myself hit her on the back of the head with a two-pound ball hammer. She stretched out the way animals do when struck, her legs quivered, and then she went limp. I skinned her while she was still warm, as it's much easier then, and then I cut her up for a stew. Mildred cried. The dog looked on, not at all sorry to see the kink go. She had never understood our interest in it. It was difficult to think of Annie going the same way, which she did two days later. This was a very difficult thing to do because killing a dog is a form of murder.

Dogs have been associated with man for so long, a million years perhaps, that they no longer, in the full sense, count as animals; they are extensions of man—inventions of man like the spinning jenny, the Queen Mary and the atomic bomb. Breeding live-stock has always interested me, and I have learned a great deal about it since I have lived alone in the world with animals. Domestic dogs, as we knew them, were bred by continually discarding dogs that were not tractable, but my dogs now are bred two ways: The dogs of my hunting pack, which have been bred for strength and courage alone, would be capable of pulling me down if they were really starving, while my personal dogs are almost human, having been bred for both brains and courage.

In taming any animal, you must replace the mother of the young animal so that it fixes its affection on you instead of on its dam; or, in the case of animals that hunt in packs, you must become the leader of the pack, set it on to find game.

This is what I do when I hunt with my hounds. Though I carry a rifle, a knife, and a pistol, I would not try to handle my pack without a bullwhip and a short club. Every now and then a young dog, never a bitch, challenges me. Weighing as much as, or more than I do, he might pull me down if I were not ready for him. On one occasion I killed—with my bare hands—a dog that weighed two hundred and five pounds (I had the curiosity to weigh him). His name was Racketeer, and if I remember rightly his breeding was Great Dane, police dog, Saint Bernard and Afghan. The dogs were named, as foxhounds are, with names that are easy to call, such as Boxer, Lavender, Sailor, Tinker, Rover, Red Boy, Spot, Foxy, Fiddler.

Racketeer was a lovely beast, but suddenly he challenged me. I had put the pack onto a bear spoor. It was spring, and the spoor was very clear in the moist ground, but Racketeer wanted to follow a lynx. When I began to whip him off—this was before I carried a club—he turned on me, while the pack waited to see which would be master. I saw him crouch for the jump, and as he leaped for my throat I struck him straight in the nose with my fist. As he fell I jumped on him; leaping into the air, I brought both feet down on him, smashing his ribs. Then I raised him in my arms and threw him back to the waiting pack, who broke him up, leaving nothing of him but the skull. I relate this incident to show the association I had with dogs and to suggest the relationship between man and his servants, and to demonstrate how they at times attempt to master him, be they animals or engines. This struggle is certain; it happens with every horse, with every dog, with every woman. It is the "showdown," and the one who loses might as well be dead—a moral that all husbands should take to heart if there are any husbands left alive, for there is no animal so dangerous as a woman, even a small good woman with a heart of gold.

But all this discourse has been an evasion of the description of the death of Annie, my pinscher. The past is still too near to make it easy to discuss. But the way it went was this: I held her on my knee, with my left hand over her shoulder, and brought the hammer down on her skull, cracking it with a single blow. I then cleaned and skinned her and we ate her, for though we had canned food we were trying to conserve it for the days that were to come. When it became known that I had killed my pets and eaten them, a woman burst into the apartment and called me a cannibal and a brute. She said it was like eating a human being, and I said, "We may be doing that yet." There had been cannibalism in the German concentration camps at Dachau and elsewhere, but this good woman had forgotten or had never believed it. On the other side of the same penny were the people who wanted me to kill their dogs for them because they could not bring themselves to do it. I killed a number of dogs that I had known quite well, many of them having lived in the hotel as long as I had. I charged half the dog for killing and dressing it, and Mildred and I became quite accustomed to dog soup and stew.

During this period the destroyed part of the city was walled off, the rubble of the fallen buildings being used to close off the streets. It made me think of the walled-off ghettos of the German occupation in Poland, and of the way situations tended to repeat themselves, death being enclosed by walls in both cases. It was a defense mechanism on our part against the knowledge that death had us hemmed, walled in, and was one of our final tributes to complacency, to the idea that if we could not see a thing we stopped its existing. See no evil, speak no evil, hear no evil, the three monkeys said. But you could not help smelling it. All over the city there was a stench of death in the air. But even this we got used to.

Order, as I say, had been for a while somewhat restored, and a few minimum services functioned, but everything worked on a kind of reflex. Policemen remained policemen because it was their habit and they did not know what else to do; for a few days garbage collectors still collected garbage for the same reason. But there was neither credit nor currency, central authority having disappeared. Local state currency was stamped out of what metals were available, but no one would accept it and so all public servants were paid in food from the stock that was available in the city warehouses, a system that obviously could not continue for long, and didn't.

There were amazing tales of the fights put up by farmers against the influx of city dwellers who had run out of the metropolis and had flung themselves upon anything edible in the country—a swarm of human locusts that the country people resisted in every manner possible. There was a pitched battle on the Canadian border in the vicinity of Niagara Falls. The Canadians appeared to be a little better off than we were, having retained their central government, and they used troops to turn back the unwelcome thousands, many of whom had known the Falls only as a honeymoon resort. We got the story from one of the survivors and his wife. She was a lovely blond nightclub singer who now looked like an old and shrunken woman; he had played a hot trumpet and was at one time internationally famous through his recordings. I recall the incident because, despite everything, he had held onto the silver trumpet that had made him famous—a remarkable young man who no doubt died with a final toot of his instrument, a single note announcing his departure from this earth and his entry into heaven.

All this took place in the first few months. I was proved to have been wise in my decision to stay in New York: there was more food here than in the country. There were still some pigeons, and there were plenty of cats, for with the departure of mankind and the failure of all city services, the rodents had increased in a phenomenal manner and naturally the city cats had increased with them. I had eaten cat as a child (our gardener in France, who trapped them, had once given me some), and both Mildred and I found them excellent. There were still some dogs in the street, which lived, literally, by dog eating dog, and these I shot with my .22. Our system of hunting was to go out together; I went a pace in front with the .22, and Mildred followed with the heavier rifle, the 303, which she, like a gunbearer in Africa, put into my hand if I asked for it. Some of the big dogs could not be stopped by a small-bore rifle; and there were human wolves, too, who had to be destroyed. Mildred was in no danger now as a woman, having, like all other surviving women, lost any visible sexual charm which she had ever had, near starvation having reduced the sexual curves that characterize women; and the sex fiends, who had run riot in the early days, raping and murdering, had either been eliminated or had been reduced by the food shortages to seeking nourishment rather than other satisfactions.

For a change, we used to fish in Central Park. Mildred, being better at it than I, would watch her float while I stood guard with the rifle. We cooked out on the roof where, when first we had taken the apartment, I had had built a little barbecue. Water was now obtained with difficulty. Some we brought from Central Park, some we collected by damming up a section of our roof. The best came from a system I devised for leading rain water from the roof above us into our bath by means of a canvas fire hose. All water had to be boiled.

At this time there were very few people left in the city—only a few thousand—because everything had broken down with the breakdown of credit. People simply would not work without money. They were not even ready to save their lives by cooperative effort. So deeply had our competitive system bitten into us that they preferred to sit around and starve, or else they ran away and starved—except the few who, like ourselves, lived on what they could find or loot from the stores. The word "loot" persists, though obviously it was no longer looting. It remained, however, an operation of some danger because of the darkness of the stores and the maniacs who had taken up their abode in many of them—savages who resented any intrusion into their territory. I remember one man that I shot at Gimbel's while Mildred held the flashlight on him. He was an immense man who ran at us roaring with rage as he brandished a meat cleaver. We had gone to Gimbel's for caviar and paté de foie gras. They had a lot of it, for apparently the other looters, having less sophisticated tastes than ours, left it alone.

For anyone who liked adventure. I suppose this would have been very interesting, but to us who had become almost sedentary and were quite unaccustomed to swift movement, hard living or even loud noises, the adjustment was most difficult. Yet in this twilight world, we succeeded in living and forming a pattern of life, even remembering the days with some semblance of accuracy. I, who had always hated a schedule of any kind, now invented one. Monday: Central Park, fishing; Wednesday and Friday: food-looting expeditions. Inevitably, though, the human instinct being what it is, more was collected than food. We found some beautiful fur coats—stone marten, blue mink. Russian sable, and ermine. The ermine came in very handy for winter hunting in the snow. We picked up some wonderful diamond rings of fifteen or twenty carats, ruby clips, necklaces and bracelets. We both looked like pirates. We were far from clean but we were dressed in suede, silk and satin; we wore rare fur coats from which I had cut the arms to give greater freedom. We had silk sashes around our waists, carried an arsenal of daggers and pistols, and over our shoulders were slung the best guns that the gun shops of New York could provide.

We had begun by this time to collect our big dogs. We needed them for protection and hunting. In the beginning we had a boxer and a police dog. We hunted other dogs to feed on. The transition of my wife from a charming, rather fastidious young American girl to a primeval savage was most interesting. She soon learned to use a knife and to skin an animal as well as I did. She was never a good shot, having difficulty in closing her left eye, so I got her a shotgun and a .32-caliber Colt. I told her that if anyone attacked, she was to wait till he was right on her, then push the muzzle of the pistol into his stomach—she would feel it go in—and then continue pulling the trigger till she passed out. No girl could have had better instructions. Fortunately, she never had to follow them. The only near disaster occurred once when I was some distance away, but her assailant was pulled down by the dogs, and when I arrived, the man who had approached her was dead. This reassured me because I had not been, until that moment, quite certain how the dogs would act, as they were young and unused to dangerous work.

This was about the time that we heard the first stories of the Red Death, the strange dancing disease that was, according to the information we had, sweeping not only the country, but the world. We soon saw evidences of it. In fact, one of these dancers was the second man our dogs killed. The disease was contagious. The first symptom was the appearance of great health and gaiety, which was followed by a mad happiness; we would see rosy-faced couples dancing and singing in the streets as the disease began to spread. In the later phase, the victim either fell into a coma or attacked anyone in the vicinity without warning. This is what happened one evening as we were about to cross Sixth Avenue: a man and a woman suddenly appeared and began pirouetting

In selecting shielding material for any shelter, sand or earth can be substituted for concrete or brick, but for each inch of solid masonry you need an inch and a half of sand or earth. Adding shielding material to a shelter will improve the protection offered by the shelter, but it also may increase the cost of the shelter.

This sand-filled lean-to basement shelter will accommodate three persons. The house itself gives partial shielding. Sandbags are used to block the end of the shelter.

This backyard plywood shelter can be built partially above ground and mounded over with earth, or be built totally below ground level.

A gravel drain under the shelter and a ditch outside help keep it dry. The family blocks the entrance with sandbags after entering the shelter.

Page 21 of the booklet, *Fallout Protection: What To Know And Do About Nuclear Attack,* published by the Departmet Of Defense, Office Of Civil Defense, December, 1961.

and jitterbugging. I hoped they would pay no attention to us, but the man saw us. I knew that we were in for trouble, for he suddenly got beyond the happy stage and became murderous. He reached me with incredible speed and had me down before I could do anything to defend myself. But as he gripped me, my wife fired three shots into him from her .32 and the dogs attacked him, the boxer grasping his thigh and the police dog his shoulder. They knocked him onto his back and quickly finished him off.

I picked up the sack I had been carrying and felt very shaken, for I was certain I had been contaminated, and now had to work out plans for a method of restraint that my wife could use which would prevent my hurting her when I reached the paroxysms of fury that were the final symptoms of the disease. I hail my own theory and was certain that if she did not touch me she would be all right. Naturally, no one knew much about the disease, but I had the idea that with restraint there was the possibility of survival, death occurring through the berserk rage, which had the effect of burning up the victim. I therefore conceived the plan of going to the local police station—we had dumped our sack of loot—and getting a pair of handcuffs and some chains. The incubation period was said to be a week, but to take no chance I found a ring bolt, fastened it in the floor of the apartment and attached the chain and handcuffs to it at once. All I had to do now, the minute I got the first symptoms, the feeling of joy and the flush that went with it, was to handcuff myself and then hope for the best. I told Mildred of this plan and gave her her instructions. She was to keep out of my reach, give me no food but plenty of water. This she was to put in a tin measuring cup and push into my reach with a long stick.

The precautions I had taken frightened my wife, and I had to spend the next few days reassuring her, telling her that there was nothing to fear and that it was all done "just in case." For my own part, I was certain that I could not have failed to contract the disease, and so we spent our time hunting furiously for more canned provisions and collecting a reserve of wood and water. I also obtained more ammunition for the shotgun, because this was the best weapon for Mildred: a scatter-gun to point in the general direction of anything that frightened her was more likely to be of use than any other gun except a blunderbuss.

What follows is all that I can remember of the days that ensued. I do not actually remember them at all and have reconstructed the story from what I remember of what Mildred told me when it was over—so there is a double twist, as it were, to the evidence, which must make it suspect to those who doubt anything but what they call fact.

It seems, according to what she said, that on the seventh day—our guess about the incubation period had apparently been right—I woke in great form in the morning and began to sing opera. The remarkable thing was that I sang in tune, which was extraordinary, for I have no ear for music. This proved that I was ill. For an hour John Charles Thomas had nothing on me. With expanded chest and wide-open mouth I stood on the roof singing to the silent city. Then I dressed, putting on a brown suit with a white pin stripe. I also put on my gaudiest tie, one that I had bought when we were working in Hollywood. It was a red-white-and-green affair made of silk, hand blocked, and about a foot wide at the wide end. I had never dared to wear it before. I then danced all by myself, tripping lightly up and down to unheard music, and then undressed and broke into a series of Zulu war dances. At this moment some glimmering of sanity must have returned to me, because Mildred said I covered my face with my hands and burst into tears; when the paroxysm was over I picked up the handcuffs, clipped them over my wrists, and lay down like a chained dog to sleep.

What came next must have been completely terrifying for my wife. I am a big man, six feet two, and I weighed two hundred pounds. Having slept for some hours, I woke in the fury that is the secondary symptom of the disease. Being a trained artist and interested in animal psychology, Mildred noted the symptoms carefully, and if I get them wrong it will be due to my faulty memory rather than to her incorrect reporting. Having circled the room to test the length of my chain, I crouched on my haunches like an animal and leaped at her. Fortunately, the ring bolt held and I was dragged back, being pulled onto my shoulders and falling on my back with my handcuffed hands between my legs. This seemed to have knocked me out for a moment, but I was only playing possum. Forgetting what I had told her, and with a wife's instinct of solicitude, she came to see if I were hurt. In a second I was up, and raising my manacled hands, I swung them down at her head in an attempt to stun her. She jumped back just in time and then decided to obey the instructions I had given her. Fetching a tin cup full of water, she pushed it into my reach with the tip of a jointed fishing rod. I seized it and tried to draw her to me, but the tip came off in my hand.

For ten days I remained in alternating states of animal fury and animal sleep. The sitting room resembled the den of a beast. Filthy, naked except for a blanket that I used not for modesty but for warmth, I growled and sulked, wringing my fingers and licking my wrists where the steel had bitten into the flesh and worn away the skin so that it was a ring of festering sores. I drank quantities of water, cup after cup, and each time I had done so I threw the cup at Mildred's head with a clumsy two-handed throw. My ribs stood out in arcs about my chest, my stomach was sunken, my eyes stared wildly; my whole skin was pink shading into red, almost scarlet; while my face and neck, in contrast to the rest of my body, were swollen, apparently suffused with blood to the point where I was unrecognizable. For some reason, the sebaceous glands were stimulated by the fever, and hair grew in great profusion all over my body. I still have it and am often glad of it in the winter, though now I look like an old silver-gray gorilla.

This, then, is the story of my illness as reported by my wife and as I remember it. On the eleventh day it ended as suddenly as it had begun. My face was now white with illness; my eyes, no longer dilated, were sunken; and, instead of having the strength of ten, I could hardly lift my hands to my head. The fever had burned itself out, and I was alive. That was my first conscious thought. I was rational. I said, "I think it's over." Mildred said, "Yes," and burst into tears. I said, "You can let me go now," and for a while it seemed doubtful that she would be able to, because she had put the handcuff key away so safely that she could not remember where it was. She found it at last in an empty flower vase.

A period of convalescence and reflection followed. It is easy to reflect when one is ill; there is nothing else to do. Our reserves of food being ample, we just sat around and talked. The ten days of my illness had been notable for the final evacuation of the hotel. As far as we knew, we were now the only people in it. The manager had decided to go with his wife and son to upper New York State.

But my mind kept going back to the atomic bomb and what we had been told about it. That it wasn't so bad as it was supposed to be; that at Bikini some trees had been left standing. Well, the world was still full of trees. Ignorant and rapacious men had brought this disaster about by their ignorance and rapacity. Because of them I was covered with hair like a damn monkey. Because of them the world was coming to an end and five thousand years—the twinkling of an eye to the Almighty God or to a geologist, but a long time for all that—had gone for nothing.

I was now the most intelligent man in the world. I knew answers that should have been obvious by implication to everyone when the first bomb burst in the New Mexican desert. I had survived the Red Death by a miracle and was therefore even more special, because a lot of people had survived the blast, but so far as I knew, I was the only man to recover from the plague. It was like being top of the class in school; like being the blue-eyed boy of the kindergarten. If, among the blind, the one-eyed man was king, among the dead the one survivor was emperor—Emperor of Nothing. The bombs used in Japan or even at Bikini had been primitive affairs —infant bombs, as it were, children's firecrackers. It did not seem to have occurred to our leaders, rulers, legislators, soldiers and sailors that bombs could be improved by other people, too—that a bomb might be made a thousand times more powerful and a hundred times as small.

All that came out of this period of reflection, during which I regained some measure of my strength, was the certainty that what had been wrong with us was nothing but stupidity. We had been too stupid to be afraid, or too afraid to acknowledge our fear. It seemed to me then that what we needed was not a world of brave men but one of cowards. If only all men had been brave enough to be afraid, there would have been no war or danger of it. Courage in young men—and beauty in young women—are two things to which we attributed too much virtue, both being much commoner than generally supposed and dependent on breeding, diet and glands. I have bred courageous dogs; there would have been no difficulty in establishing a breed of beautiful girls. They might have been rather silly, but beautiful girls have always had this tendency. It would only have fixed their beauty, as I fixed courage by selective inbreeding in my dogs. It might even have been possible to breed the girls mute. Then their dumbness would not have mattered.

I remember even now how Mildred and I tried to joke and make a play upon words, realizing that we must not lose our means of communication by neglecting word values and the finer shades of meaning. Provided we kept our vocabulary, we should remain human and probably remain sane.

I detail these discussions because they come back to me as if they had occurred only yesterday. They were our last talks together and typical of those we had had for many years, talk and ideas being the essence of all that makes man, man. Even the atomic bombs began as talk.

What I'd feared now happened. Mildred came down with the fever. Her symptoms followed the accepted pattern of dancing and singing, but considering our differences in size (she was under five feet tall and weighed only ninety-three pounds) I could not bring myself to tie her up, with the result that when she turned on me, suddenly leaping like a tiger cat onto my shoulder and sinking her teeth into my neck, I had great difficulty in escaping her. As soon as I got my hands free I threw her down and put the handcuffs on her. Her hands were so small that she wriggled out of them till I succeeded in padding them with a handkerchief. She bit, scratched, and kicked fiercely all the time I was restraining her. Having recovered from the disease, I was "salted," as we used to say in Africa of horses that had had horse sickness, and so I was able to take better care of her than she had of me. Nor was she hard to handle because she would seize any lure, like a bath towel, that I offered to her, and worry it, which kept her occupied till I could get right up to her—for a woman, like a horse or any other animal, is less dangerous when she is quite close to you. A kick or a blow has to travel to gain strength. Nevertheless, despite all my efforts—my keeping her covered and hand-feeding her—she weakened and died the day that the fever ended, curling up like a puppy in my arms so that I thought she was just sleeping and did not know she was dead till I put her down.

This description seems somewhat cold and unfeeling, but there is no way of describing such an incident except by understatement. The point was that she had been and now was not. I was almost mad with sadness and loneliness. My brave little companion was gone and her body had to be disposed of. Burial was unthinkable, for no matter how deep I might have buried her, the hunger-crazed dogs would have dug her up. So, collecting furniture from the houses in the neighborhood, I made a great pyre, rested her body on the top of it, and set it ablaze, standing watch over it with a rifle in my hands. Let those who have imagination imagine it, for I cannot describe it. Let them imagine a great heap of tables, chairs and sofas, and a man staggering to the top of the pile with a slung rifle and his dead wife over his shoulder. Imagine him putting her down, looking at her as she lies there, climbing down and setting a match to the cotton stuffing of an armchair at the bottom of the heap. Imagine all this in the street outside the house in which they have lived, and let imagination fill in the gap for each who reads it in his own way. Like a Viking, like a Hindu widow, she was burned—utterly destroyed with the household goods of those who had died before her. There were dead in many of the houses that I had brought furniture from.

It was then that I thought of suicide and, deciding against it, began to take to the bottle. Oddly enough, the dogs were of no help, the wet noses of their sympathy doing nothing to alleviate my sorrow. Some days of this, or weeks—time, which had been getting vaguer, now ceased to exist entirely, because if you are alone there is no time—and then I made my decision to leave a home which no longer held anything but memories. Seeking a place to live, I moved first to the Hotel Pierre because of its proximity to Central Park; and then ten years or so later I moved to this cave in the Chelsea because of the sylvan beauties of its surroundings—its grottoes, pool and springs attracting me profoundly.

Leaving home was a strange sensation. Each thing I looked at had a history. Given by friends, bought, inherited, each thing represented something other than what it was. They were objects certainly, some of them objects of art, but they were also memories. This man and that woman came to the surface of memory; this place and that place; this year and that year. We were in New Orleans then, I thought. We bought those little brass cannons on our honeymoon. We bought this picture in New York, that ivory Buddha in Paris. What was it they said about Buddhas? That you should never use them for anything—not as paperweights or doorstops; you should just have them to look at. This was home, a collection of objects—chairs, tables, beds, chests of drawers, china, silver, pictures, books—that had been integrated into a personality by their possessors—by us. This was home in its final phase; built up slowly, it was now suddenly disintegrated by death.

Several times I went back to look at the apartment, to walk about in it as I had walked before, to feel the things I had handled in the past. I even collected a few things as souvenirs and took them over to the Pierre. It may have been these minor objects of art, or it may have been the location of my new abode, its convenience to 57th Street, that prompted me to make a collection of the smaller and more portable pictures that were to be found in the art galleries there.

The galleries were intact, no one having bothered to loot them—jewels and gold being the things that attracted the robbers. I got some very lovely things: a Poussin, a Utrillo; I got pictures by Renoir, Ingres, Vermeer, Manet, Monet, Dali, and Winslow Homer. Later on, this picture collecting became a kind of obsession and no doubt helped me to retain my sanity, for I would hunt the more expensive apartments and houses of the city in search of works of art—pictures, bibelots, and books. I took things from museums and libraries, and so created a museum of my own in one of the large reception rooms of the hotel. The catholicity of my taste would no doubt have amazed the late curators of the Metropolitan or the Museum of Modern Art, but I have a very interesting collection to which, even now, I occasionally add an exceptional piece if I run across one. And it is very restful after a day's hunting in Central Park to drop in and look at the masterpieces of our vanished civilization and reflect upon the marvelous capacity of man for variability; and to consider the fact that I can sit here and enjoy these things, and that a few hours ago I was hunting strange and savage beasts across the Manhattan veld with a pack of immense parti-colored hounds.

It is interesting to look back now and see the devices I unknowingly employed to keep going. Had I not been alone, had Mildred lived, there might have been a great excitement in this life once we had got used to it. Even as it was, I grew to enjoy it. I see that today, when the even tenor of my life has been shattered by the sudden appearance of the strangers. Had they been men, I should unquestionably have killed them, but since they were young women I could not. That I could not was not a matter of

On March 17, 1953, more than 600 Civil Defense observers and representatives of the Nation's information media witnessed an atomic explosion at the Atomic Energy Commission's Nevada Proving Ground. Some news and radiomen called the event "Operation Doorstep." The name was appropriate, since the purpose of the program was to show the people of America what might be expected if an atomic burst took place over the doorsteps of our major cities.

"Operation Doorstep" was a combined Atomic Energy Commission, Department of Defense, and Federal Civil Defense Administration program, under the direction of a Joint Task Group made up of personnel of the three agencies.

The atomic explosion selected for the operation was one in which the Federal Civil Defense Administration had a limited test program. The program had three major projects: (1) Exposure of two typical American homes to atomic blast in order to determine what would happen to the homes, to test the effectiveness of simple basement shelters; (2) exposure of eight outdoor home-type shelters, in a joint project with AEC, to test the structural strength of such shelters; and (3) exposure of a variety of typical passenger cars to determine the amount of protection afforded to passengers, and the effect on the mechanical operation of the cars.

Both the observer and technical programs were incidental to the main purpose of the atomic detonation, which was to test an experimental nuclear device. It is important to note that the explosion was part of

the AEC developmental series. It would have taken place whether or not Civil Defense and the Department of Defense had participated.

"Operation Doorstep" marked the first time Civil Defense observers were allowed to witness a technical test program. The arrangement was made with the knowledge that it involved a certain amount of risk: that some observers might jump to conclusions, and that their conclusions might be wrong. However, the value to the Nation in demonstrating the effects of an atomic explosion on American homes and cars was so great it was believed the risk was warranted. Actually, very few persons reached wrong conclusions. These were mostly in regard to radiation hazard. The facts are contained in the preliminary report, starting on page 12.

An important angle of "Operation Doorstep" which has not received sufficient stress is the participation of industry. Without the cooperation of a number of business associations and concerns the program would have been far more limited in scope. For example, the test of passenger cars was made possible by the loan of vehicles by major manufacturers through the Automobile Manufacturers' Association and by public-spirited automobile dealers and dealers' associations. Technical evaluation of the program was provided by a special committee of the Society of Automotive Engineers. Gas and oil for the cars were donated by the Standard Oil Company of California.

Mannequins for the houses and shelters were loaned by the L. A. Darling Co. and transported to and from Las Vegas by North American Van Lines. The Atlas Trucking Co. of Las Vegas not only donated hauling service from Las Vegas to the Proving Ground but provided some items of furniture. Clothing for the mannequins was obtained from the J. C. Penney Co. through the National Retail Dry Goods Association.

Even with industry cooperation, however, the technical program was limited in the results which could be obtained.

Operation Doorstep was one of a series of atomic bomb detonations that were also media events designed to build public support for a civil defense program. The above image and the image on the following page are from the official report on Operation Doorstep produced by the FCDA. The still images of the house exploding were captured from the film images that have been used for research and as B-roll for disaster films. (Booklet from the Unites States Archives.)

RESULTS

BLAST EFFECT ON HOUSES

FCDA engineers expected that the house at 3,500 feet would collapse and that the house at 7,500 feet would sustain some damage. By placing a house in a location where collapse was expected, it would be possible to test the protective value of the basement shelters. Since no dwellings of this type had ever been exposed to atomic blast until the March 17th shot, the degree of damage to the far house could not be accurately predicted.

As shown dramatically by published sequence photos, the near house collapsed as expected. The first story was completely demolished and the second story, which was very badly damaged, dropped down on the first floor debris. The roof was blown into several sections.

The rear section of the roof was blown into the backyard. The upper half of the front part of the roof was turned upside down in the front yard while the lower part landed at some distance from the house to the rear. The gable end walls were blown apart and outward. The chimney was broken into several large masses and landed outward from the house at about a 45° angle to the rear.

The basement walls suffered some damage above grade, mostly in the rear. The front basement wall was pushed in slightly, but was not cracked except near the ends. The first floor wood girders were pushed back and the supporting pipe columns inclined to the rear.

After the blast, entry to the basement was made by test personnel at the front of the house through the gap between the first-floor framing and the basement wall. Although the living room and kitchen areas had broken through into the basement, the rest of the area was comparatively clear. Neither basement shelter suffered any damage worth noting. Mannequins in the shelters were not moved or harmed. On the other hand, mannequins in the first-floor rooms were badly damaged and some were so trapped by debris that they could not be readily removed.

The house was 90–95 percent destroyed. No portion of the house except parts of the basement walls could have been used again.

The dwelling at 7,500 feet remained standing, although it was badly damaged. The most apparent damage to this building was the destruction of doors and windows, including sash and frames. The front door disintegrated into its component parts and the doorknobs and lockset were found halfway up the stairs to the second floor. The dining room-kitchen door also disintegrated and one part of it was hurled into the plaster of the rear kitchen wall.

Principal damage to the first-floor system consisted of broken joists. Most breakage originated at knots in the lower edges of the timbers. Some studs were cracked in the front of the house. The floor joists were 2 by 8 inches, spaced 16 inches between centers, with a span of 12 feet. The front wall studs were 2 by 4 inches spaced 16 inches apart.

The second floor system suffered no apparent damage, but plaster and windows of the second story were severely damaged. Damage to the roof consisted mainly of broken rafters in the front section. All rafters except one were broken on the front side. The roof was sprung slightly at the ridge. No rafters were broken on back side of the roof. The rafters were 2 by 6 inches, spaced 16 inches between centers, with a span about 14 feet from front wall to ridge.

chivalry, for chivalry needs a social context in which to function. The force that stayed my finger—which was on the trigger—was one much older than chivalry, being the force that had given birth to it. These were young females of my own species. No factor can be more disturbing to any man or animal than a young female of his own kind.

It is hard to imagine the sport of hunting in North America at this time unless the game is described. The mutations mentioned earlier did not all appear suddenly—first one turned up and then another. I found the first sign of anything odd about six years after the blast. I was out looking for a deer in Central Park, and I came upon what looked like a dog spoor eight inches across. My dogs, however, became very excited and went off in full cry on the scent. This was their habit, and when they had brought their quarry to bay—if they could not kill it alone—they would wait for me to come up with them. With wild cattle, donkeys, or anything of that kind, if the dogs had not killed the animal by the time I reached it, I put a bullet into it and then, whipping off the hounds cut out the tongue, kidneys, sweetbreads or liver—whatever I fancied— for myself and then let them eat their fill. When I hunted a bear or a tiger, the dogs would circle it, baying, and in such an encounter I often lost one or more dogs killed and several wounded. The wounded dogs had to be protected from their companions, and isolated when I got them home, or they would have been killed. I had always been something of a veterinarian, having had to be in South Africa, and with the best drugs—sulfa, penicillin and everything else that I wanted—at my disposal, I lost very few of my wounded hounds.

This time, however, as I trotted after my pack (at that time it consisted of about fifteen couples of grown dogs, and ten half-and three-quarter-grown pups who were learning their business) I felt that they had bitten off more than they could chew. The spoor puzzled me. This was an immense beast—the stride was well over a yard—with imprints so deep that it must weigh at least half a ton. I had gone about a mile when I heard the baying of the dogs. I also heard some of them screaming the way a hurt dog does. I hurried and then, prompted by some instinct, decided to climb a tree to get a better view. It was a good thing I did because the dogs had surrounded a huge black wolf that stood as high at the withers as a horse. Three dogs were dead and, as I looked, the wolf caught another —a handsome red-colored dog called Fox—and tossed him in the air the way a good terrier does a rat. The dog fell howling with his back broken. As the wolf seized their companion, the other dogs darted in from all around to bite him, seizing his hind legs and tail, one bitch leaping at his throat. I had only the 303 with me, a rifle quite unsuited to this kind of beast had I been on the ground where he could get me, but a good enough weapon from my point of vantage in a tree. Resting the barrel along a branch, I emptied the magazine into him, and before he could decide what to do he was down and the dogs had swarmed all over him. He killed three more before he died, and hurt six. This experience taught me a very important lesson, and I never went out again without two guns, one of them a 450 express.

After seeing this animal, I was no longer surprised at the other strange beasts I saw. The atomic bomb and the radioactivity that had accompanied it were explanation enough when I thought it all out. These beasts were monsters caused by the effect of radioactivity on the genes and chromosomes of animals pregnant at the time of the blast, while other abnormal mutations were the result of some nutritional change that had taken place in the herbage. It interested me to note that I, too, felt very well and even seemed to have grown a little through eating the meat of these animals. And this diet certainly had had an effect on my hounds, the young dogs increasing in size, going up to forty inches and weighing over three hundred pounds—the size of a small lion or leopard. The aurochs, which had roamed Europe before the Romans, reappeared through some kind of throwback; and the cattle of the country—Jerseys, Guernseys, Herefords, Holsteins, and Shorthorns—bred together, increased in size, and reverted to a breed that looked like the Texas longhorn. These cattle became the chief prey of the giant parti-colored mink. I remember seeing black-and-white minks at the Sportsman's Show in Madison Square Garden years ago, and it would seem that this mutation into giantism was one which was effected by the radioactivity. These animals were fortunately rare, and I feared them greatly because of their savagery. They stood about five feet high at the shoulder and were some eighteen feet long, including the tail. But despite their size they could flatten themselves and creep along almost invisibly, the white marks helping them by breaking up the silhouette. They would creep closer and closer to their prey and then charge at it from close distance at incredible speed—the speed being fast enough to roll over an ox that was taken by surprise. Then, cutting the jugular with their immense needle teeth, they emptied the carcass of blood in a few minutes.

As far as possible, I avoided hunting such dangerous animals and confined myself to deer, wild cattle, antelopes, bison and zebras for meat for the pack and myself; and tigers, leopards, mountain lions and bears for sport and to keep my dogs in fighting trim. There is nothing more exciting than hunting some great carnivore that has taken up its abode in a house in the vicinity. Such an animal has to be killed, because nothing is so inconvenient as a tiger or leopard making a den near one's dwelling.

One of my most interesting hunts was that of a pair of tigers in the Hotel Pierre. They were a mated couple, and I was continually getting glimpses of them in the vestibule or in the passages. We avoided each other, but the situation made me nervous. And I could see that the tigers, despite the fact that they had settled down to housekeeping, were equally ill at ease. This meant that there would be a showdown sooner or later, and so one day I decided to settle them for good and all.

It should be noted that animals, unless they are hungry or sick, will seldom attack man until they are challenged. If, traveling along a narrow path, you notice a lion, you do not look at him. You suddenly take an interest in the treetops or in the flight of a passing bird. Out of the corner of your eye you will see him do the same thing. He will turn his head, something will attract him in the distance, and he will leave the path. But his face must be saved. His eye must not be met. This piece of psychology has a human application, too. There would never have been a barroom fight if two men had not looked at each other—eye to eye—so that there was no going back.

This, then, was the situation between me and the tigers. We saved one another's faces and acted with ever-increasing tact, but there was the certainty that this politeness went too far, and that when it ended, it would be with either my death or theirs. So, getting out my dogs, I divided my pack in two, selecting those that were the stupidest or that I cared for least. The balance of working hounds, about ten couples of superb animals, I left in the kennels that I had built in an adjoining flower shop. The tigers had made their den in a small pantry behind the cocktail bar; and it was the knowledge that I would lose a lot of hounds, and that any dogs would be good enough for the job provided they had courage enough to enter, which had prompted me to use my culls. I sent them into the bar. The two leaders were killed before they were through the door, the male tiger smashing them against the wall with what can only be described as a right and a left; but as he struck, I shot him, the bullet smashing his lower jaw and entering his chest. The remaining dogs went in over his body. and came out faster than they had gone in, followed by the tigress. She charged out but did not see me —I had hidden behind the bar. As she passed me I fired at her, but I missed. The dogs were now in full cry after her. As she bounded up the steps into the dining room, followed by the dogs, I got another shot in and hit her in the loins with a high shot that broke her back. I checked the dogs as well as I could —there was no point in their attacking now—but one refused to obey and was killed. Another bullet finished the tigress.

This incident was a contributory factor in my decision to move to the Chelsea. The Park was no longer important, since the whole city was now covered with grass, and the beauty of the cave I had discovered had long tempted me. There was no place near the Chelsea where large. dangerous animals could lurk, and there were excellent facilities for my dogs: a large foundation excavation with large cellars adjoining it. Nothing could have been better, and I should have moved a year earlier had I not delayed out of laziness.

This new home where I am now sitting deserves some notice. The cave has two chambers and is lighted by windows that I have pierced through the debris. There is a third room, on a lower level, which has no window. The temperature of this room rarely varies more than a few degrees, and this is where I sleep in the coldest and the hottest weather. I also keep my wine here, and the room has a pleasant rich, earthy smell of wine and dog and man that is very homelike. The second room is a combined sitting room and study: I have my best pictures and books here and some wonderful small pieces of furniture. The outside room is my kitchen and workshop. I have built myself a chimney and have a bench and carpenters' tools.

But all these conveniences could have been found in most districts in the city. It was the exterior which made the situation unique. The hotel itself had collapsed and was a voluptuous green hill covered with short, cropped grass. In fine weather I have seen a herd of zebra mixed with American bison grazing over it within a few yards of me. By some combination of accidents—the explosion that destroyed New York, the civic engineering that existed before the explosion, and certain geological factors—a lovely long, finger-shaped lake appeared in 23rd Street. It is fed from the spring which bubbles through my grotto, the water being first forced upward by natural pressure through a small crevice in the fallen masonry some fifteen feet above ground level. After I had done a little minor engineering with plumbing fixtures picked up here and there and with plants and ferns collected wherever I could find them, I had created a little paradise for myself. I should add that I did no hunting within a mile of my home, thus making a reserve because I like the game for company and I find nothing more beautiful. I also had two practical reasons, one being that if any big carnivores came along they would have no difficulty in finding a meal, and the second being that, in the event of illness, I could easily kill something to eat from my own doorstep....

Something very awkward has just occurred. My house dogs again expressed uneasiness, and, waiting till they quieted down, I went out to see what had disturbed them. What I found justified my worst fears. The girls have found my retreat. Their spoor is all around the grotto. They even rested on the grass and dipped their toes in the pool below the trickling waterfall. This infuriates me. The impertinence of these abandoned creatures—hunting out the cave of an old and respectable man and then disporting themselves at his private spring! I have been away from people too long to feel any Robinson Crusoe-like joy at discovering the footprints of these girls; besides, Friday was not a girl, much less two girls.

Bodo and Vixen worked over the grotto, quartering it, noses to the ground. stopping occasionally with backward looks at me. I followed them and found the trail to lead east and then, climbing one of the larger hillocks to get a better view, saw the smoke of a fire about half a mile away. It gave me a very strange feeling to see the smoke of another's cooking fire. I sat down and, with my dogs beside me, spent some time watching the blue smoke curl upward like a ribbon into the sky. Once a little breeze caught it, and it made a question mark. Nothing. I thought, could be more apt unless it were a period. I was overcome by a sense of finality, of foreboding. If I am not careful, my pleasant way of life may end, my habit of years be interrupted. With a certain irony I reflected on the repetition of the human pattern. As we once feared and resented the coming of atomic power, or, for that matter, universal suffrage, the liberation of the slaves or anything else that was different, I am now upset because I am no longer alone in the world. With these thoughts in my mind, I came home and cooked my supper. I had the saddle and kidneys of a yearling moose calf cooked in bear fat, a can of spaghetti with tomato sauce, and a can of green peas. I opened a bottle of port, one of the few wines which has not begun to go off after more than twenty years. I topped it off with three brandies. I have given the dogs a good meal and now sit here, pencil in hand, to record further impressions. I am now right up to date.

The brandy has done me good. I can feel my heart beating strangely.

Six months have passed since I have written a line. Although, as a novelist, I have always objected to the diary or near-diary form, I find on reading this over that it has a certain interest. Oddly enough, whether or not anyone is ever to read it appears to depend on me, because the young women are with me now. I would call them nice-looking—though it is quite hard for me to remember exactly what a pretty girl should look like.

I will describe them in greater detail later. At the moment my problem is one of biology and morals.

I am seventy years of age and, though I am healthy and remarkably strong, I am without any desire for these young creatures of my own species. My lack of interest does not appear to be reciprocated, for in them is the warmth and burgeoning of youth.

This is very embarrassing to a man of my solitary habits and advanced years. Who am I to repopulate the world with white men? And would not the world perhaps be a better place without us? On the other hand, any vanity comes in—my vanity as an author and the historian of these events: the final chapter of history as we knew it, and the opening chapter of a new kind of history. If there are to be people again, if there are to be readers again—who might someday read this diary—it appears that I must father them. The problem perturbs me; it is an issue that I find it hard to clarify. The moral question is not whether I should live with two young girls, but whether our species is worth perpetuating.

And for the life of me I cannot see what is the matter with the young Indian braves. Why can't the girls marry them, and live happily ever after without bothering me? Of course, the Indians may not think them attractive, but this seems hardly likely. In my opinion, the girls' interest in me is simply curiosity: I seem unique, and women love the rare and strange. It is also evident that I have prestige value among the Indians.

It is now spring again, and as I look back over the last few months I feel them worthy of some notice because of their personal interest to me. I will begin with today, when it really came to me in words, and go back from there.

I was galloping Prince, my big bay, over some open country in what I take to be Florida, since our war party went south and we are among palms. I have seen brown pelicans and frigate birds and so I cannot be very far wrong. Beside me on her chestnut was Helen, the smaller of the two blondes. We galloped side by side, my long white hair and beard blowing in the wind, her yellow hair flowing like a palomino's tail. Throwing my leg across a horse again after all these years has been a strange and wonderful sensation that has really reconciled me to this new way of life.

This morning, I had jumped onto Prince, the stallion I was now riding, a six-year-old standing about fifteen-three. I mounted him bareback, and used only a hackamore to control him. Unaccustomed to a white man's smell, he had been difficult at first and had played up, rearing, and then, when I put my heels into him, had gone forward in a series of leaps and plunges till I leaned forward and patted his neck, when he started moving with the great raking strides that have never ceased to give me pleasure. Bareback riding tired me at first but, once one gets used to it, it has great advantages over using a saddle. But I must go back to the day the Indians broke into my home and captured me. . . .

I had finished eating and was working on my manuscript when the dogs leaped up and went almost mad with fury. They barked and snuffled under the door. As I grabbed my rifle, the door burst open and a number of young braves, accompanied by the two girls, broke in. They were all yelling and carrying weapons. The leader killed Bodo, who jumped at him as he crossed the threshold. As I raised my rifle, one of the girls tripped me. She flung herself onto me, wrapping her arms about my legs. I fired two shots but missed with both. Looking back at the incident, I am inclined to think the three brandies may have had something to do with the poor showing I made. The brandy was wonderful '65, the so-called Napoleon, and I drank from one of those large-bellied glasses that are warmed with the hands. My missing, however, must be considered providential, for had I wounded one of the braves I might easily have been killed.

Vixen fastened her teeth onto the leg of one of the young men, but another got hold of my left arm before I could get to my feet. The Indians seemed to have decided not to hurt me and to have had a mistaken idea that I would not strike the girls if they attacked me, because the second girl now knelt on my chest. Her hair had fallen down and was hanging in my face. I was able to raise the barrel of my rifle and clip her on the jaw with it as I lay on my back, at the same time striking the other girl on the top of the head with a downward stroke from the butt. The young men now became more active, and disarmed me and tied me. I called Vixen off and gave up the battle. To tell the truth, I was curious about these Indians. I was even more curious about the two girls, who definitely were white and who spoke a kind of English—in the struggle they both swore like cavalry officers. I only hoped they did not know the meaning of the words they used. (It subsequently appeared that they did not, but had learned them from an old prospector who, having joined the Indians and finding these two orphan girls among them —their parents had died of the Red Death—had decided to pay his debt to society by teaching them his version of their own language.) The Indians were Comanches and Kiowas and had set out from Oklahoma four years ago on a kind of scouting exploration mission. They had brought the girls with them as interpreters, in case they should find any white men left alive. Their medicine men had foretold the finding of one and had said the white man would give them news. All this, naturally, came out by degrees.

I was at first tongue-tied in the presence of the girls, who seemed, once I had got used to the idea, incredibly beautiful and desirable. I have to some extent got over this phase, which I consider one of the few signs of senility I have shown. I had next to learn the language they called English. Apart from its Rabelaisian flavor, it had many Comanche words which the girls used to fill in the gaps, where they had forgotten what their prospector friend had taught them. As he died when they were about ten years old, they had developed a kind of special language, as children do. However, by degrees I got their story. They were the daughters of an Indian agent and his wife who had been living on the reservation when the blast hit us. The girls had been infants then, and so knew very little about the blast. Their mother and father had died in an accident, and an Indian squaw had adopted them. About this time, a prospector by the name of Adam K. Bell had joined forces with the tribe (he had been in the mountains for two years) and had instructed the girls in their mother tongue and in his version of history, geography and mathematics. They knew the multiplication tables and could add, subtract, divide and multiply—arts which made them invaluable to the Indians, who called them in when such obscure calculations were necessary. He had also taught them some excellent geology, though they could never figure out his interest in gold, which they said was quite common in some of the mountains they had explored; and they thought it had caused the old prospector's death through frustration, though of course they did not use that word. They said he went mad when he saw it—and to express his madness they clapped their hands, jumped up and down, and pulled at their yellow hair.

The war party that captured me had had its camp on the site of the blast. The tepees stood about where the Players Club had been. They had chosen this site because, since everything was flattened around them, they need fear no ambush. When we reached the camp, a number of warriors were seated on the grass, grazing their horses, which they held by long riatas. These were the reserve braves, as it were, who had their arms with them—bows and arrows—and could be in action in a few minutes. Farther away, other horses were being grazed under an armed, mounted guard. These men had rifles that looked like Springflelds. It appeared later that they had picked them up here and there as they crossed the country—deer rifles and the like, war souvenirs and other relatively light guns. In the United States, very heavy game rifles of the sort used in Africa have always been rare; and even if the Indians had found one, they would only have fired it once because of the kick. But even though they could have found enough ordinary rifles and enough ammunition, a great number of the braves were apparently against using them. The white man's magic had, as it were, gone out of fashion with all but the boldest. As I took in the scene, I was struck by the oddness of the combination of primitive and modern weapons in the hands of the red men, as I still called them in my Fenimore Cooper-conditioned mind. Noble savages—but I wished they had been less rough with Inc.

More men were sitting about the cooking fires in front of the tepees. My girls—I called them that already in my mind—seemed to be the only women with the party.

I was taken before the leader, a subsidiary chief or headman called Tall Eagle. He was a powerful man of about forty, and some kind of communication with him was established with the help of the girls. I did not get to know the full story of these Indians until later, when I had mastered something of their tongue, which I speak well now though I continue to mix in words of Zulu, which disconcerts them. The war party's mission was to proceed east till they came to the Great Water and then follow it south till they came to the land of the Seminoles, with whom they wished to establish contact and discuss the formation of a union of the Indian tribes that had survived, a repetition of the Six Nations alliance—if six nations were found still to exist.

They were, however, much perturbed by the great mutations that they had found in the East, and even to encounter such animals as Bengal tigers and polar bears worried them. Fortunately, the great mutations were not common. I had disposed of a number of them, for though I avoided them as much as I could, I had to kill them when I came across them, before they killed me; for these monstrosities were not, even in the animal sense, respectable members of the natural world, but were crazy—perhaps mad with hunger, their great frames needing everything that they could find to keep them going—a man or a dog being about as much use to them as a rabbit to a lion or a mouse to a cougar.

In my first week with the Indians I had the good fortune to kill a giant mink that had attacked a party of their braves, after it had killed three members of the party and sucked the blood from two of their horses. With the help of the Indians, I stripped the skin from the animal. It took ten men to drag it out so that we could peg it.

Perhaps I should describe this hunt in greater detail because it had certain interesting qualities. I was riding with one of the girls in the vicinity of my old home in 45th Street, perhaps unconsciously bidding it farewell, when from the direction of the Hudson River I heard shouts and yells which I knew must come from my new friends. I could also distinguish the scream of a giant mink. I was luckily carrying my 450. I had, in fact, fired a few shots from it just to get my horse used to the sound of a gun, something that he had not taken kindly to at first but seemed to be getting used to, as almost any horse will if he is swung sideways to the target so that a shot is not fired too close to his ears or face. At any rate, when I heard the noise I turned Prince's head toward the river and galloped down the soft grass of the street, which at this point runs downhill till it crosses Ninth Avenue, where it rises in a short hill.

I could feel Prince change his stride as the street rose; his great quarters came under him as he drove his hind hoofs into the turf. The girl stayed close behind me.

Breasting the hill, I checked the horse, pulling him up almost into a rear because, as I stopped him, I heard a terrible cry of agony from quite near by. Swinging Prince around, I pushed him up onto a ridge and saw, on the corner of what had been Tenth Avenue, the strangest sight I have ever seen.

A giant mink stood at bay with a dead Indian in his mouth. Two other Indians lay on the ground, and there was a dead horse nearby. Some mounted Indians and one loose horse were circling round the mink, who bristled with so many arrows that he looked almost like a porcupine. There were probably enough arrows to kill him in the end, but he would take days to die. The Indians with rifles were not with this party. Even if they had been, their bullets would have been too light to have much effect. The most intelligent thing the Indians could have done would have been to leave the mink alone now, because he would have settled down to suck the blood of the men and horses he had killed; but they were in no mood to give in and, uttering wild yells, they closed in on him, circling around him and shooting more arrows into him. This made it impossible for me to get a shot at him till suddenly, dropping the man he held, he did what I hoped he would do—stood up on his hind legs. He had seen me on the ridge, outlined against the sky, and wondered what I was. The mink's eyesight, fortunately, is not good. As he stood looking and sniffing, his pointed face dripping with blood, I charged down straight at him—a distance of a hundred yards or so—and, pulling up about twenty paces short of him, swung Prince broadside on and put a soft-nosed bullet into the mink's chest, midway between his short, waving forelegs. The bullet must have smashed into his backbone because he threw up his paws, almost as a man might throw up his hands, and fell backward with the Indians closing in on him, forcing their reluctant ponies up to him so that they could drive their spears into him. Once satisfied that he was dead, they expressed their pleasure.

Nothing could have suited my purpose better than this happy event, for by it I proved my value to them as a warrior. For I had realized for some time that even if they had decided to leave me behind when they left New York (they had freed me almost as soon as they caught me), I would have followed them because I needed company.

The bowl of my personal existence was shattered. Here were men again. I'd forgotten how I needed men. It was interesting how my nostrils, trained by years of hunting, now dilated at the scent of men. There were also the girls, who affected me profoundly, and the horses. Women might be a necessity in youth, but horses were a pleasure that I had never forgotten. No man was ever betrayed by a horse; no horse ever deserted him or bore false witness against him. It took me some time to explain my ideas to the Indians, and to accustom my youngest dogs to their company. The older and more savage dogs I shot after having steeled myself by drinking half a bottle of French brandy. Actually, apart from the dogs that I could not take, I regretted most leaving my wine cellar and my museum. Most of the wine had begun to go off a little by now, but the spirits were excellent except where the corks had failed to stay in a good state of preservation. But I had some beautiful dogs left; I had the bay stallion. Tall Eagle had given me; and I had the company of a hundred and fifty magnificent young Indians and two young white girls who were burned as brown as the Indians and distinguishable from them only by (their corn-colored hair and blue eyes. All this made up for what I had lost.

I was, however, faced with an ethical problem. The Indians, who had discovered heavy rifles similar to mine in some if the stores they had entered, wished me instruct them in their use. I could see nothing to be gained by such instruction, I tried to explain to them that this was white man's magic and so strong that it had destroyed all the white men in the world except me, turning its forces against them in retribution for their own misuse of its powers. I also pointed out at all they need do to have this great power at their disposal was to keep me alive and treat me well. I let one man fire a shot lying down, and the recoil broke his collarbone. This seemed to confirm all that I had said.

Until I was with people again, it had not occurred to me to consider my own appearance, because when a man is alone he has no appearance. I found a mirror and examined myself with some attention and amazement. I was as straight as I had always been, but I was much wider than I had thought possible. My arms were as big as my thighs; my chest was immense. My hair was long, reaching halfway down my back, and my beard reached my belt. Both hair and beard were snow white. My body hair, with which I was covered, was white in front of my body and shaded through silver into black along my spine. For ornament, I wore a diamond necklace around my neck; my only clothing was a khaki kilt that I wore for warmth, a leather belt in which was stuck my kukri, and a pair of leather shoes. On my upper arms I had some gold armlets made from expanding wrist-watch chains and other jeweled bracelets that I had joined together and mounted on wide leather straps—a pastime I had indulged in as a hobby. I could not think what I looked like until I suddenly remembered the steel engravings of an old Bible I had had as a child. I looked like Moses when he received the tablets. But the astonishing thing was how well I felt and how immensely strong I was—now that I had others against whom to measure myself.

My appearance does not seem to bother the Indians and it is evident that the two girls—their names are Helen and Christine—want to marry me and are even prepared to share me if necessary, much to the amusement of the braves, who, now that we know each other well, nudge me in the ribs and give me monosyllabic advice amplified by gestures. This situation is still unresolved and becomes daily more precarious.

My personal affairs have, however, no historic interest; and, having completed my story of the end of the white man's world, I can only say that I ride forward with optimism and can now laugh at the change of circumstance which hoisted my race with the petard of its own ingenuity and returned this great land to its original possessors. "America for the Americans," I say to Tall Eagle, and laugh. He says nothing. He thinks I am mad. But the girls laugh, because young girls laugh at anything, and it is spring again.

The photos on these pages are from Operation Cue, a Civil Defense exercise associated with the series of atomic bomb tests titled Operation Teapot. Operation Cue was an FCDA-controlled public relations event, attended by national media, in which an atomic bomb was detonated at 5:10 a.m. on May 5, 1955. These images of mannequins, like those from Operation Doorstep, have held the fear of atomic threat that have plagued mankind for decades; that anxiety is only amplified by the uncanny

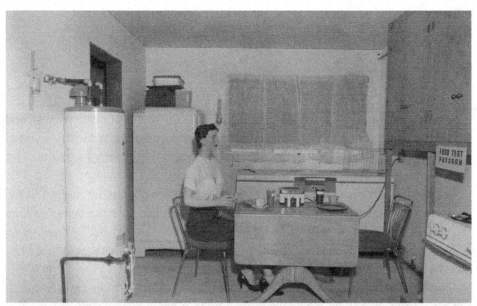

stillness of daily American life portrayed by the unnatural settings and poses that awaited the atomic blast. The goal of this test was six-fold, seeking informaton on the effects of an atomic explosion on: 1. response of residential, commerical, and industrial structures and materials; 2. food and foodstuffs; 3. shelters for civilian populations; 4. utilities, services, and associated equipment; 5. mobile housing and emergency vehicles; and 6. radiological defense. (Photos United States Archives.)

A Bad Day For Sales
Fritz Leiber

The big bright doors of the office building parted with a pneumatic whoosh and Robie glided onto Times Square. The crowd that had been watching the fifty-foot-tall girl on the clothing billboard get dressed, or reading the latest news about the Hot Truce scrawl itself in yard-high script, hurried to look.

Robie was still a novelty. Robie was fun. For a little while yet, he could steal the show. But the attention did not make Robie proud. He had no more emotions than the pink plastic giantess, who dressed and undressed endlessly whether there was a crowd or the street was empty, and who never once blinked her blue mechanical eyes. But she merely drew business while Robie went out after it.

For Robie was the logical conclusion of the development of vending machines. All the earlier ones had stood in one place, on a floor or hanging on a wall, and blankly delivered merchandise in return for coins, whereas Robie searched for customers. He was the demonstration model of a line of sales robots to be manufactured by Shuler Vending Machines, provided the public invested enough in stocks to give the company capital to go into mass production.

The publicity Robie drew stimulated investments handsomely. It was amusing to see the TV and newspaper coverage of Robie selling, but not a fraction as much fun as being approached personally by him. Those who were usually bought anywhere from one to five hundred shares, if they had any money and foresight enough to see that sales robots would eventually be on every street and highway in the country.

Robie radared the crowd, found that it surrounded him solidly, and stopped. With a carefully built-in sense of timing, he waited for the tension and expectation to mount before he began talking.

"Say, Ma, he doesn't look like a robot at all," a child said. "He looks like a turtle."

Which was not completely inaccurate. The lower part of Robie's body was a metal hemisphere hemmed with sponge rubber and not quite touching the sidewalk. The upper was a metal box with black holes in it. The box could swivel and duck.

A chromium-bright hoopskirt with a turret on top.

"Reminds me too much of the Little Joe Paratanks," a legless veteran of the Persian War muttered, and rapidly rolled himself away on wheels rather like Robie's.

His departure made it easier for some of those who knew about Robie to open a path in the crowd. Robie headed straight for the gap. The crowd whooped.

Robie glided very slowly down the path, deftly jogging aside whenever he got too close to ankles in skylon or sockassins. The rubber buffer on his hoopskirt was merely an added safeguard.

The boy who had called Robie a turtle jumped in the middle of the path and stood his ground, grinning foxily.

Robie stopped two feet short of him. The turret ducked. The crowd got quiet.

"Hello, youngster," Robie said in a voice that was smooth as that of a TV star, and was, in fact, a recording of one.

The boy stopped smiling. "Hello," he whispered.

"How old are you?" Robie asked.

"Nine. No, eight."

"That's nice," Robie observed. A metal arm shot down from his neck, stopped just short of the boy.

The boy jerked back.

"For you," Robie said.

The boy gingerly took the red polly-lop from the neatly fashioned blunt metal claws, and began to unwrap it.

"Nothing to say?" asked Robie.

"Uh—thank you."

After a suitable pause, Robie continued, "And how about a nice refreshing drink of Poppy Pop to go with your polly-lop?" The boy lifted his eyes, but didn't stop licking the candy. Robie waggled his claws slightly. "Just give me a quarter and within five seconds—"

A little girl wriggled out of the forest of legs. "Give me a polly-lop, too, Robie," she demanded.

"Rita, come back here!" a woman in the third rank of the crowd called angrily.

Robie scanned the newcomer gravely. His reference silhouettes were not good enough to let him distinguish the sex of children, so he merely repeated, "Hello, youngster."

"Rita!"

"Give me a polly-lop!"

Disregarding both remarks, for a good salesman is single-minded and does not waste bait, Robie said winningly, "I'll bet you read *Junior Space Killers*. Now I have here—"

"Uh-uh, I'm a girl. He got a polly-lop."

At the word "girl," Robie broke off. Rather ponderously, he said, "I'll bet you read *Gee-Gee Jones, Space Stripper*. Now I have here the latest issue of that thrilling comic, not yet in the stationary vending machines. Just give me fifty cents and within five—"

"Please let me through. I'm her mother."

A young woman in the front rank drawled over her powder-sprayed shoulder, "I'll get her for you," and slithered out on six-inch platform shoes. "Run away, children," she said nonchalantly. Lifting her arms behind her head, she pirouetted slowly before Robie to show how much she did for her bolero half-jacket and her form-fitting slacks that melted into skylon just above the knees. The little girl glared at her. She ended the pirouette in profile.

At this age-level, Robie's reference silhouettes permitted him to distinguish sex, though with occasional amusing and embarrassing miscalls. He whistled admiringly. The crowd cheered.

Someone remarked critically to a friend, "It would go over better if he was built more like a real robot. You know, like a man."

The friend shook his head. "This way it's subtler."

No one in the crowd was watching the newscript overhead as it scribbled, "Ice Pack for Hot Truce? Vanadin hints Russ may yield on Pakistan."

Robie was saying, ". . . in the savage new glamor-tint we have christened Mars Blood, complete with spray applicator and fit-all fingerstalls that mask each finger completely except for the nail. Just give me five dollars—uncrumpled bills may be fed into the revolving rollers you see beside my arm—and within five seconds—"

"No, thanks, Robie," the young woman yawned.

"Remember," Robie persisted, "for three more weeks, seductivizing Mars Blood will be unobtainable from any other robot or human vendor."

"No, thanks."

Robie scanned the crowd resourcefully. "Is there any gentleman here…" he began just as a woman elbowed her way through the front rank.

"I told you to come back!" she snapped at the little girl.

"But I didn't get my polly-lop!"

"…who would care to…"

"Rita!"

"Robie cheated. Ow!"

Meanwhile, the young woman in the half bolero had scanned the nearby gentlemen on her own. Deciding that there was less than a fifty per cent chance of any of them accepting the proposition Robie seemed about to make, she took advantage of the scuffle to slither gracefully back into the ranks. Once again the path was clear before Robie.

He paused, however, for a brief recapitulation of the more magical properties of Mars Blood, including a telling phrase about "the passionate claws of a Martian sunrise."

But no one bought. It wasn't quite time. Soon enough silver coins would be clinking, bills going through the rollers faster than laundry, and five hundred people struggling for the privilege of having their money taken away from them by America's first mobile sales robot.

But there were still some tricks that Robie had to do free, and one certainly should enjoy those before starting the more expensive fun.

So Robie moved on until he reached the curb. The variation in level was instantly sensed by his under-scanners. He stopped. His head began to swivel. The crowd watched in eager silence. This was Robie's best trick.

Robie's head stopped swiveling. His scanners had found the traffic light. It was green. Roble edged forward. But then the light turned red. Robie stopped again, still on the curb. The crowd softly ahhed its delight.

It was wonderful to be alive and watching Robie on such an exciting day. Alive and amused in the fresh, weather-controlled air between the lines of bright skyscrapers with their winking windows and under a sky so blue you could almost call it dark.

(But way, way up, where the crowd could not see, the sky was darker still. Purple-dark, with stars showing. And in that purple-dark, a silver-green something, the color of a bud, plunged down at better than three miles a second. The silver-green was a newly developed paint that foiled radar.)

Robie was saying, "While we wait for the light, there's time for you youngsters to enjoy a nice refreshing Poppy Pop. Or for you adults—only those over five feet tall are eligible to buy—to enjoy an exciting Poppy Pop fizz. Just give me a quarter or—in the case of adults, one dollar and a quarter; I'm licensed to dispense intoxicating liquors—and within five seconds…"

But that was not cutting it quite fine enough. Just three seconds later, the silver-green bud bloomed above Manhattan into a globular orange flower. The skyscrapers grew brighter and brighter still, the brightness of the inside of the Sun. The windows winked blossoming white fire-flowers.

The crowd around Roble bloomed, too. Their clothes puffed into petals of flame. Their heads of hair were torches.

The orange flower grew, stem and blossom. The blast came. The winking windows shattered tier by tier, became black holes. The walls bent, rocked, cracked. A stony dandruff flaked from their cornices. The flaming flowers on the sidewalk were all leveled at once. Robie was shoved ten feet. His metal hoopskirt dimpled, regained its shape.

The blast ended. The orange flower, grown vast, vanished overhead on its huge, magic bean-stalk. It grew dark and very still. The cornice-dandruff pattered down. A few small fragments rebounded from the metal hoop-skirt.

Robie made some small, uncertain movements, as if feeling for broken bones. He was hunting for the traffic light, but it no longer shone either red or green.

He slowly scanned a full circle. There was nothing anywhere to interest his reference silhouettes. Yet whenever he tried to move, his under-scanners warned him of low obstructions. It was very puzzling.

The silence was disturbed by moans and a crackling sound, as faint at first as the scampering of distant rats.

A seared man, his charred clothes fuming where the blast had blown out the fire, rose from the curb. Robie scanned him.

"Good day, sir," Robie said. "Would you care for a smoke? A truly cool smoke? Now I have here a yet-unmarketed brand…"

But the customer had run away, screaming, and Robie never ran after customers, though he could follow them at a medium brisk roll. He worked his way along the curb where the man had sprawled, carefully keeping his distance from the low obstructions, some of which writhed now and then, forcing him to jog. Shortly he reached a fire hydrant. He scanned it. His electronic vision, though it still worked, had been somewhat blurred by the blast.

"Hello, youngster," Robie said. Then, after a long pause, "Cat got your tongue? Well, I have a little present for you. A nice, lovely polly-lop.

"Take it, youngster," he said after another pause. "It's for you. Don't be afraid."

His attention was distracted by other customers, who began to rise up oddly here and there, twisting forms that confused his reference silhouettes and would not stay to be scanned properly. One cried, "Water," but no quarter clinked in Robie's claws when he caught the word and suggested, "How about a nice refreshing drink of Poppy Pop?"

The rat-crackling of the flames had become a jungle muttering. The blind windows began to wink fire again.

A little girl marched, stepping neatly over arms and legs she did not look at. A white dress and the once taller bodies around her had shielded her from the brilliance and the blast. Her eyes were fixed on Robie. In them was the same imperious confidence, though none of the delight, with which she had watched him earlier.

"Help me, Robie," she said. "1 want my mother."

"Hello, youngster," Robbie said. "What would you like? Comics? Candy?"

"Where is she, Robie? Take me to her."

"Balloons? Would you like to watch me blow up a balloon?"

The little girl began to cry. The sound triggered off another of Robie's novelty circuits, a service feature that had brought in a lot of favorable publicity.

"Is something wrong?" he asked. "Are you in trouble? Are you lost?"

"Yes, Robie. Take me to my mother."

"Stay right here," Roble said reassuringly, "and don't be frightened. I will call a policeman." He whistled shrilly, twice.

Time passed. Robie whistled again. The windows flared and roared. The little girl begged, "Take me away, Robie," and jumped onto a little step in his hoopskirt.

"Give me a dime," Robie said.

The little girl found one in her pocket and put it in his claws.

"Your weight," Robie said, "is fifty-four and one-half pounds."

"Have you seen my daughter, have you seen her?" a woman was crying somewhere. "I left her watching that thing while I stepped inside—Rita!"

"Robie helped me," the little girl began babbling at her. "He knew I was lost. He even called the police, but they didn't come. He weighed me, too. Didn't you, Roble?"

But Robie had gone off to peddle Poppy Pop to the members of a rescue squad which had just come around the corner, more robotlike in their asbestos suits than he in his metal skin.

Daybroke
Robert Bloch

Up in the sky the warheads whirled, and the thunder of their passing shook the mountain.

Deep in his vaulted sanctuary he sat, godlike and inscrutable, marking neither the sparrow's or the missile's fall. There was no need to leave his shelter to stare down at the city.

He knew what was happening—had known ever since early in the evening when the television flickered and died. An announcer in the holy, white garb of the healing arts had been delivering an important message about the world's most popular laxative—the one most people preferred, the one four out of five doctors used themselves. Midway in his praise of this amazing new medical discovery he had paused and advised the audience to stand by for a special bulletin.

But the bulletin never came; instead the screen went blank and the thunder boomed.

All night long the mountain trembled, and the seated man trembled too; not with anticipation but with realization. He had expected this, of course, and that was why he was here. Others had talked about it for years; there had been wild rumors and solemn warnings and much muttering in taverns. But the rumor-mongers and the warning-sounders and the tavern-mutterers had made no move. They had stayed in the city and he alone had fled.

Some of them, he knew. had stayed to stave off the inevitable end as best they could, and these he saluted for their courage. Others had attempted to ignore the future, and these he detested for their blindness. And all of them he pitied.

For he had realized, long ago, that courage was not enough and that ignorance was no salvation. Wise words and foolish words are one—they will not halt the storm. And when the storm approaches, it is best to flee.

So he had prepared for himself this mountain retreat, high over the city, and here he was safe; would be safe for years to come. Other men of equal wealth could have done the same, but they were too wise or too foolish to face reality. So while they spread their rumors and sounded their warnings and muttered in their cups, he built his sanctuary: lead-guarded, amply provisioned, and stocked with every need for years to come, including even a generous supply of the world's most popular laxative.

Dawn came at last and the echoes of the thunder died, and he went to a special, shielded place where he could sight his spyglass at the city. He stared and he squinted, but there was nothing to be seen—nothing but swirling clouds that billowed blackly and rolled redly across the hazed horizon. Then he knew that he must go down to the city if he wanted to find out, and made due preparations.

There was a special suit to wear, a cunning seamless garment of insulated cloth and lead, difficult and costly to obtain. It was a top secret suit; the kind only Pentagon generals possess. They cannot procure them for their wives, and they must steal them for their mistresses. But he had one. He donned it now.

An elevated platform aided his descent to the base of the mountain, and there his car was waiting. He drove out, the shielded doors closing automatically behind him, and started for the city. Through the eyepiece of his insulated helmet he stared out at a yellowish fog, and he drove slowly, even though he encountered no traffic nor any sign of life.

After a time the fog lifted, and he could see the countryside. Yellow trees and yellow grass stood stiffly silhouetted against a yellow sky in which great clouds writhed and whirled.

Van Gogh's work, he told himself, knowing it was a lie. For no artist's hand had smashed the windows of the farmhouses, peeled the paint from the sides of the barns, or squeezed the warm breath from the herds huddling in the fields, standing fright-frozen but dead.

He drove along the broad arterial leading to the city; an arterial which ordinarily swarmed with the multicolored corpuscles of motor vehicles. But there were no cars moving today, not in this artery.

Not until he neared the suburbs did he see them, and then he rounded a curve and was halfway upon the vanguard before he panicked and halted in a ditch.

The roadway ahead was packed with automobiles as far as the eye could see—a solid mass, bumper to bumper, ready to descend upon him with whirring wheels.

But the wheels were not turning.

The cars were dead. The further stretches of the highway were an automotive graveyard. He approached the spot on foot, treading with proper reverence past the Cadillac-corpses, the cadavers of Chevrolets, the bodies of Buicks. Close at hand he could see the evidence of violent ends; the shattered glass, the smashed fenders, the battered bumpers and twisted hoods.

The signs of struggle were often pitiable to observe; here was a tiny Volkswagen, trapped and crushed between two looming Lincolns; there an MG had died beneath the wheels of a charging Chrysler. But all were still now. The Dodges dodged no longer, the Hornets had ceased their buzzing, and the Ramblers would never ramble again.

It was hard for him to realize with equal clarity the tragedy that had overtaken the people inside these cars—they were dead, too, of course, but somehow their passing seemed insignificant. Maybe his thinking had been affected by the attitude of the age, in which a man tended to be less and less identified as an individual and more and more regarded on the basis of the symbolic status of the car he drove. When a stranger rode down the street, one seldom thought of him as a person; one's only immediate reaction was, "There goes a Ford—there goes a Pontiac—there goes one of those big goddam Imperials." And men bragged about their cars instead of their characters. So somehow the death of the automobiles seemed more important than the death of their owners. It didn't seem as though human beings had perished in this panic-stricken effort to escape from the city; it was the cars which had made a dash for final freedom and then failed.

He skirted the road now and continued along the ditch until he came to the first sidewalks of the suburbs. Here the evidence of destruction was accentuated. Explosion and implosion had done their work. In the country, paint had been peeled from the walls, but in the suburbs walls had been peeled from the buildings. Not every home was leveled. There were still plenty of ranch houses standing, though no sign of a rancher in a gray flannel suit. In some of the picturesquely modern white houses, with their light lines and heavy mortgages, the glass side walls remained unshattered, but there was no sign of happy, busy suburban life within—the television sets were dead.

Now he found his progress impeded by an increasing litter. Apparently a blast had swept through this area; his way was blocked by a clutter of the miscellaneous debris of Exurbia.

He waded through or stepped around:

Boxes of Kleenex, artificial shrunken heads which had once dangled in the windows of station-wagons, crumpled shopping-lists and scribbled notices of appointments with psychiatrists.

He stepped on an Ivy League cap, nearly tripped over a twisted barbecue grille, got his feet tangled in the straps of foam-rubber falsies. The gutters were choked with the glut from a bombed-out drugstore; bobbie-pins, nylon bobby-socks, a spate of pocket-books, a carton of tranquilizers, a mass of suntan lotion, suppositories, deodorants, and a big cardboard cutout of Harry Belafonte obscured by a spilled can of hot fudge.

He shuffled on, through a welter of women's electric shavers, Book-of-the-Month-Club bonus selections, Presley records, false teeth, and treatises on Existentialism. Now he was actually approaching the city proper. Signs of devastation multiplied.

Trudging past the campus of the university he noted, with a start of horror, that the huge football stadium was no more. Nestled next to it was the tiny Fine Arts building, and at first he thought that it too had been razed. Upon closer inspection, however, he realized it was untouched, save for the natural evidence of neglect and decay.

He found it difficult to maintain a regular course, now, for the streets were choked with wrecked vehicles and the sidewalks often blocked by beams or the entire toppled fronts of buildings. Whole structures had been ripped apart, and here and there were freakish variations where a roof had fallen in or a single room smashed to expose its contents. Apparently the blow had come instantly, and without forewarning, for there were few bodies on the streets and those he glimpsed inside the opened buildings gave indication that death had found them in the midst of their natural occupations.

Here, in a gutted basement, a fat man sprawled over the table of his home work-shop, his sightless eyes fixed upon the familiar calendar exhibiting entirely the charms of Marilyn Monroe. Two flights above him, through the empty frame of a bathroom window, one could see his wife, dead in the tub, her hand still clutching a movie magazine with a Rock Hudson portrait on the cover. And up in the attic, open to the sky, two young lovers stretched on a brass bed, locked naked in headless ecstasy.

He turned away, and as his progress continued he deliberately avoided looking at the bodies. But he could not avoid seeing them now, and with familiarity the revulsion softened to the merest twinge. It then gave way to curiosity.

Passing a school playground he was pleased to see that the end had come without grotesque or unnatural violence. Probably a wave of paralyzing gas had swept through this area. Most of the figures were frozen upright in normal postures. Here were all of the aspects of ordinary childhood—the big kid punching the little kid, both leaning up against a fence where the blast had found them; a group of six youngsters in uniform black leather jackets piled upon the body of a child wearing a white leather jacket.

Beyond the playground loomed the center of the city. From a distance the mass of shattered masonry looked like a crazy garden-patch turned by a mad plowman. Here and there were tiny blossoms of flame sprouting forth from the interstices of huge clods, and at intervals he could see lopped, stemlike formations, the lower stories of sky-scrapers from which the tops had been sheared by the swish of a thermonuclear scythe.

He hesitated, wondering if it was practical to venture into this weird welter. Then he caught sight of the hillside beyond, and of the imposing structure which was the new Federal Building. It stood there, somehow miraculously untouched by the blast, and in the haze he could see the flag still fluttering from its roof. There would be life here, and he knew he would not be content until he reached it.

But long before he attained his objective, he found other evidences of continued existence. Moving delicately and deliberately through the debris, he became aware that he was not entirely alone here in the central chaos.

Wherever the flames flared and flickered, there were furtive figures moving against the fire. To his horror, he realized that they were actually kindling the blazes; burning away barricades that could not otherwise be removed, as they entered shops and stores to loot. Some of the scavengers were silent and ashamed, others were boisterous and drunken; all were doomed.

It was this knowledge which kept him from interfering. Let them plunder and pilfer at will, let them quarrel over the spoils in the shattered streets; in a few hours or a few days, radiation and fallout would take their inevitable toll.

No one interfered with his passage; perhaps the helmet and protective garment resembled an official uniform. He went his way unhindered and saw:

A barefooted man wearing a mink coat, dashing through the door of a cocktail lounge and passing bottles out to a bucket-brigade of four small children—

An old woman standing in a bombed-out bank vault, sweeping stacks of bills into the street with her broom. Over in one corner lay the body of a white-haired man, his futile arms outstretched to embrace a heap of coins. Impatiently, the old woman nudged him with her broom. His head lolled, and a silver dollar popped out of his open mouth——

A soldier and a woman wearing the armband of the Red Cross, carrying a stretcher to the blocked entrance of a partially-razed church. Unable to enter, they bore the stretcher around to the side, and the soldier kicked in one of the stained-glass windows—

An artist's basement studio, open to the sky; its walls still intact and covered with abstract paintings. In the center of the room stood the easel, but the artist was gone. What was left of him was smeared across the canvas in a dripping mass, as though the artist had finally succeeded in putting something of himself into his picture—

A welter of glassware that had once been a chemical laboratory, and in the center of it a smocked figure slumped over a microscope. On the slide was a single cell which the scientist had been intently observing when the world crashed about his ears—

A woman with the face of a Vogue model, spread-eagled in the street. Apparently she had been struck down while answering the call of duty, for one slim, aristocratic hand still gripped the strap of her hatbox. Otherwise, due to some prank of explosion, the blast had stripped her quite naked; she lay there with all her expensive loveliness exposed, and a pigeon nested in her golden pelvis—

127

A thin man, emerging from a pawnshop and carrying an enormous tuba. He disappeared momentarily into a meat market nextdoor, then came out again, the bell of his tuba stuffed with sausages—

A broadcasting studio, completely demolished, its once immaculate sound stage littered with the crumpled cartons of fifteen different varieties of America's Favorite Cigarette and the broken bottles of twenty brands of America's Favorite Beer. Protruding from the wreckage was the head of America's Favorite Quizmaster, eyes staring glassily at a sealed booth in the corner which now served as the coffin for a nine-year-old boy who had known the batting averages of every team in the American and National Leagues since 1882—

A wild-eyed woman sitting in the street, crying and crooning over a kitten cradled in her arms—

A broker caught at his desk, his body mummified in coils of ticker-tape—

A motorbus, smashed into a brick wall; its passengers still jamming the aisles; standees clutching straps even in rigor mortis—

The hindquarters of a stone lion before what had once been the Public Library; before it, on the steps, the corpse of an elderly lady whose shopping-bag had spewed its contents over the street—two murder-mysteries, a rental copy of *Peyton Place*, and the latest issue of the *Reader's Digest*—

A small boy wearing a cowboy hat, who levelled a toy pistol at his little sister and shouted, "Bang! You're dead!"

(She was.)

He walked slowly now, his pace impeded by obstacles both physical and of the spirit. He approached the building on the hillside by a circuitous route; avoiding repugnance, overcoming morbid curiosity, shunning pity, recoiling from horror, surmounting shock.

He knew there were others about him here in the city's core, some bent on acts of mercy, some on heroic rescue. But he ignored them all, for they were dead. Mercy had no meaning in this mist, and there was no rescue from radiation. Some of those who passed called out to him, but he went his way unheeding, knowing their words were mere death-rattles.

But suddenly, as he climbed the hillside, he was crying. The salty warmth ran down his cheeks and blurred the inner surface of his helmet so that he no longer saw anything clearly. And it was thus he emerged from the inner circle; the inner circle of the city, the inner circle of Dante's hell. His tears ceased to flow and his vision cleared. Ahead of him was the proud outline of the Federal Building, shining and intact—or almost so.

As he neared the imposing steps and gazed up at the façade, he noted that there were a few hints of crumbling and corrosion on the surface of the structure. The freakish blast had done outright damage only to the sculptured figures surmounting the great arched doorway; the symbolic statuary had been partially shattered so that the frontal surface had fallen away. He blinked at the empty outlines of the three figures; somehow he never had realized that Faith, Hope and Charity were hollow.

Then he walked inside the building. There were tired soldiers guarding the doorway, but they made no move to stop him, probably because he wore a protective garment even more intricate and impressive than their own.

Inside the structure a small army of low clerks and high brass moved antlike in the corridors; marching grim-faced up and down the stairs. There were no elevators, of course—they'd ceased functioning when the electricity gave out. But he could climb.

He wanted to climb now, for that was why he had come here. He wanted to gaze out over the city. In his gray insulation he resembled an automaton, and like an automaton he plodded stiffly up the stairways until he reached the topmost floor.

But there were no windows here, only walled-in offices. He walked down a long corridor until he came to the very end. Here, a single large cubicle glowed with gray light from the glass wall beyond.

A man sat at a desk, jiggling the receiver of a field telephone and cursing softly. He glanced curiously at the intruder, noted the insulating uniform, and returned to his abuse of the instrument in his hand.

So it was possible to walk over to the big window and look down.

It was possible to see the city, or the crater where the city had been.

Night was mingling with the haze on the horizon, but there was no darkness. The little incendiary blazes had been spreading, apparently, as the wind moved in, and now he gazed down upon a growing sea of flame. The crumbling spires and gutted structures were drowning in red waves. As he watched, the tears came again, but he knew there would not be enough tears to put the fires out.

So he turned back to the man at the desk, noting for the first time that he wore one of the very special uniforms reserved for generals.

This must be the commander, then. Yes, he was certain of it now, because the floor around the desk was littered with scraps of paper. Maybe they were obsolete maps, maybe they were obsolete plans, maybe they were obsolete treaties. It didn't matter now.

There was another map on the wall behind the desk, and this one mattered very much. It was studded with black and red pins, and it took but a moment to decipher their meaning. The red pins signified destruction, for there was one affixed to the name of this city. And there was one for New York, one for Chicago, Detroit, Los Angeles—every important center had been pierced.

He looked at the general, and finally the words came.

"It must be awful," he said.

"Yes, awful," the general echoed.

"Millions upon millions dead."

"Dead."

"The cities destroyed, the air polluted, and no escape. No escape anywhere in the world."

"No escape."

He turned away and stared out the window once more, stared down at Inferno. Thinking, *this is what it has come to, this is the way the world ends.*

He glanced at the general again, and then sighed.

"To think of our being beaten," he whispered.

The red glare mounted, and in its light he saw the general's face, gleeful and exultant.

"What do you mean, man?" the general said proudly, the flames rising. "We won!"

Blunder
Philip Wylie

There is no record of the exact date...

It was probably a morning in late May, or possibly in early June, when Carl Everson and Hugh Dunn rode up from the abandoned nickel mine on its creaky hoist and stood with their hands over their eyes, spreading their fingers apart slowly, to become accustomed to the outdoor brilliance. Late May or early June—since this was the latitude of the "midnight sun" and there had been no dark. Around the two men was an enormous clearing which stretched from a solid wall of spruces to boulders fringing the polar ocean; an expanse of weeds, birches, wild grass and young conifers gradually obliterating a village near the mine and steadily overgrowing high, rusty cones of tailings.

Everson and Dunn had invested their life savings here. The region suited their needs: a mine in hard rock, deep enough, with extensive lateral galleries, close to the sea. Here, moreover, on a Pole-facing promontory of the North Cape, was utter isolation—necessary because some risk was involved in their work and they did not wish to endanger human beings. Indeed, the harming of a person would have ruined their purpose, which was essentially as commercial as it was scientific.

Carl Everson held the Chair of Physics in the Oslo Institute; Hugh Dunn was Dean of Engineering at Glasgow, and a Nobel Laureate, besides. The scheme on which they had long plotted together was ingenious and, basically, quite simple.

It depended upon two facts. First, that volcanic phenomena are radioactive in nature. Second, that certain types—the steam-producing types—are usable as a power source: at least one Italian city had drawn its electricity from steam that gushed out of a volcanic vent, since the 1920s. Everson and Dunn intended to disintegrate a bismuth "bomb" in the mine gallery in such a way as to start a slow, hot, atomic chain reaction. The process, according to their calculations, would not "burn out" for centuries and the conjunction of the sea would guarantee production of superheated steam which, they believed, could be "harnessed." As owners of such a source, the two scientists knew that they could furnish to all of northern Scandinavia, and much of Finland, extremely cheap electrical power. In doing so, they would make their fortunes.

The venture had one unfavorable aspect: Research in physics was sequestered by individual national governments. For many years, new information had been released only after the security authorities in the "nation-of-discovery" had assured themselves it was no longer, actually, "new." Thus, scientific advances made in Britain, Russia, America, China and elsewhere were not always added to the body of common human knowledge but often retained as "military secrets." Owing to that situation, Everson and Dunn had long argued the wisdom of carrying out their plan.

"Bismuth fission," the Norwegian had often said, "is something new under the sun. We'll be the first to do it—maybe. We think we know what will happen. But are we sure? Evans is apparently working on it. Chandra Lalunal, at Delhi. And Stackpole. Maybe we'd better wait for their further reports. They've hinted at progress—"

And the Scot would generally reply, "Aye. Wait. Wait how long? For the rest of our lives? Wait until generals and statesmen decide the knowledge has leaked, or their spies have learnt it? Suppose we do fail, Carl? What then?"

"Then we'll jointly own a big puddle of hot rock that nobody can approach for centuries."

"Right." The Scot would chuckle. "Right. And be the precious fools of physics, too! Well, get on with it, Carl. Fine times, these, for what they used to call a free man!"

The times. The date. It was May or early June, but the year is not on the record, either. The vague monographs concerning bismuth fission, by Evans and Lalunal and Stackpole, had been published twenty-eight years after the first appalling rainbow of transmuted mass flashed onto (and into) the barrens of New Mexico, U.S.A. The famed "atomic bomb." So the date was a springtime later than 1973. 'Seventy-four, perhaps. Everson and Dunn had offered a questioning paper, too, in the hope of getting more data for their experiment. But it had been held up by Norwegian censorship. That it had finally been released, and was even now in print, they could not know for they had camped in solitude for some weeks.

They stood in the sunshine a moment—in the stillness—in the subarctic morning. The two men could see, now. They put out the miner's lights on their hats and walked, quickly, through the grass, following a cable that snaked from the mine shaft.

They came to a detonator and stood over it, reluctantly: a pair of tall thoughtful men—the Scot redheaded, the Norwegian blond as glass. Good men.

"Touch it off," the Scot said.

"I hate to."

Dunn chuckled and rammed home the plunger. The mine shaft grunted repeatedly. Small shocks vibrated the weedy ground. A wisp of smoke—then a cloud—puffed out of the vertical bowel. The hoist dropped out of sight; the housing over it collapsed. All down the deep intestine, dynamite exploded; its sides caved in and tumbled, blocking heavily the gallery in which a mechanism the size of a piano ticked and ticked, undisturbed by this choking of exit.

"Done," said Everson.

They strode into the forest, following a path that was the remnant of a heavy-duty highway. The trucks of Norwegians, then Germans, then Russians, had rolled here long ago, hauling off nickel ore for the violent purposes of World War II. Everson, who was less sanguine than his colleague, contemplated a goldheaded fly that lighted on his Mackinaw. It was, he thought, a perfect creature—sterile as the northern woods, efficient as nature, germane to the region—which man had never been. Man had left the bleaching wreckage of the mine town and the corroded heaps of ore; the fly brought only a living goldness into this place, this sprucy fragrance, this green churchliness.

Their car faced south. They removed its tarpaulin and drove, swiftly, to the main road. At an inn some fifty miles from the mine, they stopped and entered the dining room. Their waitress had long, silvery braids and she let them fall invitingly over the shoulders of Hugh Dunn while he peered at the menu. But he did not notice. Everson, finally, translated the list of dishes and did the ordering; Dunn spoke Norwegian badly. This is usually so: the citizens of the weak countries learn the tongues of the stronger…

Morning in Scandinavia was afternoon in India. Chandra Lalunal neither resisted nor resented the heat; he accepted it. He sat watching garden shadows stretch across a dry lawn and listening to the spatter of a fountain. The sound should have contributed psychological, coolness; it failed; it made the young man think of the mammoth humidity which seemed to be the entire substance of the day. Chandra's apartment was a unit in a file of one-story white buildings which quartered down a hill, parallel to a garden—the work of some landscape architect who had fancied the Ficus. These trees, with small leaves and with great, standing tall and growing a tangle of root exposed in low, stalactite-crowded caves, all glittered alike in the hazy sunshine.

Chandra could look over their tops, here and there, at the domes and spicules of the city and the square, huge walls of the government buildings. He sat in a doorway not because there was a breeze, but in case there might be one. Occasionally, he turned a page of the newly arrived journal in his lap. It was called, *The International Physical Quarterly*. Much of its text was printed not in words but in diagrams and mathematical symbols. His dark profile had a remarkable sharpness, so that, viewed from the side, it seemed akin to the keener animals. With a full-face view, however, this predatory look was overmastered by his eyes—bright, black and yet dreaming in subjective peace. His brown fingers turned another page.

The eyes glanced down, held, changed shape minutely. "Inquiries into the Binding Fractions of Bismuth," the article said. Its authors were known by reputation to the Indian: Carl Everson and Hugh Dunn. Chandra, also, had made some "inquiries" into the atom of bismuth. Now, his brain commenced its common, human, utterly astonishing function. Words and symbols became electrical patterns within it; these took meaning. related to apparatus in Chandra's own laboratory, represented similar pages of figures he had written, and spelled thoughts, concepts, actual experiments. An hypothesis, begun two generations before by a dead and greatly honored savant named Albert Einstein, was the starting place of the electronic panoply that informed the young man's reading mind. Chandra checked, cross-checked, opened his lips to say an unsaid word of disapproval, and presently came to the end of the monograph.

Now, he looked for some time at the gardens. Far away, the temples brayed— slat-ribbed priests riding on the bell ropes. Chandra did not notice. The Delhi plane slanted overhead, fast, quiet. He saw it—and did not see. At last he rose. He crossed the marble floor of his living room, picked up a white hand set, dialed. He asked for Lord Polt and, after a time, talked to him.

"But it may be very important," Chandra finally said. "I know it is late. But this is pressing, sir."

The other man changed his mind. Chandra presently drove his car through the heat walls and among the slow snarl of people to the government buildings.

Lord Polt wanted to get to his air-conditioned home. He wanted tea. He wanted to change his linen. He wanted to forget the harangue he'd had that day from the leader of the Eastern Conference. He wanted to get out of the drab, damned, sweating institutional chamber where he rotted away his life. He wanted to go home to England.... He said all that, pushing his tall bulkiness around despairfully behind his desk, wiping his sweated forehead with a white handkerchief, envying Chandra his appearance of dryness. He finally said, "What the devil it, son?"

Chandra put the periodical on the governor's desk. "It is this."

Lord Polt looked at it and his vexation returned. "Talk sense, Chandra, for the love of heaven! 'This'! What is it? Runes! Hieroglyphics!"

"It's got a mistake in it," Chandra said. His voice belonged to his eyes. "A quite bad mistake."

The Englishman was too deeply exasperated now and, paradoxically, too fond of the young physicist, to maintain his damp vehemence. "You'll have to do better than that, Chandra," he said slowly. "A mistake? Thousands of you birds make millions of 'em. Are you asking me to correct the papers of a couple of Oslo and Glasgow chemists? I mean—what do you want?"

"I want," Chandra answered, "to have you requisition the world network, at once. Tonight. For at least an hour. I would like to be put on the air to explain this—error in mathematics."

Lord Polt's eyes bulged. "Are you mad, son? The world—!"

"It is a most hazardous mistake. Time shouldn't be lost. There may be much time. Years. But there may be no time at all."

"Time, in the name of the Eternal, for what?"

"To prevent any accident." Chandra smiled slightly. "In the name of the Eternal, as you say, sir."

A choleric disposition was not the reason for which the Foreign Office had sent Lord Polt to India; he had brains. He said, after a moment, "See here, Chandra. If this mistake is so important, how'd the Board miss it? How does it come to be in print?"

The dark youth showed his teeth; only a man who knew Indians well would have understood it was more than an easy smile. "There are branches of mathematics and of physical research which are pursued by a few people, only. Branches which have been thoroughly investigated and abandoned, long ago. This is one. Besides—even with mathematics, it is possible to—to—"

"Dissemble?" The man's head nodded.

"—to publish papers which would mean one thing to most scientists—and a little more, perhaps, to a few others." Chandra sighed. "That is another reason why it is sad—and vain—to imagine that science can be searched, censored and deleted—like soldiers' mail."

They were silent. The Englishman used his handkerchief again. "Chandra, the heat's affected you. It would require an emergency order from London to get the world network tonight. Or any night. I couldn't ask for it, to let you lecture on physics. And even if I could, whatever you want to say would have to be reviewed first by the Board. You know that. The Board is two years behind. Censoring your stuff is difficult—"

"I assure you, sir, the peril is—is of a magnitude—"

Lord Polt was annoyed again. "The devil with the peril! People in your business have gone around muttering about peril for thirty years! Send your blasted corrections through channels!"

For, a long moment, the liquid Indian eyes rested upon the bright blue eyes. Dark eyes —fatigued with subjugation, fatalistic, fatal. Then Chandra said, "I'm sorry I troubled you, sir. Perhaps it isn't urgent."

The governor nodded. "You're on the ragged side. Take a week off, son. Go up in the hills. If your school president's sticky about it, phone me."

Chandra thanked him.

He went back to his apartment and sat, again in the doorway, looking at the many kinds of Ficus trees and their increasing shadows....

Stackpole—Jeffry Stackpole, of Atlanta, Georgia, Harvard University, and Massachusetts Institute of Technology, now, and for a long time, far from home—learned of the blunder in the Everson-Dunn equations from a subordinate. Stackpole was chief engineer of Plant Number 5, Chiang Kai-shek Memorial Uranium Works. His subordinate, Plummer, knocked and entered his office without waiting. He had *The International Physical Quarterly* in his hand. Plummer was fresh from the States—recently a good quarterback but now a better nuclear physicist—and what he had discovered amused him.

"Look at this, chief," he said. "I just opened it. Dunn may have won a Nobel Prize, but he and Everson—the Oslo Everson—have sure taken a fall in bismuth-radiation-effect."

Stackpole was young, reputation and achievements considered—forty-two. A lean man with brown eyes, bald on top; a man with big hands and feet and a big, placid voice. The kind of man to whom a stranger would talk in a bar; the kind for whom a lost old lady would look, in order to inquire the right direction.... He put aside a cost report. The spark in his eye showed he was not so formal as to resent Plummer's hasty entrance; the slight pursing of his lips, that Plummer's statement interested him.

"Bismuth?" Stackpole repeated. "Radiation? Let's look."

Plummer went on enthusiastically, "They missed the proper description of k as the infinite constant under special pressure circumstances—"

"Hold on, Plum"— There was still faint Georgia in Stackpole's voice—"I can read, myself."

He read. For five minutes, ten, fifteen. His long face became insensitive fixity. Plummer lost his excitement, watching, and, after a time, gasped suddenly: "You mean, Jeffry—that you think they might—?"

"They might. Who mightn't—figuring it that way?"

"What are you going to do?" The young man's voice was low, meager.

COMMONWEALTH OF PENNSYLVANIA
STATE COUNCIL OF CIVIL DEFENSE
HARRISBURG, PENNSYLVANIA
RICHARD GERSTELL, DIRECTOR

Pennsylvania Motorists:

Your State Council of Civil Defense, through your Department of Revenue, furnishes you the Official Air Raid Warning Instructions printed on the other side of this card. Memorize them. They are designed for your survival.

John S. Fine

JOHN S. FINE, *Governor*

When You Hear The Air Raid Warning
FOLLOW THESE OFFICIAL INSTRUCTIONS

1. Pull to the side of the road and stop.

2. Leave lanes open for emergency vehicles and keep all intersections clear.

3. Shut off motor and lights.

4. Get out and take cover, if handy; otherwise, crouch or lie down in vehicle.

5. Resume travel on "All Clear," unless otherwise directed.

(KEEP THIS CARD IN YOUR CAR)

COMMONWEALTH OF PENNSYLVANIA
STATE COUNCIL OF CIVIL DEFENSE
HARRISBURG, PENNSYLVANIA

This is to certify that

_____
(*Name*)

_____
(*Address*)

is duly enrolled in_____
(*Name of county or local civil defense organization*)

assigned for duty with the_____service.

County of_____

Enrollment No._____   *Richard Gerstell*

Date of Issue_____, 19____   State Director of Civil Defense

Countersigned by: | *Signature of Issuing Director*

LOYALTY OATH

I do solemnly swear (or affirm) that I will support and defend the Constitution of the United States and the Constitution of the State of Pennsylvania against all enemies, foreign and domestic, that I will bear true faith and allegiance to the same; that I take this obligation freely without any mental reservation or purpose of evasion and that I will well and faithfully discharge the duties upon which I am about to enter;

And I do further swear (or affirm) that I do not advocate nor am I a member or an affiliate of any organization, group or combination of persons that advocates the overthrow of the Government of the United States or of this State by force or violence, and that during such time as I am a member of the Civil Defense organization listed on the face of this card I will not advocate nor become a member nor an affiliate of any organization, group or combination of persons that advocates the overthrow of the Government of the United States or of this State by force or violence.

....
(Date)   (Signature)

Cards issued through the Pennsylvania State Council of Civil Defense to the citizens of Pennsylvania, early 1950s. The card at the top was to be carried in the wallet as a reminder of what to do when an air raid siren sounded warning of an impending atomic bomb. The bottom card is a stark reminder of the Second Red Scare.

Stackpole closed the scientific journal. "Tell May to call my car, Plum. I'll see the general tonight. Maybe—just maybe—this is what we've waited for. Maybe this one'll convince them that they can't keep knowledge in a lot of different pockets. Keep us in their pockets, either. I'll see if the general will let me get through to Oslo, or Glasgow. Wherever Dunn and Everson are. And we'll plan a general announcement. Others must be catching onto the fumble—right this minute."

He put on a hat and took a raincoat from a hidden closet. There were no windows in his office: the light was indirect, the ventilation mechanical and the furnishings ultra-modern. He knew he needed a raincoat only because a small panel, set in his desktop, constantly reported the weather outside. Plummer had gone. Stackpole crossed the room, switched off the lights, and went out, also. A Chinese girl in a red dress was sitting at a desk in the anteroom.

"I sent for the car," she said.

He noticed, with the vacant acuity that accompanies crisis moods, how beautiful she was. "Thank you, May. Good night."

His long legs scissored in the scintillant corridors; his big feet fell hard on the plastic flooring. He went through the main lobby and out onto the steps. The rain hit him, then—the wind whipped his coat—lightning split his vision—thunder followed. His nerves burned with crucial fire. And with hope....

Now, on the shimmery black paving, the car came. But now, his mind was elsewhere—in many elsewheres, moving swiftly with a nearly simultaneous consciousness. He was on Peace Street. He was in the M.I.T. high-tension lab. He was saying goodby to a New York City girl who wouldn't marry him and go to live in China but who still said she loved him. He was glancing—just glancing—at May Tom. Cheng blew the musical horn; Stackpole went down the steps at a run.

They drove past the plant, after he'd told Cheng to go to the general's home—past the solid mile of cubic architecture that turned masses of uranium into energy for a great and growing people. The structures, seen in headlights, seen in lightning flashes, were, somehow, both critical of nature and anti-human. He tried conversation to dispel the shadows. "How are you tonight, Cheng?"

The chauffeur lifted one shoulder. "Not good, Dr. Stackpole."

"Girl trouble?"

The head shook in the murk. "Just full of nothing. Doctor. Who isn't? It is a disease people have now, I guess. A pain of emptiness. We have been afraid too long. And we cannot get used to it."

Stackpole gave up the idea of conversation. Nameless terror, or named terror, year after year: it was a world disease, all right. Better to glance away from the squat, streaming, soundless mills of twentieth century man. Better to look out the car window on the other side, where, in the relatively feeble flare of lightning, the Yangtze River labored beneath a hectic wind....

Chicago's Herbert Evans was the third scientist who, in the opinion of Everson and Dunn, might have contributed valuable data to the experiment in the nickel mine. It was just dawn, in Chicago, at the time the Norwegian and the Scot were taking lunch, the Indian was staring with fatigue and fatalism over his hot valley, and the Georgian was racing on his errand in central China.

Dawn pleased Evans: it was the period he usually chose to go home from work. Home, for him, was a shabby, outmoded, two-room hotel apartment where a bachelor could accumulate unanswered mail, old clothes and the patina of pipe-smoke without human rebuke or even the implied protest of neater quarters. Home was not where he hung his hat, but where he had tossed it—ever since he'd gone to work in the university as instructor and laboratory assistant. Work, for Evans, had then been in a stuffy roomful of hurriedly made gadgets. Down the years, that informal shop had turned into a gleaming hall where apparatus worth zillions was ranged in a vast stupefying geometry.

Evans left this chamber as the sky grayed. He went down the street whistling—a chubby little man, a merry, grandpa-looking man, who wore a smile and carried his hands in his pockets. He had coffee and Danish pastry in a cheap, all-night restaurant. He walked on to his hotel, went up in the antediluvian elevator, and found the *Review* with his morning paper, inside the door on the floor.

Naturally, he read it—as the others had—immediately. Evans could remember the life of scientists in the presecrecy days. People didn't leap for journals, then. Journals weren't raked clean of all sorts of data by governments, either. Scientific news was just news—and, even though the modern journals were distributed all over the world at the same time, it wasn't any advantage. For every scientist had turned into a man who snatched at crumbs.

Evans could easily remember the spirit of science before the Fear—and the old, free great who served it. He'd even talked to Einstein, once.

He lay down on his bed, fully clothed, and read. When he came to the article about bismuth, the youthfulness and rosiness went out of him. He recognized the error and he shut his eyes, thinking hard. If anybody should set up the experiment suggested here—!

What could one man do? He considered a direct call to the seat of government and knew, even while he thought of it, that the people in Washington would demur, temporize, doubt, ask for additional opinion—unwilling all the while to smash an international habit that was like hysteria carved in marble.

He was in the same predicament as Chandra. As Stackpole. Only a higher authority could act. But Evans knew one very high authority; he knew the President of the United States. For a long time, the old man lay there, wondering how it would be possible to compel the President to break through international silence and tell the whole world, immediately, not to do so-and-so; not to try this; not to set up that equipment in such-and-such a way. Tell the world—even though it meant giving up certain useful data belonging to the U.S.

Finally, Evans got up. He went to the telephone and reserved a seat on the seven o'clock to Washington. He sent word to Charlie Trent to make an appointment for him with the President that same morning. Then he began throwing old clothes—mildewed, mothy, forgotten—from the bottom drawer of a big bureau. What he found underneath was a shoulder holster, a revolver, a waxed box of shells.

Nobody would search him; they knew him at the White House. It was just possible—just—that, if the President didn't believe him, he could draw the gun suddenly enough and threaten him long enough to make him speak certain orders into his desk instruments. The President wouldn't believe him, he felt.

Evans smiled very sorrowfully. This rash idea would doubtless fail. Perhaps, though, its very attempt and failure would attract political interest in the obscure data in the journal. His scheme came from long ago—from his boyhood—from motion pictures about gangsters. Even the revolver was obsolete, nowadays. A museum piece. He smiled again, whimsically; broke the gun, loaded it, and before he put it in its holster, noticed with vague surprise that it had been manufactured in Worcester, Massachusetts, U.S.A....

There was no Worcester, any more, of course. No Massachusetts. No New England. From Lake Champlain and the Hudson River down to the Atlantic Ocean stretched what nowadays was called, "The New England Wastes." In the Sahara, there are oases; here, were none.

The cities were scoured away, for the most part stone sinks, some filled with water. Wherever buildings remained, they were halved, quartered, toppled, bleached. What had not vaporized had burned or melted or blanched in a hideous heat. Nothing grew; nothing. No trees on the White Mountains and no reeds around the stale ponds. No anemone blossomed in the deepest cranny of rock. From time to time the great

Connecticut River flash-flooded. The event went all unnoticed. In summer, the river was partly dry. No insects danced above it; never a trout or bass spilled its surface in climbing attack. No squatting frog croaked there, or peeper trilled. Even ducks had learned not to migrate over this immense region—and gulls, not to fly in from the sea. The lonely land eroded; the continental skeleton steadily emerged; the aspect of it grew lunar—suggesting hauntingly, horribly, that some similar catastrophe had stripped the moon of air and pitted its ground like this; some fiend's bombardment, some deliberate boiling of the moonmen's land—a million years ago.

New England had vanished in eight minutes, during the infamous "sneak punch" of World War III, now called the "Short War"—as though man still awaited a longer. On Christmas Eve, in 1966, the rockets broke a hundred miles above, and their bomb-contents homed accurately. What they did not destroy in that infernal period was left radioactive. The thousands of survivors who drove and flew out of the holocaust also died—slowly—of leukemia, of cancer, of ray burns which ate their extremities to stumps and gradually along the stumps to vital portions.

There existed, in central Europe, another region like The New England Wastes, but larger—as large as the Ukraine. It had been created three hours after the obliteration of New England, by the answering American salvo—a blow of a strength not foreseen by the treacherous assailants; a blow that had set diplomats chattering over the international wave bands and brought armistice before morning. Armistice. Armed truce. Armed vigilance. Armed secrecy. That had lasted till this very hour....

Man was stubbornly attempting to reclaim the lost domain. Even as Evans noted the legend on his revolver, the effort got under way. A prodigious machine broke over a hilltop on the edge of the Wastes. It came clanking from a woods where the leaves were fresh, flowers bloomed, bees buzzed and morning was late May-like, or early June-like. Its caterpillar treads stamped pungency from the grass. It descended upon the barren earth, cumbersome, buglike; wherever it went, it left behind a row of planted saplings, like a harvester that worked backwards.

Inside this contrivance, protected from the radioactivity of the ground by lead shields, two men watched instruments that told how the holes were being dug, the water poured, the small trees set, the earth packed around their roots.

They were ordinary men—farmer-mechanics—and by and by they stopped to survey their accomplishment through quartz slits. They lighted cigarettes and looked at each other.

"I bet they die, too, Ed."

"Want to put up dough, Curley?"

"Well—"

"Those birches are a new strain," Ed said. "Some professor developed 'em. They're supposed to stand twice as much rays as there is around here. Stand 'em—and grow."

"And drop seeds? And make little birches in this hellhole?"

"There—you've got me. Let's start her up."

"Take a lot of birches," Curley said, "to cover New England. And then what have you got?" He spat over a shield, taking care not to expose his face....

At the seaside inn, on the North Cape, Everson and Dunn compared watches. Their luncheon—sampled, cold—sat at their heavy elbows. In the last half hour they had scarcely communicated—and yet, each man knew that the other had reached a passionate and belated decision. A decision that the experiment was a mistake. A decision that they had acted beyond their rights; that they should have waited until they possessed all possible information concerning bismuth.

As the two watches pushed time along on the pine table, Dunn showed abrupt anger. He doubled his fist and made the dishes jump. "If this goes wrong—if this makes another shambles like New England—it's justice! It will teach the whole idiotic world that you cannot monopolize knowledge! Or own scientists! I say, Carl, we'll either be rich men, soon—or the authors of a lesson people need as badly as they need air to breathe!"

Everson only said, "Five seconds."

In the gallery of the choked mine, the piano-sized mechanism stopped ticking. For a moment—a moment in the infinite darkness—nothing happened. Then a flame sputtered. It shot shadows down the man-hewn corridor. Minerals glinted. The flame brightened. Now, lead began to melt—to dribble like pure silver onto the dust-deep floor. As it flowed, it made a flake of beryllium accessible to particles streaking from a tube of radon. This was the first step. It took a minute or so.

New particles sprang from the beryllium into a series of sheets of pure uranium. The atoms of this substance split in two. They drove into the bismuth blocks and their containing cadmium. For a certain time, very short. the purest light surged through the cavern and became brighter than the sun. Now, as the bismuth commenced to split, the rock walls were bombarded by the three rays—alpha, beta and gamma—and by a spreading storm of atomic fragments. The light—visible light, light invisible, and light that would blind human eyes—swelled within the region, drove through the walls, and reflected, here and there, from the sleazy stuff of the world. For another, equally brief moment, the rock-jammed throat of the mine acted as a tamper. It half held in the acumulating temperatures and pressures.

The interval of compression was very short. Everson and Dunn had calculated that it would produce one new effect: As each bismuth atom divided, the additional pressure violence, swifter-paced than that of the resonance of half nuclei, would shake from each another neutron—a small, additional quantum. This, they assumed, would be the necessary "torch" to set a, slow, enduring "fire" to the mineral walls; a perpetual chain reaction.

It was there that Everson and Dunn had erred: the tamper changed all resonance. The bismuth flew apart entirely. Its disintegration destroyed surrounding structures in the same fashion. The thing envisaged by Chandra Lalunal, Jeffry Stackpole and Herbert Evans now took place under the spruce forest and the sea edge. An atomic glare began to penetrate the earth and to race across the chords of it. Energy, driving up through the White Sea, boiled it, vaporized it, atomized it, broke its atoms and pushed against the ocean that might otherwise have driven toward the now empty place.

Vertical surge traversed the atmosphere and the stratosphere and broke into space. Here, cosmic particles, traveling at the velocity of a harmonic—since they were unslowed, unmuffled, by the air—destroyed certain fragments in the rising plane of atomic debris. These produced the "omega ray," hypothesized and variously named by Lalunal, Stackpole and Evans. (But still on the restricted lists, while London and Washington separately cogitated its possible military value.) An atmosphere would have shielded the earth from the omega ray. But, in place of atmosphere, there was now an expanding region of disintegration, and the ray penetrated it, shattering even the crushed, abnormal atomic structures in the central globe beneath....

In London, in the House of Parliament, Jeremy Hathcoat had commenced an oration on a proposal to restrict certain areas of research. One of the most brilliant orators in England's long history, he had finished a solemn period and was maturing his pace when the House of Parliament was closed forever. In Pennsylvania, in the United States, hundreds of Boy Scouts were assembling outside Philadelphia to search a deep and fragrant forest for an heiress who had been missing from her nearby mansion for three days; their excited voices, the confident instructions of their scout-masters, the barking of dogs which were to accompany them—all these were ended. Gunner McPhey, the greatest pitcher in a decade, was enjoying an early workout in the empty ball park in Washington, D. C. He raised his left foot, circled it gracefully, and flung a ball that never smacked the catcher's mitt. In Missouri, farmers rising at the bird-chittery interval before dawn, finished their breakfasts, many of them—but few reached their stables or their fields. Few of the stay-out revelers in Hollywood, California, ever saw their homes again.

Busy afternoon for Europe—morning for South America, for Gauchos on the plains, poison-dart blowers in deep jungles, astronomers studying the sun on Andes tip—night and sleep on the Pacific. In darkened Seattle, a jealous wife approached her snoring husband, step by step, with a blade that caught the light of half a moon: a death she meant to deal was done for her and she perished, also—no murderess. To dancers in cabarets and to lollers on beaches, to night watchmen and men pitching hay—it came alike.

The North Polar icecap melted. The sea boiled away. The Scandinavian Peninsula cracked open. The seam ran down Europe and, in Africa, met radiance emerging there. The hot contents of the earth extruded in the north, but it was as if the molten mass emerged and was laid bare simultaneously. Of all habitable places. Tasmania last experienced the advent of energy and the accompanying transmutation of its island mass.

When the event occurred, Chandra was still sitting in his wicker chair, staring at the banyan trees with an expression of almost aggressive fatalism. He had the journal in his hand. Stackpole and his driver, Cheng, were watching a boatman fight the hard current of the storm-pounded Yangtze Kiang River. Their sight was extinguished—the boatman's hands did not even slip from the tiller as vision and thought were joined amongst the temperatures. To Evans, flying toward Washington at eight hundred miles an hour—to this oddly armed, cherubic old man—there came horrible suspicion—a presentiment that his errand would be futile. On The New England Wastes, Ed got halfway through a sentence intended to state that birches were better than nothing. Everson and Dunn, of course, were among the first victims.

If Mars had inhabitants, they certainly rejoiced, for there was created in their chilly firmament a small but profligate sun where the earth had circled, blue-green, for two billion years. A little sun that grew large—and a million times brighter than earth—and sent to them, across the reaches, additional heat and more light for their dim, red sandstone plains. To the Martians came the spectacular comfort of a new, radiant companion. If there were thoughtful creatures alive in the steaming hurricanes of Venus, they must have marveled and perhaps worried over the phenomenon: it is dangerous to be too near a sun birth. It is dangerous, when a close neighbor grows ten times its size and spurts incredible energy into space. If the Martians became glad, surely the Venutians grew anxious.

In due course, the earth's moon was engulfed and added as fuel to the atomic holocaust. Due course. It was not long. The atomic principle involves velocities which the average terrestrial man had not taken the trouble to understand, even at the year of his dissolution.

Indeed, the time which elapsed after the first, great light sprang from the Everson-Dunn machine, and until the earth became an expanding sphere heated to trillions of degrees, was slightly less than one nineteenth of a second.

The first radioactive symbol used at The University of California, Berkeley, 1946.
(Photo by Jimmy J. Pack Jr. from the lobby exhibit at The Dept. of Energy, Washington, D.C.)

Atom War
Rog Phillips

[Amazing Stories'] EDITOR'S NOTE —With the discovery of the atomic bomb and its use by the United States against Japan in 1945, a new type of war became possible. That of surprise attack by an aggressor who remains secret. The advantage of this form opening is, of course, obvious. The attacked nation cannot know where to center its counterattack until it is too late to bring any decisive strength into action.

In order to succeed, the aggressor must have secret bases from which to launch rocket bombs, sufficient numbers of bombs to insure the crippling of the attacked nation at once, if need be, and sufficient reserves in bombs and bases to paralyze the key centers of the entire world if that becomes necessary.

The technique is simplicity itself. A sudden destruction, without warning, of several important but not vital points within the country being attacked, followed by an ultimatum to surrender at once unconditionally or be totally destroyed, the conditions of surrendering immediate alliance with and military support of the aggressor without reservation.

The integrity, or in this case stupidity, of the attacked nation is the key to success or failure of this method, for the identity of the attacking power cannot be kept secret more than a few days, and the victim is still in possession of most of his military strength if he agrees to the surrender terms at once.

If the initial phase succeeds, rapid occupation of the control centers of the defeated nation, followed by a declaration to the rest of the world that the victor will rest on his laurels, completes the war successfully, for then no single nation will risk national suicide for a profitless attempt at rescue.

FALLACY OF FORCE, wrld crt, A.D. 2637, first published by the United States Army in 2165 A.D. was and is the greatest force for peace in the world. It contains the complete analysis of every type of warfare, its weaknesses, and how to checkmate it. Since the first publication of this book it has been revised and brought up to date whenever necessary. No potential aggressor could possibly hope to succeed in keeping either his gains or his own power in a war after reading this book, so no war has been fought since the beginning of the twenty-third century.

"You know how they used to believe the world was flat and rested on the back of an elephant to keep from falling?" Gar Winfield was talking earnestly to his friend, Johnny Baker, and those of his fellow officers sprawling around the club room who were interested enough to listen. "And how they believed the elephant stood on the back of a giant turtle so he wouldn't fall, and the turtle floated in a giant sea so it wouldn't fall? Then they conveniently left it at that because they couldn't see how they could end the endless series? Well, the whole trouble was that they couldn't conceive of the *existence* of infinity. They had to have a beginning and an end to everything."

"What's that got to do with the size of the universe?" asked Johnny, his uniform-clad body sunk deep in the cushions of a large chair and his feet stretched out across the rug.

"Well, nothing, really, except that you think the universe has to have a finite size. It doesn't. It has no ending in any direction," Gar said earnestly.

"Wait a minute," broke in Johnny, glancing around at the circle of faces and sprawling figures, "there is a finite number of atoms of matter in the earth isn't there?"

"Yes," replied Gar.

"Well—" Johnny sat up to deliver what he thought would be the coup de grace—"if you say the universe is infinite then you have to say that there are an infinite number of atoms in space and since infinity is not a number but means beyond number, you arrive at a contradiction."

"Oh, no," Gar answered. "There isn't any contradiction. You just have a finite number of atoms in any finite volume of space, but an infinite number in any infinite volume of space!" At that moment the radio screen lit up with motion and the announcer's voice became excited. "Watch it folks! There is going to be a crash."

The three-by-four screen showed a large, four-motor freight plane headed nose down toward a wooded section of a hill. A second after the picture came into sharp focus the plane ploughed into the trees. In that second before the crash the lettering on the fuselage could be made out. The large blue letters spelled out ACME MOVERS.

The announcer, during all this, was speaking in a swift, low monotone, his words clear and distinct despite the speed of his sentences. "The pilot and co-pilot just bailed out before our on-the-spot pickup plane reached the spot. The freighter is an Acme Furniture plane carrying the furnishings of Mr. J. C. Gildow of Seattle, Washington, to his new home in Schenectady, New York. The valve stuck on the second gas tank so that the plane ran out of fuel without warning. In a moment, as soon as the crash is shown in full, we will take you to the pilot in his chute as he is floating to the earth. As you can see, the wings are shearing off the tops of the trees as it ploughs through them. The strong, main girder through the wings will do no more than bend slightly under the blows of the tree trunks. The crash is interesting mainly because of trees. Now you can see that the plane has come to a stop in its forward flight through the trees and is settling to the ground. There will probably be some damage to the load it carries, but not too much. Let's switch to the pilot and see what he has to say."

Instantly the scene changed and a man hanging in the harness of a parachute covered the screen. Also a new voice took over.

"This is Milton Downing at the microphone, folks. I am in a Tellenewscast on-the-spot pickup plane at the scene of this crash in South Dakota. In a moment we will see what the pilot, Gus Crawford, has to say. While we are getting a focus on his voice I will turn you over to Cliff Edwards in the studio."

With no appreciable break in the flow of words the voice of Cliff Edwards took over the mike. "This is Cliff Edwards talking. This on-the-spot newscast is a regular feature of the National Newscast Corporation and is brought to you through the facilities of the National Broadcasting Corporation.

"And this is your local station, KQZ, bringing you this regular news program through the courtesy of the Sooner Candy Company." Without a change in tempo a sonovox song began which ended with the words, "I'd Sooner eat Sooners than later." A unanimous groan came from the listeners in the room—and no doubt that groan was repeated in front of thousands of radio receivers. The symphony of color that accompanied this sonovox song vanished to be replaced by the man in the parachute harness again. The focused bank of microphones on the pickup plane were now trained on his face. His expression was one of embarrassment and caution. "I am Crawford, the pilot of the plane that just crashed. It is my first crash and, I hope, my last. I don't think I had better say anything about the causes of the accident. The examiners will be in a better position to make a statement on that when they arrive."

The figure of Cliff Edwards replaced that of the pilot on the screen and his million-dollar voice took over. "Don't forget to listen to our hourly summary of the latest news. Every hour on the hour." His voice and figure faded as the commercials again took over.

"I see what you mean," Johnny Baker took up the conversation where it had been interrupted by the newscast. "Then you say that space is the classical Euclidean type, infinite in all directions, and is completely filled throughout by the material universe, so that actually there is an infinity of suns and planets in existence right now."

"That's right," replied Gar.

"Well then—" Johnny wrinkled his forehead in concentration—"if there is an infinity of planets and suns right now in the universe, doesn't it follow that somewhere there is another planet on which a civilization as great as ours exists right now?"

"Right again, Johnny," Gar said, grinning. "And since the universe could have no beginning and there always were an infinity of planets, even though any individual planet had a beginning and will have an end, it is also certain that somewhere in the universe is a race of intelligent beings who, as a race, have always existed even though they must have had a beginning!" Gar's grin broadened as he tossed this bombshell.

"Huh?" Johnny gasped. The rest of the men laughed. All of them except Johnny were graduate officers in the army defense forces. Johnny was an undergraduate. A sophomore in the New Chicago Military Academy, he had dropped in to the officers club to see his older brother. His brother not being there, he had found himself before long in the company of these august and hoary graduate officers who were part of the machinery for the defense of the capitol city, New Chicago. Since there was nothing to defend the capitol from, their duties were more theoretical than actual.

Having been through the academy himself, Gar knew that he could startle Johnny with his discourse on certain aspects of modern theory which were not taught until the senior year.

The television screen came to life again and the figure of Cliff Edwards took shape. His face was tense and his voice as it came from the loudspeaker was unusually excited. "Hold on to your seats, folks. Something very unusual has happened. All telephone and radio communication with San Diego, California, suddenly ceased just two and a half minutes ago. We are checking on telegraph right now. Just a minute. Here is the report from Western Union. Their teletype machine in contact with San Diego stopped receiving at exactly the same instant.

"That can mean only one thing, folks. And I hate even to think of it. Our pickup plane from Los Angeles will be there in a moment. Wait a minute. Here's a report from Los Angeles. Come in, Los Angeles."

A new figure took the screen. "Hello, folks. This is Jack Haley in Los Angeles. A violent shock just occurred. A report now coming in from the seismologist at the university says that the quake came from the direction of San Diego and had all the characteristics of a gigantic explosion. Already, from our studio windows you can see a giant mushroom of white smoke growing by the second down San Diego way. We will switch you now to Jerry Anderson who is rapidly nearing San Diego and has his scanner trained on the explosion. Come in, Jerry Anderson."

On the screen a giant cloud of white appeared. A seething, black inferno within the white outer layer boiled to the surface in various spots. The cloud was ascending and expanding in all directions with the speed of a stratoplane.

A quiet voice sounded over the loudspeaker. "This is Jerry Anderson, folks. It is obvious now that this cloud is from the explosion of an atomic bomb. Something the whole world has been dreading for twenty years. We might as well face the grim reality. San Diego is no more!"

As one man Gar, Johnny, and the rest stood up in amazement. It couldn't happen, but here it was. An unprovoked attack by an unknown enemy. The television screen now went mad. One scene after another flashed on to be replaced a moment later by another, and still another. Bonneville Dam on the lower Columbia River had been bombed. While the pickup plane was showing the torrents of flood water galloping toward Portland and Vancouver, the scene was blotted out by an even more terrible spectacle. Grand Coulee Dam had also been destroyed and gigantic walls of angry water were dashing at express train speed across the reclaimed fields and the homes of the settlers. For the first time in fifty thousand years the Columbia reached its high water mark, engraved in the canyon walls of the Coulee.

Again the scene changed. This time it was just blurred sky. But wait! Isn't that streak in the screen taking shape? It enlarges. Swiftly its outlines become sharp and clear. It is a giant stratorocket bomb! Its forward deflection plate is glowing cherry red. Up into the screen the familiar landscape of Detroit flashes for one split second. Then, for the thousandth part of a second a holocaust seems to reach out its hands and dive through the screen. Everyone in front of the screen flinched and threw up his hands. In that instant the screen went blank. In the next it showed the destruction of Detroit from a distance.

The announcer's voice was hoarse, his words lagging behind the picture by half a minute. But no one was listening to him anyway. The horrors of the screen needed no explanation.

A sudden thought struck them all at once. Would the next target be the capitol? As one man, the officers dashed out of the room. Only Johnny remained.

Seconds later Gar and his companions were seated in a tube car in the subbasement of the club. As the tube car started to move, its door closed with a swishing sound, sealing the interior against outside pressure. Each man was strapping himself to his seat. Five gravities pressed each man against the back of his seat as the enormous pressure behind the car in the sealed tube shot it ahead. Midway toward their destination the seats swivelled half around, and by the time they had locked in their new position the tube car was braking to a halt, compressing the gasses at the destination end and recovering some of the energy expended in their start.

In less time than it takes to tell the car had traversed the twenty miles of perfect bore under the capitol city and reached station number three of the defense system. As it came into position under the exit port huge hooks swung out behind it and secured it against the tremendous pressure it had built up in the bore's dead end. The exit port and the door to the tube car opened together and the men piled out, Gar in the lead.

But no longer were they men. Now they had become just cogs in the defense machine. Specialized actions and knowledge drilled into their conscious and subconscious minds, engraved indelibly on their very souls, took over now. Thought could not be tolerated. It was too slow. Meter boards and scanner screens, fed by the surface towers above occupied their senses, and would continue to fill their alert minds until they were relieved from duty. Thus the years of training had prepared them, and when the emergency arrived they were ready.

The intercom came to life and the loud voice of the central office I.C. officer erupted into the still efficiency of the room. "Stand by for a special communication. Our unknown attacker is going to deliver his ultimatum."

At once a new voice, smooth and cool, sounded. Without relaxing their vigilance the men listened. The intonations of the voice were mathematically exact, spoken by a foreigner, but not even an expert would be able to tell what his nationality was.

"This message, broadcast to the entire world, is an ultimatum to the government of the United States of America. We have just destroyed the cities of San Diego and Detroit, and the dams of Bonneville and Grand Coulee. We have done this with regret, knowing that it was necessary to convince the responsible authorities of your government that delay on their part to reach an immediate decision in regard to the terms we are about to set forth will mean immediate national suicide for its country.

"We are prepared to destroy at once every city of two-hundred thousand or more population, and every key power source in the United States and are fully determined to do so unless we receive the formal capitulation of the responsible government by midnight tonight, Central Standard time. This capitulation must be complete and unconditional, with the assurance and guarantee of these responsible parties that effective immediately the government of the United States will turn over to us the control of all military forces and ally herself with us to the fullest extent in case it becomes necessary to repel the hostile advances of other nations foolhardy enough to court destruction by attacking as when our identity becomes known.

"If this capitulation is not forthcoming by the time limit, we will visit further destruction on unspecified targets within one hour after the deadline. Then the ultimatum will be repeated with certain further demands made which will become increasingly stringent as the destruction proceeds.

"To the rest of the world we give this assurance and also a warning. We have no military designs against any country other than the United States of America. With her subjection our aggressive program is ended. However, if any nation is foolhardy enough to attack us, we are prepared to at once destroy utterly and without hesitation every city and public utility of that nation. Take heed."

After a moment of silence the voice of the I.C. officer sounded. "That message was broadcast from several different sources at once and on the same wavelength. There is no way of determining the exact locations of the transmitters. Our bearings give us a sixth power equation with imaginary roots, indicating that the enemy has solved the problem of hiding the source of transmission. Keep to your posts, men. We have no assurance that the enemy will wait until an hour after the deadline. And remember, the future of the country is in your hands as well as those higher up. That is all."

Silence descended again like a shroud. Gar's mind was in a daze. Things had happened so fast that it would be weeks before he would be able to think straight again. And the worst was yet to come.

The hours passed slowly. Twice, once at ten o'clock and again at eleven-thirty, the radar picked up signs of approaching objects from the stratosphere, but each time it was a meteor.

At eleven-forty-five the intercom came to life and the same alien voice repeated the previous message and added the warning not to wait until the last minute because the capitol itself would receive the next blow. Midnight came and went. The men, like dripping machines, stayed at their posts. Beads of perspiration stood out on their foreheads and ran in crazy rivulets over their faces.

Each was thinking, over and over, "Any minute now. Any minute now. Any minute now." And still no bomb came.

The days of blood-and-guts warfare were gone for good. But every man in that room would have traded his comfortable stool in front of an instrument board for the mental relaxation of the old type of warfare at that moment.

Then it came. The radars picked up five stratobombs coming in from almost directly overhead. Two were aiming toward the Chicago Loop and the other three for New Chicago. Thin, twin-pencil fingers of pale luminescence reached out from the towers surrounding the two cities to kiss each bomb lightly and cling to it with desperate tenacity. One bomb began to glow with pale red heat. Then another and another, until all five were glowing and leaving a trail of sparks in its wake.

Suddenly the nearest one swerved in its flight and headed directly for tower number three. It struck with a dull booming sound and the underground control room shook slowly and deliberately, as though it were trying to shrug off the molten and relatively harmless hulk that had been an atomic bomb capable of destroying a Grand Coulee dam by itself. Molten or not, it had struck at a velocity of eight miles a second and plowed itself deeply into the earth and concrete that protected control center number three.

As the last tremor ceased there came the sound of screaming metal and hissing air. The hooks that held the tube car had been shaken loose with the exit hatch still open. Two thousand cubic feet of air under twelve hundred pounds pressure to the square inch forced its way through the small opening into the underground rooms and sought the ventilation shafts.

Gar felt a sharp pain as his lungs collapsed under the sudden pressure. For perhaps two seconds it rose to a maximum of two hundred pounds and then slowly subsided as the compressed air roared up the ventilation shafts. Every man in the room was on the floor, moaning feebly and holding his hands over his solar plexus.

Five minutes after the pressure had returned to normal, Gar climbed painfully into his chair. His eyes felt as if knives had been plunged into them, his head seemed to be split wide open, and a pink froth bubbled out of the left corner of his mouth. Then a rivulet of red crept out of his right ear and slowly trickled down to the lobe where it collected into a drop that was not quite large enough to let go. By some strange miracle his left ear drum had stood the pressure so that he could still hear.

The name Helen Crawford is a common enough name, as names go. But Helen herself belied the commonness of her name. A commercial artist, she had spent most of the day trying to capture just the right touch for a magazine-cover picture, but somehow it had eluded her. So she had given up and hopped into her coupe for a ride out in the open spaces.

Her ride had taken her in a large circle through the southern part of the state. The lights of Chicago had grown to cover the entire horizon on her return before she decided to stop and have something to eat. Marty's Rendezvous, written in large neon letters over the front of a cozily, lighted, one-story stucco affair, had attracted her.

A glance at her wristwatch showed that it was eleven-fifty-five when she entered and settled herself in a booth near the back. The radio was blaring the latest news of the attack, but Helen, immersed in her own thoughts and unaware that the country was being attacked, remained blithely oblivious to the air of excitement in the cafe.

At two minutes and twenty-three seconds after midnight she was sitting comfortably relaxed, her arms on the table, her head against the leather back of the booth wall. Her mouth, a shade too wide for beauty, accentuated the perfect symmetry of her face. Her brown hair, carelessly combed, draped down on her shoulders. Her grey suit coat was unbuttoned and the red sweater underneath. closely hugged the contours of her figure. Her eyes were closed. At two minutes and twenty-four seconds after midnight the molten blob that had been an atomic bomb pushed the front part of Marty's Rendezvous ahead of it into the underground headquarters of control center number three. Helen opened her eyes a brief instant before the shock of the concussion reached her. Then a wave of darkness engulfed her.

She did not stir as the plaster and boards above her booth dropped around her.

Gar was bent over the wash basin, cold water from the tap dripping through his hair. He straightened, reached for a towel, and began to briskly rub his face and scalp. It made him feel much better.

The rest of the men were in various stages of recovery from the effects of the surge of compressed air. The intercom loudspeaker came to life asking for a report on the damage. Gar ignored it and the others seemed not to hear it. It dawned on Gar that in all probability his left eardrum was the only unbroken one in the outfit. He went over to the intercom and flicked the mike switch.

"This is Gar Winfield in three. A dud came in. The extent of damage is unknown, but the compressed air storage tube let go. All personnel injured to some extent by the escaping air. All equipment seems, offhand, to be in working order, but will report in detail later." He flicked the switch again and the voice came from the other end.

"Okay, Gar. Number three is the only military casualty. All bombs were killed before they landed, but get back to your posts as soon as you can. A second wave is reported about twenty minutes away. Number three is now cut out of coordination but you can freelance with your sterio (the dual beam hysteresis ray) until tests on your equipment are completed."

Gar glanced at the others. They were huddled in a group in the center of the room, a dull look of puzzlement on their faces.

"All of you that can hear, speak up," he requested. Not a one of them answered. Gar shrugged hopelessly and spoke into the mike.

"Sorry, sir. All personnel excepting myself have broken eardrums. We can operate the sterio, but coordination is out of the question without replacements."

"Replacements on the way by surface car. Inspect damage and report." A loud click followed, indicating that the intercom was now cut off.

Gar walked over to the desk and wrote on a pad, tearing off the note and handing it to the nearest man who read it and passed it on. The note said, "Take it easy. Help coming. I'm going to inspect the damage."

Gar's journey of inspection showed that the tube could not be made to operate again without weeks of work, and the surface exit into the base of the tower was blocked by debris. The six inch conduit that contained all the wires leading into the station had been uncovered by the bomb as it ploughed in, and had been bent, but was otherwise not damaged.

He went back to the control room and scribbled another note asking for volunteers to open the exit shaft. Soon they were all busy pulling dirt and broken concrete out of the tunnel that led to the surface.

New Chicago was built by the military government of the United States on the southern end of Lake Michigan east of Chicago proper. After the second world war it was realized that atomic explosives made the old capitol city, Washington, D. C., too vulnerable.

Underground vaults and offices for the nation's vital administrative offices were built, safe from every conceivable form of attack. The construction genius of the country had turned out a masterpiece. Office and vault structures were of welded steel plate, riding on springs so as to nullify any heavy shock. Each structure was completely surrounded by fabulous amounts of reinforced concrete which served the double purpose of protecting these underground centers and acting as foundations for the skyscrapers that reared their heads above the clouds from the surface.

Chicago and New Chicago, together with the resident suburban areas, thus formed a gigantic industrial and governmental hub covering an area of almost two thousand square miles with a population of over sixty million.

Things never dreamed of before 1940 made this giant possible. The visiphone, a television telephone, came in as standard equipment in 1947. Slip-on wings, a unit weighing only twelve pounds, made up of a jacket that could be put on just like an ordinary zipper jacket, to which was attached a pair of robot muscled wings complete with cellophane feathers, powered by a small power pack whose case was studded by buttons for controlling the type of muscular rhythm in the wings, started coming

155

off the assembly line early in 1948. With this gadget the office worker could hop off the pavement after breakfast and reach his office, twenty or thirty miles away on the eighty-sixth floor, in half an hour.

Slip-ons, as they came to be called, took the entire country by storm. People took to the air like birds at the rate of a hundred a day in October, 1947. By October 1948 they were taking to the air at the rate of over a thousand a day as the factories expanded their output to try to keep up with the growing demand.

Completely foolproof, designed for every type of flying and landing, even a beginner could fly as easily as a bird. And they took no more space than an overcoat when hung in the closet.

The robot muscle created a gigantic industry almost overnight. In the entertainment field they became a sensation. Fantastic creatures appeared on the vaudeville stage and the screen. Interplanetary plots for stories became the rule. Mad creations sprang up to thrill and chill every type of audience.

Specialization in radio broadcasting started with the National Newscast Corporation. One station in each large city was devoted exclusively to on-the-spot news broadcasts with an hourly summary of the highlights of the news. This was followed almost immediately by the Screen Guild Network, devoted exclusively to the latest and best plays. It followed the movie program of two or three plays lasting two to two and a half hours, repeated over again continuously, with a complete new program every day. The Screen Guild rapidly took over every station not owned by N.N.C.

History repeated itself. In the twenties the stage had fallen from its high estate to the low one of training ground for would-be moving picture artists. By 1949 the cinema had descended to the same position in relation to the radio screen. And no one ever went to the movies anymore. The daylight television screen eliminated the necessity for semi-darkness in television reception. Every worthwhile movie played continuously on screens in cafes, beer parlors, department stores and even the waiting rooms in doctors' offices.

The double shaft, air cushion elevator came in early in 1947, making possible continuous elevator service for any heighth. Obsolete skyscrapers were torn down and new ones built with ten stories underground and fifty to a hundred and fifty on top.

Instead of being pulled up by cable the new elevator rested on a cushion of compressed air in smooth shaft. In a second shaft the counter piston rode up and down. Hundreds of details went into the perfection of this elevator.

City planning came into its own after New Chicago paved the way. Moving sidewalks on every third level connected each building with its neighbor. A person could travel all over the downtown area from building to building on the twenty-first level, for example, without descending to the street.

Yes, the coordinated super-city of 1960 was a far cry from the stupidly put together city of 1945 with each unit made as an unrelated part of an uncoordinated whole.

The military dictator of the United States sat at his desk in emergency headquarters a hundred feet under the heart of New Chicago. Forming a semicircle in front of him were seven ten-by-twelve visiscreens, and in back of them was a scanner to send his image along with his voice to any part of the world.

The clock set in the wall facing him showed just fifteen minutes past midnight. At twelve-thirty-seven, five more strato bombs would dive upon the Chicago area. If just one of them landed the destruction would be incalculable. Not only would hundreds of buildings be wiped out, thousands of them would be made unsafe and have to be torn down.

The dictator had not been idle since that ultimatum by the enemy. Those seven screens facing him had all been filled most of the time. And a plan had been born. Born of desperation and dire necessity. He was reviewing that plan now.

Surrender was unavoidable. If it were delayed destruction would be so great that it would endanger the entire world. So it was not a question of whether the United States should surrender or not, but of what should take place after that surrender.

Upon surrender the unknown enemy would make itself known. But not before she had control of the attack bases of the U. S. That much was certain. But *could* she take possession of our attack arsenals without giving away her identity in the operation? And when her identity became known could we destroy her before it was too late?

Honoring the surrender was out of the question because the question forced upon the governments of the world could find no answer in the field of honor. It had not been propounded there.

A face appeared on the center screen and a voice sounded. "The hookup is now open, sir." The dictator nodded. Then, as a red flash across the screen signalled that he was on the air, he spoke.

"To my fellow citizens and countrymen I address the first half of this message. We are about to surrender the sovereign rights of nationhood. We may never regain them. It has been a hard decision to make. For my part, death would be preferable to loss of honor, but I could not include in that statement death to millions of women and children. Should I ask you to give your opinion? Surely you should have a right personally to decide between death and enslavement, but there isn't time. At this very moment stratobombs are only five minutes away from the capitol. If only one of them gets through you may be without a government. If I do not decide for you here and now the decision will still not be for you to make. So I must make it.

"I hold out no promise or hope for the future. But do I need to say more than that I know my people? Remember, each of you, that you are your brother's keeper. Weigh the cost of your actions at all times. Weigh them carefully.

"And now, to the unknown government who has visited us with destruction, I address myself. Our surrender goes into effect at this instant. Our military forces have instructions to obey your every command henceforth. If I survive the attack to take place in less than a minute I will await your pleasure here in New Chicago."

As he finished his speech the dictator glanced up, as if trying to pierce the ceiling and watch the silent, deadly arrows of destruction now only a few miles above the capitol.

The enemy had reckoned without the sterio ray, but he had ingenuity. When the first attack against the Chicago area had flopped he knew that some secret defense weapon had been used, and since the atomic bomb had only one weakness the cause of the failure was at once obvious. He had immediately gone to work. The very safeguards that protected the bomb from premature explosion were its undoing. They could not be changed on short notice.

But the location and number of radar towers in the Chicago area were known to him. Assuming that the new defense weapon was a ray, and assuming that it took time to kill a bomb, it was a simple matter of arithmetic to get at least one bomb through. Arithmetic and mathematics.

The atom bomb was taken out of ten stratobombs and ballast substituted. Then the ten duds and five live bombs were sent from the secret bases, in waves of five each, to arrive in the Chicago area at the same time but at different speeds and on different courses. The live bombs were to come in at the greatest speed and a little later than the duds.

One bomb got through and landed half way between Chicago and New Chicago, just thirty-five miles from the center of each, and two miles from the Lake Michigan shore. It could not have landed in a worse place, for contained in the area it destroyed were the telephone cables, power cables, and nerve centers of both cities.

Gar was seated at the switchboard in the control station when the lights went out. For a second he thought the conduit bad been injured after all, then the shock of the atom blast picked him up and gently laid him over the switchboard. After a moment it again picked him up and gently laid him on the floor. The whole operation seemed to him unreal. The work of some invisible, deliberating spirit. Like he might be a piece of furniture being moved about.

The sense of unreality ended abruptly with the realization of what these motions meant. He had read of atom blasts. These deliberate movements were not of himself, but of the earth.

With this realization came the memory of his companions. He dashed to the tunnel through the darkness. It was cleared but he could see no sign of them. Climbing upward he emerged into a weird glow. The overcast sky, the air itself, and all the buildings of New Chicago in the distance seemed to glow with a light of their own. This he knew would wear off in a few hours.

His fellow officers lay about him at the mouth of the tunnel. He bent over them one by one. None was alive. About fifty feet away was the remains of the roadside cafe, Marty's Rendezvous. He stumbled over to it. The caved-in front and the hole in the ground, told him plainly that the dud had struck there.

Impulse made him move around the hole and climb into the ruins. He walked as if guided by fate to a pile of rubble and began pulling fallen boards aside. He heard a soft moan and redoubled his efforts.

In a moment a feminine shoe could be seen in the eerie light. A few minutes later he was bending over the unconscious figure of Helen Crawford, the wreckage that had saved her from the full force of the atom blast cleared away. A terrific emotion was shaking Gar. It was almost as though he were the last man on earth and had found a companion after having given up all hope. And perhaps he and Helen were the only two people left alive in the Chicago area. He did not know, but in the desolate wreckage of the two cities revealed by the unearthly radioactive light from where he was frantically chafing Helen's wrists and patting her face with the vague helplessness of a man in the presence of a woman, it did not seem likely that many survivors could be found.

In later years, as Gar looked back on that night, his most vivid memory was the unreality of it all. But when Helen opened her eyes and looked at him for the first time her clear, blue eyes seemed the most real thing he had ever seen.

Her voice—cool, with an undertone of humor—asked, "What goes, bo?"

Gar aped her mood. "The end of the worl', girl."

Helen looked around wonderingly. Then she struggled to her feet in amazement, looked toward New Chicago, whirled around, taking in the wreckage all about her. "I believe you," she said. "Well, what do we do about it—stand here?"

Gar grinned. "I hadn't thought that far ahead," he replied.

Helen suddenly became aware of the look of admiration in Gar's eyes. She noticed for the first time that he was clean cut, had an air of quiet power about him, and that his face was handsome in a distinctly masculine sort of way. Much different than the assorted sizes, ages, and shapes that had held that look in their eyes before in her experience. She smiled.

"My name is Gar Winfield," Gar said in pleasurable embarrassment.

"Mine is Helen Crawford," Helen answered, holding out her hand. They shook hands, laughing over the ceremony of introduction under such unusual circumstances.

"Well, what do we do now?" Helen asked, repeating her question of a minute before.

Gar looked around, frowning in thought. "I guess we had better see if one of these cars will work. If it will we had better drive away from Chicago and find a house where there is a radio and a phone so that we can find out what is going on. Maybe the war is over already."

"What war?" Helen asked.

"Didn't you know the United States was being attacked?" Gar asked in amazement.

"No! Is it? By whom?" Helen fired at him.

While they were examining the parked cars in search of one not too badly damaged to run, Gar brought her up to date.

They found a Buick convertible with its tires up but its top gone. Its tank was nearly full and after a couple of tries the motor came to life. Backing it around a pile of wreckage they got onto the highway and headed south. The going was slow for several miles, and often they had to swing around bits of debris that had been blown out to the highway by the explosion.

Once Gar stopped the car when he saw an arm sticking up over the edge of the drainage ditch by the road. Helen climbed out of the car to investigate and climbed back feeling sick. The arm had no body attached to it.

They drove on in silence, and after a while the eerie light of their surroundings was replaced by normal darkness, split by their headlights. Suddenly the haze overhead ended and the stars came out. Helen sniffled quietly.

Without being aware of doing it, Gar found his arm around Helen's shoulder. He drove swiftly, his eyes straight ahead, not daring to look at Helen lest she become aware of his arm and move away.

It was almost with regret that Gar pulled up in front of a lighted farmhouse. As he came to a stop the front door opened and a man and woman poked their heads out. They remained that way as Gar and Helen walked up the path to the porch.

As they started up the steps the man cried out, "Wait, you can't come in here."

"Why not?" Gar asked in surprise.

"Look at yourselves," the man commanded.

Gar and Helen looked at each other. They were glowing softly. They looked at the car on the road. It too was glowing with a soft, radioactive light.

"That won't hurt you," Gar said. "We were in the area of the explosion. We've got to get rid of these clothes before they burn us and also wash all over to get the radioactive ash off our skin. Do you understand?"

He and Helen started up the steps, and the farmer and his wife moved back silently to make way for them.

As they entered the living room they saw that the farmer and his wife were of the shiftless variety. No rug on the floor, worn out furniture, dirty curtains, and the odor of a dozen meals and as many Monday washes hanging in, the air. But there was a radio.

Gar turned it on, then headed for the kitchen. He ignored the farmer and his wife. They were evidently afraid of his uniform and stupified by the explosion they had heard. While he and Helen were washing in the kitchen sink the radio came to life.

"… from Sydney, Australia. The capitol of Xsylvania was completely wiped out by four atomic bombs. Other bombs are being directed in a geometrical pattern over the enemy at the rate of one every five minutes.

"Here is a bulletin from Moscow. The United States Ambassador has just been called to the Kremlin for a consultation. Will the U.S.S.R. join the battle against Xsylvania? The way Australia is going there won't be much of Xsylvania left by tomorrow!

"Flash! The Yrrian Republic just declared war on Australia, effective immediately, stating that Australia has violated the United Nations Charter in attacking Xsylvania without first exhausting every peaceful channel in attempts to settle whatever differences exist between the two countries. The Yrrian President called on all members of the United Nations to fulfill their obligations under the treaty by following suit! Imagine that, folks. A murderer breaks loose and when a law-abiding citizen tries to end his spree of killing, the 'respectable' Yrria says the bad law-abiding citizen of the world of nations should write a letter to the authorities asking them to call a board meeting and decide what should be done about this murderer who is cutting innocent throats right and left!

"A newsflash from Sydney, Australia is now coming in. In a moment we will be able to see what it is. Things are happening fast. Too fast for comprehension. The world has gone mad. We may be living the last few days of our existence. There have been seventy-seven atom bomb explosions in the last twenty-four hours—or rather, twelve hours, for believe it or not, folks, that is all the older this war is.

"Did I say seventy-seven? It is now ninety-two. And Australia is now helpless. Her three bomb launching centers have just been wiped out.

"Two things are now certain. The first is rather trivial in a way. There is not a single sheet of photographic film left in the world that is any good, unless it is in a box lined with lead sheeting. The second is perhaps the most tragic fact we will have to face in our lifetime. There is now enough radioactive material loose in the atmosphere by actual calculation to shorten the life span of every living creature on earth by several years.

"The next generation will, according to the most eminent authorities, contain a high percentage of mutations and freaks. Perhaps I shouldn't say this, but it might be better if the war is carried on to its logical conclusion now. Race suicide."

The radio became silent. Gar and Helen stood in front of it, their arms over each other's shoulders, horror written on their young faces. The radio, after a moment of silence came to life again. A new voice took over.

"This is a different commentator, folks. Because this station is violating the rules pertaining to defeated nations in keeping on the air, and our lives will be forfeit if we are caught, I am not giving my name. The previous announcer lost his head. I don't blame him, really, but he was talking nonsense. The radioactive residue of an atomic bomb explosion loses its power after a few hours. There is no danger, so don't lose your heads."

Gar snapped off the radio and said to Helen, "Let's go."

They left the house without a glance at the inmates nor even thanking them for their passive hospitality. Gar drove the car silently, heading south again. Helen too seemed to be in deep thought.

"Gar," she finally said.

"Yes?" "Do you think that first commentator was right?"

"Right about what?" Gar asked.

"About mutants and freaks being born from now on because of the radioactives in the atmosphere."

Gar did not answer for a while. Finally he spoke. "I don't know," he said slowly. "It is known that x-rays can cause mutations. But I have never heard of any experiments where radioactive elements were used in a study of mutation. Offhand I would say that if such mutations do take place now they stand just as much of a chance of being for the better as for the worse. Mutation generally occurs in the newest factor of a gene pattern. In the human the newest is the forebrain and the soul.

"They, are also the most important, because the physical form does not mean too much. It may be that children will be born now who are so much more intelligent than we that there can be no comparison. Or it may be that a race will come into existence now which has no soul. A race of intelligent beasts. Or maybe all possible mutants will be born and segregate themselves into hostile camps and fight to exterminate one another. The old survival-of-the-fittest philosophy.

"All I can say is that we must not think of that until it comes. If you and I should marry, we must not be afraid to have children. If you marry someone else, Helen, you must not be afraid to have children. Understand?" And he flashed her a quick smile.

"I understand," Helen replied, and an enigmatical smile tugged at the corners of her mouth for several minutes.

After a time the road turned toward the east. Then the dim light of early dawn began to spread over the landscape. Just as the top edge of the sun crept above the horizon they entered the outskirts of Logansport.

A policeman stepped out into the middle of the street and stopped them. "You're from the area of the explosion, ain't you?" he asked, and then without waiting for an answer. "Not many left alive, I guess. Not many came through. Turn to the right at the next corner and go a block and a half. You'll see the place. You can wash up and get fresh clothes there and a bite to eat."

Gar and Helen thanked him profusely. He shrugged off their thanks and motioned them to move on.

A half hour later Gar and Helen were sitting at the counter of a cheery restaurant gulping hot, black coffee.

Helen's freshly washed hair was combed straight back, reaching down to her shoulders. The print dress she had chosen from the small stock of the local dress shop gave her a clean, dairy-maid appearance.

Gar had been provided with a new uniform. He would have looked as if nothing had happened except for the hint of suffering in his eyes and the lines of fatigue on his face.

The waitress brought their breakfast of bacon and eggs. With a sigh of relief and exhaustion they began to eat.

The radio came to life. Its screen remained blank, but the loudspeaker blared loudly. "At a moment's notice we may have to get off the air, folks. It is reported that planes have landed at several spots with Xsylvanian troops.

"Remember what you have been told to do. The invasion cannot reach important proportions. The end is already in sight. Xsylvania is almost totally destroyed now. Australia will be avenged a hundredfold.

"The government broadcast of the details of the sterio ray will soon make it impossible to use atom bombs on any effective scale. There are thousands of amateur radio hounds throughout the country making sterio ray machines at this moment. In every country all over the world there are other thousands doing the same.

"The nations of the world are meeting over the conference table today to decide the fate of the unholy three. The war isn't over yet, but its end is certain. So look up. Look to the future. I am not asking you to forget what has happened. Seventy-five million Americans have lost their lives in the past fifteen hours, but never again will such a horrible thing be possible."

Gar and Helen left the restaurant and started a tour of the town. The air was hazy and the sun shown through a mile-thick cloud of fine dust that had been drawn into the air by the explosion the night before. Several of the shop windows showed cracks and the local department store already had several of its show windows boarded up.

A block away a crowd was gathering about a man standing on a box. Gar and Helen hastened their steps to hear what he was saying.

"… time to end this dictatorship that makes slaves of honest people. Do you want some rat-faced stooge of the army dictator to keep on telling you where you are to work and what you are to do all your life?"

Gar grinned and, taking Helen's arm, moved on.

"Aren't you going to stop him?" Helen asked in alarm.

"No," Gar answered. "I might stop him, but there are thousands of him right now. He won't get anyplace."

Another crowd was gathering at the next corner. As Gar and Helen hurried forward to see what was going on, a band started to play. Then several shrill voices began to sing "Shall We Gather at the River."

When Gar and Helen reached the fringes of the crowd a white-haired old man climbed onto a packing box and began to shout, "The end of the world is coming. You are living in the last days. This is the Battle of Armageddon and it will end only with the coming of the Lord.

"Give your hearts to the Lord, my friends. 'Ask and it shall be given unto you.' Ask the Lord to forgive your sins. 'Ye must be born again.'"

The band took up the tune and the uniformed followers of the old man began to sing softly, "Ye must be born, again, ye must be born again—"

Gar and Helen walked on. After a few steps they looked back. Most of the crowd was drifting away. And the crowd around the first speaker had almost vanished. Gar grinned at Helen. "You see?" He pointed. "They aren't any threat. Rabble rousers can't get anywhere any more. Come on, let's go over to the local military headquarters. I have to report to duty.

They walked slowly, their arms linked together. Finally they came to a white marble building fronted by a tier of long steps. Gar and Helen walked slowly up the steps and went in through a revolving door.

Marines prepare to charge an objective seconds after an atomic explosion at the Atomic Proving Grounds, Yucca Flat, Nevada. Defense Dept. Photo—Marine Corps. (Photograph—United States Archives).

The Day the Bomb Fell
Leslie A. Croutch

Johnny kicked his way to school that bright spring morning, punishing a small round stone unmercilessly as he vented his boyish spleen.

"I wish I didn't have to go to school," he was grumbling. "I wish it'd burn down. I wish the teacher'd get the mumps, or chicken pox, or somethin'."

He halted to look into the window of the big hardware store. What a fine display of fishing tackle they had. Leaning against the curved corner where it turned in toward the entrance, he could hear the radio set on display within. Absent-mindedly he listened to the voice of the newscaster.

"… President Green remained in his office during the night, awaiting the latest reports of the tense European situation. Orders have gone out to all airdromes, cancelling all leaves…"

Johnny yawned. Ho hum! Adults were funny, sticking around a radio like that when it was so nice out. The sun was sure hot today. He'd like to go fishin'. He wondered if Pop would be home early like he said, to paint the garage. He liked painting.

The school bell yammered, its amplified electronic voice snapping him to awareness of the world he was a part of. He started to run, books swinging from the strap, banging against his legs, striking passersby who turned to look after him, smiling.

He just made it. Luckily the school was just around the next corner. Puffing like one of the obsolete steam engines they had in the amusement park, he raced up the broad concrete walk and through the closing front doors. The caretaker shook his head at the human jet plane that shot by him, up the stairs, round the corner, into the room, to flop breathlessly into a seat halfway up the aisle.

As the class mumbled its prayers, led by Miss Wilkinson, Johnny scanned the room, furtively, out of the corners of his eyes, wondering if any of his classmates had had the nerve to skip. Yep, Bert White was missing—and by golly, so was Torn Ketcheson. He counted them off in his mind: eight, nine, ten—gee-willikers, fifteen of them absent!

When the prayer was over, and the salute to the flag, the door opened, allowing a boy to slip in. Miss Wilkinson saw him.

"You're late, Torn," she said, gently reproachful.

"Yes, Miss Wilkinson. My father had to leave."

They all knew what that meant. Things must be bad, thought Johnny, if they had had to send for Tom's pop. He was a colonel in the new air force, and had been home on leave. Suddenly he remembered the other boys' fathers were also officers, or enlisted men. Had they been sent for, was that why they hadn't come to school?

Miss Wilkinson was nervous. She kept dropping her chalk, and she made some funny mistakes in arithmetic that made the class snicker. And when some of the kids kept looking out of the windows, to the horizon and up at the sky, she said nothing. In fact, while they were studying, once, she stood near one of them, looking kind of white and scared. Johnny began wishing he'd listened to the radio with his mother and dad that morning. Something had come over it to make them worried, too. He wondered what it was.

At ten-thirty something happened that he knew he would never forget. He was sitting, his head on his hand, half asleep, looking out of the open windows. Far away, over the tall buildings of the downtown section, he could see needle-like fingers poking into the sky. They were the tall stacks of the huge plants about twenty miles away, staining the heat ridden horizon with smudgy stains. Suddenly, a terrifically bright light lit up the whole sky, making his eyes hurt. While he was rubbing them, he felt a blow, a hot, heavy, pushy feeling. Then the noise came. The whole school shook and decorative, pastel-toned tile fell from the high ceiling. The girls started to cry and even Miss Wilkinson had tears in her eyes.

When Johnny could see again, he looked toward the place he had seen the light and there was a huge black cloud rising high in the sky. It was small down near the ground, but up above it rolled and boiled and swelled so it looked like the biggest toadstool ever.

As he watched, openmouthed, there came another terrible flash of the intense brightness, followed by the heavy breath of heat and the soul-shaking sound. This one came from another point on the line that divided earth and sky, over toward where there were more big factories, making very secret things that people didn't know much about. He scratched irritably. His skin was prickling and felt like he had a pretty bad case of sunburn. Another heavy cloud, big-topped, slim-based, was slowly climbing.

A wailing sound rose through the still morning air. It sounded kind of spooky, like a wind blowing through trees at night. Then he realized it was the sound of many people shouting and crying.

Miss Wilkinson shook him by the shoulder and pointed toward the door. He saw the others were leaving, hurried, yet orderly.

They got down the wide stairs and outside to be greeted by a new sound, equally frightening. It was a distant sighing, high up, that was steadily growing louder, nearer. He looked up, but could see nothing.

"Run!" Miss Wilkinson was suddenly crying. "Get into the cellars. Quickly now. There isn't a second to lose."

The children ran toward the concrete frames in the ground. Johnny and his chums had made many boyish wagers as to their purpose. What interest they had caused, when, only a few short weeks before, crews of men had suddenly invaded the grounds, disturbing the classes with their loud voices and clanking machinery. Then they had departed, as mysteriously as they had come, leaving behind them the deep, concrete-walled, concrete-roofed rooms. The principal had talked over the amplifying system, telling them they were for special classes to be held underground some day. He had said when the time to use them came, the teachers would tell them to go to the cellars quickly, and they must—without hesitation, without delay.

Johnny stumbled, lurching sideways. He threw out his arm to catch himself, then the ground opened up and he tumbled into the deep cut that bad been made for a new water main to the school. The breath jarred from him. He struggled to his feet and looked up.

He could see the bright blue sky and he was starting to shout when suddenly the blue was wiped out by a terrible wave of liquid fire washing overhead. The ground shook, sending him sprawling again. He could see—for one short second—pieces of boards, bits of clothing, even chunks of masonry sailing by. He thought for one brief instant, "It must be a tornado," before everything went black.

When he came to, it was night. Sitting up, he nursed his aching head. His skin felt dry and burned and he had a terrible thirst. He got to his feet and found that, by standing on a large chunk of concrete that had fallen in, missing him by but a few inches, he could just reach the brink of the hole. He clawed for some time, hardly knowing what he was doing. Finally he managed to get a hold and drew himself out.

The school—where was the school? It was gone. In its place was nothing but a strewn mass of broken masonry. He stumbled toward it, beset by a sudden sense of loss.

"Jeepers!" he thought. "I didn't really mean it!"

Turning slowly, he looked about and saw he could see for a long ways. For a minute this didn't strike as being unusual. Then he cried aloud. Everywhere was desolation, utter ruin, half obscured here and there by columns of smoke, through which red tongues licked.

Suddenly he was afraid. He wanted to get home to see if his mother was all right. He started to run, but progress was slow, halting. Rubble tripped him up. Fires forced lengthy detours. Twisted piles of scrap that had once been automobiles huddled here and there. Once he passed something that sat on a fragment of curbstone, clad in tattered shreds of clothing, moaning as it rocked to and fro. He saw its face, briefly, and his stomach turned over painfully.

There seemed to be hardly anything alive. A dog ran shrieking from his path, caroming blindly off wreckage, rolling over and over in the dust when its legs failed it.

Eventually he reached the street he lived on, almost beyond feeling. It was no better. Here and there a bit of wall still stood, miraculous paradox amid ruin. He stumbled wearily down what had once been a neat tree-lined street, until he reached where his home had stood.

But there was nothing left. Not a wall remained, not a shrub of the hedge his father had so lovingly tended. It looked as though a giant steam roller had passed this way, flattening everything, grinding it to dust, leaving only a hole where the cellar had been, from which a twisted bit of piping beckoned like a skeletal finger.

He didn't cry. He couldn't cry. Walking toward what had once been a comfortable home, he stared straight ahead, eyes dry, a tight feeling in his throat.

The front steps were still there, leading up their four steps to the platform formed of flat stone slabs, before which a door had been. A door with tiny stained glass windows and a huge, funny looking brass knocker. He gulped.

Slowly he sat down. Chin dropped to rest in a grimy hand. Eyes sought the horizon, bespeckled with peaceful looking stars, a pale glow heralding a rising moon.

A huge grey cat poked a frightened head around some debris, meowed disconsolately, looked up at him, then ran up the steps to crawl into his lap. Fingers caressed the fur and a friendly purr answered his administrations.

"You lonesome, too?" he asked. The cat rubbed his head against his leg. "Guess maybe your folks are gone too, huh?"

Far off toward where the harbor lay, where the big factory town was, he saw the beam of a searchlight shoot up, explore the night sky tentatively, then flick off. Then he heard the sighing sound of many planes, shooting high overhead. He strained his eyes but was unable to see any riding lights.

"I wonder if Pop will come," he murmured. The cat stirred, licked his fingers.

Slowly the night passed the way of all nights since the world began, retreating finally before a lighting western sky. When it was light enough to see, he rose and, carrying the cat, walked slowly down the walk, turned up the street and, without a backward look, headed toward the open country. He wasn't sure why he took that direction. He knew only that some faint compulsion seemed to force him to leave the shambles that had been a living, breathing community a short, time before.

He walked for a long time, hardly conscious of his surroundings. Gradually he became aware of a gnawing hunger, a torturing thirst. And above it all, deadening his sensibilities, an aching loneliness that made him embrace the animal tightly from time to time. He saw nothing but wreckage, and the odd human, poking blindly about, stunned, unfeeling. He wondered for a time over what looked like a ghostly shadow, imprinted faintly on what was left of a concrete wall. He found a hole in the pavement filled with water by a slowly leaking main, and drank from it.

Once the sound of planes made him huddle in a ditch beside the road. He didn't know what he must fear. Only the knowledge that everything was strange. They shot by overhead, many of them, bearing no insignia, ominous, unfamiliar.

All this time he carried the animal, seeking in it comfort to fend off the loneliness that gnawed at his mind. Only once did he put it down, and that to drink. The cat didn't go away, but huddled close against his body and mourned softly until he picked it up again.

His skin itched and he scratched a great deal, but it only made the sensation worse. Finally he gave up.

It was late in the afternoon, judging by the sun, when he worked his way up a gradual slope and saw the farmhouse. It was all that remained of the buildings.. He didn't know how it had escaped, since the other structures lay scattered for yards and yards over the fields.

Looking for signs of life, he slowly approached the door. A dog lay in the front yard, lifeless. The door, which faced the city, swung on one hinge, blackened, blistered as though from intense heat. No glass remained in any of the windows.

Johnny called out, loudly, listened, then called again and again. Peeking inside he saw a room filled with dust, littered with broken plaster from the ceiling and walls, the furniture strewn about.

He went around to the back. There he found a horse, huddled against the wall as though for comfort. It sensed his presence and tried to whinny but all that came forth was a sort of sobbing sound that made Johnny feel bad. Dried blood stained the animal's nostrils, and the hair on its foreparts was all gone, leaving the skin red and boiled looking, like the lobsters his mother used to prepare for dinner. It stretched its neck, slamming its head against the wall. It was blind.

The back door was closed. Placing his hand against it, he shoved it open on hinges that were well oiled. Inside he found a kitchen, with pots still on the stove, rolled-out dough on the table, a carton of smashed eggs on the floor.

Hunger grew sharply in him and he searched the kitchen for food. There was bread in the pantry and he took it out, also some cooked meat and a whole bologna sausage. This he tied up in a towel from a drawer in the table. In a frying pan in the warming closet of the stove he found some raw liver, which the cat did away with with great dispatch and efficiency.

He was about to leave when the door leading to the rest of the house swung open and a girl appeared. She was about his own age, he reckoned, and she had red hair and a lot of freckles across her nose and she looked pretty scared.

"Who are you?" Johnny asked.

"I'm Marianne. This is my home."

"I guessed that," he told her with all the superiority of the youthful male.

"Then why did you ask?"

He wasn't going to get anywhere this way, he told himself.

"Where's your mom and pop?" he asked.

Her face, which had been showing some animation stiffened and her upper lip trembled. She brushed the back of her hand across it and gave a sort of sniff.

"I guess they're kinda dead."

"Kinda dead? Doncha know if they are or not?"

She nodded.

"Dad's down by the barn." She looked out of the window and amended her statement. "Where the barn was, I mean. I saw him go into it and then the big noise came and it wasn't there anymore."

"Where's your mom?"

"She was going to make a pie when we saw the cloud way off there. We went to the window to see better, only she was right up close. I guess that's why I didn't get hurt. I was looking around her when the light came. She threw up her hands and made a funny sound, then she started to run around, bumping into things and falling down. I led her to the bedroom and she fell down and never got up again."

He tilted his head, listening. The planes were coming again, or maybe they were different ones. And there was another sound. A heavy kind of rumbling, like big guns, only more steady. Going to the window, he looked out. Toward the city he could see a low cloud of dust coming this way. Then, where the road went up over a little elevation, he saw the big things, a lot of them. They looked like the tanks they had pictures of in the books at school, only these were much bigger. They were coming pretty fast, too.

"I guess we better go somewhere else," he said, and she nodded. They ran from the house, hand in hand.

"Maybe we can hide there." She pointed to what looked like a small bush, leading back from the house.

"It's Pop's orchard. There's a kind of cave there, too, that an old river ran into before it dried up."

When they were safely among the neat rows of tree corpses, they halted and looked back, gasping for breath.

The cavalcade of tanks rolled up and one of them turned out and approached the house. Some men in strange uniforms got out. From where they were they looked black, like the planes, and were comprised of a baggy pair of breeches, sloppy coat with a belt and a brimless sort of hat or cap. There were markings on the collars but Johnny couldn't make them out. Some went into the house while the rest either stood and talked or prowled around, kicking pieces of rubble and laughing loudly. One of them found the old horse and called to his companions. They took outside arms and made practice shots at it till it finally fell.

"I hate them!" sobbed Marianne, intensely. Johnny nodded mutely.

"I guess maybe they're the ones who killed our parents," he said. "They're not our soldiers."

Smoke started coming out of the door, followed by red flame. Marianne would have jumped up if he hadn't held her down.

"They're burning my mom," she cried.

He watched the house bum and hot tears rolled down his dusty face. The cat, sensing his grief, cried softly and crept close.

"I guess maybe they're gonna burn everything," he whispered, little realizing how full of prophecy the words were. "I reckon this is war, Marianne, like the history books tell about. Only worse."

She nodded. The tank started up with a muted roar and rolled off down the highway after the others.

Johnny watched it go. Looking up, his boyish shoulders straightened.

"Wasn't long ago," he said, "that I was wishin' the school'd burn down—that summer vacation was here." He sighed heavily. "I guess, Marianne," he went on, taking her hand and starting off into the orchard, "maybe vacation has come a little early this year."

HELP PROTECT OUR COUNTRY

REPORT THESE MATTERS DIRECT TO FBI

The public should be alert to report all information directly to the FBI which relates to the following specific matters:

1. Allegations of espionage, sabotage, or subversive activities.
2. Foreign submarine landings.
3. Suspicious parachute landings.
4. Possession and distribution of foreign-inspired propaganda.
5. Theft or unauthorized possession or purchase of large quantities of firearms, ammunition or explosives, or short- wave transmitters ond receivers.
6. Poisoning of public water supplies.
7. Chartering of airplanes for flights over restricted areas.
8. Fires and explosions of an unusual nature affecting any phase of the defense program.
9. Suspicious individuals loitering near restricted areas.
10. Possession of radio-active materials.

J. EDGAR HOOVER

Excerpted from the Greater Boston Civil Defense Manual, American Radio Publication, 1952.

AN OUTLINE FOR FAMILY EMERGENCY PLANNING

The nearest public fallout shelter to our home is located at

....

The best route from our home to this shelter is

....

The location in our home that offers the greatest fallout protection

is ....

Our Emergency Broadcast System (EBS) Station is ....

Its dial setting is ....

NAMES OF FAMILY MEMBERS				
Nearest shelter to work/school				
Best route planned?				
Is assistance to shelter needed?				
Who will provide?				
CD Training Completed:				
Personal and Family Survival				
Medical Self-Help				
Home Nursing				
First Aid				
Shelter Management				
Radiological Monitoring				
Firefighting				

Outline from Personal and Family Survival Civil Defense Handbook, November, 1966.

After the Sirens
Hugh Hood

They heard the sirens first about four forty-five in the morning. It was still dark and cold outside and they were sound asleep. They heard the noise first in their dreams and, waking, understood it to be real.

"What is it?" she asked him sleepily, rolling over in their warm bed. "Is there a fire?"

"I don't know," he said. The sirens were very loud. "I've never heard anything like that before."

"It's some kind of siren," she said, "downtown. It woke me up."

"Go back to sleep!" he said. "It can't be anything."

"No," she said, "I'm frightened. I wonder what it is. I wonder if the baby has enough covers." The wailing was still going on. "It couldn't be an air-raid warning, could it?"

"Of course not," he said reassuringly, but she could hear the indecision in his voice.

"Why don't you turn on the radio," she said, "just to see? Just to make sure. I'll go and see if the baby's covered up." They walked down the hall in their pajamas. He went into the kitchen, turned on the radio and waited for it to warm up. There was nothing but static and hum.

"What's that station?" he called to her. "Conrad, or something like that."

"That's 640 on the dial," she said, from the baby's room. He twisted the dial and suddenly the radio screamed at him, frightening him badly.

"This is not an exercise. This is not an exercise. This is not an exercise," the radio blared. *"This is an air-raid warning. This is an air-raid warning. We will be attacked in fifteen minutes. We will be attacked in fifteen minutes. This is not an exercise."* He recognized the voice of a local announcer who did an hour of breakfast music daily. He had never heard the man talk like that before. He ran into the baby's room while the radio shrieked behind him : *"We will be attacked in fifteen minutes. Correction. Correction. In fourteen minutes. In fourteen minutes. We will be attacked in fourteen minutes. This is not an exercise."*

"Look," he said, "don't ask me any questions, please, just do exactly what I tell you and don't waste any time." She stared at him with her mouth open. "Listen," he said, "and do exactly as I say. They say this is an air-raid and we'd better believe them." She looked frightened nearly out of her wits. "I'll look after you," he said; "just get dressed as fast as you can. Put on as many layers of wool as you can. Get that?"

She nodded speechlessly.

"Put on your woolen topcoat and your fur coat over that. Get as many scarves as you can find. We'll wrap our faces and hands. When you're dressed, dress the baby the same way. We have a chance, if you do as I say without wasting time." She ran off up the hall to the coat closet and he could hear her pulling things about.

"This will be an attack with nuclear weapons. You have thirteen minutes to take cover," screamed the radio. He looked at his watch and hurried to the kitchen and pulled a cardboard carton from under the sink. He threw two can openers into it and all the canned goods he could see. There were three loaves of bread in the breadbox and he crammed them into the carton. He took everything that was wrapped and solid in the refrigerator and crushed it in. When the carton was full he took a bucket which usually held a garbage bag, rinsed it hastily, and filled it with water. There was a plastic bottle in the refrigerator. He poured the tomato juice out of it and rinsed it and filled it with water.

"This will be a nuclear attack." The disc-jockey's voice was cracking with hysteria. *"You have nine minutes, nine minutes, to take cover. Nine minutes."* He ran into the dark hall and bumped into his wife who was swaddled like a bear.

"Go and dress the baby," he said. "We're going to make it, we've just got time. I'll go and get dressed." She was crying, but there was no time for comfort. In the bedroom he forced himself into his trousers, a second pair of trousers, two shirts and two sweaters. He put on the heaviest, loosest jacket he owned, a topcoat, and finally his overcoat. This took him just under five minutes. When he rejoined his wife in the living room, she had the baby swaddled in her arms, still asleep.

"Go to the back room in the cellar, where your steamer trunk is," he said, "and take this." He gave her a flashlight which they kept in their bedroom. When she hesitated he said roughly, "Go on, get going."

"Aren't you coming?"

"Of course I'm coming," he said. He turned the radio up as far as it would go and noted carefully what the man said. *"This will be a nuclear attack. The target will probably be the aircraft company. You have three minutes to take cover."* He picked up the carton and balanced the bottle of water on it. With the other hand he carried the bucket. Leaving the kitchen door wide open, he went to the cellar, passed through the dark furnace room, and joined his wife.

"Put out the flashlight," he said. "We'll have to save it. We have a minute or two, so listen to me." They could hear the radio upstairs. *"Two minutes,"* it screamed.

"Lie down in the corner of the west and north walls,""he said quickly. "The blast should come from the north if they hit the target, and the house will blow down and fall to the south. Lie on top of the baby and I'll lie on top of you!"

She cuddled the sleeping infant in her arms. "We're going to die right now," she said, as she held the baby closer to her.

"No, we aren't," he said, "we have a chance. Wrap the scarves around your face and the baby's, and lie down." She handed him a plaid woolen scarf and he tied it around his face so that only his eyes showed. He placed the water and food in a corner and then lay down on top of his wife, spreading his arms and legs as much as possible, to cover and protect her.

"Twenty seconds," shrieked the radio. *"Eighteen seconds. Fifteen."*

He looked at his watch as he fell. "Ten seconds," he said aloud. "It's five o'clock. They won't waste a megaton bomb on us. They'll save it for New York." They heard the radio crackle into silence and they hung onto each other, keeping their eyes closed tightly.

Instantaneously the cellar room lit up with a kind of glow they had never seen before, the earthen floor began to rock and heave, and the absolutely unearthly sound began. There was no way of telling how far off it was, the explosion. The sound seemed to be inside them, in their bowels; the very air itself was shattered and blown away in the dreadful sound that went on and on and on.

They held their heads down, hers pushed into the dirt, shielding the baby's scalp, his face crushed into her hair, nothing of their skin exposed to the glow, and the sound went on and on, pulsing curiously, louder than anything they had ever imagined, louder than deafening, quaking in their eardrums, louder and louder until it seemed that what had exploded was there in the room on top of them in a blend of smashed, torn air, cries of the instantly dead, fall of steel, timber, and brick, crash of masonry and glass—they couldn't sort any of it out—all were there, all imaginable noises of destruction synthesized. It was like absolutely nothing they had ever heard before and it so filled their skulls, pushing outward from the brainpan, that they could not divide it into its parts. All that they could understand, if they understood anything, was that this was the ultimate catastrophe, and that they were still recording it, expecting any second to be crushed into blackness, but as long as they were recording it they were still living. They felt, but did not think, this. They only understood it instinctively and held on tighter to each other, waiting for the smash, the crush, the black.

But it became lighter and lighter, the glow in the cellar room, waxing and intensifying itself. It had no color that they recognized through their tightly-shut eyelids. It might have been called green, but it was not green, nor any neighbor of green. Like the noise, it was a dreadful compound of ultimately destructive fire, blast, terrible energy released from a bursting sun, like the birth of the solar system. Incandescence beyond an infinite number of lights swirled around them.

The worst was the nauseous rocking to and fro of the very earth beneath them, worse than an earthquake, which might have seemed reducible to human dimensions, those of some disaster witnessed in the movies or on television. But this was no gaping, opening seam in the earth, but a threatened total destruction of the earth itself, right to its core, a pulverization of the world. They tried like animals to scrabble closer and closer in under the north cellar wall even as they expected it to fall on them. They kept their heads down, waiting for death to take them as it had taken their friends, neighbors, fellow workers, policemen, firemen, soldiers; and the dreadful time passed and still they did not die in the catastrophe. And they began to sense obscurely that the longer they were left uncrushed, the better grew their chances of survival. And pitifully, slowly their feelings began to resume their customary segmented play amongst themselves, while the event was still unfolding. They could not help doing the characteristic, the human thing, the beginning to think and struggle to live.

Through their shut eyelids the light began to seem less incandescent, more recognizably a color familiar to human beings and less terrifying because it might be called a hue of green instead of no-color-at-all. It became green, still glowing and illuminating the cellar like daylight, but anyway green, nameable as such and therefore familiar and less dreadful. The light grew more and more darkly green in an insane harmony with the rocking and the sound.

As the rocking slowed, as they huddled closer and closer in under the north foundation, a split in the cellar wall showed itself almost in front of their hidden faces, and yet the wall stood and did not come in on top of them. It held and, holding, gave them more chance for survival although they didn't know it. The earth's upheaval slowed and sank back and no gaps appeared in the earth under them, no crevasse to swallow them up under the alteration of the earth's crust. And in time the rocking stopped and the floor of their world was still, but they would not move, afraid to move a limb for fear of being caught in the earth's mouth.

The noise continued, but began to distinguish itself in parts, and the worst, basic element attenuated itself; that terrible crash a part of the atmosphere under the bomb had stopped by now, the atmosphere had parted to admit the ball of radioactivity, had been blown hundreds of miles in every direction and had rushed back to regain its place, disputing that place with the ball of radioactivity, so that there grew up a thousand-mile vortex of cyclonic winds around the hub of the displacement. The cyclone was almost comforting, sounding, whistling, in whatever stood upright, not trees certainly, but tangled steel beams and odd bits of masonry. The sound of these winds came to them in the cellar. Soon they were able to name sounds, and distinguish them from others which they heard, mainly sounds of fire—no sounds of the dying, no human cries at all, no sounds of life. Only the fires and cyclonic winds.

Now they could feel, and hear enough to shout to each other over the fire and wind.

The man tried to stir, to ease his wife's position. He could move his torso as far as the waist or perhaps the hips. Below that, although he was in no pain and not paralyzed, he was immobilized by a heavy weight. He could feel his legs and feet; they were sound and unhurt, but he could not move them. He waited, lying there trying to sort things out, until some sort of ordered thought and some communication was possible, when the noise should lessen sufficiently. He could hear his wife shouting something into the dirt in front of her face and he tried to make it out.

"She slept through it," he heard, "she slept through it," and he couldn't believe it, although it was true. The baby lived and recollected none of the horror.

"She slept through it," screamed the wife idiotically, "she's still asleep." It couldn't be true, he thought, it was impossible, but there was no way to check her statement until they could move about. The baby must have been three feet below the blast and the glow, shielded by a two-and-a-half-foot wall of flesh, his and his wife's, and the additional thickness of layers of woolen clothing. She should certainly have survived, if they had, but how could she have slept through the noise, the awful light, and the rocking? He listened and waited, keeping his head down and his face covered.

Supposing that they had survived the initial blast, as seemed to be the case; there was still the fallout to consider. The likelihood, he thought (he was beginning to be able to think) was that they were already being eaten up by radiation and would soon die of monstrous cancers, or plain, simple leukemia, or rottenness of the cortex. It was miraculous that they had lived through the first shock; they could hardly hope that their luck would hold through the later dangers. He thought that the baby might not have been infected so far, shielded as she was, and he began to wonder how she might be helped to evade death from radiation in the next few days. Let her live a week, he thought, and she may go on living into the next generation, if there is one.

Nothing would be the same in the next generation; there would be few people and fewer laws, the national boundaries would have perished—there would be a new world to invent. Somehow the child must be preserved for that, even if their own lives were to be forfeited immediately. He felt perfectly healthy so far, untouched by any creeping sickness as he lay there, forcing himself and the lives beneath him deeper into their burrow. He began to make plans; there was nothing else for him to do, just then.

The noise of the winds had become regular now and the green glow had subsided; the earth was still and they were still together and in the same place, in their cellar, in their home. He thought of his books, his checkbook, his phonograph records, his wife's household appliances. They were gone, of course, which didn't matter. What mattered was that the way they had lived was gone, the whole texture of their habits. The city would be totally uninhabitable. If they were to survive longer, they must get out of the city at once. They would have to decide immediately when they should try to leave the city, and they must keep themselves alive until that time.

"What time is it?" gasped his wife from below him in a tone pitched in almost her normal voice. He was relieved to hear her speak in the commonplace, familiar tone; he had been afraid that hysteria and shock would destroy their personalities all at once. So far they had held together. Later on, when the loss of their whole world sank in, when they appreciated the full extent of their losses, they would run the risk of insanity or, at the least, extreme neurotic disturbance. But right now they could converse, calculate, and wait for the threat of madness to appear days, or years, later.

He looked at his watch. "Eight-thirty," he said. Everything had ended in three-and-a-half hours. "Are you all right?" he asked.

"I think so," she said, "I don't feel any pain and the baby's fine. She's warm and she doesn't seem frightened."

He tried to move his legs and was relieved to see that they answered the nervous impulse. He lifted his head fearfully and twisted it around to see behind him. His legs were buried under a pile of loose brick and rubble which grew smaller toward his thighs; his torso was quite uncovered. "I'm all right," he said, beginning to work his legs free; they were undoubtedly badly bruised, but they didn't seem to be crushed or broken; at the worst he might have torn muscles or a bad sprain. He had to be very careful, he reasoned, as he worked at his legs. He might dislodge something and bring the remnant of the house down around them. Very, very slowly he lifted his torso by doing a push-up with his arms. His wife slid out from underneath, pushing the baby in front of her. When she was free she laid the child gently to one side, whispering to her and promising her food. She crawled around to her husband's side and began to push the bricks off his legs.

"Be careful," he whispered. "Take them as they come. Don't be in too much of a hurry."

She nodded, picking out the bricks gingerly, but as fast as she could. Soon he was able to roll over on his back and sit up. By a quarter to ten he was free and they took time to eat and drink. The three of them sat together in a cramped, narrow space under the cellar beams, perhaps six feet high and six or seven feet square. They were getting air from somewhere although it might be deadly air, and there was no smell of gas. He had been afraid that they might be suffocated in their shelter.

"Do you suppose the food's contaminated?" she asked.

"What if it is?" he said. "So are we, just as much as the food. There's nothing to do but risk it. Only be careful what you give the baby."

"How can I tell?"

"I don't know," he said. "Say a prayer and trust in God." He found the flashlight, which had rolled into a corner, and tried it. It worked very well.

"What are we going to do? We can't stay here."

"I don't even know for sure that we can get out," he said, "but we'll try. There should be a window just above us that leads to a crawl-space under the patio. That's one of the reason why I told you to come here. In any case we'd be wise to stay here for a few hours until the very worst of the fallout is down."

"What'll we do when we get out?"

"Try to get out of town. Get our outer clothes off, get them all off for that matter, and scrub ourselves with water. Maybe we can get to the river."

"Why don't you try the window right now so we can tell whether we can get out?"

"I will as soon as I've finished eating and had a rest. My legs are very sore."

He could hear her voice soften. "Take your time," she said.

When he felt rested, he stood up. He could almost stand erect and with the flashlight was able to find the window quickly. It was level with his face. He piled loose bricks against the wall below it and climbed up on them until the window was level with his chest. Knocking out the screen with the butt of the flashlight, he put his head through and then flashed the light around; there were no obstructions that he could see, and he couldn't smell anything noxious. The patio, being a flat, level space, had evidently been swept clean by the blast without being flattened. They could crawl out of the cellar under the patio, he realized, and then kick a hole in the lath and stucco which skirted it.

He stepped down from the pile of brick and told his wife that they would be able to get out whenever they wished, that the crawl space was clear.

"What time is it?"

"Half-past twelve."

"Should we try it now?"

"I think so," he said. "At first I thought we ought to stay here for a day or two, but now I think we ought to try and get out from under the fallout. We may have to walk a couple of hundred miles."

"We can do it," she said and he felt glad. She had always been able to look unpleasant issues in the face.

He helped her through the cellar window and handed up the baby, who clucked and chuckled when he spoke to her. He pushed the carton of food and the bucket of water after them. Then he climbed up and they inched forward under the patio.

"I hear a motor," said his wife suddenly.

He listened and heard it too.

"Looking for survivors," he said eagerly. "Probably the Army or Civil Defense. Come on."

He swung himself around on his hips and back and kicked out with both feet at the lath and stucco. Three or four kicks did it. His wife went first, inching the baby through the hole. He crawled after her into the daylight; it looked like any other day except that the city was leveled. The sky and the light were the same; everything else was gone. They sat up, muddy, scratched, nervously exhausted, in a ruined flower bed. Not fifty feet away stood an olive-drab truck, the motor running loudly. Men shouted to them.

"Come on, you!" shouted the men in the truck. "Get going!" They stood and ran raggedly to the cab, she holding the child and he their remaining food and water. In the cab was a canvas-sheeted, goggled driver, peering at them through huge eyes. "Get in the back," he ordered. "We've got to get out right away. Too hot." They climbed into the truck and it began to move instantly.

"Army Survival Unit," said a goggled and hooded man in the back of the truck. "Throw away that food and water; it's dangerous. Get your outer clothing off quick. Throw it out!" They obeyed him without thinking, stripping off their loose outer clothes and dropping them out of the truck.

"You're the only ones we've found in a hundred city blocks," said the soldier. "Did you know the war's over? There's a truce."

"Who won?"

"Over in half an hour," he said, "and nobody won."

"What are you going to do with us?"

"Drop you at a check-out point forty miles from here. Give you the scrub-down treatment, wash off the fallout. Medical check for radiation sickness. Clean clothes. Then we send you on your way to a refugee station."

"How many died?"

"Everybody in the area. Almost no exceptions. You're a statistic, that's what you are. Must have been a fluke of the blast."

"Will we live?"

"Sure you will. You're living now, aren't you?"

"I guess so," he said.

"Sure you'll live! Maybe not too long. But everybody else is dead! And you'll be taken care of." He fell silent.

They looked at each other, determined to live as long as they could. The wife cuddled her child close against her thin silk blouse. For a long time they jolted along over rocks and broken pavement without speaking. When the pavement smoothed out the husband knew that they must be out of the disaster area. In a few more minutes they were out of immediate danger; they had reached the check-out point. It was a quarter to three in the afternoon.

"Out you get," said the soldier. "We've got to go back." They climbed out of the truck and he handed down the baby. "You're all right now," he said. "Good luck."

"Good-by," they said.

The truck turned about and drove away and they turned silently, hand in hand, and walked toward the medical tents. They were the seventh, eighth, and ninth living persons to be brought there after the sirens.

Fallout!

Fallout; whether it is the literal or the metaphorical, atomic weapons have changed the course of human history. In our stories the results of the use of atomic weapons sometimes end in the fantastical, while others end mankind with Eliot's final whimper.

Time Enough at Last
Lynn Venable

For a long time, Henry Bemis had had an ambition. To read a book. Not just the title or the preface, or a page somewhere in the middle. He wanted to read the whole thing, all the way through from beginning to end. A simple ambition perhaps, but in the cluttered life of Henry Bemis, an impossibility.

Henry had no time of his own. There was his wife, Agnes who owned that part of it that his employer, Mr. Carsville, did not buy. Henry was allowed enough to get to and from work—that in itself being quite a concession on Agnes' part.

Also, nature had conspired against Henry by handing him with a pair of hopelessly myopic eyes. Poor Henry literally couldn't see his hand in front of his face. For a while, when he was very young, his parents had thought him an idiot. When they realized it was his eyes, they got glasses for him. He was never quite able to catch up. There was never enough time. It looked as though Henry's ambition would never be realized. Then something happened which changed all that.

Henry was down in the vault of the Eastside Bank & Trust when it happened. He had stolen a few moments from the duties of his teller's cage to try to read a few pages of the magazine he had bought that morning. He'd made an excuse to Mr. Carsville about needing bills in large denominations for a certain customer, and then, safe inside the dim recesses of the vault he had pulled from inside his coat the pocket size magazine.

He had just started a picture article cheerfully entitled "The New Weapons and What They'll Do To YOU," when all the noise in the world crashed in upon his eardrums. It seemed to be inside of him and outside of him all at once. Then the concrete floor was rising up at him and the ceiling came slanting down toward him, and for a fleeting second Henry thought of a story he had started to read once called "The Pit and The Pendulum." He regretted in that insane moment that he had never had time to finish that story to see how it came out. Then all was darkness and quiet and unconsciousness.

When Henry came to, he knew that something was desperately wrong with the Eastside Bank & Trust. The heavy steel door of the vault was buckled and twisted and the floor tilted up at a dizzy angle, while the ceiling dipped crazily toward it. Henry gingerly got to his feet, moving arms and legs experimentally. Assured that nothing was broken, he tenderly raised a hand to his eyes. His precious glasses were intact, thank God! He would never have been able to find his way out of the shattered vault without them. He made a mental note to write Dr. Torrance to have a spare pair made and mailed to him. Blasted nuisance not having his prescription on file locally, but Henry trusted no one but Dr. Torrance to grind those thick lenses into his own complicated prescription. Henry removed the heavy glasses from his face. Instantly the room dissolved into a neutral blur. Henry saw a pink splash that he knew was his hand, and a white blob come up to meet the pink as he withdrew his pocket handkerchief and carefully dusted the lenses. As he replaced the glasses, they slipped down on the bridge of his nose a little. He had been meaning to have them tightened for some time.

He suddenly realized, without the realization actually entering his conscious thoughts, that something momentous had happened, something worse than the boiler blowing up, something worse than a gas main exploding, something worse than anything that had ever happened before. He felt that way because it was so quiet. There was no whine of sirens, no shouting, no running, just an ominous and all pervading silence.

Henry walked across the slanting floor. Slipping and stumbling on the uneven surface, he made his way to the elevator. The car lay crumpled at the foot of the shaft like a discarded accordion. There was something inside of it that Henry could not look at, something that had once been a person, or perhaps several people, it was impossible to tell now.

Feeling sick, Henry staggered toward the stairway. The steps were still there, but so jumbled and piled back upon one another that it was more like climbing the side of a mountain than mounting a stairway. It was quiet in the huge chamber that had been the lobby of the bank. It looked strangely cheerful with the sunlight shining through the girders where the ceiling had fallen. The dappled sunlight glinted across the silent lobby, and everywhere there were huddled lumps of unpleasantness that made Henry sick as he tried not to look at them.

"Mr. Carsville," he called. It was very quiet. Something had to be done, of course. This was terrible, right in the middle of a Monday, too. Mr. Carsville would know what to do. He called again, more loudly, and his voice cracked hoarsely, "Mr. Carrrrsville!" And then he saw an arm and shoulder extending out from under a huge fallen block of marble ceiling. In the buttonhole was the white carnation Mr. Carsville had worn to work that morning, and on third finger of that hand was a massive signet ring, also belonging to Mr. Carsville. Numbly, Henry realized that the rest of Mr. Carsville was under that block of marble.

Henry felt a pang of real sorrow. Mr. Carsville was gone, and so was the rest of the staff—Mr. Wilkinson and Mr. Emory and Mr. Prithard, and the same with Pete and Ralph and Jenkins and Hunter and Pat the guard and Willie the doorman. There was no one to say what was to be done about the Eastside Bank & Trust except Henry Bemis, and Henry wasn't worried about the bank, there was something he wanted to do.

He climbed carefully over piles of fallen masonry. Once he stepped down into something that crunched and squashed beneath his feet and he set his teeth on edge to keep from retching. The street was not much different from the inside, bright sunlight and so much concrete to crawl over, but the unpleasantness was much, much worse. Everywhere there were strange, motionless lumps that Henry could not look at.

Suddenly, he remembered Agnes. He should be trying to get to Agnes, shouldn't he? He remembered a poster he had seen that said, "In event of emergency do not use the telephone, your loved ones are as safe as you." He wondered about Agnes. He looked at the smashed automobiles, some with their four wheels pointing skyward like the stiffened legs of dead animals. He couldn't get to Agnes now anyway, if she was safe, then, she was safe, otherwise… of course, Henry knew Agnes wasn't safe. He had a feeling that there wasn't anyone safe for a long, long way, maybe not in the whole state or the whole country, or the whole world. No, that was a thought Henry didn't want to think, he forced it from his mind and turned his thoughts back to Agnes.

She had been a pretty good wife, now that it was all said and done. It wasn't exactly her fault if people didn't have time to read nowadays. It was just that there was the house, and the bank, and the yard. There were the Jones' for bridge and the Graysons' for canasta and charades with the Bryants. And the television, the television Agnes loved to watch, but would never watch alone. He never had time to read even a newspaper. He started thinking about last night, that business about the newspaper.

Henry had settled into his chair, quietly, afraid that a creaking spring might call to Agnes' attention the fact that he was momentarily unoccupied. He had unfolded the newspaper slowly and carefully, the sharp crackle of the paper would have been a clarion call to Agnes. He had glanced at the headlines of the first page. "Collapse Of Conference Imminent." He didn't have time to read the article. He turned to the second page. "Solon Predicts War Only Days Away." He flipped through the pages faster, reading brief snatches here and there, afraid to spend too much time on one item. On a back page was a brief article entitled, "Prehistoric Artifacts Unearthed In Yucatan." Henry smiled to himself and carefully folded the sheet of paper into fourths. That would be interesting, he would read all of it. Then it came, Agnes' voice.

"Henrrreee!" And then she was upon him. She lightly flicked the paper out of his hands and into the fireplace. He saw the flames lick up and curl possessively around the unread article. Agnes continued, "Henry, tonight is the Jones' bridge night. They'll be here in thirty minutes and I'm not dressed yet, and here you are ... reading." She had emphasized the last word as though it were an unclean act. "Hurry and shave, you know how smooth Jasper Jones' chin always looks, and then straighten up this room." She glanced regretfully toward the fireplace. "Oh dear, that paper, the television schedule ... oh well, after the Jones leave there won't be time for anything but the late-late movie and . . . Don't just sit there, Henry, hurrreeee!"

Henry was hurrying now, but hurrying too much. He cut his leg on a twisted piece of metal that had once been an automobile fender. He thought about things like lockjaw and gangrene and his hand trembled as he tied his pocket-handkerchief around the wound. In his mind, he saw the fire again, licking across the face of last night's newspaper. He thought that now he would have time to read all the newspapers he wanted to, only now there wouldn't be any more. That heap of rubble across the street had been the Gazette Building. It was terrible to think there would never be another up to date newspaper. Agnes would have been very upset, no television schedule. But then, of course, no television. He wanted to laugh but he didn't. That wouldn't have been fitting, not at all.

He could see the building he was looking for now, but the silhouette was strangely changed. The great circular dome was now a ragged semi-circle, half of it gone, and one of the great wings of the building had fallen in upon itself. A sudden panic gripped Henry Bemis. What if they were all ruined, destroyed, every one of them? What if there wasn't a single one left? Tears of helplessness welled in his eyes as he painfully fought his way over and through the twisted fragments of the city.

He thought of the building when it had been whole. He remembered the many nights he had paused outside its wide and welcoming doors. He thought of the warm nights when the door had been thrown open and he could see the people inside, see them sitting at the plain wooden tables with the stacks of books beside them. He used to think then, what a wonderful thing a public library was, a place where anybody, anybody at all could go in and read.

He had been tempted to enter many times. He had watched the people through the open doors, the man in greasy work clothes who sat near the door, night after night, laboriously studying, a technical journal perhaps, difficult for him, but promising a brighter future. There had been an aged, scholarly gentleman who sat on the other side of the door, leisurely paging, moving his lips a little as he did so, a man having little time left, but rich in time because he could do with it as he chose.

Henry had never gone in. He had started up the steps once, got almost to the door, but then he remembered Agnes, her questions and shouting, and he had turned away. He was going in now though, almost crawling, his breath coming in stabbing gasps, his hands torn and bleeding. His trouser leg was sticky red where the wound in his leg had soaked through the handkerchief. It was throbbing badly but Henry didn't care. He had reached his destination.

Part of the inscription was still there, over the now doorless entrance. P U B C L I B R . The rest had been torn away. The place was in shambles. The shelves were overturned, broken, smashed, tilted, their precious contents spilled in disorder upon the floor. A lot of the books, Henry noted gleefully, were still intact, still whole, still readable. He was literally knee deep in them, he wallowed in books. He picked one up. The title was "Collected Works of William Shakespeare." Yes, he must read that, sometime. He laid it aside carefully. He picked up another. Spinoza. He tossed it away, seized another, and another, and still another. Which to read first… there were so many.

He had been conducting himself a little like a starving man in a delicatessen— grabbing a little of this and a little of that in a frenzy of enjoyment.

But now he steadied away. From the pile about him, he selected one volume, sat comfortably down on an overturned shelf, and opened the book.

Henry Bemis smiled.

There was the rumble of complaining stone. Minute in comparison which the epic complaints following the fall of the bomb. This one occurred under one corner of the shelf upon which Henry sat. The shelf moved; threw him off balance. The glasses slipped from his nose and fell with a tinkle.

He bent down, clawing blindly and found, finally, their smashed remains. A minor, indirect destruction stemming from the sudden, wholesale smashing of a city. But the only one that greatly interested Henry Bemis.

He stared down at the blurred page before him. He began to cry.

SURVIVOR REGISTRATION AND INFORMATION

After emergence from shelter, everyone will undoubtedly want to obtain information and help. Such assistance will be available at the nearest location designated by local government. Police officers may be available to give directions, with auxiliary police assisting regular police officers. It will be important to obey directions of those on police duty, whether or not they are in uniform. While walking in a suspected contaminated area, a person should try to stay in the middle of streets or roads and avoid contact with anything that might be contaminated.

FIGURE 62.—Auxiliary policeman keeps two people from dangerous area.

If traveling in an automobile should be possible, the windows and vents should be kept closed. Cars may pass rescue teams at work getting people out of buildings or other structures where they have been trapped. The driver or other passengers should not pause to assist members of rescue teams unless they specifically ask for help.

Upon arrival at the welfare center, which may be located in a school, a community shelter, a hospital, a factory, or a government building,

104

In the Department of Defense/Office of Civil Defense handbook, Personal and Family Survival: Civil Defense Adult Education Course Student Manual, revised May 1963, chapter VII discusses what to do once local authorities have declared it is safe to leave the fallout shelter. The tone of the booklet is optimistic and offers a plan to start getting one's life back together after an atomic war. Once a person has relocated, they can send a quick postcard to let their loved ones know where they are. Images of the postcards are on the following page.

advice will be available on where to obtain food, water, and medical assistance. It is advisable to check bulletin boards, signs, or posters in the welfare center, because valuable information may be posted at entrances or in corridors. All notices should be read carefully.

Depending on the size of the community, there will probably be some delays in completing registration for assistance. If so, patience is essential. Those who are taking names must be extremely careful as they note down information from and for people. It is of greatest importance that this information be correct for the sake of the individual as well as for the community. Everyone will want to find out about relatives and friends. They, in turn, will want to know what has happened to their loved ones.

Among other forms that may be filled out during registration are a Post Office Emergency Change of Address and Safety Notification Form. This form will help people to locate loved ones and friends in other areas by mail.

SAFETY NOTIFICATION CARD—NO POSTAGE REQUIRED

DIRECTIONS.—Fill in this card and mail it immediately after evacuation or attack to any person who might be concerned about your safety. Cards may be obtained free at Civil Defense registration points and Post Offices.

I AM
WE ARE SAFE AND CAN BE REACHED AT THIS ADDRESS UNTIL FURTHER NOTICE

_____
(IF UNABLE TO GIVE DEFINITE MAIL ADDRESS SHOW "GENERAL DELIVERY")

_____   _____
(POST OFFICE)   (STATE)

MEMBERS OF FAMILY INCLUDED IN THIS NOTIFICATION (IF NOT INDIVIDUAL SIGNER ONLY)

_____   _____

_____   _____

_____   _____

DATE _____ SIGNATURE _____
POD Form 810 (Feb. 1959)   ☆GPO: 1966 O—799-066

POST OFFICE DEPARTMENT
OFFICIAL BUSINESS

PENALTY FOR PRIVATE USE TO AVOID
PAYMENT OF POSTAGE. $300

(This card for use ONLY in Civil Defense Emergency as indicated on reverse side)

THIS SIDE OF CARD IS FOR ADDRESS

POSTMASTER: THIS CARD MUST BE GIVEN PRIORITY
IN DISTRIBUTION AND DISPATCH

That Only a Mother
Judith Merill

Margaret reached over to the other side of the bed where Hank should have been. Her hand patted the empty pillow, and then she came altogether awake, wondering that the old habit should remain after so many months. She tried to curl up, cat-style, to hoard her own warmth, found she couldn't do it anymore, and climbed out of bed with a pleased awareness of her increasingly clumsy bulkiness.

Morning motions were automatic. On the way through the kitchenette, she pressed the button that would start breakfast cooking—the doctor had said to eat as much breakfast as she could—and tore the paper out of the facsimile machine. She folded the long sheet carefully to the "National News" section, and propped it on the bathroom shelf to scan while she brushed her teeth.

No accidents. No direct hits. At least none that had been officially released for publication. *Now, Maggie, don't get started on that. No accidents. No hits. Take the nice newspaper's word for it.*

The three clear chimes from the kitchen announced that breakfast was ready. She set a bright napkin and cheerful colored dishes on the table in a futile attempt to appeal to a faulty morning appetite. Then, when there was nothing more to prepare, she went for the mail, allowing herself the full pleasure of prolonged anticipation, because today there would surely be a letter.

There was. There were. Two bills and a worried note from her mother: "Darling. Why didn't you write and tell me sooner? I'm thrilled, of course, but, well, one hates to mention these things, but are you certain the doctor was right? Hank's been around all that uranium and thorium or whatever it is all these years, and I know you say he's a designer, not a technician, and he doesn't get near anything that might be dangerous, but you know he used to, back at Oak Ridge. Don't you think… well, of course, I'm just being a foolish old woman, and I don't want you to get upset. You know much more about it than I do, and I'm sure your doctor was right. He should know…"

Margaret made a face over the excellent coffee, and caught herself refolding the paper to the medical news.

Stop it, Maggie, stop it! The radiologist said that Hank's job couldn't have exposed him. And the bombed area we drove past… No, no. Stop it, now! Read the social notes or the recipes, Maggie girl.

A well-known geneticist, in the medical news, said that it was possible to tell with absolute certainty, at five months, whether the child would be normal, or at least whether the mutation was likely to produce anything freakish. The worst cases, at any rate, could be prevented. Minor mutations, of course, displacements in facial features, or changes in brain structure could not be detected. And there had been some cases recently, of normal embryos with atrophied limbs that did not develop beyond the seventh or eighth month. But, the doctor concluded cheerfully, the worst cases could be predicted and prevented.

"Predicted and prevented." We predicted it, didn't we? Hank and the others, they predicted it. But we didn't prevent it. We could have stopped it in '46 and '47. Now...

Margaret decided against the breakfast. Coffee had been enough for her in the morning for ten years; it would have to do for today. She buttoned herself into the interminable folds of material that, the salesgirl had assured her, was the only comfortable thing to wear during the last few months. With a surge of pure pleasure, the letter and newspaper forgotten, she realized that she was on the next to last button. It wouldn't be long now.

The city in the early morning had always been a special kind of excitement for her. Last night it had rained, and the sidewalks were still damp-gray instead of dusty. The air smelled fresher, to a city-bred woman, for the occasional pungency of acrid factory smoke. She walked the six blocks to work, watching the lights go out in the all-night hamburger joints, where the plate glass walls were already catching the sun, and the lights go on in the dim interiors of cigar stores and dry-cleaning establishments.

The office was in a new Government building. In the rolovator, on the way up, she felt, as always, like a frankfurter roll in the ascending half of an old-style rotary toasting machine. She abandoned the air-foam cushioning gratefully at the fourteenth floor, and settled down behind her desk, at the rear of a long row of identical desks.

Each morning the pile of papers that greeted her was a little higher. These were, as everyone knew, the decisive months. The war might be won or lost on these calculations as well as any others. The manpower office had switched her here when her old expediter's job got to be too strenuous. The computer was easy to operate, and the work was absorbing, if not as exciting as the old job. But you didn't just stop working these days. Everyone who could do anything at all was needed.

And—she remembered the interview with the psychologist—*I'm probably the unstable type. Wonder what sort of neurosis I'd get sitting home reading that sensational paper...*

She plunged into work without pursuing the thought.

February 18.

Hank darling,

Just a note—from the hospital, no less. I had a dizzy spell at work, and the doctor took it to heart. Blessed if I know what I'll do with myself lying in bed for weeks, just waiting—but Dr. Boyer seems to think it may not be so long.

There are too many newspapers around here. More infanticides all the time, and they can't seem to get a jury to convict any of them. It's the fathers who do it. Lucky thing you're not around, in case—

Oh darling, that wasn't a very *funny* joke, was it? Write as often as you can, will you? I have too much time to think. But there really isn't anything wrong, and nothing to worry about.

Write often, and remember I love you.

Maggie.

SPECIAL SERVICE TELEGRAM
FEBRUARY 21, 1953
22:04 LK37G
FROM: TECH. LIEUT. H. MARVELL.
X47-016 GCNY
TO: MRS. H. MARVELL
WOMEN'S HOSPITAL
NEW YORK CITY
HAD DOCTOR'S GRAM STOP WILL ARRIVE FOUR OH TEN STOP
SHORT LEAVE STOP YOU DID IT MAGGIE STOP LOVE HANK

February 25.

Hank dear,

So you didn't see the baby either? You'd think a place this size would at least have visiplates on the incubators, so the fathers could get a look, even if the poor benighted mommas can't. They tell me I won't see her for another week, or maybe more—but of course, mother always warned me that if I didn't slow my pace, I'd probably even have my babies too fast. Why must she always be right?

Did you meet that battle-ax of a nurse they put on here? I imagine they save her for people who've already had theirs, and don't let her get too near the prospectives—but a woman like that simply shouldn't be allowed in a maternity ward. She's obsessed with mutations, can't seem to talk about anything else. Oh, well, ours is all right, even if it was in an unholy hurry.

I'm tired. They warned me not to sit up so soon, but I *had* to write you. All my love, darling,

Maggie.

February 29.

Darling,

I finally got to see her! It's all true, what they say about new babies and the face that only a mother could love—but it's all there, darling, eyes, ears, and noses—no, only one!—all in the right places. We're so lucky, Hank.

I'm afraid I've been a rambunctious patient. I kept telling that hatchet-faced female with the mutation mania that I wanted to see the baby. Finally the doctor came in to "explain" everything to me, and talked a lot of nonsense, most of which I'm sure no one could have understood, any more than I did. The only thing I got out of it was that she didn't actually have to stay in the incubator; they just thought it was "wiser."

I think I got a little hysterical at that point. Guess I was more worried than I was willing to admit, but I threw a small fit about it. The whole business wound up with one of those hushed medical conferences outside the door, and finally the Woman in White said: "Well, we might as well. Maybe it'll work out better that way."

I'd heard about the way doctors and nurses in these places develop a God complex, and believe me it is as true figuratively as it is literally that a mother hasn't got a leg to stand on around here.

I *am* awfully weak, still. I'll write again soon. Love,

Maggie

March 8.

Dearest Hank,

Well, the nurse was wrong if she told you that. She's an idiot anyhow. It's a girl. It's easier to tell with babies than with cats, and I *know*. How about Henrietta?

I'm home again, and busier than a betatron. They got *everything* mixed up at the hospital, and I had to teach myself how to bathe her and do just about everything else. She's getting prettier, too. When can you get a leave, a *real* leave?

Love,
Maggie

May 26.

Hank dear,

You should see her now—and you shall. I'm sending you along a reel of color movie. My mother sent her those nighties with drawstrings all over. I put one on, and right now she looks like a snow-white potato sack with that beautiful, beautiful flower-face blooming on top. Is that *me* talking? Am I a doting mother? But wait till you see her!

July 10.

… Believe it or not, as you like, but your daughter can talk, and I don't mean baby talk. Alice discovered it—she's a dental assistant in the WACs, you know—and when she heard the baby giving out what I thought was a string of gibberish, she said the kid knew words and sentences, but couldn't say them clearly because she has no teeth yet. I'm taking her to a speech specialist.

September 13.

… We have a prodigy for real! Now that all her front teeth are in, her speech is perfectly clear and—a new talent now—she can sing! I mean really carry a tune! At seven months! Darling my world would be perfect if you could only get home.

November 19.

… at last. The little goon was so busy being clever, it took her all this time to learn to crawl. The doctor says development in these cases is always erratic…

SPECIAL SERVICE TELEGRAM
DECEMBER 1, 1953
08:47 LK59F
FROM: TECH. LIEUT. H. MARVELL
X47-016 GCNY
TO: MRS. H. MARVELL
APT. K-17
504 E. 19 ST.
N.Y. N.Y

WEEK'S LEAVE STARTS TOMORROW STOP WILL ARRIVE AIRPORT TEN
OH FIVE STOP DON'T MEET ME STOP LOVE LOVE LOVE HANK

Margaret let the water run out of the bathinette until only a few inches were left, and then loosed her hold on the wriggling baby.

"I think it was better when you were retarded, young woman," she informed her daughter happily. "You *can't* crawl in a bathinette, you know."

"Then why can't I go in the bathtub?" Margaret was used to her child's volubility by now, but every now and then it caught her unawares. She swooped the resistant mass of pink flesh into a towel, and began to rub.

"Because you're too little, and your head is very soft, and bathtubs are very hard."

"Oh. Then when can I go in the bathtub?"

"When the outside of your head is as hard as the inside, brainchild." She reached toward a pile of fresh clothing. "I cannot understand," she added, pinning a square of cloth through the nightgown, "why a child of your intelligence can't learn to keep a diaper on the way other babies do. They've been used for centuries, you know, with perfectly satisfactory results."

The child disdained to reply; she heard it too often. She waited patiently until she had been tucked, clean and sweet-smelling, into a white-painted crib. Then she favored her mother with a smile that inevitably made Margaret think of the first golden edge of the sun bursting into a rosy predawn. She remembered Hank's reaction to the color pictures of his beautiful daughter, and with the thought, realized how late it was.

"Go to sleep, puss. When you wake up, you know, your *Daddy* will be here."

"Why?" asked the four-year-old mind, waging a losing battle to keep the ten-month-old body awake.

Margaret went into the kitchenette and set the timer for the roast. She examined the table, and got her clothes from the closet, new dress, new shoes, new slip, new everything, bought weeks before and saved for the day Hank's telegram came. She stopped to pull a paper from the facsimile, and, with clothes and news, went into the bathroom, and lowered herself gingerly into the steaming luxury of a scented tub.

She glanced through the paper with indifferent interest. Today at least there was no need to read the national news. There was an article by a geneticist. The same geneticist. Mutations, he said, were increasing disproportionately. It was too soon for recessives; even the first mutants, born near Hiroshima and Nagasaki in 1946 and 1947 were not old enough yet to breed. *But my baby's all right.* Apparently, there was some degree of free radiation from atomic explosions causing the trouble. *My baby's fine. Precocious, but normal.* If more attention had been paid to the first Japanese mutations, he said...

There was that little notice in the paper in the spring of '47. That was when Hank quit at Oak Ridge. "Only 2 or 3 percent of those guilty of infanticide are being caught and punished in Japan today..." *But* MY BABY'S *all right.*

She was dressed, combed, and ready to the last light brush-on of lip paste, when the door chime sounded. She dashed off for the door, and heard for the first time in eighteen months the almost-forgotten sound of a key turning in the lock before the chime had quite died away.

"Hank!"

"Maggie!"

And then there was nothing to say. So many days, so many months, of small news piling up, so many things to tell him, and now she just stood there, staring at a khaki uniform and a stranger's pale face. She traced the features with the finger of memory. The same high-bridged nose, wide-set eyes, fine feathery brows; the same long jaw, the hair a little farther back now on the high forehead, the same tilted curve to his mouth. Pale... Of course he'd been underground all this time. And strange, stranger because of lost familiarity than any newcomer's face could be.

She had time to think all that before his hand reached out to touch her, and spanned the gap of eighteen months. Now, again, there was nothing to say, because there was no need. They were together, and for the moment that was enough.

"Where's the baby?"

"Sleeping. She'll be up any minute."

No urgency. Their voices were as casual as though it were a daily exchange, as though war and separation did not exist. Margaret picked up the coat he'd thrown down on the chair near the door, and hung it carefully in the hall closet. She went to check the roast, leaving him to wander through the rooms himself, remembering and coming back. She found him, finally, standing over the baby's crib.

She couldn't see his face, but she had no need to.

"I think we can wake her just this once." Margaret pulled the covers down and lifted the white bundle from the bed. Sleepy lids pulled back heavily from smoky brown eyes.

"Hello." Hank's voice was tentative.

"Hello." The baby's assurance was more pronounced.

He had heard about it, of course, but that wasn't the same as hearing it. He turned eagerly to Margaret. "She really can—?"

"Of course she can, darling. But what's more important, she can even do nice normal things like other babies do, even stupid ones. Watch her crawl!" Margaret set the baby on the big bed.

For a moment young Henrietta lay and eyed her parents dubiously.

"Crawl?" she asked.

"That's the idea. Your daddy is new around here, you know. He wants to see you show off."

"Then put me on my tummy."

"Oh, of course." Margaret obligingly rolled the baby over.

"What's the matter?" Hank's voice was still casual, but an undercurrent in it began to charge the air of the room. "I thought they turned over first."

"This baby," Margaret would not notice the tension. "*This* baby does things when she wants to."

The baby's father watched with softening eyes while the head advanced and the body hunched up propelling itself across the bed.

"Why, the little rascal." He burst into relieved laughter. "She looks like one of those potato-sack racers they used to have on picnics. Got her arms pulled out of the sleeves already." He reached over and grabbed the knot at the bottom of the long nightie.

"I'll do it, darling." Margaret tried to get there first.

"Don't be silly, Maggie. This may be *your* first baby, but *I* had five kid brothers." He laughed her away, and reached with his other hand for the string that closed one sleeve. He opened the sleeve bow, and groped for an arm.

"The way you wriggle," he addressed his child sternly, as his hand touched a moving knob of flesh at the shoulder, "anyone might think you are a worm, using your tummy to crawl on, instead of your hands and feet."

Margaret stood and watched, smiling. "Wait till you hear her sing, darling—"

His right hand traveled down from shoulder the shoulder to where he thought an arm would be, traveled down, and straight down, over firm small muscles that writhed in an attempt to move against the pressure of his hand. He let his fingers drift up again to the shoulder. With infinite care he opened the knot at the bottom of the nightgown. His wife was standing by the bed, saying, "She can do 'Jingle Bells,' and—"

His left hand felt along the soft knitted fabric of the gown, up toward the diaper that folded, flat and smooth, across the bottom end of his child. No wrinkles. No kicking. *No…*

"Maggie." He tried to pull his hands from the neat fold in the diaper, from the wriggling body.

"Maggie." His throat was dry; words came hard, low, and grating. He spoke very slowly, thinking the sound of each word to make himself say it. His head was spinning, but he had to know before he let it go.

"Maggie, why... didn't you... tell me?"

"Tell you what, darling?" Margaret's poise was the immemorial patience of a woman confronted with the man's childish impetuosity. Her sudden laugh sounded fantastically easy and natural in that room; it was all clear to her now. "Is she wet? I didn't know."

She didn't know. His hands, beyond control, ran up and down the soft-skinned baby body, the sinuous, limbless body. *Oh God, dear God*—his head shook and his muscles contracted in a bitter spasm of hysteria. His fingers tightened on his child—*Oh God, she didn't know...*

Still image from one of the houses used in Operation Cue, fully decorated with a father and baby mannequin as test subjects. (Photograph—United States Archives.)

About Time To Go South
Douglas Angus

The two men walked along the wide, empty street, their heavy shoes crunching on the endless shards of glass.

"I thought it would be easy," the tall one said, "but there aren't any signs."

"The signs were always printed on the second-story windows," the short, redheaded one said. "Don't you remember? And now there aren't any windows, so there aren't any signs." As he spoke, his mouth, as much of it as showed through his fox-brush beard, seemed to squirm around to one side of his face.

They continued on through the silence. Once the tall one stooped and picked up a fragment of brick to throw at three crows perched on a crumbling cornice, but before the jagged crumble of clay left his hand, the soot-colored birds went flapping down the street between the high buildings. "Haw, haw, haw!" they went. They sounded as if they were inside a huge barrel.

"They're so damn smug," the tall one said.

They stopped at a corner where the wind came up cold and salty from the water. Above their heads a rusty sign swung slowly back and forth with long, melancholy groans.

"Reminds me of my grandfather's old farm," the tall one said. "It was by the sea. What a lonely place! Something used to creak like that all the time. The funny thing is I never found out what it was. Something loose high up among the eaves of the barns—like a creaking in the sky. It was the noise that made the place so lonely."

"They liked to have their offices on corners like this," the short one said. "You can see how that would be. Then people coming along both streets could see the signs on the windows, and people waiting for the light to change would look up and see them, and people getting off the buses—"

"There was a big book in the parlor with pictures—one book besides the Bible," the tall one went on. "I read it through every summer on rainy afternoons, because there was nothing else to do. It was called *The Holy War*, by a man named Bunyan. Imagine a name like Bunyan."

"*The Holy War*, eh." The short one stared hard at the second-story window openings, trying to see into the darkness of the rooms. "That's a good one. They were all holy wars."

"Unholy, you mean."

"Holy, unholy. What's the difference now."

The tall one looked at him for a moment. "Hurts, eh?"

"Like holy hell. Like someone was pounding it with a red-hot poker."

"You want me to try up there?" The tall one nodded toward the windows above their heads.

"Yeah—do you mind? I'll try the ones across the street."

They separated, the short one crossing the street, the tall one stepping right through a door that had once contained a full-length panel of glass. It was dark on the steps and pitch black in the upper hallway. He moved cautiously. You never could tell what you would stumble over in the darkness. And as he moved along the wall, he felt for doorknobs and each time he found one he swung the door open, letting in a shaft of gray light and the cool, strong wind. Papers and dust swirled down the hail behind him. Then he found what he was looking for—a door with a name, DR. EUGENE SPRAGUE, and under it the one word, DENTIST. He walked quickly through the waiting room with its wicker furniture and its moldy copies of *The Saturday Evening Post* and *Life* to the inner office, and there it was: the familiar chair, the adjustable round light—dead—the little trays and the basin with the hooked silver spout—dry—and swinging loose on its cantilever, with its little wheels and cords, that instrument of torture. Staring at that he suddenly remembered, years ago, when he was a small boy, the old dentist holding the drill daintily like a pencil and saying, "If they would just let me at Hitler with this for five minutes!" He had been shocked at the expression on the face of the old man dedicated to the easing of pain—the big outside hate breaking through to his little-boy world. He walked over to the cabinet and began pulling out the small drawers until he found what he wanted, the squat, evil-beaked, silver-plated forceps. For a long moment he held the thing in his hand, looking at it, until his wrist began to ache and he realized that he had been gripping the handle with all his strength.

He leaned out of the glassless window and, when his companion appeared on the sidewalk, he called down, "I've found it."

For half a minute the red face between the red hair and the red beard was turned up to him, and the words came reluctantly. "OK, I'll come up."

The man in the office turned around. He brushed away the cobwebs hanging between the arms of the chair, and swung it around to face the window sill; he opened the forceps and clamped it with gentle pressure onto the index finger of his left hand, after a while increasing the pressure until the pain grew intense. It hung there like a predatory bird. He shivered slightly and looked up to see the short one standing just inside the door with his eyes fixed on the forceps.

"Do you still want to go through with it?" the tall one said.

"Got to. No way out of it. Got to take out the tooth or chop off my head. It's one or the other." He came forward and rested his arm on the arm of the chair.

"I haven't the slightest idea of how to go about it, you know," the tall one said.

"There can't be much to it. Just get a good grip and pull. Let's see the damn thing." The man by the chair reached out for the forceps and turned it over and over, examining it with fascination. "They used to keep it out of sight," he said. "They'd come sidling up with one hand behind them, sort of absent-minded, and say, 'Open,' in a soft voice, and the next thing you knew your jaw was cracking in—two—not hurting, just cracking and you could feel a big hunk of you leaving you." He looked up briefly. "That was all right with me then—not seeing it, I mean." He peered closer at the instrument in his hand. "You see those grooves ?" He pointed with stubby fingers. "They're turned back like shark's teeth." He closed the forceps and rested his fingers on the curved space between the jaw. "Curved. To cup right around the tooth. There must be different ones for different teeth." He looked up again. "This the only one you found?"

"Yes, the only one."

"Well—" The short man fingered his beard with one hand, then handed over the forceps. For a few seconds he stood as if rooted, looking down at the seat of the chair. At last he seemed to jerk forward like a marionette; at the same time he reached into his breast pocket and pulled out a pint bottle of whisky. "I don't know whether this will really do any good. I read about it somewhere. I swallow as much as I can take in one long gulp and then, while my mouth is still open and I'm gasping for air, you yank her out."

"Why, that's no good," the tall man said. "No good at all. That isn't the way they did it. You drank and drank until you passed out. One swallow isn't going to help any."

The short man looked at him with helpless, appealing eyes. "Jesus," he said. "I don't think I can go through with it. I'm scared out of my wits." He pulled himself forward and sank into the seat. "I've gotten soft. We all got soft. All those drugs— aspirin, ether. They spoiled us. They used to tell me my great-aunt had all her lowers pulled out at one sitting by a horse doctor, without batting an eye."

"Well, I don't want to discourage you," the tall man said. "A long swig might help at that. It does sort of hit you like a sledgehammer—the whisky, I mean." He leaned forward. "Let me see the tooth again. I wouldn't want to pull out the wrong one." He grinned slightly.

The man in the chair opened his mouth and inserted a forefinger.

The other nodded. "Let me try the forceps on it—just for hold." There was a slight moisture on his forehead, which he wiped away with the back of his hand. He bent forward and inserted the forceps clumsily, turning it this way and that, his eye almost inside the stretched lips. "Can't you open any wider?" he said.

The red beard quivered violently and a faint squeak came from deep in the throat.

The tall man shifted his hold on the forceps to his left hand. Then he took it in both hands and began to pull.

"Feel anything?" he asked.

The short man shook his head.

The tall man braced a foot against the chair and leaned back slowly, his eyes resting on the eyes of the other. The face of the man in the chair began to get red again, and all at once he put up his hand.

The tall man straightened up. "I had a good grip on it," he said. "I should have yanked her out."

"Oh, no. Not before I get this whisky into me." The man in the chair lifted the bottle. His hand shook a little. He drew a deep breath, closed his eyes and tipped the bottle. As the fiery liquor ran down his throat his face grew a deeper and deeper red and the veins in his neck swelled. Suddenly he pulled the bottle away with a loud gasp, his mouth open, his lips drawn back, baring his teeth in a wide grin.

Swiftly the tall man leaned forward, both hands on the forceps. He was crouched over like a rigid question mark, his head sideways, his forehead brushed by the red beard. When he had the tooth in the forceps, he gripped the handle so hard that the muscles of his forearms bulged like tennis balls. His own lips drew back in a mimetic grin as tigerish as that of his patient. Bracing himself he gave the forceps a terrific jerk, and the man in the chair rose straight up on his arms, uttered an ear-splitting yell, and then slumped back against the padded seat.

"I got it," the tall one said, then stopped short, regarding the forceps. "Christ!" he said softly. "It must have broken off."

The crumpled figure in the chair stared with dismayed eyes at the forceps. After a while he pushed himself up straight. "It's no use," he said. "I can't go through with it again."

"Whisky didn't help much, eh?" The tall man carefully dropped the fragment of tooth onto the white glass tray.

"No." The redheaded man's face was as white as paper again. His eyes roved around the office, like the eye of a starving bird. Suddenly his glance stopped on a small object lying almost hidden among the cluster of bottles on the cabinet shelf. For a long moment he stared at it. Then a deep sigh that was almost a groan, but a groan of relief, escaped his lips.

His whole body seemed to relax, and his eyes grew bright and fresh like the eyes of a man suddenly coming out of a deep fever. "What have we been thinking of!" he exclaimed, and his voice was such a joy to hear that the tall man looked at him in sudden dismay. "All you have to do is give me a shot of novocain. There must be some around here somewhere." In a moment he was out of the chair fumbling among the innumerable little phials that filled the shelves of the cabinet. As he searched he mopped his forehead and neck with a handkerchief. "I can't find it," he said. "Where the devil did the bastard keep the stuff?"

"It doesn't matter," the other said. "If we don't find any here, we will in some other office."

Suddenly the short one held up a small green bottle. "Ah!" he said. He peered at the label with shining eyes. Then he held the bottle up to the light, staring at it as if it were the very elixir of life. With his free hand he reached for the needle.

"That will have to be sterilized," the tall one said.

"We could boil it."

The tall one shook his head. "Might break it, and then where would we be?"

The short one looked around. He spied a bottle of alcohol. "Here we are," he said. "This will do the trick."

Back in the chair, he waited, relaxed, while the tall man, holding the needle gingerly, peered into his mouth. Then he shifted his head away slightly and said, "Don't drop it whatever you do."

The tall one moved the needle slowly in. "I think about there," he said.

"You make a little ring of them right around the tooth," the short one said, gripping the arms of the chair again.

The tall one held the needle as if it were a coral snake that might turn around and sting him in the finger. "Ready?" he asked.

The short one nodded. He quivered slightly as the needle went home. His eyes were wide open, staring at the ceiling.

The tall one stood back and the air escaped from his lungs with a loud gasp. "So far, so good," he said.

"I think it's going to work," the short one said.

"Let's not count our chickens." The tall one inserted the needle again. He made four insertions, using up all the novocain in the little bottle. Then he sat back on the window ledge and lit a cigarette. His hand shook like a leaf. "How does it feel?" he asked.

The other probed his gums with his finger. "Fine," he said. "I don't feel a thing. You've froze it up good. It feels like a hunk of cement."

"All right. Let's go." The tall one tossed his cigarette out into the street and picked up the forceps. He worked away at the other's mouth, then leaned back for a moment, breathing hard.

"I think you're beginning to enjoy this," the man in the chair said.

"I've lost about five pounds, that's all." The tall man leaned forward. "Here, open your damn trap." He worked away some more. Once he started to pull, but the forceps slipped off and he cursed softly. He tried again, pulling gently and then with all his strength. The man in the chair grew as rigid as a board. Suddenly the forceps came away, and there before their eyes was the source of evil—the yellowish brown tooth, blunt, decayed, one corner broken. They bent over it curiously. At the root was a white pustule.

The man in the chair leaned over and spat into the basin. His face was radiant. "I'm a new man," he said. "I feel like a million dollars." He stepped down from the chair.

"If you don't mind," the tall one said, "I'll take a swig from that bottle."

"Why, sure." The short one thrust out the bottle. "Take it all. Anything I have is yours. You saved my life."

"The novocain did the trick," the tall one said. "You thank the man who invented the novocain." He tipped the bottle and swallowed.

"By God, I do—with all my heart. Of all the men who ever lived—"

They walked out through the door and down the dark stairway. "I guess you did suffer more than I did," the short one said.

"I sweated a little. I hope you'll do the same for me some day."

"We ought to eat nuts and roots instead of all this canned stuff. We got to live more like animals."

"You know I even think I could handle that drill," the tall one said.

They came out onto the street and stood for a moment on the corner.

"What street is this anyway?" the short one said. "It might be good to know."

"I doubt we'll ever pass here again." The tall man peered up at the sign. "Broadway and One Hundred and Twenty-fifth," he said.

The short one pulled up his coat collar. "It's gotten dark," he said, "and colder."

"Yes." The tall one looked up at the gray sky. "We've stayed up here long enough. It's about time to go South."

Members of The Atomic Energy Commission view the detonation of an atomic bomb as part of Operation Cue. (Photograph—United States Archives.)

To Pay the Piper

James Blish

The man in the white jacket stopped at the door marked "Re-Education Project—Col. H. H. Mudgett, Commanding Officer" and waited while the scanner looked him over. He had been through that door a thousand times, but the scanner made as elaborate a job of it as if it had never seen him before.

It always did, for there was always in fact a chance that it had never seen him before, whatever the fallible human beings to whom it reported might think. It went over him from grey, crew-cut poll to reagent-proof shoes, checking his small wiry body and lean profile against its stored silhouettes, tasting and smelling him as dubiously as if he were an orange held in storage two days too long.

"Name?" it said at last.

"Carson, Samuel, 32-434-0698."

"Business?"

"Medical director, Re-Ed One."

While Carson waited, a distant, heavy concussion came rolling down upon him through the mile of solid granite above his head. At the same moment, the letters on the door—and everything else inside his cone of vision—blurred distressingly, and a stab of pure pain went lancing through his head. It was the supersonic component of the explosion, and it was harmless—except that it always both hurt and scared him.

The light on the door-scanner, which had been glowing yellow up to now, flicked back to red again and the machine began the whole routine all over; the sound-bomb had reset it. Carson patiently endured its inspection, gave his name, serial number and mission once more, and this time got the green. He went in, unfolding as he walked the flimsy square of cheap paper he had been carrying all along.

Mudgett looked up from his desk and said at once: "What now?" The physician tossed the square of paper down under Mudgett's eyes. "Summary of the press reaction to Hamelin's speech last night," he said. "The total effect is going against us, Colonel. Unless we can change Hamelin's mind, this outcry to re-educate civilians ahead of soldiers is going to lose the war for us. The urge to live on the surface again has been mounting for ten years; now it's got a target to focus on. Us."

Mudgett chewed on a pencil while he read the summary; a blocky, bulky man, as short as Carson and with hair as grey and close-cropped. A year ago, Carson would have told him that nobody in Re-Ed could afford to put stray objects in his mouth even once, let alone as a habit; now Carson just waited. There wasn't a man—or a woman or a child—of America's surviving thirty-five million "sane" people who didn't have some such tic. Not now, not after twenty-five years of underground life.

"He knows it's impossible, doesn't he?" Mudgett demanded abruptly.

"Of course he doesn't," Carson said impatiently. "He doesn't know any more about the real nature of the project than the people do. He thinks the 'educating' we do is in some sort of survival technique—that's what the papers think, too, as you can plainly see by the way they loaded that editorial."

"Um. If we'd taken direct control of the papers in the first place—"

Carson said nothing. Military control of every facet of civilian life was a fact, and Mudgett knew it. He also knew that an appearance of freedom to think is a necessity for the human mind—and that the appearance could not be maintained without a few shreds of the actuality.

"Suppose we do this," Mudgett said at last. "Hamelin's position in the State Department makes it impossible for us to muzzle him. But it ought to be possible to explain to him that no unprotected human being can live on the surface, no matter how many Merit Badges he has for woodcraft and first aid. Maybe we could even take him on a little trip topside; wager he's never seen it."

"And what if he dies up there?" Carson said stonily. "We lose three-fifths of every topside party as it is and Hamelin's an inexperienced—"

"Might be the best thing, mightn't it?"

"*No*," Carson said. "It would look like we'd planned it that way. The papers would have the populace boiling by the next morning."

Mudgett groaned and nibbled another double row of indentations around the barrel of the pencil. "There must be something," he said.

"There is."

"Well?"

"Bring the man here and show him just what we *are* doing. Re-educate *him*, if necessary. Once we told the newspapers that he'd taken the course... well, who knows, they just might resent it. Abusing his clearance privileges and so on."

"We'd be violating our basic policy," Mudgett said slowly. "'Give the Earth back to the men who fight for it.' Still, the idea has some merits..."

"Hamelin is out in the antechamber right now," Carson said. "Shall I bring him in?"

The radioactivity never did rise much beyond a mildly hazardous level, and that was only transient, during the second week of the war —the week called the Death of Cities. The small shards of sanity retained by the high commands on both sides dictated avoiding weapons with a built-in backfire: no cobalt bombs were dropped, no territories permanently poisoned. Generals still remembered that unoccupied territory, no matter how devastated, is still unconquered territory.

But no such considerations stood in the way of biological warfare. It was controllable: you never released against the enemy any disease you didn't yourself know how to control. There would be some slips, of course, but the margin for error…

There were some slips. But for the most part, biological warfare worked fine. The great fevers washed like tides around and around the globe, one after another. In such cities as had escaped the bombings, the rumble of truck convoys carrying the puffed heaped corpses to the mass graves became the only sound except for sporadic small-arms fire; and then that too ceased, and the trucks stood rusting in rows.

Nor were human beings the sole victims. Cattle fevers were sent out. Wheat rusts, rice molds, corn blights, hog choleras, poultry enteritises fountained into the indifferent air from the hidden laboratories, or were loosed far aloft, in the jet stream, by rocketing fleets. Gelatin capsules pullulating with gill-rots fell like hail into the great fishing grounds of Newfoundland, Oregon, Japan, Sweden, Portugal. Hundreds of species of animals were drafted as secondary hosts for human diseases, were injected and released to carry the blessings of the laboratories to their mates and litters. It was discovered that minute amounts of the tetracycline-series of antibiotics, which had long been used as feed supplements to bring farm animals to full market weight early, could also be used to raise the most whopping Anopheles and Aëdes mosquitoes anybody ever saw, capable of flying long distances against the wind and of carrying a peculiarly interesting new strains of the malarial parasite and the yellow fever virus…

By the time it had ended, everyone who remained alive was a mile underground. For good.

"I still fail to understand why," Hamelin said, "if, as you claim, you have methods of reeducating soldiers for surface life, you can't do so for civilians as well. Or instead."

The under-secretary, a tall, spare man, bald on top, and with a heavily creased forehead, spoke with the odd neutral accent—untinged by regionalism—of the trained diplomat, despite the fact that there had been no such thing as a foreign service for nearly half a century.

"We're going to try to explain that to you," Carson said. "But we thought that, first of all, we'd try to explain once more why we think it would be bad policy—as well as physically out of the question.

"Sure, everybody wants to go topside as soon as it's possible. Even people who are reconciled to these endless caverns and corridors hope for something better for their children—a glimpse of sunlight, a little rain, the fall of a leaf. That's more important now to all of us than the war, which we don't believe in any longer. That doesn't even make any military sense, since we haven't the numerical strength to occupy the enemy's territory any more, and they haven't the strength to occupy ours. We understand all that. But we also know that the enemy is intent on prosecuting the war to the end. Extermination is what they say they want, on their propaganda broadcasts, and your own Department reports that they seem to mean what they say. So we can't give up fighting them; that would be simple suicide. Are you still with me?"

"Yes, but I don't see—"

"Give me a moment more. If we have to continue to fight, we know this much: that the first of the two sides to get men on the surface again—so as to be able to attack important targets, not just keep them isolated in seas of plagues—will be the side that will bring this war to an end. They know that, too. We have good reason to believe that they have a re-education project, and that it's about as far advanced as ours is."

"Look at it this way," Col. Mudgett burst in unexpectedly. "What we have now is a stalemate. A saboteur occasionally locates one of the underground cities and lets the pestilences into it. Sometimes on our side, sometimes on theirs. But that only happens sporadically, and it's just more of this mutual extermination business—to which we're committed, willy-nilly, for as long as they are. If we can get troops onto the surface first, we'll be able to scout out their important installations in short order, and issue them a surrender ultimatum with teeth in it. They'll take it. The only other course is the sort of slow, mutual suicide we've got now."

Hamelin put the tips of his fingers together. "You gentlemen lecture me about policy as if I had never heard the word before. I'm familiar with your arguments for sending soldiers first. You assume that you're familiar with all of mine for starting with civilians, but you're wrong, because some of them haven't been brought up at all outside the Department. I'm going to tell you some of them, and I think they'll merit your close attention."

Carson shrugged. "I'd like nothing better than to be convinced, Mr. Secretary. Go ahead."

"You of all people should know, Dr. Carson, how close our underground society is to a psychotic break. To take a single instance, the number of juvenile gangs roaming these corridors of ours has increased 400% since the rumors about the Re-Education Project began to spread. Or another: the number of individual crimes without motive—crimes committed, just to distract the committer from the grinding monotony of the life we all lead—has now passed the total of all other crimes put together.

"And as for actual insanity—of our thirty-five million people still unhospitalized, there are four million cases of which we know, each one of which should be committed right now for early paranoid schizophrenia—except that were we to commit them, our essential industries would suffer a manpower loss more devastating than anything the enemy has inflicted upon us. Every one of those four million persons is a major hazard to his neighbors and to his job, but how can we do without them? And what can we do about the unrecognized, subclinical cases, which probably total twice as many? How long can we continue operating without a collapse under such conditions?"

Carson mopped his brow. "I didn't suspect that it had gone that far."

"It has gone that far," Hamelin said icily, "and it is accelerating. Your own project has helped to accelerate it. Col. Mudgett here mentioned the opening of isolated cities to the pestilences. Shall I tell you how Louisville fell?"

"A spy again, I suppose," Mudgett said.

"No, Colonel. Not a spy. A band of—of vigilantes, of mutineers. I'm familiar with your slogan, 'The Earth to those who fight for it.' Do you know the counter-slogan that's circulating among the people?"

They waited. Hamelin smiled and said: "'Let's die on the surface.'"

"They overwhelmed the military detachment there, put the city administration to death, and blew open the shaft to the surface. About a thousand people actually made it to the top. Within twenty-four hours the city was dead—as the ringleaders had been warned would be the outcome. The warning didn't deter them. Nor did it protect the prudent citizens who had no part in the affair."

Hamelin leaned forward suddenly. "People won't wait to be told when it's their turn to be re-educated. They'll be tired of waiting, tired to the point of insanity of living at the bottom of a hole. They'll just go.

"And that, gentlemen, will leave the world to the enemy... or, more likely, the rats. They alone are immune to everything by now."

There was a long silence. At last Carson said mildly: "Why aren't we immune to everything by now?"

"Eh? Why—the new generations. They've never been exposed."

"We still have a reservoir of older people who lived through the war: people who had one or several of the new diseases that swept the world, some as many as five, and yet recovered. They still have their immunities; we know; we've tested them. We know from sampling that no new disease has been introduced by either side in over ten years now. Against all the known ones, we have immunization techniques, antisera, antibiotics, and so on. I suppose you get your shots every six months like all the rest of us; we should all be very hard to infect now, and such infections as do take should run mild courses." Carson held the under-secretary's eyes grimly. "Now, answer me this question why is it that, despite all these protections, every single person in an opened city dies?"

"I don't know," Hamelin said, staring at each of them in turn. "By your showing, some of them should recover."

"They should," Carson said. "But nobody does. Why? Because the very nature of disease has changed since we all went underground. There are now abroad in the world a number of mutated bacterial strains which can bypass the immunity mechanisms of the human body altogether. What this means in simple terms is that, should such a germ get into your body, your body wouldn't recognize it as an invader. It would manufacture no antibodies against the germ. Consequently, the germ could multiply without any check, and—you would die. So would we all."

"I see," Hamelin said. He seemed to have recovered his composure extraordinarily rapidly. "I am no scientist, gentlemen, but what you tell me makes our position sound perfectly hopeless. Yet obviously you have some answer."

Carson nodded. "We do. But it's important for you to understand the situation, otherwise the answer will mean nothing to you. So: is it perfectly clear to you now, from what we've said so far, that no amount of re-educating a man's brain, be he soldier or civilian, will allow him to survive on the surface?"

"Quite clear," Hamelin said, apparently ungrudgingly. Carson's hopes rose by a fraction of a millimeter. "But if you don't re-educate his brain, what can you re-educate? His reflexes, perhaps?"

"No," Carson said. "His lymph nodes, and his spleen."

A scornful grin began to appear on Hamelin's thin lips. "You need better public relations counsel than you've been getting," he said. "If what you say is true—as of course I assume it is—then the term 're-educate' is not only inappropriate, it's downright misleading. If you had chosen a less suggestive and more accurate label in the beginning, I wouldn't have been able to cause you half the trouble I have."

"I agree that we were badly advised there," Carson said. "But not entirely for those reasons. Of course the name is misleading; that's both a characteristic and a function of the names of top secret projects. But in this instance, the name 'Re-Education', bad as it now appears, subjected the men who chose it to a fatal temptation. You see, though it is misleading, it is also entirely accurate."

"Word-games," Hamelin said.

"Not at all," Mudgett interposed. "We were going to spare you the theoretical reasoning behind our project, Mr. Secretary, but now you'll just have to sit still for it. The fact is that the body's ability to distinguish between its own cells and those of some foreign tissue—a skin graft, say, or a bacterial invasion of the blood—isn't an inherited ability. It's a learned reaction. Furthermore, if you'll think about it a moment, you'll see that it has to be. Body cells die, too, and have to be disposed of; what would happen if removing those dead cells provoked an antibody reaction, as the destruction of foreign cells does? We'd die of anaphylactic shock while we were still infants.

"For that reason, the body has to learn how to scavenge selectively. In human beings, that lesson isn't learned completely until about a month after birth. During the intervening time, the newborn infant is protected by antibodies that it gets from the colostrum, the 'first milk' it gets from the breast during the three or four days immediately after birth. It can't generate its own; it isn't allowed to, so to speak, until it's learned the trick of cleaning up body residues without triggering the antibody mechanisms. Any dead cells marked 'personal' have to be dealt with some other way."

"That seems clear enough," Hamelin said. "But I don't see its relevance."

"Well, we're in a position now where that differentiation between the self and everything outside the body doesn't do us any good any more. These mutated bacteria have been 'selfed' by the mutation. In other words, some of their protein molecules, probably desoxyribonucleic acid molecules, carry configurations or 'recognition-units' identical with those of our body cells, so that the body can't tell one from another."

"But what has all this to do with re-education?"

"Just this," Carson said. "What we do here is to impose upon the cells of the body—all of them—a new set of recognition-units for the guidance of the lymph nodes and the spleen, which are the organs that produce antibodies. The new units are highly complex, and the chances of their being duplicated by bacterial evolution, even under forced draught, are too small to worry about. That's what Re-Education is. In a few moments, if you like, we'll show you just how it's done."

Hamelin ground out his fifth cigarette in Mudgett's ashtray and placed the tips of his fingers together thoughtfully. Carson wondered just how much of the concept of recognition-marking the under-secretary had absorbed. It had to be admitted that he was astonishingly quick to take hold of abstract ideas, but the self-marker theory of immunity was—like everything else in immunology—almost impossible to explain to laymen, no matter how intelligent.

"This process," Hamelin said hesitantly. "It takes a long time?"

"About six hours per subject, and we can handle only one man at a time. That means that we can count on putting no more than seven thousand troops into the field by the turn of the century. Every one will have to be a highly trained specialist, if we're to bring the war to a quick conclusion."

"Which means no civilians," Hamelin said. "I see. I'm not entirely convinced, but—by all means let's see how it's done."

Once inside, the under-secretary tried his best to look everywhere at once. The room cut into the rock was roughly two hundred feet high. Most of it was occupied by the bulk of the Re-Education Monitor, a mechanism as tall as a fifteen-story building, and about a city block square. Guards watched it on all sides, and the face of the machine swarmed with technicians.

"Incredible," Hamelin murmured. "That enormous object can process only one man at a time?"

"That's right," Mudgett said. "Luckily it doesn't have to treat all the body cells directly. It works through the blood, re-selfing the cells by means of small changes in the serum chemistry."

"What kind of changes?"

"Well," Carson said, choosing each word carefully, "that's more or less a graveyard secret, Mr. Secretary. We can tell you this much: the machine uses a vast array of crystalline, complex sugars which behave rather like the blood group-and-type proteins. They're fed into the serum in minute amounts, under feedback control of second-by-second analysis of the blood. The computations involved in deciding upon the amount and the precise nature of each introduced chemical are highly complex. Hence the size of the machine. It is, in its major effect, an artificial kidney."

"I've seen artificial kidneys in the hospitals," Hamelin said, frowning. "They're rather compact affairs."

"Because all they do is remove waste products from the patient's blood, and restore the fluid and electrolyte balance. Those are very minor renal functions in the higher mammals. The organ's main duty is chemical control of immunity. If Burnet and Fenner had known that back in 1949, when the selfing theory was being formulated, we'd have had Re-Education long before now."

"Most of the machine's size is due to the computation section," Mudgett emphasized. "In the body, the brain-stem does those computations, as part of maintaining homeostasis. But we can't reach the brain-stem from outside; it's not under conscious control. Once the body is re-selfed, it will re-train the thalamus where we can't."

Suddenly, two swinging doors at the base of the machine were pushed apart and a mobile operating table came through, guided by two attendants. There was a form on it, covered to the chin with a sheet. The face above the sheet was immobile and almost as white.

Hamelin watched the table go out of the huge cavern with visibly mixed emotions. He said: "This process—it's painful?"

"No, not exactly," Carson said. The motive behind the question interested him hugely, but he didn't dare show it. "But any fooling around with the immunity mechanisms can give rise to symptoms—fever, general malaise, and so on. We try to protect our subjects by giving them a light shock anesthesia first."

"Shock?" Hamelin repeated. "You mean electroshock? I don't see how—"

"Call it stress anesthesia instead. We give the man a steroid drug that counterfeits the anesthesia the body itself produces in moments of great stress—on the battlefield, say, or just after a serious injury. It's fast, and free of after-effects. There's no secret about that, by the way; the drug involved is 21-hydroxypregnane-3,20 dione sodium succinate, and it dates all the way back to 1955."

"Oh," the under-secretary said. The ringing sound of the chemical name had had, as Carson had hoped, a ritually soothing effect.

"Gentlemen," Hamelin said hesitantly. "Gentlemen, I have a—a rather unusual request. And, I am afraid, a rather selfish one." A brief, nervous laugh. "Selfish in both senses, if you will pardon me the pun. You need feel no hesitation in refusing me, but…"

Abruptly he appeared to find it impossible to go on. Carson mentally crossed his fingers and plunged in.

"You would like to undergo the process yourself?" he said.

'Well, yes. Yes, that's exactly it. Does that seem inconsistent? I should know, should I not, what it is that I'm advocating for my following? Know it intimately, from personal experience, not just theory? Of course I realize that it would conflict with your policy, but I assure you I wouldn't turn it to any political advantage—none whatsoever. And perhaps it wouldn't be too great a lapse of policy to process just one civilian among your seven thousand soldiers.'

Subverted, by God! Carson looked at Mudgett with a firmly straight face. It wouldn't do to accept too quickly.

But Hamelin was rushing on, almost chattering now. "I can understand your hesitation. You must feel that I'm trying to gain some advantage, or even to get to the surface ahead of my fellowmen. If it will set your minds at rest, I would be glad to enlist in your advance army. Before five years are up, I could surely learn some technical skill which would make me useful to the expedition. If you would prepare papers to that effect, I'd be happy to sign them."

"That's hardly necessary," Mudgett said. "After you're Re-Educated, we can simply announce the fact, and say that you've agreed to join the advance party when the time comes."

"Ah," Hamelin said. "I see the difficulty. No, that would make my position quite impossible. If there is no other way—"

"Excuse us a moment," Carson said. Hamelin bowed, and the doctor pulled Mudgett off out of earshot.

"Don't overplay it," he murmured. "You're tipping our hand with that talk about a press release, Colonel. He's offering us a bribe—but he's plenty smart enough to see that the price you're suggesting is that of his whole political career. He won't pay that much."

"What then?" Mudgett whispered hoarsely.

"Get somebody to prepare the kind of informal contract he suggested. Offer to put it under security seal so we won't be able to show it to the press at all. He'll know well enough that such a seal can be broken if our policy ever comes before a presidential review—and that will restrain him from forcing such a review. Let's not demand too much. Once he's been re-educated, he'll have to live the rest of the five years with the knowledge that he can live topside any time he wants to try it—and he hasn't had the discipline our men have had. It's my bet that he'll goof off before the five years are up—and good riddance."

They went back to Hamelin, who was watching the machine and humming in a painfully abstracted manner.

"I've convinced the Colonel," Carson said, "that your services in the army might well be very valuable when the time comes, Mr. Secretary. If you'll sign up, we'll put the papers under security seal for your own protection, and then I think we can fit you into our treatment program today."

"I'm grateful to you, Dr. Carson," Hamelin said. "Very grateful indeed."

Five minutes after his injection, Hamelin was as peaceful as a flounder and was rolled through the swinging doors. An hour's discussion of the probable outcome, carried on in the privacy of Mudgett's office, bore very little additional fruit, however.

"It's our only course," Carson said. "It's what we hoped to gain from his visit, duly modified by circumstances. It all comes down to this: Hamelin's compromised himself, and he knows it."

"But," Mudgett said, "suppose he was right? What about all that talk of his about mass insanity?"

"I'm sure it's true," Carson said, his voice trembling slightly despite his best efforts at control. "It's going to be rougher than ever down here for the next five years, Colonel. Our only consolation is that the enemy must have exactly the same problem; and if we can beat them to the surface—"

"Hsst!" Mudgett said. Carson had already broken off his sentence. He wondered why the scanner gave a man such a hard time outside that door, and then admitted him without any warning to the people on the other side. Couldn't the damned thing be trained to knock?

The newcomer was a page from the haemotology section. "Here's the preliminary rundown on your 'Student X', Dr. Carson," he said.

The page saluted Mudgett and went out. Carson began to read. After a moment, he also began to sweat.

"Colonel, look at this. I was wrong after all. Disastrously wrong. I haven't seen a blood-type distribution pattern like Hamelin's since I was a medical student, and even back then it was only a demonstration, not a real live patient. Look at it from the genetic point of view—the migration factors."

He passed the protocol across the desk. Mudgett was not by background a scientist, but he was an enormously able administrator, of the breed that makes it its business to know the technicalities on which any project ultimately rests. He was not much more than halfway through the tally before his eyebrows were gaining altitude like shock-waves.

"Carson, we can't let that man into the machine! He's—"

"He's already in it, Colonel, you know that. And if we interrupt the process before it runs to term, we'll kill him."

"Let's kill him, then," Mudgett said harshly. "Say he died while being processed. Do the country a favor."

"That would produce a hell of a stink. Besides, we have no proof." Mudgett flourished the protocol excitedly.

"That's not proof to anyone but a haemotologist."

"But Carson, the man's a saboteur!" Mudgett shouted. "Nobody but an Asiatic could have a typing pattern like this! And he's no melting-pot product, either—he's a classical mixture, very probably a Georgian. And every move he's made since we first heard of him has been aimed directly at us—aimed directly at tricking us into getting him into the machine!"

"I think so too," Carson said grimly. "I just hope the enemy hasn't many more agents as brilliant."

"One's enough," Mudgett said. "He's sure to be loaded to the last cc of his blood with catalyst poisons. Once the machine starts processing his serum, we're done for —it'll take us years to re-program the computer, if it can be done at all. It's got to be stopped!"

"Stopped?" Carson said, astonished. "But it's, already stopped. That's not what worries me. The machine stopped it fifty minutes ago."

"It can't have! How could it? It has no relevant data!"

"Sure it has." Carson leaned forward, took the cruelly chewed pencil away from Mudgett, and made a neat check beside one of the entries on the protocol. Mudgett stared at the checked item.

"Platelets Rh VI?" he mumbled. "But what's that got to do with... Oh. Oh, I see. That platelet type doesn't exist at all in our population now, does it? Never seen it before myself, at least."

"No," Carson said, grinning wolfishly. "It never was common in the West, and the pogrom of 1981 wiped it out. That's something the enemy couldn't know. But the machine knows it. As soon as it gives him the standard anti-IV desensitization shot, his platelets will begin to dissolve—and he'll be rejected for incipient thrombocytopenia." He laughed. "For his own protection! But—"

"But he's getting nitrous oxide in the machine, and he'll be held six hours under anesthesia anyhow—also for his own protection," Mudgett broke in. He was grinning back at Carson like an idiot. "When he comes out from under, he'll assume that he's been re-educated, and he'll beat it back to the enemy to report that he's poisoned our machine, so that they can be sure they'll beat us to the surface. And he'll go the fastest way: overland."

"He will," Carson agreed. "Of course he'll go overland, and of course he'll die. But where does that leave us? We won't be able to conceal that he was treated here, if there's any sort of an inquiry at all. And his death will make everything we do here look like a fraud. Instead of paying our Pied Piper—and great jumping Jehosophat, look at his name! They were rubbing our noses in it all the time! Nevertheless, we didn't pay the piper; we killed him. And 'platelets Rh VI' won't be an adequate excuse for the press, or for Hamelin's following."

"It doesn't worry me," Mudgett rumbled. "Who'll know? He won't die in our labs. He'll leave here hale and hearty. He won't die until he makes a break for the surface. After that we can compose a fine obituary for the press. Heroic government official, on the highest policy level—couldn't wait to lead his followers to the surface—died of being too much in a hurry—Re-Ed Project sorrowfully reminds everyone that no technique is foolproof—"

Mudgett paused long enough to light a cigarette, which was a most singular action for a man who never smoked. "As a matter of fact, Carson," he said. "It's a natural."

Carson considered it. It seemed to hold up. And 'Hamelin' would have a death certificate as complex as he deserved—not officially, of course, but in the minds of everyone who knew the facts. His death, when it came, would be due directly to the thrombocytopenia which had caused the Re-Ed machine to reject him—and thrombocytopenia is a disease of infants. Unless ye become as little children...

That was a fitting reason for rejection from the new kingdom of Earth: anemia of the newborn.

His pent breath went out of him in a long sigh. He hadn't been aware that he'd been holding it. "It's true," he said softly. "That's the time to pay the piper."

"When?" Mudgett said.

"When?" Carson said, surprised. "Why, before he takes the children away."

EMERGENCY MASS FEEDING
instructor course

JOINTLY DEVELOPED AND SPONSORED BY

THE DEPARTMENT OF DEFENSE AND THE
FEDERAL CIVIL DEFENSE ADMINISTRATION

The Department of Defense, working with the FCDA, created a course designed to teach local authorities how to feed survivors (the introduction to the booklet is pictured on the following pages). Yet The Department of Defense/Office of Civil Defense handbook, Personal and Family Survival: Civil Defense Adult Education Course Student Manual, revised May 1963, offers little on how to obtain food, relying solely on localities to build their own stockpiles: "Food and water will probably be the greatest survivor need after emerging from shelter. At the same time, it will be important to limit the possible adverse effects of eating heavily contaminated food and water. Therefore, food and water supplies will be controlled and checked by local authorities. Survivors will be fed in large groups at feeding centers or will be issued approved rations as appropriate. Individuals should cooperate with the control measures set up by the local Civil Defense organization by avoiding unnecessary contact with radioactive materials and by not consuming unchecked food and water unless necessary for survival."

JOINT ARMY-FCDA TRAINING PROGRAM ON IMPROVISATION IN EMERGENCY FEEDING

INTRODUCTION TO COURSE OF INSTRUCTION

Feeding Problems

In any general natural or man-made disaster—whether it be fire, flood, hurricane, tornado, earthquake or atomic, thermo-nuclear, or saturation bombing—certain emergency conditions will generally prevail.

Wholesale destruction of dwellings, stores, or warehouses by enemy attack will leave thousands of people not only homeless, but without sources of food and feeding facilities. It is essential that provision be made for feeding facilities to be placed in operation immediately after attack. The program must be planned and operated to take care of hungry people wherever they may be. The fundamental importance of any such emergency feeding program automatically gives its organization and development a high priority in civil defense planning.

The content of this course was determined only after considerable discussion between the Federal Civil Defense Administration and the Quartermaster Corps of the Department of the Army. It has also had the benefit of the criticisms, suggestions, and recommendations of the representatives of the organizations and agencies who participated in the pilot program.

The course content includes lessons on sanitation and water purification. In a civil defense emergency, emergency feeding will look to the engineering and health services to provide safe water for cooking and drinking purposes, and to provide adequate facilities for disposal of wastes. It will also look to the health services for assistance on all other matters relating to sanitation. T h e engineering and health services will, in turn, depend upon the existing water works and sewerage utilities organizations to assume leadership in necessary repair or reconstruction work and the existing public health organizations to assure quality of the water and adequacy

of sanitary facilities. It is expected that these services will be properly organized to render effective support to the emergency feeding program. However, it may be necessary for an interim period after attack to feed people without the support of the civil defense engineering and health services. It is for this reason that the course content of this training program includes lessons on sanitation, water purification, and similar subjects. The importance of feeding people is so vital to civil defense that emergency feeding personnel must be trained to operate even under the most adverse conditions.

For purposes of this instruction, certain assumptions are made. These include:

a. That the major portion of public utilities, including electricity, gas, transportation and fuel, will be destroyed.

b. That homes, restaurants, cafeterias, food equipment, and storage facilities will be unusable.

c. That the sewage system has been destroyed.

d. That some food supplies, unaffected by the damage, are available.

e. That water is available and may be used if purified.

f. That salvage materials will be available.

g. That responsibility for feeding will rest upon civilian agencies.

The problem, then, is to establish mass feeding facilities utilizing field expedients, including cooking and eating utensils and waste disposal systems in lieu of normal food service equipment. For full effectiveness, emer-

iii

gency feeding must start immediately after attack.

Major consideration must be given to the selection of a site for such operations. Certain fundamentals must be considered in the selection of a kitchen and eating site in order to attain maximum efficiency. These will be explained in detail in the instruction.

Simplicity must be the keyword in an operation dependent solely on expedients for the preparation and serving of food to large groups of people.

The expedients developed for demonstration can be made from material normally available.

These facilities and utensils are of a type that can be made in the shortest possible time with a minimum of tools.

Groups of people with little or no mechanical ability can be instructed in the rudiments of this improvisation without difficulty.

The material covered is considered to be the minimum essential information necessary to meet the requirements of a disaster situation. Particular attention is called to the subjects of water purification, personal hygiene, sanitation, and food poisoning, as the rules pertaining to these are the ones most susceptible to violation.

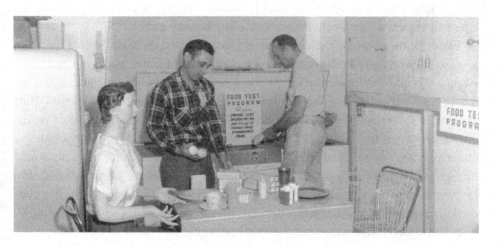

Members of The Atomic Energy Commission prepare a model kitchen for an atomic bomb test.
(Photograph—United States Archives.)

The Last of the Deliveries
Poul Anderson

When I was nine years, old, we still had a crazy man living in our town. He was very old, almost a hundred I suppose, and all his kin were dead. But in those days every town still had a few people who did not belong to any family.

Uncle Jim was wrong in the head, but harmless. He cobbled for us. His shop was in the front room of his house, always prim and neat, and when you stood there among the good smells of leather and oil, you could see his living room beyond. He did not have many books, but shelf after shelf was loaded with tall bright sheafs cased in plastic—old as himself, and as cracked and yellow with their age. He called them his magazines, and if we children were good he sometimes let us look at the pictures in them, but we had to be very careful. After he was dead I had a chance to read the texts, which didn't make sense. Nobody would worry about the things the people in those magazines, made such a fuss over. He also had a big antique television set, though why he kept it when there was nothing to receive but official calls and the town had a perfectly good set for them, I don't know. But he was crazy.

Every morning his long stiff figure went for a walk down Main Street. The Trees there were mostly elms, grown tall enough to overshadow it and speckle the pavement with cool bright sunflecks. Uncle Jim was always dressed in his ancient clothes, no matter how hot the day, and summer in Ohio can get plenty hot. He wore frayed white shirts with scratchy, choky collars, and long trousers and a clumsy kind of jacket, and narrow shoes that pinched his feet. It was ugly, but he kept it painfully clean. We children, being young and therefore cruel, thought at first that because we never saw him unclothed he must be hiding some awful deformity, and teased him about it. But my auntsbrother John made us stop, and uncle Jim never held it against us. He even used to give us candy he had made himself, till the town dentist complained; then all of us had solemn talks with our fathers and found out that sugar rots the teeth.

Finally we decided that Uncle Jim—we called him that, without saying on which side he was anyone's uncle, because he wasn't really—wore all those clothes as a sort of background for his button that said WIN WITH WILLARD. He told me once, when I asked, that Willard had been the last Republican President of the United States and a very great man who tried to avert disaster but was too late because the people were already far gone in sloth and decadence. That was a big lading for a nine-year-old head, and I still don't really understand it, except that once the towns did not govern themselves and the country was divided between two big groups who were not even clans but who more or less took turns furnishing a President; and the President was not an umpire between towns and states, but ran everything.

Uncle Jim used to creak down Main Street past Townhall and the sunpower plant, then turn at the fountain and go by my fathergreatuncle Conrad's house to the edge of town where the fields and Trees rolled to the blue rim of the world. At the airport he would turn and come back by Joseph Arakelian's, where he always looked in at the hand looms and sneered with disgust and talked about automatic machinery; though what he had against the looms I don't know, because Joseph's weavery was famous. He also made harsh remarks about our ratty little airport and the town's half-dozen flitters. That wasn't fair: we had a very good airport, surfaced with concrete blocks ripped out of the old highway, and there were enough flitters for all our longer trips. You'd never get more than six groups going anywhere at any one time in a town this size.

But I wanted to tell about the Communist.

This was in the spring. The snow had melted and the ground begun to dry and our farmers were out planting. The rest of our town bustled with preparations for the Fete, cooking and baking, oh such a smell as filled the air, women trading recipes from porch to porch, artisans hammering and sawing and welding, the washlines afire with Sunday-best clothes taken out of winter chests, lovers hand in hand whispering of the festivals to come. Red and Bob and Stinky and I were playing marbles by the airport. It used to be mumbletypeg, but some of the kids flipped their knives into Trees and the Elders made a rule that no kid could carry a knife unless a grownup was with him.

So it was a fair sweet morning, the sky a dizzy-high arch of blue, sunlight bouncing off puffy white clouds and down to the earth, and the first pale whisper of green had been breathed across the hills. Dust leaped where our marbles hit, a small wind blew up from the south and slid across my skin and rumpled my hair, the world and the season and we were young.

We were about to quit, fetch our guns and take into the woods after rabbit; when a shadow fell across us and we saw Uncle Jim and my mothercousin Andy. Uncle Jim wore a long coat above all his other clothes, and still shivered as he leaned on his cane, and the shrunken hands were blue with cold. Andy wore a kilt, for the pockets, and sandals. He was our town engineer, a stocky man of forty, but once in the prehistoric past before I was born he had been on an expedition to Mars, and this made him a hero for us kids. We never understood why he was not a swaggering corsair. He owned three thousand books at least, more than twice the average in our town. He spent a lot of time with Uncle Jim too, and I didn't know why. Now I see that he was trying to learn about the past from him, not the dead past mummified in the history books but the people who had once been alive.

The old man looked down at us and said: "You boys aren't wearing a stitch. You'll catch your death of cold." He had a high, thin voice, but it was steady. In all the years alone, he must have learned how to be firm with himself.

"Oh, nonsense," said. Andy. "I'll bet it's sixty in the sun."

"We was going after rabbits," I said importantly. "I'll bring mine to your place and your wife can make us a stew." Like all children, I spent as much time with kinfolk as I did with my orthoparents, but I favored Andy's home. His wife was a wonderful cook, his oldest son was better than most on the guitar, and his daughter's chess was just about my speed, neither too good nor too bad.

I'd won most of the marbles this game, so now I gave them back. "When I was a boy," said Uncle Jim, "we played for keeps."

"What happened after the best shooter had won all the marbles in town?" asked Stinky. "It's hard work making a good marble, Uncle Jim. I can't hardly replace all I lose anyway."

"You could have bought some more," he told him. "There were stores where you could buy anything."

"But who made all those marbles?"

"There were factories—"

Imagine that! Big grown men spending their lives making colored glass balls!

We were almost ready to leave when the Communist showed up. We saw him as he rounded the clump of Trees at the north quarter-section, which was pasture that year. He was on the Middleton road, and dust scuffed up from his bare feet.

A stranger in town is always big news, and we kids started running to meet him till Andy recalled us with a sharp word and reminded us that he was entitled to proper courtesy. So we waited, with our eyes bugging out, till he reached us.

But this was a woebegone stranger. He was tall and thin, like Uncle Jim, but his cape hung in rags about a narrow chest where you could count all the ribs, and under a bald dome of a head was a dirty white beard down to his waist. He walked heavily, leaning on a staff, heavy as Time, and even then I sensed the loneliness like a weight on his thin shoulders.

Andy stepped forward and bowed. "Greetings and welcome, Freeborn," he said. "I am Andrew Jackson Welles, town engineer, and on behalf of the Folks I bid you stay, rest, and refresh yourself." He didn't just rattle the words off as he would for someone he knew, but declaimed them with great care.

Uncle Jim smiled then, a smile like thawing after a nine year's winter, for this man was as old as himself and born in the same forgotten world. He trod forth and held out his hand. "Hello, sir," he said. "My name is Robbins. Pleased to meet you." They didn't have very good manners in his day.

"Thank you, Comrade Welles, Comrade Robbins," said the stranger. His smile was lost somewhere in that tangled mold of whiskers. "I'm Harry Miller."

"Comrade?" Uncle Jim spoke it slowly, like a word out of a nightmare, and his hand crept back again. "What do you mean?"

The newcomer wanderer straightened and looked at us in a way that frightened me. "I meant what I said," he answered. "I don't make any bones about it. Harry Miller, of the Communist Party of the United States of America!"

Uncle Jim sucked in a long breath. "But—" he stammered, "but I thought… at the very least, I thought all you rats were dead."

"Now hold on," said Andy. "Your pardon, Freeborn Miller. Our friend isn't, uh, isn't quite himself. Don't take it personally, I beg you."

There was a grimness in Miller's chuckle. "Oh, I don't mind. I've been called worse than that."

"And deserved it!" I had never seen Uncle Jim angry before. His face got red and he stamped his cane in the dust. "Andy, this, this man is a traitor. D'you hear? He's a foreign agent!"

"You mean you come clear from Russia?" murmured Andy, and we boys clustered near with our ears stiff in the breeze, because a foreigner was a seldom sight.

"No," said Miller. "No, I'm from Pittsburgh. Never been to Russia. Wouldn't want to go. Too awful there—they had Communism once."

"Didn't know anybody was left in Pittsburgh," said Andy. "I was there last year with a salvage crew, after steel and copper, and we never saw anything but birds."

"A few. A few. My wife and I—But she died, and I couldn't stay in that rotting empty shell of a city, so I went out on the road."

"And you can go back on the road," snarled Uncle Jim.

"Now, please be quiet," said Andy. "Come on into town, Freeborn Miller—Comrade Miller, if you prefer. May I invite you to stay with me?"

Uncle Jim grabbed Andy's arm. He shook like a dead leaf in fall, under the heartless fall winds. "You can't!" he shrieked. "Don't you see, he'll poison your minds, he'll subvert you, we'll end up slaves to him and his gang of bandits!"

"It seems you've been doing a little mind-poisoning of your own, Mister Robbins," said Miller.

Uncle Jim stood for a moment, head bent to the ground, and the quick tears of an old man glimmered in his eyes. Then he lifted his face and pride rang in the words: "I am a Republican."

"I thought so." The Communist glanced around and nodded to himself. "Typical bourgeois pseudo-culture. Look at those men, each out on his own little tractor in his own field, hugging his own little selfishness to him."

Andy scratched his head. "What are you talking about, Freeborn?" he asked. "Those are town machines. Who wants to be bothered with keeping his own tractor and plow and harvester?"

"Oh... you mean—" I could see a light of wonder in the Communist's eyes, and he half stretched out his hands. They were aged hands, I could see the bones just under the dried-out skin. "You mean you do work the land collectively ?"

"Why, no. What on earth would be the point of that?" replied Andy. "A man's entitled to what he raises himself, isn't he?"

"So the land, which should be the property of all the people, is parceled among those kulaks!" flared Miller.

"How in hell's name can land be anybody's property? It's... it's land! You can't put forty acres in your pocket and walk off with them." Andy took a long breath. "You must have been pretty well cut off from things in Pittsburgh—ate the ancient canned stuff, didn't you? I thought so. It's easy enough to explain. Look, that section out there is being planted in corn by my mothercousin Glenn. It's his corn, that he swaps for whatever else he needs. But next year, to conserve the soil, it'll be put in alfalfa, and my sisterson Willy takes care of it then. As for garden truck and fruit, most of us raise our own, just to get outdoors each day."

The light faded in our visitor. "It doesn't make sense," said Miller, and I could hear how tired he was. It must have been a long hike from Pittsburgh, living off handouts from gypsies and the Lone Farmers.

"I quite agree," said Uncle Jim with a stiff kind of smile. "In my father's day—" He closed his mouth. I knew his father had died in Korea, in some war when he was just a baby, and Uncle Jim had been left to keep the memory and the sad barren pride of it. I remembered my history, which Freeborn Levinsohn taught in our town because he knew it best, and a shiver crept in my skin. A Communist! Why, they had killed and tortured Americans... only this was a faded rag of a man, he couldn't kill a puppy. It was very odd.

229

We started toward Townhall. People saw us and began to crowd around, staring and whispering as much as decorum allowed. I strutted with Red and Bob and Stinky, right next to the stranger, the real live Communist, under the eyes of all the other kids.

We passed Joseph's weavery, and his family and apprentices came out to join the goggle eyes. Miller spat in the street. "I imagine those people are hired!" he said.

"You don't expect them to work for nothing, do you?" asked Andy.

"They should work for the common good."

"But they do. Every time somebody needs a garment or a blanket, Joseph gets his boys together and they make one. You can buy better stuff from him than most women can make at home."

"I knew it. The bourgeois exploiter—"

"I only wish that were the case," said Uncle Jim, tight-lipped.

"You would," snapped Miller.

"But it isn't. People don't have any drive these days. No spirit of competition. No desire to improve their living standard. No... they buy what they need, and wear it while it lasts—and it's made to last damn near forever." Uncle Jim waved his cane in the air. "I tell you, Andy, the country's gone to hell. The economy is stagnant. Business has become a bunch of miserable little shops and people making for themselves what they used to buy!"

"I think we're pretty well fed and clothed and housed," said Andy.

"But where's your... your drive? Where's the get-up-and-go, the hustling, that made America great? Look—your wife wears the same model of gown her mother wore. You use a flitter that was built in your father's time. Don't you want anything *better?*"

"Our machinery works well enough," said Andy. He spoke in a bored voice, this was an old argument to him while the Communist was new. I saw Miller's tattered cape swirl into Si Johansen's carpenter shop and followed.

Si was making a chest of drawers for George Hulme, who was getting married this spring. He put down his tools and answered politely.

"Yes... yes, Freeborn... sure, I work here.... Organize? What *for*? Social-like, you mean ? But my apprentices got too damn much social life as it is. Every third day a holiday, damn near. . . No, they *ain't* oppressed. Hell, they're my own kin!... But there ain't any people who haven't got good furniture. Not unless they're lousy carpenters and too uppity to get help—"

"But the people all over the world!" screamed Miller. "Don't you have any heart, man? What about the Mexican peons?"

Si Johansen shrugged. "What about them? If they want to run things different down there, it's their own business." He put away his electric sander and hollered to his apprentices that they could have the rest of the day off. They'd have taken it anyway, of course, but Si was a little bit bossy.

Andy got Miller out in the street again, and at Townhall the Mayor came in from the fields and received him. Since good weather was predicted for the whole week, we decided there was no hurry about the planting and we'd spend the afternoon welcoming our guest.

"Bunch of bums!" snorted Uncle Jim. "Your ancestors stuck by a job till it was finished."

"This'll get finished in time," said the Mayor, like he was talking to a baby. "What's the rush, Jim?"

"Rush? To get on with it—finish it and go on to something else. Better things for better living!"

"For the benefit of your exploiters," cackled Miller. He stood on the Townhall steps like a starved and angry rooster.

"What exploiters?" The Mayor was as puzzled as me.

"The... the big businessmen, the—"

"There aren't any more businessmen," said Uncle Jim, and a little more life seemed to trickle out of him as he admitted it. "Our shopkeepers... no. They only want to make a living. They've never heard of making a profit. They're too lazy to expand."

"Then why haven't you got socialism?" Miller's red eyes glared around as if looking for some hidden enemy. "It's every family for itself. Where's your solidarity?"

"We get along pretty well with each other, Freeborn," said the Mayor. "We got courts to settle any arguments."

"But don't you want to go on, to advance, to—"

"We got enough," declared the Mayor, patting his belly. "I couldn't eat any more than I do."

"But you could wear more!" said Uncle Jim. He jittered on the steps, the poor crazy man, dancing before all our eyes like the puppets in a traveling show. "You could have your own car, a new model every year with beautiful chrome plate all over it, and new machines to lighten your labor, and—"

"—and to buy those shoddy things, meant only to wear out, you would have to slave your lives away for the capitalists," said Miller. "The People must produce for the People."

Andy traded a glance with the Mayor. "Look, Freeborns," he said gently, "you don't seem to get the point. We don't want all those gadgets. We have enough. It isn't worthwhile scheming and working to get more than we have, not while there are girls to love in springtime and deer to hunt in the fall. And when we do work, we'd rather work for ourselves, not for somebody else, whether you call the somebody else a capitalist or the People. Now let's go sit down and take it easy before lunch."

Wedged between the legs of the Folks, I heard Si Johansen mutter to Joseph Arake-lian: "I don't get it. What would we do with all this machinery? If I had some damn machine to make furniture for me, what'd I do with my hands?"

Joseph lifted his shoulders. "Beats me, Si. Personally, I'd go nuts watching two people wear the same identical pattern."

"It might be kind of nice at that," said Red to me. "Having a car like they show in Uncle Jim's magazines."

"Where'd you go in it?" asked Bob.

"Gee, I dunno. To Canada, maybe. But shucks, I can go to Canada any time I can talk my dad into borrowing a flitter."

"Sure," said Bob. "And if you're going less than a hundred miles, you got a horse, haven't you? Who wants an old car?"

I wriggled through the crowd toward the Plaza, where the women were setting up outdoor tables and bringing food for a banquet. The crowd was so thick around our guest where he sat that I couldn't get near, but Stinky and I skun up into the Plaza Tree, a huge gray oak, and crawled along a branch till we hung just above his head. It was a bare and liver-spotted head, wobbling on a thread of neck, but he darted it around and spoke shrill.

Andy and the Mayor sat near him, puffing their pipes, and Uncle Jim was there too. The Folks had let him in so they could watch the fireworks. That was perhaps a cruel and thoughtless thing to do, but how could we know? Uncle Jim had always been so peaceful, and we'd never had two crazy men in town.

"I was still young," Comrade Miller was saying, "I was only a boy, and there were still telecasts. I remember how my mother cried, when we knew the Soviet Union was dissolved. On that night she made me swear to keep faith, and I have, I have, and now I'm going to show you the truth and not a pack of capitalist lies."

"Whatever did happen to Russia?" wondered Ed Mulligan. He was the town psychiatrist, he'd trained at Henninger clear out in Kansas. "I never would have thought the Communists would let their people go free, not from what I've read of them."

"The Communists were corrupted," said Miller fiercely. "Filthy bourgeois lies and money."

"Now that isn't true," said Uncle Jim. "They simply got corrupt and easygoing of their own accord. Any tyrant will. And so they didn't foresee what changes the new technology would make, they blithely introduced it, and in the course of one generation their Iron Curtain rusted away. Nobody *listened* to them anymore."

"Pretty correct, Jim," said Andy. He saw my face among the twigs, and winked at me. "There was some violence, it was more complicated than you think, but that's essentially what happened. Trouble is, you can't seem to realize that it happened in the U.S.A. also."

Miller shook his withered head. "Marx proved that technological advances mean inevitable progress toward socialism," he said. "Oh, the cause has been set back, but the day is coming."

"Why, maybe you're right up to a point," said Andy. "But you see, science and society went beyond that point. Maybe I can give you a simple explanation."

"If you wish," said Miller, grumpy-like.

"Well, I've studied the period. Technology made it possible for a few people and acres to feed the whole country, so there were millions of acres lying idle; you could buy them for peanuts. Meanwhile the cities were over-taxed, under-represented, and choked by their own traffic. Along came the cheap sunpower unit and the high-capacity accumulator. Those made it possible for a man to supply most of his own wants, not work his heart out for someone else to pay the inflated prices demanded by an economy where every single business was subsidized or protected at the taxpayer's expense. Also, by living in the new way, a man cut down his money income to the point where he had to pay almost no taxes—so he actually lived better on a shorter work week.

"More and more, people tended to drift out and settle in small country communities. They consumed less, so there was a great depression, and that drove still more people out to fend for themselves. By the time big business and organized labor realized what was happening and tried to get laws passed against what they called un-American practices, it was too late; nobody was interested. It all happened so gradually, you see but it happened, and I think we're happier now."

"Ridiculous!" said Miller. "Capitalism went bankrupt, as Marx foresaw two hundred years ago, but its vicious influence was still so powerful that instead of advancing to collectivism you went back to being peasants."

"Please," said the Mayor. I could see he was annoyed, and thought that maybe peasants were somebody not Freeborn. "Uh, maybe we can pass the time with a little singing."

Though he had no voice to speak of, courtesy demanded that Miller be asked to perform first. He stood up and quavered out something about a guy named Joe Hill. It had a nice tune, but even a nine-year-old like me knew it was lousy poetics. A childish *a-b-c-b-* scheme of masculine rhymes and not a double metaphor anywhere. Besides, who cares what happened to some little tramp when there are hunting songs and epics about interplanetary explorers to make? I was glad when Andy took over and gave us some music with muscle in it.

Lunch was called, and I slipped down from the Tree and found a seat nearby. Comrade Miller and Uncle Jim glowered at each other across the table, but nothing was said till after the meal, a couple of hours later. People had kind of lost interest in the stranger as they learned he'd spent his life huddled in a dead city, and wandered off for the dancing and games. Andy hung around, not wanting to but because he was Miller's host.

The Communist sighed and got up. "You've been nice to me," he said.

"I thought we were all a bunch of capitalists," sneered Uncle Jim.

"It's man I'm interested in, wherever he is and whatever conditions he has to live under," said Miller.

Uncle Jim lifted his voice with his cane: "Man! You claim to care for man, you who only killed and enslaved him?"

"Oh, come off it, Jim," said Andy. "That was a long time ago. Who cares at this late date?"

"*I* do!" Uncle Jim started crying, but he looked at Miller and walked up to him, stiff-legged, hands clawed. "They killed my father! Men died by the tens of thousands—for an ideal! And you don't care! The whole damn country has lost its guts!"

I stood under the Tree, one hand on the cool rough comfort of its bark. I was a little afraid, because I did not understand. Surely Andy, who had been sent by the United Townships Research Foundation all the long black way to Mars, just to gather knowledge, was no coward. Surely my father, a gentle man and full of laughter, did not lack guts. What was it we were supposed to want?

"Why, you bootlicking belly-crawling lackey," yelled Miller. "It was you who gutted them! It was you who murdered working men, and roped their sons into your dummy unions, and... and... what about the Mexican peons?"

Andy tried to come between them. Miller's staff clattered on his head. Andy stepped back, wiping the blood off, looking helpless, as the old crazy men howled at each other. He couldn't use force—he might hurt them.

Perhaps, in that moment, he realized. "It's all right, Freeborns," he said quickly. "It's all right. We'll listen to you. Look, you can have a nice debate tonight, right in Townhall, and we'll all come and—"

He was too late. Uncle Jim and Comrade Miller were already fighting, thin arms locked, and dim eyes full of tears because they had no strength left to destroy what they hated. But I think, now, that the hate arose from a baffled love. They both loved us in a queer maimed fashion, and we did not care, we did not care.

Andy got some men together and separated the two and they were led off to different houses for a nap. But when Dr. Simmons looked in on Uncle Jim a few hours later, he was gone. The doctor hurried off to find the Communist, and he was gone too.

I only learned that afterward, since I went off to play tag and pom-pom-pullaway with the other kids down where the river flowed cool and dark. It was in the same river, next morning, that Constable Thompson found the Communist and the Republican. Nobody knew what had happened. They met under the Trees, alone, at dusk when bonfires were being lit and the Elders making merry around them and lovers stealing off into the woods. That's all anybody knows. We gave them a nice funeral.

It was the talk of the town for a week, and in fact the whole state of Ohio heard about it, but then the talk died and the old crazy men were forgotten. That was the year the Brotherhood came into power in the north, and men worried what it could mean. The next spring they learned, and there was an alliance made and war went across the hills. For the Brotherhood gang, just as it had threatened, planted no Trees at all, and such evil cannot go unpunished.

An FCDA Civil Defense poster produced for rural areas of the United States.

Road to Nightfall

Robert Silverberg

The dog snarled, and ran on. Katterson watched the two lean, fiery-eyed men speeding in pursuit, while a mounting horror grew in him and rooted him to the spot. The dog suddenly bounded over a heap of rubble and was gone; its pursuers sank limply down, leaning on their clubs, and tried to catch their breath.

"It's going to get much worse than this," said a small, grubby-looking man who appeared from nowhere next to Katterson. "I've heard the official announcement's coming today, but the rumor's been around for a long time."

"So they say," answered Katterson slowly. The chase he had just witnessed still held him paralyzed. "We're all pretty hungry."

The two men who had chased the dog got up, still winded, and wandered off. Katterson and the little man watched their slow retreat.

"That's the first time I've ever seen people doing that," said Katterson. "Out in the open like that—"

"It won't be the last time," said the grubby man. "Better get used to it, now that the food's gone."

Katterson's stomach twinged. It was empty, and would stay that way till the evening's food dole. Without the doles, he would have no idea of where his next bite of food would come from. He and the small man walked on through the quiet street, stepping over the rubble, walking aimlessly with no particular goal in mind.

"My name's Paul Katterson," he said finally. "I live on 47th Street. I was discharged from the Army last year."

"Oh, one of those," said the little man. They turned down 15th Street. It was a street of complete desolation; not one pre-war house was standing, and a few shabby tents were pitched at the far end of the street. "Have you had any work since your discharge?"

Katterson laughed. "Good joke. Try another."

"I know. Things are tough. My name is Malory; I'm a merchandiser."

"What do you merchandise?"

"Oh... useful products."

Katterson nodded. Obviously Malory didn't want him to pursue the topic, and he dropped it. They walked on silently, the big man and the little one, and Katterson could think of nothing but the emptiness in his stomach. Then his thoughts drifted to

237

the scene of a few minutes before, the two hungry men chasing a dog. Had it come to that so soon, Katterson asked himself? What was going to happen, he wondered, as food became scarcer and scarcer and finally there was none at all.

But the little man was pointing ahead. "Look," he said. "Meeting at Union Square."

Katterson squinted and saw a crowd starting to form around the platform reserved for public announcements. He quickened his pace, forcing Malory to struggle to keep up with him.

A young man in military uniform had mounted the platform and was impassively facing the crowd. Katterson looked at the jeep nearby, automatically noting it was the 2036 model, the most recent one, eighteen years old. After a minute or so the soldier raised his hand for silence, and spoke in a quiet, restrained voice.

"Fellow New Yorkers, I have an official announcement from the Government. Word has just been received from Trenton Oasis—"

The crowd began to murmur. They seemed to know what was coming.

"Word has just been received from Trenton Oasis that, due to recent emergency conditions there, all food supplies for New York City and environs will be temporarily cut off. Repeat: due to recent emergency in the Trenton Oasis, all food supplies for New York and environs will temporarily be cut off."

The murmuring in the crowd grew to an angry, biting whisper as each man discussed this latest turn of events with the man next to him. This was hardly unexpected news; Trenton had long protested the burden of feeding helpless, bombed-out New York, and the recent flood there had given them ample opportunity to squirm out of their responsibility. Katterson stood silent, towering over the people around him, finding himself unable to believe what he was hearing. He seemed aloof, almost detached, objectively criticizing the posture of the soldier on the platform, counting his insignia, thinking of everything but the implications of the announcement, and trying to fight back the growing hunger.

The uniformed man was speaking again. "I also have this message from the Governor of New York, General Holloway: he says that attempts at restoring New York's food supply are being made, and that messengers have been dispatched to the Baltimore Oasis to request food supplies. In the meantime the Government food doles are to be discontinued effective tonight, until further notice. That is all."

The soldier gingerly dismounted from the platform and made his way through the crowd to his jeep. He climbed quickly in and drove off. Obviously he was an important man, Katterson decided, because jeeps and fuel were scarce items, not used lightly by anyone and everyone.

Katterson remained where he was and turned his head slowly, looking at the people around him—thin, half-starved little skeletons, most of them, who secretly begrudged him his giant frame. An emaciated man with burning eyes and a beak of a nose had gathered a small group around himself and was shouting some sort of harangue. Katterson knew of him—his name was Emerich, and he was the leader of the colony living in the abandoned subway at 14th Street. Katterson instinctively moved closer to hear him, and Malory followed.

"It's all a plot!" the emaciated man was shouting. "They talk of an emergency in Trenton. What emergency? I ask you, what emergency? That flood didn't hurt them. They just want to get us off their necks by starving us out, that's all! And what can we do about it? Nothing. Trenton knows we'll never be able to rebuild New York, and they want to get rid of us, so they cut off our food."

By now the crowd had gathered round him. Emerich was popular; people were shouting their agreement, punctuating his speech with applause.

"But will we starve to death? We will not!"

"That's right, Emerich!" yelled a burly man with a beard.

"No," Emerich continued, "we'll show them what we can do. We'll scrape up every bit of food we can find, every blade of grass, every wild animal, every bit of shoe leather. And we'll survive, just the way we survived the blockade and the famine of '47 and everything else. And one of these days we'll go out to Trenton and—and— roast them alive!"

Roars of approval filled the air. Katterson turned and shouldered his way through the crowd, thinking of the two men and the dog, and walked away without looking back. He headed down Fourth Avenue, until he could no longer hear the sounds of the meeting at Union Square, and sat down wearily on a pile of crushed girders that had once been the Carden Monument.

He put his head in his big hands and sat there. The afternoon's events had numbed him. Food had been scarce as far back as he could remember—the twenty-four years of war with the Spherists had just about used up every resource of the country. The war had dragged on and on. After the first rash of preliminary bombings, it had become a war of attrition, slowly grinding the opposing spheres to rubble.

Somehow Katterson had grown big and powerful on hardly any food, and he stood out wherever he went. The generation of Americans to which he belonged was not one of size or strength—the children were born undernourished old men, weak and wrinkled. But he had been big, and he had been one of the lucky ones chosen for the Army. At least there he had been fed regularly.

Katterson kicked away a twisted bit of slag, and saw little Malory coming down Fourth Avenue in his direction. Katterson laughed to himself, remembering his Army days. His whole adult life had been spent in a uniform, with soldier's privileges. But it had been too good to last; two years before, in 2052, the war had finally dragged to a complete standstill, with the competing hemispheres both worn to shreds, and almost the entire Army had suddenly been mustered out into the cold civilian world. He had been dumped into New York, lost and alone.

"Let's go for a dog-hunt," Malory said, smiling, as he drew near.

"Watch your tongue, little man. I might just eat you if I get hungry enough."

"Eh? I thought you were so shocked by two men trying to catch a dog."

Katterson looked up. "I was," he said. "Sit down, or get moving, but don't play games," he growled. Malory flung himself down on the wreckage near Katterson and tried to straighten his tangled, thinning hair.

"Looks pretty bad," Malory said.

"Check," said Katterson. "I haven't eaten anything all day."

"Why not? There was a regular dole last night, and there'll be one tonight."

"You hope," said Katterson. The day was drawing to a close, he saw, and evening shadows were falling fast. Ruined New York looked weird in twilight; the gnarled girders and fallen buildings seemed ghosts of long-dead giants.

"You'll be even hungrier tomorrow," Malory said. "There isn't going to be any dole, any more."

"Don't remind me, little man."

"I'm in the food-supplying business, myself," said Malory, as a weak smile rippled over his lips.

Katterson picked up his head in a hurry.

"Playing games again?"

"No," Malory said hastily. He scribbled his address on a piece of paper and handed it to Katterson. "Here. Drop in on me any time you get really hungry. And—say, you're a pretty strong fellow, aren't you? I might even have some work for you, since you say you're unattached."

The shadow of an idea began to strike Katterson. He turned so he faced the little man, and stared at him. "What kind of work?" Malory paled. "Oh, I need some strong men to obtain food for me. You know," he whispered.

Katterson reached over and grasped the small man's thin shoulders. Malory winced. "Yes, I know," Katterson repeated slowly. "Tell me, Malory," he said carefully. "What sort of food do you sell?"

Malory squirmed. "Why—why —now look, I just wanted to help you, and—"

"Don't give me any of that." Slowly Katterson stood up, not releasing his grip on the small man. Malory found himself being dragged willy-nilly to his feet. "You're in the meat business, aren't you, Malory? *What kind of meat do you sell?*"

Malory tried to break away. Katterson shoved him with a contemptuous half-open fist and sent him sprawling back into the rubble-heap. Malory twisted away, his eyes wild with fear, and dashed off down 13th Street into the gloom. Katterson stood for a long time watching him retreat, breathing hard and not daring to think. Then he folded the paper with Malory's address on it and put it in his pocket, and walked numbly away.

Barbara was waiting for him when he pressed his thumb against the doorplate of his apartment on 47th Street, an hour later.

"I suppose you've heard the news," she said as he entered. "Some spic-and-span lieutenant came by and announced it down below. I've already picked up our dole for tonight, and that's the last one. Hey—anything the matter ?" She looked at him anxiously as he sank wordlessly into a chair.

"Nothing, kid. I'm just hungry—and a little sick to my stomach."

"Where'd you go today? The Square again?"

"Yeah. My usual Thursday afternoon stroll, and a pleasant picnic that turned out to be. First I saw two men hunting a dog—they couldn't have been much hungrier than I am, but they were chasing this poor scrawny thing. Then your lieutenant made his announcement about the food. And then a filthy meat peddler tried to sell me some 'merchandise' and give me a job."

The girl caught her breath. "A job? Meat? What happened? Oh, Paul—"

"Stow it," Katterson told her. "I knocked him sprawling and he ran away with his tail between his legs. You know what he was selling? You know what kind of meat he wanted me to eat?"

She lowered her eyes. "Yes, Paul."

"And the job he had for me—he saw I'm strong, so he would have made me his supplier. I would have gone out hunting in the evenings. Looking for stragglers to be knocked off and turned into tomorrow's steaks."

"But we're so hungry, Paul—when you're hungry that's the most important thing."

"What?" His voice was the bellow of an outraged bull. "What? You don't know what you're saying, woman. Eat before you go out of your mind completely. I'll find some other way of getting food, but I'm not going to turn into a bloody cannibal. No longpork for Paul Katterson."

She said nothing. The single light-glow in the ceiling flickered twice.

"Getting near shut-off time. Get the candles out, unless you're sleepy," he said. He had no chronometer, but the flickering was the signal that eight-thirty was approaching. At eight-thirty every night electricity was cut off in all residence apartments except those with permission to exceed normal quota.

Barbara lit a candle.

"Paul, Father Kennen was back here again today."

"I've told him not to show up here again," Katterson said from the darkness of his corner of the room.

"He thinks we ought to get married, Paul."

"I know. I don't."

"Paul, why are you—"

"Let's not go over that again. I've told you often enough that I don't want the responsibility of two mouths to feed, when I can't even manage keeping my own belly full. This way is the best—each of us our own."

"But children, Paul—"

"Are you crazy tonight?" he retorted. "Would you dare to bring a child into this world? Especially now that we've even lost the food from Trenton Oasis. Would you enjoy watching him slowly starve to death in all this filth and rubble, or maybe growing up into a hollow-cheeked little skeleton? Maybe you would. I don't think I'd care to."

He was silent. She sat watching him, sobbing quietly.

"We're dead, you and I," she finally said. "We won't admit it, but we're dead. This whole world is dead—we've spent the last thirty years committing suicide. I don't remember as far back as you do, but I've read some of the old books, about how clean and new and shiny this city was before the war. The war! All my life, we've been at war, never knowing who we were fighting or why. Just eating the world apart for no reason at all."

"Cut it, Barbara," Katterson said. But she went on in a dead monotone. "They tell me America once went from coast to coast, instead of being cut up into little strips bordered by radioactive no-man's-land. And there were farms, and food, and lakes and rivers, and men flew from place to place. Why did this have to happen? Why are we all dead? Where do we go now, Paul?"

"I don't know, Barbara. I don't think anyone does." Wearily, he snuffed out the candle, and the darkness flooded in and filled the room.

Somehow he had wandered back down to Union Square again, and he stood on 14th Street, rocking gently back and forth on his feet and feeling the light-headedness which is the first sign of starvation. There were just a few people in the streets, morosely heading for whatever destinations claimed them. The sun was high overhead, and bright.

His reverie was interrupted by the sound of yells and an unaccustomed noise of running feet. His Army training stood him in good fashion, as he dove into a gaping trench and hid there, wondering what was happening.

After a moment he peeked out. Four men, each as big as Katterson himself, were roaming up and down the now deserted streets. One was carrying a sack.

"There's one," Katterson heard the man with the sack yell harshly. He watched without believing as the four men located a girl cowering near a fallen building.

She was a pale, thin, ragged looking girl, perhaps twenty at the most, who might have been pretty in some other world. But her cheeks were sunken and coarse, her eyes dull and glassy, her arms bony and angular.

As they drew near she huddled back, cursing defiantly, and prepared to defend herself. *She doesn't understand, Katterson thought. She thinks she's going to be attacked.*

Perspiration streamed down his body, and he forced himself to watch, kept himself from leaping out of hiding. The four marauders closed in on the girl. She spat, struck out with her clawlike hand.

They chuckled and grabbed her clutching arm. Her scream was suddenly ear-piercing as they dragged her out into the open. A knife flashed; Katterson ground his teeth together, wincing, as the blade struck home.

"In the sack with her, Charlie," a rough voice said.

Katterson's eyes steamed with rage. It was his first view of Malory's butchers—at least, he suspected it was Malory's gang. Feeling the knife at his side, in its familiar sheath, he half-rose to attack the four meat-raiders, and then, regaining his senses, he sank back into the trench.

So soon? Katterson knew that cannibalism had been spreading slowly through starving New York for many years, and that few bodies of the dead ever reached their graves intact—but this was the first time, so far as he knew, that raiders had dragged a man living from the streets and killed him for food. He shuddered. The race for life was on, then.

The four raiders disappeared in the direction of Third Avenue, and Katterson cautiously eased himself from the trench, cast a wary eye in all directions, and edged into the open. He knew he would have to be careful; a man his size carried meat for many mouths.

Other people were coming out of the buildings now, all with much the same expression of horror on their faces. Katterson watched the marching skeletons walking dazedly, a few sobbing, most of them past the stage of tears. He clenched and unclenched his fists, angry, burning to stamp out this spreading sickness and knowing hopelessly that it could not be done.

A tall, thin man with chiseled features was on the speaker's platform now. His voice was choked with anger. "Brothers, it's out in the open now. Men have turned from the ways of God, and Satan has led them to destruction. Just now you witnessed four of His creatures destroy a fellow mortal for food—the most terrible sin of all.

"Brothers, our time on Earth is almost done. I'm an old man—I remember the days before the war, and, while some of you won't believe it, I remember the days when there was food for all, when everyone had a job, when these crumpled buildings were tall and shiny and streamlined, and the skies teemed with jets. In my youth I traveled all across this country, clear to the Pacific. But the War has ended all that, and it's God's hand upon us. Our day is done, and soon we'll all meet our reckoning.

"Go to God without blood on your hands, brothers. Those four men you saw today will burn forever for their crime. Whoever eats the unholy meat they butchered today will join them in Hell. But listen a moment, brothers, listen! Those of you who aren't lost yet, I beg of you: save yourselves! Better to go without food at all, as most of you are doing, than to soil yourselves with this kind of new food, the most precious meat of all."

Katterson stared at the people around him. He wanted to end all this; he had a vision of a crusade for food, a campaign against cannibalism, banners waving, drums beating, himself leading the fight. Some of the people had stopped listening to the old preacher, and some had wandered off. A few were smiling and hurling derisive remarks at the old man, but he ignored them.

"Hear me! Hear me, before you go. We're all doomed anyway; the Lord has made that clear. But think, people—this world will shortly pass away, and there is the greater world to come. Don't sign away your chance for eternal life, brothers! Don't trade your immortal soul for a bite of tainted meat!"

The crowd was melting away, Katterson noted. It was dispersing hastily, people quickly edging away and disappearing. The preacher continued talking. Katterson stood on tiptoes and craned his neck past the crowd and stared down towards the east. His eyes searched for a moment, and then he paled. Four ominous figures were coming with deliberate tread down the deserted street.

POST-BOMB DISASTER RESCUE AND RELIEF

IN CASE OF ATTACK, the State Plan calls for such preliminary action as locating the bomb strike; determining the size of the bomb and whether it was a ground or air burst; and estimating the amount of radiation present in areas of destruction and damage. As soon as these steps have been taken, the Civil Defense director in charge of relief operations will assign areas of responsibility to the various Civil Defense leaders that are available to him. He will issue orders and instructions for Civil Defense operating forces to be made available to the various area directors. When the assistance needed is beyond local capabilities and outside aid is required, State and Federal Governments will be called upon.

All the services of Civil Defense will be needed in these relief operations, and large quantities of medical supplies and first aid equipment and many emergency hospitals must be made available. Transportation for moving the injured quickly to the hospitals will be vitally needed. Transportation will be needed also to evacuate the homeless, sick and injured to prepared facilities located in the support area. Food, water, clothing, bedding and personal first aid kits will be needed in great quantity.

We have stored within the State, 3,000 Emergency First Aid Units, 200 Emergency Hospitals with a capacity of two hundred beds each, as well as much blood-collecting equipment. The Federal Government has stored in various parts of our State vast quantities of medical supplies and public works equipment which will be made available when needed.

The explosion of a nuclear weapon may cause the contamination of thousands of square miles in our state by radioactive fallout. To determine the presence of this fallout, trained Civil Defense personnel are available to measure with detection instruments the degree of this

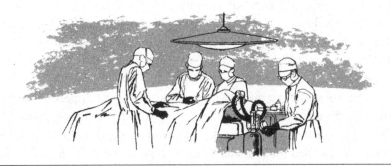

From *You and Civil Defense*, State of New York Executive Dept., Civil Defense Commission.

hazard. In this way, the people may be warned of the presence of fallout, and if the radiation is excessive, they may be evacuated to safer areas.

There will be at least two fixed monitor stations and a mobile survey team in each of the towns. Each of the several Civil Defense services will have especially trained monitors to work with their Civil Defense operating teams. A system of communication, mostly by telephone, is being set up so that the radiation readings of the monitors can be communicated to county Civil Defense directors. The radiation group at the county control center will record, compute, evaluate and plot the information made known to them on the Civil Defense director's operations map. This will enable the Civil Defense director to inform and instruct the people and the Civil Defense workers on what is required of them at any given moment.

RECOVERY WHEN ATTACKS HAVE ENDED, Civil Defense will undertake to cope with the initial problems of recovery and eventual return, as far as possible, to pre-attack conditions. This means restoration of public utilities, rehabilitation of transportation and communications facilities, and re-establishment of industry — all of which will require the combined efforts of local, State and Federal Defense organizations and other governmental agencies.

The supply of food, water, clothing, financial assistance, the restoration of banking facilities and the utilization of available manpower are some of the many problems Civil Defense forces will be called upon to solve in the recovery period after attack. All of this involves positive programs for the management of available resources and the production of essential commodities.

Almost everyone had seen them now. They were walking four abreast down the center of the street, the tallest holding an empty sack. People were heading hastily in all directions, and as the four figures came to the corner of 14th Street and Fourth Avenue only Katterson and the preacher still stood at the platform.

"I see you're the only one left, young man. Have you defiled yourself, or are you still of the Kingdom of Heaven?"

Katterson ignored the question. "Old man, get down from there!" he snapped. "The raiders are coming back. Come on, let's get out of here before they come."

"No. I intend to talk to them when they come. But save yourself, young man, save yourself while you can."

"They'll kill you, you old fool," Katterson whispered harshly.

"We're all doomed anyway, son. If my day has come, I'm ready."

"You're crazy," Katterson said. The four men were within speaking distance now. Katterson looked at the old man for one last time and then dashed across the street and into a building. He glanced back and saw he was not being followed.

The four raiders were standing under the platform, listening to the old man. Katterson couldn't hear what the preacher was saying, but he was waving his arms as he spoke. They seemed to be listening intently. Katterson stared. He saw one of the raiders say something to the old man, and then the tall one with the sack climbed up on the platform. One of the others tossed him an unsheathed knife.

The shriek was loud and piercing. When Katterson dared to look out again, the tall man was stuffing the preacher's body into the sack. Katterson bowed his head. The trumpets began to fade; he realized that resistance was impossible. Unstoppable currents were flowing.

Katterson plodded uptown to his apartment. The blocks flew past, as he methodically pulled one foot after another, walking the two miles through the rubble and deserted, ruined buildings. He kept one hand on his knife and darted glances from right to left, noting the furtive scurryings in the side streets, the shadowy people who were not quite visible behind the ashes and the rubble. Those four figures, one with the sack, seemed to lurk behind every lamppost, waiting hungrily.

He cut into Broadway, taking a shortcut through the stump of the Parker Building. Fifty years before, the Parker Building had been the tallest in the Western world; its truncated stump was all that remained. Katterson passed what had once been the most majestic lobby in the world, and stared in. A small boy sat on the step outside, gnawing a piece of meat. He was eight, or ten; his stomach was drawn tight over his ribs, which showed through like a basket. Choking down his revulsion, Katterson wondered what sort of meat the boy was eating.

He continued on. As he passed 44th Street, a bony cat skittered past him and disappeared behind a pile of ashes. Katterson thought of the stories he had heard of the Great Plains, where giant cats were said to roam unmolested, and his mouth watered.

The sun was sinking low again, and New York was turning dull gray and black. The sun never really shone in late afternoon anymore; it sneaked its way through the piles of rubble and cast a ghostly glow on the ruins of New York. Katterson crossed 47th Street and turned down towards his building.

He made the long climb to his room—the elevator's shaft was still there, and the frozen elevator, but such luxuries were beyond dream—and stood outside for just a moment, searching in the darkness for the doorplate. There was the sound of laughter from within, a strange sound for ears not accustomed to it, and a food-smell crept out through the door and hit him squarely. His throat began to work convulsively, and he remembered the dull ball of pain that was his stomach.

Katterson opened the door. The food-odor filled the little room completely. He saw Barbara look up suddenly, white-faced, as he entered. In his chair was a man he had met once or twice, a scraggly-haired, heavily-bearded man named Heydahl.

"What's going on ?" Katterson demanded. Barbara's voice was strangely hushed. "Paul, you know Olaf Heydahl, don't you? Olaf, Paul?"

"What's going on?" Katterson repeated.

"Barbara and I have just been having a little meal, Mr. Katterson," Heydahl said, in a rich voice. "We thought you'd be hungry, so we saved a little for you."

The smell was overpowering, and Katterson felt it was all he could do to keep from foaming at the lips. Barbara was wiping her face over and over again with the napkin; Heydahl sat contentedly in Katterson's chair.

In three quick steps Katterson crossed to the other side of the room and threw open the doors to the little enclosed kitchenette. On the stove a small piece of meat sizzled softly. Katterson looked at the meat, then at Barbara.

"Where did you get this?" he asked. "We have no money."

"I—I—"

"I brought it," Heydahl said quietly. "Barbara told me how little food you had, and since I had more than I wanted I brought over a little gift."

"I see. A gift. No strings attached?"

"Why, Mr. Katterson! Remember I'm Barbara's guest."

"Yes, but please remember this is my apartment, not hers. Tell me, Heydahl—what kind of payment do you expect for this—this gift? And how much payment have you had already?"

Heydahl half-rose in his chair. "Please, Paul," Barbara said hurriedly. "No trouble, Paul. Olaf was just trying to be friendly."

"Barbara's right, Mr. Katterson," Heydahl said, subsiding. "Go ahead, help yourself. You'll do yourself some good, and you'll make me happy too."

Katterson stared at him for a moment. The half-light from below trickled in over Heydahl's shoulder, illuminating his nearly-bald head and his flowing beard. Katterson wondered just how Heydahl's cheeks managed to be quite so plump.

"Go ahead," Heydahl repeated. "We've had our fill."

Katterson turned back to the meat. He pulled a plate from the shelf and plopped the piece of meat on it, and unsheathed his knife. He was about to start carving when he turned to look at the two others.

Barbara was leaning forward in her chair. Her eyes were staring wide, and fear was shining deep in them. Heydahl, on the other hand, sat back comfortably in Katterson's chair, with a complacent look on his face that Katterson had not seen on anyone's features since leaving the Army.

A thought hit him suddenly and turned him icy-cold. "Barbara," he said, controlling his voice, "what kind of meat is this? Roast beef or lamb?"

"I don't know, Paul," she said uncertainly. "Olaf didn't say what—"

"Maybe roast dog, perhaps? Filet of alleycat? Why didn't you ask Olaf what was on the menu. *Why don't you ask him now?*"

Barbara looked at Heydahl, then back at Katterson.

"Eat it, Paul. It's good, believe me—and I know how hungry you are."

"I don't eat unlabeled goods, Barbara. Ask Mr. Heydahl what kind of meat it is, first." She turned to Heydahl. "Olaf—"

"I don't think you should be so fussy these days, Mr. Katterson," Heydahl said. "After all, there are no more food doles, and you don't know when meat will be available again."

"I like to be fussy, Heydahl. What kind of meat is this?"

"Why are you so curious? You know what they say about looking gift horses in the mouth, heh heh."

"I can't even be sure this is horse, Heydahl. What kind of meat is it?" Katterson's voice, usually carefully modulated, became a snarl. "A choice slice of fat little boy? Maybe a steak from some poor devil who was in the wrong neighborhood one evening?"

Heydahl turned white.

Katterson took the meat from the plate and hefted it for a moment in his hand. "You can't even spit the words out, either of you. They choke in your mouths. Here—cannibals!"

He hurled the meat hard at Barbara; it glanced off the side of her cheek and fell to the floor. His face was flaming with rage. He flung open the door, turned, and slammed it again, rushing blindly away. The last thing he saw before slamming the door was Barbara on her knees, scurrying to pick up the piece of meat.

Night was dropping fast, and Katterson knew the streets were unsafe. His apartment, he felt, was polluted; he could not go back to it. The problem was to get food. He hadn't eaten in almost two days. He thrust his hands in his pocket and felt the folded slip of paper with Malory's address on it, and, with a wry grimace, realized that this was his only source of food and money. But not yet—not so long as he could hold up his head.

Without thinking he wandered toward the river, toward the huge crater where, Katterson had been told, there once had been the United Nations buildings. The crater was almost a thousand feet deep; the United Nations had been obliterated in the first bombing, back in 2028. Katterson had been just one year old then, the year the war began. The actual fighting and bombing had continued for the next five or six years, until both hemispheres were scarred and burned from combat, and then the long war of attrition had begun. Katterson had turned eighteen in 2045—nine long years, he reflected—and his giant frame made him a natural choice for a soft Army post. In the course of his Army career he had been all over the section of the world he considered his country—the patch of land bounded by the Appalachian radioactive belt on one side, by the Atlantic on the other. The enemy had carefully constructed walls of fire partitioning America into a dozen strips, each completely isolated from the next. An airplane could cross from one to another, if there were any left. But science, industry, technology, were dead, Katterson thought wearily, as he stared without seeing at the river. He sat down on the edge of the crater and dangled his feet.

What had happened to the brave new world that had entered the Twenty-First Century with such proud hopes? Here he was, Paul Katterson, probably one of the strongest and tallest men in the country, swinging his legs over a great devastated area, with a gnawing pain in the pit of his stomach. The world was dead, the shiny streamlined world of chrome plating and jet planes. Someday, perhaps, there would be new life. Someday.

Katterson stared at the waters beyond the crater. Somewhere across the seas there were other countries, broken like the rest. And somewhere in the other direction were rolling plains, grass, wheat, wild animals, fenced off by hundreds of miles of radioactive mountains. The War had eaten up the fields and pastures and livestock, had ground all mankind under.

He got up and started to walk back through the lonely streets. It was dark now, and the few gaslights cast a ghostly light, like little eclipsed moons. The fields were dead, and what was left of mankind huddled in the blasted cities, except for the lucky ones in the few Oases scattered by chance through the country. New York was a city of skeletons, each one scrabbling for food, cutting corners and hoping for tomorrow's bread.

A small man bumped into Katterson as he wandered unseeing. Katterson looked down at him and caught him by the arm. A family man, he guessed, hurrying home to his hungry children.

"Excuse me, sir," the little man said, nervously, straining to break Katterson's grip. The fear was obvious on his face; Katterson wondered if the worried little man thought this giant was going to roast him on the spot.

"I won't hurt you," Katterson said. "I'm just looking for food, citizen."

"I have none."

"But I'm starving," Katterson said. "You look like you have a job, some money. Give me some food and I'll be your bodyguard, your slave, anything you want."

"Look, fellow, I have no food to spare. Ouch! Let go of my arm!"

Katterson let go, and watched the little man go dashing away down the street. People always ran away from other people these days, he thought. Malory had made a similar escape.

The streets were dark and empty. Katterson wondered if he would be someone's steak by morning, and he didn't really care. His chest itched suddenly, and he thrust a grimy hand inside his shirt to scratch. The flesh over his pectoral muscles had almost completely been absorbed, and his chest was bony to the touch. He felt his stubbly cheeks, noting how tight they were over his jaws.

He turned and headed uptown, skirting around the craters, climbing over the piles of the rubble. At 50th Street a Government jeep came coasting by and drew to a stop. Two soldiers with guns got out.

"Pretty late for you to be strolling, Citizen," one soldier said.

"Looking for some fresh air."

"That all?"

"What's it to you?" Katterson said.

"Not hunting some game too, maybe?" Katterson lunged at the soldier. "Why, you little punk—"

"Easy, big boy," the other soldier said, pulling him back. "We were just joking."

"Fine joke," Katterson said. "You can afford to joke—all you have to do to get food is wear a monkey suit. I know how it is with you Army guys."

"Not any more," the second soldier said.

"Who are you kidding?" Katterson said. "I was a Regular Army man for seven years, until they broke up our outfit in '52. I know what's happening."

"Hey—what regiment?"

"306th Exploratory, soldier."

"You're not Katterson, Paul Katterson?"

"Maybe I am," Katterson said slowly. He moved closer to the two soldiers. "What of it?"

"You know Mark Leswick?"

"Damned well I do," Katterson said. "But how do you know him?"

"My brother. Used to talk of you all the time—Katterson's the biggest man alive, he'd say. Appetite like an ox."

Katterson smiled. "What's he doing now?"

The other coughed. "Nothing. He and some friends built a raft and tried to float to South America. They were sunk by the Shore Patrol just outside the New York Harbor."

"Oh. Too bad. Fine man, Mark. But he was right about that appetite. I'm hungry."

"So are we, fellow," the soldier said. "They cut off the soldier's dole yesterday."

Katterson laughed, and the echoes rang in the silent street. "Damn them anyway! Good thing they didn't pull that when I was in service; I'd have told them off."

"You can come with us, if you'd like. We'll be off-duty when this patrol is over, and we'll be heading downtown."

"Pretty late, isn't it? What time is it? Where are you going?"

"It's quarter to three," the soldier said, looking at his chronometer. "We're looking for a fellow named Malory; there's a story he has some food for sale, and we just got paid yesterday." He patted his pocket smugly.

Katterson blinked. "You know what kind of stuff Malory's selling?"

"Yeah," the other said. "So what? When you're hungry, you're hungry, and it's better to eat than starve. I've seen some guys like you—too stubborn to go that low for a meal. But you'll give in, sooner or later, I suppose. I don't know—you look stubborn."

"Yeah," Katterson said, breathing a little harder than usual. "I guess I am stubborn. Or maybe I'm not hungry enough yet. Thanks for the lift, but I'm afraid I am going uptown."

And he turned and trudged off into the darkness.

There was only one friendly place to go.

Hal North was a quiet, bookish man who had come in contact with Katterson fairly often, even though North lived almost four miles uptown, on 114th Street.

Katterson had a standing invitation to come to North at any time of day or night, and, having no place else to go, he headed there. North was one of the few scholars who still tried to pursue knowledge at Columbia, once a citadel of learning. They huddled together in the crumbling wreck of one of the halls, treasuring moldering books and exchanging ideas. North had a tiny apartment in an undamaged building on 114th Street, and he lived surrounded by books and a tiny circle of acquaintances.

Quarter to three, the soldier said. Katterson walked swiftly and easily, hardly noticing the blocks as they flew past. He reached North's apartment just as the sun was beginning to come up, and he knocked cautiously on the door. One knock, two, then another a little harder.

Footsteps within. "Who's there?" in a tired, high-pitched voice.

"Paul Katterson," Katterson whispered. "You awake?"

North slid the door open. "Katterson! Come on in! What brings you up here?"

"You said I could come whenever I needed to. I need to." Katterson sat down on the edge of North's bed. "I haven't eaten in two days, pretty near."

North chuckled. "You came to the right place, then. Wait—I'll fix you some bread and oleo. We still have some left."

"You sure you can spare it, Hal?"

North opened a cupboard and took out a loaf of bread, and Katterson's mouth began to water. "Of course, Paul. I don't eat much anyway, and I've been storing most of my food doles. You're welcome to whatever's here, for as long as you like."

A sudden feeling of love swept through Katterson, a strange, consuming emotion which seemed to enfold all mankind for a moment, then withered and died away. "Thanks, Hal. Thanks."

He turned and looked at the tattered, thumb-stained book lying open on North's bed. Katterson let his eye wander down the tiny print, and read softly aloud.

"The emperor of the sorrowful
realm was there,
Out of the girding ice be stood
breast-high,
And to his arm alone the giants
were
Less comparable than to
giant I."

North brought a little plate of food over to where Katterson was sitting. "I was reading that all night," he said. "Somehow I had thought of browsing through it again, and I started it last night and read till you came."

"Dante's *Inferno*," Katterson said. "Very appropriate. Someday I'd like to look through it again too. I've read so little, you know; soldiers don't get much education."

"Whenever you want to read, Paul, the books are still here." North smiled, a pale smile on his wan face. He pointed to the bookcase, where grubby, frayed books leaned at all angles. "Look, Paul: Rabelais, Joyce, Dante, Enright, Voltaire, Aeschylus, Homer, Shakespeare. They're all here, Paul, the most precious things of all. They're my old friends; those books have been my breakfasts and my lunches and my suppers many times when no food was to be had for any price."

"We may be depending on them alone, Hal. Have you been out much these days?"

"No," North said. "I haven't been outdoors in over a week. Henriks has been picking up my food doles and bringing them here, and borrowing books. He came by yesterday—no, two days ago—to get my volume of Greek tragedies. He's writing a new opera, based on a play of Aeschylus."

"Poor crazy Henriks," Katterson said. "Why does he keep on writing music when there are no orchestras, no records, no concerts? He can't even hear the stuff he writes."

North opened the window and the morning air edged in. "Oh, but he does, Paul. He hears his music in his mind, and that satisfies him. It doesn't really matter; he'll never live to hear it played."

"The doles have been cut off," Katterson said.

"I know."

"The people out there are eating each other. I saw a man killed for food yesterday—butchered just like a cow."

North shook his head and straightened a tangled, whitened lock. "So soon? I thought it would take longer than that, once the food ran out."

"They're hungry, Hal."

"Yes, they're hungry. So are you. In a day or so my supply up here will be gone, and I'll be hungry too. But it takes more than hunger to break down the taboo against eating flesh. Those people out there have given up their last shred of humanity now; they've suffered every degradation there is, and they can't sink any lower. Sooner or later we'll come to realize that, you and I, and then we'll be out there hunting for meat too."

"Hal!"

"Don't look so shocked, Paul." North smiled patiently. "Wait a couple of days, till we've eaten the bindings of my books, till we're finished chewing our shoes. The thought turns my stomach, too, but it's inevitable. Society's doomed; the last restraints are breaking now. We're more stubborn than the rest, or maybe we're just fussier about our meals. But our day will come too."

"I don't believe it," Katterson said, rising.

"Sit down. You're tired, and you're just a skeleton yourself now. What happened to my big, muscular friend Katterson? Where are his muscles now?" North reached up and squeezed the big man's biceps. "Skin, bones, what else? You're burning down, Paul, and when the spark is finally out you'll give in too."

"Maybe you're right, Hal. As soon as I stop thinking of myself as human, as soon as I get hungry enough and dead enough, I'll be out there hunting like the rest. But I'll hold out as long as I can."

He sank back on the bed and slowly turned the yellowing pages of Dante.

Henriks came back the next day, wild-eyed and haggard, to return the book of Greek plays, saying the times were not ripe for Aeschylus. He borrowed a slim volume of poems by Ezra Pound. North forced some food on Henriks, who took it gratefully and without any show of diffidence. Then he left, staring oddly at Katterson.

Others came during the day—Komar, Goldman, de Metz—all men who, like Henriks and North, remembered the old days, before the long war. They were pitiful skeletons, but the flame of knowledge burned brightly in each of them. North introduced Katterson to them, and they looked wonderingly at his still-powerful frame before pouncing avidly on the books.

But soon they stopped coming. Katterson would stand at the window and watch below for hours, and the empty streets remained empty. It was now four days since the last food had arrived from Trenton Oasis. Time was running out.

A light snowfall began the next day, and continued throughout the long afternoon. At the evening meal North pulled his chair over to the cupboard, balanced precariously on its arm, and searched around in the cupboard for a few moments. Then he turned to Katterson.

"I'm even worse off than Mother Hubbard," he said. "At least she had a dog."

"Huh?"

"I was referring to an incident in a children's book," North said. "What I meant was we have no more food."

"None?" Katterson asked dully.

"Nothing at all." North smiled faintly. Katterson felt the emptiness stirring in his stomach, and leaned back, closing his eyes.

Neither of them ate at all the next day. The snow continued to filter lightly down. Katterson spent most of the time staring out the little window, and he saw a light, clean blanket of snow covering everything in sight. The snow was unbroken.

The next morning Katterson arose and found North busily tearing the binding from his copy of the Greek plays. With a sort of amazement Katterson watched North put the soiled red binding into a pot of boiling water.

"Oh, you're up? I'm just preparing breakfast."

The binding was hardly palatable, but they chewed it to a soft pulp anyway, and swallowed the pulp just to give their tortured stomachs something to work on. Katterson retched as he swallowed his final mouthful.

One day of eating bookbindings.

"The city is dead," Katterson said from the window without turning around. "I haven't seen anyone come down this street yet. The snow is everywhere."

North said nothing.

"This is crazy, Hal," Katterson said suddenly. "I'm going out to get some food."

"Where?"

"I'll walk down Broadway and see what I can find. Maybe there'll be a stray dog. I'll look. We can't hold out forever up here."

"Don't go, Paul."

Katterson turned savagely. "Why? Is it better to starve up here without trying than to go down and hunt? You're a little man; you don't need food as much as I do. I'll go down to Broadway; maybe there'll be something. At least we can't be any worse off than now."

North smiled. "Go ahead, then."

"I'm going."

He buckled on his knife, put on all the warm clothes he could find, and made his way down the stairs. He seemed to float down, so lightheaded was he from hunger. His stomach was a tight hard knot.

The streets were deserted. A light blanket of snow lay everywhere, mantling the twisted ruins of the city. Katterson headed for Broadway, leaving tracks in the unbroken snow, and began to walk downtown.

At 96th Street and Broadway he saw his first sign of life, some people at the following corner. With mounting excitement he headed for 95th Street, but pulled up short.

There was a body sprawled over the snow, newly dead. And two boys of about twelve were having a duel to the death for its possession, while a third circled warily around them. Katterson watched them for a moment, and then crossed the street and walked on.

He no longer minded the snow and the solitude of the empty city. He maintained a steady, even pace, almost the tread of a machine. The world was crumbling fast around him, and his recourse lay in this solitary trek.

He turned back for a moment and looked behind him. There were his footsteps, the long trail stretching back and out of sight, the only marks breaking the even whiteness. He ticked off the empty blocks.

90th. 87th. 85th. At 84th he saw a blotch of color on the next block, and quickened his pace. When he got to close range, he saw it was a man lying on the snow. Katterson trotted lightly to him and stood over him.

He was lying face-down. Katterson bent and carefully rolled him over. His cheeks were still red; evidently he had rounded the corner and died just a few minutes before. Katterson stood up and looked around. In the window of the house nearest him, two pale faces were pressed against the pane, watching greedily.

He whirled suddenly to face a small, swarthy man standing on the other side of the corpse. They stared for a moment, the little man and the giant. Katterson noted dimly the other's burning eyes and set expression. Two more people appeared, a ragged woman and a boy of eight or nine. Katterson moved closer to the corpse and made a show of examining it for identification, keeping a wary eye on the little tableau facing him.

Another man joined the group, and another. Now there were five, all standing silently in a semi-circle. The first man beckoned, and from the nearest house came two women and still another man. Katterson frowned; something unpleasant was going to happen.

A trickle of snow fluttered down. The hunger bit into Katterson like a red-hot knife, as he stood there uneasily waiting for something to happen. The body lay fence-like between them.

The tableau dissolved into action in an instant. The small swarthy man made a gesture and reached for the corpse; Katterson quickly bent and scooped the dead man up. Then they were all around him, screaming and pulling at the body.

The swarthy man grabbed the corpse's arm and started to tug, and a woman reached up for Katterson's hair. Katterson drew up his arm and swung as hard as he could, and the small man left the ground and flew a few feet, collapsing into a huddled heap in the snow.

All of them were around him now, snatching at the corpse and at Katterson. He fought them off with his one free hand, with his feet, with his shoulders. Weak as he was and outnumbered, his size remained a powerful factor. His fist connected with someone's jaw and there was a rewarding crack; at the same time he lashed back with his foot and felt contact with breaking ribs.

"Get away!" he shouted. "Get away! This is mine! Away!" The first woman leaped at him, and he kicked at her and sent her reeling into the snowdrifts. "Mine! This is mine!"

They were even more weakened by hunger than he was. In a few moments all of them were scattered in the snow except the little boy, who came at Katterson determinedly, made a sudden dash, and leaped on Katterson's back.

He hung there, unable to do anything more than cling. Katterson ignored him, and took a few steps, carrying both the corpse and the boy, while the heat of battle slowly cooled inside him. He would take the corpse back uptown to North; they could cut it in pieces without much trouble. They would live on it for days, he thought. They would—

He realized what had happened. He dropped the corpse and staggered a few steps away, and sank down into the snow, bowing his head. The boy slipped off his back, and the little knot of people timidly converged on the corpse and bore it off triumphantly, leaving Katterson alone.

"Forgive me," he muttered hoarsely. He licked his lips nervously, shaking his head. He remained there kneeling for a long time, unable to get up.

"No. No forgiveness. I can't fool myself; I'm one of them now," he said. He arose and stared at his hands, and then began to walk. Slowly, methodically, he trudged along, fumbling with the folded piece of paper in his pocket, knowing now that he had lost everything.

The snow had frozen in his hair, and he knew his head was white from snow—the head of an old man. His face was white too. He followed along Broadway for a while, then cut to Central Park West. The snow was unbroken before him. It lay covering everything, a sign of the long winter setting in.

"North was right," he said quietly to the ocean of white that was Central Park. He looked at the heaps of rubble seeking cover beneath the snow. "I can't hold out any longer." He looked at the address—Malory, 218 West 42nd Street—and continued onward, almost numb with the cold.

His eyes were narrowed to slits, and lashes and head were frosted and white. Katterson's throat throbbed in his mouth, and his lips were clamped together by hunger. 70th Street, 65th. He zigzagged and wandered, following Columbus Avenue, Amsterdam Avenue for a while. Columbus, Amsterdam—the names were echoes from a past that had never been.

What must have been an hour passed, and another. The streets were empty. Those who were left stayed safe and starving inside, and watched from their windows the strange giant stalking alone through the snow. The sun had almost dropped from the sky as he reached 50th Street. His hunger had all but abated now; he felt nothing, knew just that his goal lay ahead. He faced forward, unable to go anywhere but ahead.

Finally 42nd Street, and he turned down toward where he knew Malory was to be found. He came to the building. Up the stairs, now, as the darkness of night came to flood the streets. Up the stairs, up another flight, another. Each step was a mountain, but he pulled himself higher and higher.

At the fifth floor Katterson reeled and sat down on the edge of the steps, gasping. A liveried footman passed, his nose in the air, his green coat shimmering in the half-light. He was carrying a roasted pig with an apple in its mouth, on a silver tray. Katterson lurched forward to seize the pig. His groping hands passed through it, and pig and footman exploded like bubbles and drifted off through the silent halls.

Just one more flight. Sizzling meat on a stove, hot, juicy, tender meat filling the hole where his stomach had once been. He picked up his legs carefully and set them down, and came to the top at last. He balanced for a moment at the top of the stairs, nearly toppled backwards but seized the banister at the last second, and then pressed forward.

There was the door. He saw it, heard loud noise coming from behind it. A feast was going on, a banquet, and he ached to join it. Down the hall, turn left, pound on the door.

Noise growing closer.

"Malory! Malory! It's me, Katterson, big Katterson! I've come to you! Open up, Malory!"

The handle began to turn.

"Malory! Malory!"

Katterson sank to his knees in the hall and fell forward on his face when the door opened at last.

There Will Come Soft Rains
Ray Bradbury

In the living room the voice-clock sang, *Tick-tock seven o'clock, time to get up, time to get up, seven o'clock!* as if it were afraid that nobody would. The morning house lay empty. The clock ticked on, repeating and repeating its sounds into the emptiness. *Seven-nine, breakfast time, seven-nine!*

In the kitchen the breakfast stove gave a hissing sigh and ejected from its warm interior eight pieces of perfectly browned toast, eight eggs sunnyside up, sixteen slices of bacon, two coffees, and two cool glasses of milk.

"Today is August 4, 2057," said a second voice from the kitchen ceiling, "in the city of Allendale, California." It repeated the date three times for memory's sake. "Today is Mr. Featherstone's birthday. Today is the anniversary of Tilita's marriage. Insurance is payable, as are the water, gas, and light bills."

Somewhere in the walls, relays clicked, memory tapes glided under electric eyes.

Eight-one, tick-tock, eight-one o'clock, off to school, off to work, run, run, eight-one!" But no doors slammed, no carpets took the soft tread of rubber heels. It was raining outside. The weather box on the front door sang quietly: "Rain, rain, go away; rubbers, raincoats for today…" And the rain tapped on the empty house, echoing.

Outside, the garage chimed and lifted its door to reveal a waiting car. After a long wait the door swung down again.

At eight-thirty the eggs were shriveled and the toast was like stone. An aluminum wedge scraped them into the sink, where hot water whirled them down a metal throat which digested and flushed them away to the distant sea. The dirty dishes were dropped into a hot washer and emerged twinkling dry.

Nine-fifteen, sang the clock, *time to clean.*

Out of warrens in the wall, tiny robot mice darted. The rooms were acrawl with the small cleaning animals, all rubber and metal. They thudded against chairs, whirling their mustached runners, kneading the rug nap, sucking gently at hidden dust. Then, like mysterious invaders, they popped into their burrows. Their pink electric eyes faded. The house was clean.

Ten o'clock. The sun came out from behind the rain. The house stood alone in a city of rubble and ashes. This was the one house left standing. At night the ruined city gave off a radioactive glow which could be seen for miles.

Ten-fifteen. The garden sprinklers whirled up in golden founts, filling the soft morning air with scatterings of brightness. The water pelted windowpanes, running down the charred west side where the house had been burned evenly free of its white paint. The entire west face of the house was black, save for five places. Here the silhouette in paint of a man mowing a lawn. Here, as in a photograph, a woman bent to pick flowers. Still farther over, their images burned on wood in one titanic instant, a small boy, hands flung into the air; higher up, the image of a thrown ball, and opposite him a girl, hands raised to catch a ball which never came down.

The five spots of paint—the man, the woman, the children, the ball—remained. The rest was a thin charcoaled layer.

The gentle sprinkler rain filled the garden with falling light.

Until this day, how well the house had kept its peace. How carefully it had inquired, "Who goes there? What's the password?" and, getting no answer from lonely foxes and whining cats, it had shut up its windows and drawn the shades in an old-maidenly preoccupation with self-protection which bordered on a mechanical paranoia.

It quivered at each sound, the house did. If a sparrow brushed a window, the shade snapped up. The bird, startled, flew off! No, not even a bird must touch the house!

The house was an altar with ten thousand attendants, big, small, servicing, attending, in choirs. But the gods had gone away, and the ritual of the religion continued senselessly, uselessly.

Twelve noon.

A dog whined, shivering, on the front porch.

The front door recognized the dog voice and opened. The dog, once huge and fleshy, but now gone to bone and covered with sores, moved in and through the house, tracking mud. Behind it whirled angry mice, angry at having to pick up mud, angry at inconvenience.

For not a leaf fragment blew under the door but what the wall panels flipped open and the copper scrap rats flashed swiftly out. The offending dust, hair, or paper, seized in miniature steel jaws, was raced back to the burrows. There, down tubes which fed into the cellar, it was dropped into the sighing vent of an incinerator which sat like evil Baal in a dark corner.

The dog ran upstairs, hysterically yelping to each door, at last realizing, as the house realized, that only silence was here.

It sniffed the air and scratched the kitchen door. Behind the door, the stove was making pancakes which filled the house with a rich baked odor and the scent of maple syrup.

The dog frothed at the mouth, lying at the door, sniffing, its eyes turned to fire. It ran wildly in circles, biting at its tail, spun in a frenzy, and died. It lay in the parlor for an hour.

Two o'clock, sang a voice.

Delicately sensing decay at last, the regiments of mice hummed out as softly as blown gray leaves in an electrical wind.

Two-fifteen.

The dog was gone.

In the cellar, the incinerator glowed suddenly and a whirl of sparks leaped up the chimney.

Two thirty-five.

Bridge tables sprouted from patio walls. Playing cards fluttered onto pads in a shower of pips. Martinis manifested on an oaken bench with egg-salad sandwiches. Music played.

But the tables were silent and the cards untouched.

At four o'clock the tables folded like great butterflies back through the paneled walls.

Four-thirty.

The nursery walls glowed.

Animals took shape: yellow giraffes, blue lions, pink antelopes, lilac panthers cavorting in crystal substance. The walls were glass. They looked out upon color and fantasy. Hidden films clocked through well-oiled sprockets, and the walls lived. The nursery floor was woven to resemble a crisp, cereal meadow. Over this ran aluminum roaches and iron crickets, and in the hot still air butterflies of delicate red tissue wavered among the sharp aroma of animal spoors! There was the sound like a great matted yellow hive of bees within a dark bellows, the lazy bumble of a purring lion. And there was the patter of okapi feet and the murmur of a fresh jungle rain, like other hoofs, falling upon the summer-starched grass. Now the walls dissolved into distances of parched weed, mile on mile, and warm endless sky. The animals drew away into thorn brakes and water holes.

It was the children's hour.

Five o'clock. The bath filled with clear hot water.

Six, seven, eight o'clock. The dinner dishes manipulated like magic tricks, and in the study a click. In the metal stand opposite the hearth where a fire now blazed up warmly, a cigar popped out, half an inch of soft gray ash on it, smoking, waiting.

Nine o'clock. The beds warmed their hidden circuits, for nights were cool here.

Nine-five. A voice spoke from the study ceiling:

"Mrs. McClellan, which poem would you like this evening?"

The house was silent.

The voice said at last, "Since you express no preference, I shall select a poem at random." Quiet music rose to back the voice. "Sara Teasdale. As I recall, your favorite….

"There will come soft rains and the smell of the ground,
And swallows circling with their shimmering sound;

And frogs in the pools singing at night,
And wild plum trees in tremulous white;

Robins will wear their feathery fire,
Whistling their whims on a low fence-wire;

And not one will know of the war, not one
Will care at last when it is done.

Not one would mind, neither bird nor tree,
If mankind perished utterly;

And Spring herself, when she woke at dawn
Would scarcely know that we were gone."

The fire burned on the stone hearth and the cigar fell away into a mound of quiet ash on its tray. The empty chairs faced each other between the silent walls, and the music played.

At ten o'clock the house began to die.

The wind blew. A falling tree bough crashed through the kitchen window. Cleaning solvent, bottled, shattered over the stove. The room was ablaze in an instant!

"Fire!" screamed a voice. The house lights flashed, water pumps shot water from the ceilings. But the solvent spread on the linoleum, licking, eating, under the kitchen door, while the voices took it up in chorus: "Fire, fire, fire!"

The house tried to save itself. Doors sprang tightly shut, but the windows were broken by the heat and the wind blew and sucked upon the fire.

The house gave ground as the fire in ten billion angry sparks moved with flaming ease from room to room and then up the stairs. While scurrying water rats squeaked from the walls, pistoled their water, and ran for more. And the wall sprays let down showers of mechanical rain.

But too late. Somewhere, sighing, a pump shrugged to a stop. The quenching rain ceased. The reserve water supply which had filled baths and washed dishes for many quiet days was gone.

The fire crackled up the stairs. It fed upon Picassos and Matisses in the upper halls, like delicacies, baking off the oily flesh, tenderly crisping the canvases into black shavings.

Now the fire lay in beds, stood in windows, changed the colors of drapes!

And then, reinforcements.

From attic trapdoors, blind robot faces peered down with faucet mouths gushing green chemical.

The fire backed off, as even an elephant must at the sight of a dead snake. Now there were twenty snakes whipping over the floor, killing the fire with a clear cold venom of green froth.

But the fire was clever. It had sent flames outside the house, up through the attic to the pumps there. An explosion! The attic brain which directed the pumps was shattered into bronze shrapnel on the beams.

The fire rushed back into every closet and felt of the clothes hung there.

The house shuddered, oak bone on bone, its bared skeleton cringing from the heat, its wire, its nerves revealed as if a surgeon had torn the skin off to let the red veins and capillaries quiver in the scalded air. Help, help! Fire! Run, run! Heat snapped mirrors like the brittle winter ice. And the voices wailed Fire, fire, run, run, like a tragic nursery rhyme, a dozen voices, high, low, like children dying in a forest, alone, alone. And the voices fading as the wires popped their sheathings like hot chestnuts. One, two, three, four, five voices died.

In the nursery the jungle burned. Blue lions roared, purple giraffes bounded off. The panthers ran in circles, changing color, and ten million animals, running before the fire, vanished off toward a distant steaming river....

Ten more voices died. In the last instant under the fire avalanche, other choruses, oblivious, could be heard announcing the time, playing music, cutting the lawn by remote-control mower, or setting an umbrella frantically out and in the slamming and opening front door, a thousand things happening, like a clock shop when each clock strikes the hour insanely before or after the other, a scene of maniac confusion, yet unity; singing, screaming, a few last cleaning mice darting bravely out to carry the horrid ashes away! And one voice, with sublime disregard for the situation, read poetry aloud in the fiery study, until all the film spools burned, until all the wires withered and the circuits cracked.

The fire burst the house and let it slam flat down, puffing out skirts of spark and smoke.

In the kitchen, an instant before the rain of fire and timber, the stove could be seen making breakfasts at a psychopathic rate, ten dozen eggs, six loaves of toast, twenty dozen bacon strips, which, eaten by fire, started the stove working again, hysterically hissing!

The crash. The attic smashing into kitchen and parlor. The parlor into cellar, cellar into sub-cellar. Deep freeze, armchair, film tapes, circuits, beds, and all like skeletons thrown in a cluttered mound deep under.

Smoke and silence. A great quantity of smoke.

Dawn showed faintly in the east. Among the ruins, one wall stood alone. Within the wall, a last voice said, over and over again and again, even as the sun rose to shine upon the heaped rubble and steam:

"Today is August 5, 2057, today is August 5, 2057, today is…"

The results of a "modern-built" house being exposed to an atomic bomb detonation as part of Operation Cue, 1955. (Photograph—United States Archives.)

Last Testament

Carol Amen

If I sound calm as I begin this, I'm not. Numb would be more like it. Drained, nearly hopeless. I'm writing to try to hold onto my sanity. It's something to do, a discipline. I will make every effort to tell what happened, no matter how painful the telling is. I want this record to be accurate, and in sequence.

March 23. Tonight as I fixed dinner and wrestled with self-pity because Tom had phoned saying he'd be staying late in San Francisco, the entire Eastern Seaboard was wiped out.

I had the TV in the kitchen tuned to the evening news from New York. When the video went off there was a bright pop. Then the screen went dark.

I moved to jiggle the knobs, expecting the usual apology about "technical difficulties," although now that I think of it, the sound was off, too. No static, no flickers—nothing.

Suddenly the picture came back, with an excited San Francisco announcer shouting, "Listen! Listen! We're being attacked!" The man's voice rose and broke. His manner bore no resemblance to the typical modulated accounts of international intrigue, assassination, natural disasters.

"Radar sources confirm. Many Eastern cities have already been destroyed."

The East, I thought, panic rising in my throat. My brother's Atlanta home. There must be some mistake.

Mary Liz and Brad, our older children, stared with me at the television. If only Tom were here. Maybe he would tell us it was a stunt, some Orson Welles trick for audience reaction. But as I looked at the TV crew, I knew it was no prank.

The announcer was hysterical. Sometimes the camera wasn't even focused. Over and over we could hear, "Massive retaliation." Was my brother's family really gone? I refused to think it was true.

Then came the same flash on the screen, only this time we could see it all around us. An eerie light coursed and flickered hideously.

"Tom!" I screamed. "Tom!" *Was that San Francisco?* Scottie, almost three, began wailing as Mary Liz, Brad, and I ran outside. Brad, who's twelve and very logical, questioned whether we should look south toward the intense light. At fourteen, Mary Liz seems infinitely older than I. She didn't move her gaze for a second.

I thought it would be like a giant mushroom, but it was more of an inverted mountain. I stood transfixed as its funnel pulled life from the place my husband had been at three o'clock. "Tom. Oh, Tom," I whispered.

Other explosions, more distant, erupted like visual echoes to the first. I think there were six or seven.

Scottie whimpered and clung to my legs. Automatically I picked him up, just as the ground trembled beneath us. Earthquake. Oh, God, not that, too!

"Daddy might have left early, after all," Mary Liz whispered. "Sometimes he does. He could be halfway home by now for all we know." Mary Liz is like that. A dreamer, always hopeful.

"Daddy will come to us." I paused. "He will—if he can."

We went inside. I held Scottie close. "Brad, get the transistor and turn it to the Civil Defense station. Somebody will tell us what's happening."

All my life I've heard that "should there be an actual alert" we would be given emergency instructions. Back and forth we twisted the dials on the little radio, straining for the sound of authority, someone in charge. Nothing.

I ached to talk to my mother. She used to console me when I had nightmares. I reached for the phone, but there was no dial tone. Our electricity was off.

Brad spoke excitedly. "Mom, Mr. Halliday's radio set! He's got emergency power. He let our Scout troup talk to some Explorers up in Idaho."

In case Tom arrived, I left a note recording my intentions—to go over to Ab and Betty's—and the date and time: March 23. 7:15 P.M.

The scene at the Hallidays' was like something from a bad movie. As the minutes and hours dragged by, more and more people arrived. The room where Ab, Betty, Tom, and I had played so many games of pinochle was jammed shoulder to shoulder.

Ab was at his set and Betty darted in and out carrying terse bulletins. "Seattle gone." Or, "Just raised Yuba City. All safe." The brotherhood of "hams" was on duty—those that were alive.

We drank coffee, spoke inanely to one another, and tried to comfort the children. Around 11:00, Ab took a break and staggered out. Betty hurried to stand beside him. I felt his eyes bore into my very soul. He and Tom fished together. Betty had my husband bring back sourdough bread whenever he went in to the city.

"San Francisco's gone," Ab said hoarsely. "The entire Bay Area. I can't raise anyone there. We're on the fringe. I've found only one ham closer to San Francisco than us.

Sacramento is silent—utterly silent. Southern California, too. A fellow in Twain Harte thinks they hit Yosemite. The sky is black with splinters—trees and rocks coming down like rain. It must've been a mistake. There's nothing strategic there. I can't even tell you some of the things I've heard." He swayed, and Betty tightened her embrace.

The room was deadly quiet. "We're the lucky ones. Survivors. Folks I reached in Northern California and Oregon. Rural areas. Small towns. Not near industrial or military installations. We may be cut off, but we're not crippled or dead. We're lucky."

I gathered the children and came home. I thought of stories I've read where a woman had lost a beloved husband. Those women shrieked, tore their clothes. I felt every bit as deranged as any story heroine I ever read about.

My husband. Oh, Tom. The dearest human being in the world. My rock. I am raw. My insides ripped out without anesthetic.

For hours I sat in Tom's chair by the window, trying to remember. I could almost see the flecks of amber in his eyes, feel the bristly little hairs that grew on the back of his hands. Once I thought I caught his unique scent. But I couldn't remember whether we had said, "I love you," when he left at six that morning.

I don't know what to do. Probably there is nothing to do. Before going to bed, I started this journal.

March 24, Parts of the day blurred. We ate. Washed dishes. Contacted friends. Feared the weather.

The sky is yellow and dark—almost like liquid instead of air. And hot. Nothing like normal for a northern coastal town in March. I am afraid. I would like to erase Ab's words, "We are the lucky ones."

Brad and I decided that if by some miracle Tom is on his way home, we might need gas to drive to a safer place. We went down to our regular station.

A ripple of fear shot through me when I saw Slim perched on a stool by the pumps with a rifle across his knees, directing his son in filling the tank of a battered Chevy.

For a minute I considered driving away, but Slim came over and spoke politely.

"Mornin', missus," he said. Your mister get home last night?"

"He'd planned to stay late in the city. We thought for a while—" I took a firmer grip on the wheel. "It looks like he didn't get out."

I saw pain on the weathered face. Tom often took Teddy, Slim's retarded son, along on his fishing trips. I used to begrudge, occasionally, that Tom spent precious time with this boy when his own children seldom saw him. Then I would feel guilty for my resentment.

269

"Gas, missus?"

"What are you charging?"

"It's free to my regular customers," Slim replied. "Don't figure credit cards is much good now."

"But I can pay. This is your business, not a charity."

"I done some thinkin' last night, missus. Me and Teddy don't need much. Food and a roof. When the gas is gone, we'll plant a garden. Go fishin'."

Brad leaned across the seat as Slim's son unscrewed our gas cap. "Then how come you've got that rifle, Mr. Sutton?"

"Just because I'm givin' gas away don't mean I'm a fool. There's been people here wantin' fill-ups. Them that's never seen the inside of this station, nor didn't have the time of day for Teddy."

My face burned and I chose my words carefully. "I'll accept the gas, Slim, if you'll let me have you and Teddy over for a meal. I want to repay you somehow."

"This gas's been paid for, missus. More than once. I just hope you can use it."

On the way home, we saw a crowd at the Catholic church, and went in. The mayor was huffing and puffing. Robbery of drugs from the pharmacy. Gas $100 a gallon at some stations. Might have to invoke martial law. He also advised drinking only bottled water and eating canned food.

I felt like laughing. A bomb that could level a city and shoot debris into the sky 150 miles away probably wouldn't have much trouble finding its way into my apricots.

The mood lifted a little when the clergy took over. Father Sweeney and our Methodist minister, Reverend Jansen, led us in prayer. Their faith is somehow heartening. They wear it like armor.

March 27. Our tree. Our tree. I cannot write today…

March 29. I thought to find some relief for us. We packed lunch and pulled Scottie in his wagon. Intended to walk to the beach. But then we saw our tree.

Several years ago, families contributed trees and shrubs for roadside beautification. Ours was a flowering plum and Tom had dug the hole himself. Proudly we watched it through seasons of bloom, purple leaf, and bare branch. Just a couple of weeks ago we photographed the little beauty under a corona of blossoms. What delicate color. Then, the other day, as we crested the hill, we saw it again. Apparently it had come to leaf since our photo, but this didn't look like a plum tree in spring. It was—it was—

Papery tatters hung like shrouds from its limbs.

Mary Liz and Brad stared, uncomprehending at first. Then Brad murmured, "We're going to die, too, aren't we, Mom?"

We huddled together, trying not to look at the ashy leaves. I thought of those Exposure to Communicable Disease forms teachers sometimes send home when there's an outbreak of mumps or measles. The paper lists various diseases and the incubation period of each, and the teacher checks the appropriate box so the parent can be prepared. We have seen a plum tree—Nature's Exposure to Disease warning.

March 31. The first to go was the three-week-old infant of Cathy Pitkin, our former babysitter.

At a town meeting/prayer service, someone said tiny Susie's death was probably due to birth defects. I hurried over to see Cathy and her husband and found the young mother sobbing quietly.

"We thought we were so lucky," John muttered. "Didn't seem like there'd be any more bombs. Then poor little Susie had to get sick and die. 'Course I've tried to tell Cathy we're young. We can have another baby."

He said something about it being up to the survivors to continue, to repopulate the earth. I can't remember exactly. I just stared at him, wanting to reach over and pull his eyelids down over the indecent innocence in his eyes. Not even Brad is as naive as this boy.

"Don't know why she won't talk to you. She admires you. Had to nurse Susie just because you always nursed your babies."

She nursed?"

"Oh, yeah. Susie hadn't had so much as a spoonful of cereal or canned baby food yet. Cathy was so proud of having plenty of milk. We gave her water, but we boiled it. You don't suppose the water was contaminated?"

"I think everything's contaminated, John. Try to comfort Cathy. Tell her Susie is better off. In a few weeks I think she'll understand."

April 2. Mary Liz is sure she heard a robin today. I wonder.

April 5. Twenty-some have died, and many more are sick. The symptoms vary. High fever, itching, dry skin. Some nausea. I thought hair would fall out, but perhaps they went too quickly for that.

At the time of the baby's death, I suspected it was an omen, just the beginning. When the others were stricken, though, I tried to pretend, to clutch at coincidence.

It took a walk on the beach to convince me what I knew all along. I didn't tell the children what I saw, nor will I recount it here. My magnificent ocean. I pray God will forgive us for what we have done.

I resent having no one to talk to. My friends? Tell aloud the horrors I picture over and over? I think not. The journal helps a little.

April 7. I am worried about Scottie.

April 8. Scottie is feverish. Repeatedly he asks for the story of Peter Pan. Mary Liz sings, "I can fly, I can fly, I can fly." I cannot bear to listen. But I cannot bear to be far from him.

April 9. By turns Mary Liz and I bathe Scottie. Still the fever won't come down. I don't think he hears the crooning. My baby. My baby.

Many in town are dead. Most businesses are closed, as is the school. The newspaper comes out weekly now, only a single sheet with survival information. Garbage pickup continues irregularly, due to the gas shortage. Other services dependent on gas or electricity have been discontinued.

Two supermarkets and three tiny groceries are operational. The proprietors inventoried canned goods and are rationing them out fairly. They tell us that after everything returns to normal we can pay them back.

There is a theory that only the young and old will die. A few feel they are somehow strong, invulnerable. Ab Halliday came over. The Hallidays have lost two of their four children, but Ab is far from giving up. He is at the radio at least eighteen hours a day. By relay he has found people alive as far east as Nebraska.

My parents live (or is it lived?) in Iowa. In recent days I've caught myself talking out loud to my mother, asking her what she would do, leaning on her for advice and strength.

Ab has discovered that deaths are occurring everywhere, even in remote areas, yet he is determined all is not lost. I envy him his fiction.

April 11. Scott died yesterday at 1:30 P.M.

The three of us dug a deep hole in the back yard near the browning rose bushes. The cemetery is unspeakable. Rev. Jansen came and prayed with us. Mostly, he and the Catholic priest are conducting mass burials. About 700 so far.

Ironically, I think Reverend Jansen took as much comfort from us as we did from him. We became close when Tom's parents were killed in the car crash, and then again during my depression before Scottie was born. He is a good man.

In the midst of our pitiful little service, I thought of a night several years ago. It was right after a winter's rain, and I stood alone on the front porch. All the stars in the world, it seemed, had come out—thousands and thousands of them. I felt so alive. I remember standing on tiptoe to get closer to the beauty. "Life is good!" I shouted. For once I was glad of the solitude, for I would have been embarrassed if even Tom had heard me.

Then yesterday, in our back yard, I spoke of that moment. "Have you ever felt like that?" I looked at them one by one.

Mr. Jansen seemed to come back from a long way off. "I have been very happy at times. It's important that you remind us of such good feelings. Especially now." His voice seemed infinitely sad. "The past weeks I've felt so helpless."

He turned to Brad. "Have you ever experienced the feeling your mother described— glad to be alive?"

My son was silent a moment. "Maybe. Once up on the Hallidays' diving board, just before I jumped in. I don't mean diving—exactly. It was—oh, I can't explain. But I guess I know what Mom means."

Mary Liz reached for my hand. "For me, it was when Daddy came home from a trip. I loved us being together, with everything the way it belonged. Now I'd be satisfied just to see the stars."

Mr. Jansen gave each of us a brief pat, then walked slowly from the yard…

April 12. At least 1,300 gone. More than half our population. Beale's Contracting picks up the bodies in one of their large dump trucks and bulldozes communal graves on the east edge of town. That's since the cemetery can't handle it any more.

Brad and Mary Liz fall into petty bickering at times and I want to scream, "We are dying! Can't you, for God's sake, love each other a few minutes?" Then without a word on my part, they make up and we sit together quietly, at peace.

After Scottie died, Brad kept proposing projects, games, brain teasers. But it didn't work. Nor can I find comfort in my garden. My plants are dead, and the only fragrance in the air is a stench—the smell of death from San Francisco, from Canada, from China, for all I know.

Then Brad had another idea. It happened after Larry's parents died and he moved in with us. Maybe to keep his friend busy, Brad suggested we organize a work detail for our street. He proposed that the four of us—he and Larry, Mary Liz and I—working by teams, make a morning check at each house in the neighborhood.

I had reservations about squandering our slight strength on others. But the people we visited seemed so grateful.

When we first called on a woman I'd quarreled with years ago, I thought I couldn't go through with it. She and I had fought over a supposedly stolen ball—claimed by each family of youngsters. We'd not spoken in ten years. Larry and I carried a jar of soup to her porch, waited down her hostile stare, then followed her inside.

She led me back to a bedroom where her daughter, once Mary Liz's playmate, lay in a stupor. For a terrible, timeless moment we forgot the past, in which we had been stupid, and the future, when we would be dead. It was the present. Two mothers helpless in front of a stricken child. Our arms groped for each other, and we clung together a long time, crying and inhaling the girl's cloying breath.

I asked Larry to finish rounds without me. At the end of our road, I fell to the dry grass of a vacant lot. I tore the earth. Retched. Screamed. I have no idea the length of time. I was demented. But I knew enough not to let the children see me.

April 14. We three need to be near, and: Larry's presence doesn't intrude. Sometimes when we're resting one will tell a family story, recall a trip, something funny. "Remember the quilt in Grandma's guest room?" "Remember Monopoly?" "Remember Daddy?"

We're all getting slower now, and we wondered about the rounds. Mary Liz pointed out, "Their eyes light up so when we go in." We voted to continue. Because of the deaths we have fewer houses to call at but it takes us longer. We have brought two young children to Scottie's old room. They will not be here long, I'm afraid.

April 15. This used to be Income Tax Day. Now it marks Beale's switch from bulldozing to burning. It takes less strength to torch the bodies than it does to drive the big cat that opened the graves.

April 24. Larry died suddenly a day or two ago. He had gone in the morning on rounds and that afternoon crawled into his bunk and died. I regret not noticing how quiet he had become. His mother was my friend and our boys have been close for years. I wish I had told her I'd take care of Larry, but she died too soon.

We pulled the body of that sweet, uncomplaining boy over to the corner for pickup and I remembered some lines of Millay's.

Down, down, down into the darkness of the grave

274

Gently they go, the beautiful, the tender, the kind;
Quietly they go, the intelligent, the witty, the brave.
I know. But I do not approve. And I am not resigned.

Odd how close I feel to all poets, craftsmen, and workers who have ever tried to make a statement. Will anyone survive to gaze at Michelangelo's creations, a Navajo rug, or my own scribblings?

May 1. Mary Liz collapsed today. As I sit beside her and write, I suspect that with her also the battle will be brief. She calls out for reassurance I cannot muster.

I was strong with Scottie. But I cannot seem to steel myself for this. I long for those days when I could afford depression, tantrums, counseling, and comfort in Tom's arms.

This is my firstborn. My beautiful daughter. She brushes hot fingers against the sheet. Who will comfort me when she is gone? She asks for a drink. Something I can give. She asks for her Daddy. Something I can't.

When she was little, she reacted in outrage if she were hurt or frustrated. I can see her stamping her small foot, throwing back her head to challenge Tom or me. Or was it Brad who stamped his foot, and Mary Liz the docile one? It's hard to remember.

From his rounds alone today, Brad brought home a man. This sick creature is a pitiful shell. Occasionally he staggers from his bed to the kitchen to grab food and hoard it in his room. Why can't he trust us to care for him? I have no pity to spare. Brad says it's better to have him here than go a block and a half to check him several times a day.

Later, after resting, Brad walked clear over to the Hallidays' for news. There is no one left to drive Beale's truck. Dear Betty Halliday and all their children are gone. Ab sent word with Brad we should move over there. He dares not leave his radio. The fool. Nearly all his hams are silent now. But he thinks some miracle may save us yet.

Is Mary Liz alive? She is so still. Oh, Tom, I scream in my soul. Tom, you are the lucky one not to have to watch our children die!

I am sick myself. It is so hard to concentrate. Perhaps I don't make sense. Sometimes I read back over what I have written and the words swim. What was my point? Why do I not save my strength? I keep arguing the journal is important. My link to sanity, to civilization.

Probably May 3. Mary Liz is gone. I made a winding sheet and Brad and I dragged her to the back yard, to the raw dirt on top of Scottie's grave. We sat beside her, staring, waiting for some ease to the pain. After forever, Brad began, "Our Father, who art in heaven—" It took us a long time to say it. We kept forgetting and had to start again and again.

I am getting sicker, but Brad shows no signs of weakening. I will try to hold on a while longer. I think I can manage.

Brad tries so hard to be a man. No, he is a man. He's so like you, Tom. He went out again yesterday, right after Mary Liz—I cannot say the word that means the end of our daughter. But Brad went out. He says Mr. Jansen died several days ago. He found the priest staggering. He and Jansen had promised each other they would call at every home and pray with the sick. Brad helped him for a while. They found three people alive.

May 5, I think. Today Brad brought home Teddy from the gas station. He reminds me of Scottie in his confusion. Slim must have died days ago. Brad said their house was in an awful state.

Days later. Yesterday, in Brad's walk, he found Ab like a zombie at the radio set. He had to slap him to get a response. The man hadn't left his radio for four days or nights. In all that time—silence.

It finished him, Tom. His hope lasted longer than anybody's. Brad says Ab asked to come over here. He started up out of his chair. Then fell to the floor. No pulse.

Brad walked home. Told me about Ab. Admitted he is sick now, too. Our time surely must be short. I thought to end it for us three together, in the garage. Slim had hoped we could use the gas. And that way no one would be left alone at the end.

I went out to check the car. The battery is still alive. How ironic the inanimate objects fare so much better. Such effort to start the car. Each movement laborious, slow motion. Then back to get Teddy and Brad. Teddy had found Tom's favorite fishing rod. Held it clutched to his cheek like a security blanket. Brad sitting nearby, eyes closed.

I thought there could be no surprises left. But I find I cannot do it. What right have I? We will go soon enough. I pray God will help me stay awake, take them first.

Final entry. If survivors come here. Want them to know something. We didn't act like animals. Most people were good. Helped. Tried.

If only we could have lived as well as we have died.

I wish—

The Federal Civil Defense Administration had set up a pattern of national civil defense in the early 1950s. By the early 1970s this plan of accounbtability no longer existed, as the narrator in Amen's story finds out.

CIVIL DEFENSE

FOR

SCHOOLS

STATE COUNCIL
OF CIVIL DEFENSE
HARRISBURG, PENNSYLVANIA
1952

Civil Defense for Schools was a booklet published by the State of Pennsylvania Council of Civil Defense in 1952. Advanced copies were sent out to school districts in January 1952 seeking feedback. The following pages are excerpted from the final published booklet.

3. Principal Duties of the Administrator

The school administrator's civil defense duties generally comprise seven primary steps, namely:

a. Appointment of a School Civil Defense Council, responsible for the development of general policies and procedures. (Should be chosen from parents, school personnel and other interested individuals.)

b. Appointment of a Civil Defense Director for each school building. (Should be a faculty member or full-time employee working within the building.)

c. Appointment of three persons (with designated order of responsibility) who shall act for the Civil Defense Director in the event he is either absent or unable to act.

d. Appointment (from faculty, administrative personnel or student body) of emergency committees in each school, responsible for activities relating to:

> (1) Air raid warnings
> (2) Shelter
> (3) Fire fighting
> (4) First aid
> (5) Emergency feeding
> (6) Public relations

e. Procurement and supply of civil defense equipment and materials required for protection of each school building. (Fire extinguishers, ladders, rope, hand tools, stretchers, cots, blankets, first aid materials, flashlights, battery-powered radios and similar essentials.)

f. Periodic appraisal of the civil defense program, including the inspection of equipment and facilities.

g. Maintenance of complete and accurate records for each school building. (Personnel lists, inventories, records of drills and training activities, etc.)

4. Provisions for Shelter

Every school should *provide and clearly mark shelter areas* adequate for the temporary housing of all occupants of the school. (See Page 28, "Standard Signs For Civil Defense Use.")

5. Establishment of Standard Air Raid Precaution Procedure

Every school should establish a standard procedure to be followed in case of enemy attack. This should be designed to take all occupants of the building to designated shelter areas as quickly as possible and with a minimum of confusion. (See Section B, "Shelter Areas," below.)

B. SHELTER AREAS

1. Essential Characteristics

a. School shelter areas are selected spaces providing the maximum, readily available protection from bomb blast and heat. In general, they should be comparatively strong-walled, heavily-roofed rooms (or corridors) located in the lower portion of the building.

b. They should embrace the least possible amount of glass and provide not less than four to six square feet of floor space for each assigned occupant.

2

c. Every area should have a minimum of two entryways and at least one emergency exit, preferably leading directly to the outside of the building.

d. Drinking water and toilet facilities should be readily available.

e. Where necessary, special provisions should be made for protection from possible dangers resulting from rupture of steam, gas and water mains.

2. *Utilization of Existing Facilities*

a. Insofar as possible, existing facilities should be used for school shelter areas.

b. New, or special, structures should be constructed only if existing facilities are considered grossly inadequate.

c. Rooms and corridors with ceilings resting on inside, rather than outside, walls should be utilized for shelter purposes.

d. Ideally, the tops and sides of such areas should be capable of withstanding "wind" pressures of roughly 100 pounds per square foot.

(For technical details see *The Effects of Atomic Weapons*, U. S. Government Printing Office, Washington 25, D. C. 1951, $1.25.)

3. *General Suggestions*

The following suggestions are offered as guides for use in the selection and preparation of shelter areas, keeping in mind the fact that safety of the children should receive *first* priority—safety of property, *second*:

a. Always take full advantage of basement spaces and interior corridors on the ground floor.

b. Areas with skylights, as well as upper floor rooms and corridors, are especially hazardous and should not be used for shelter purposes.

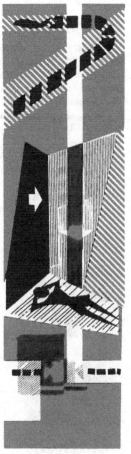

The same holds true for most auditoriums, gymnasiums and other large "open" spaces, particularly those with high, outside walls and large, or numerous, windows.

c. Boiler rooms, steam pipe "tunnels" and similar places should never be used as shelter areas.

d. Possible dangers from broken window glass may be greatly lessened by installation of wooden shutters, fine-mesh screen, or even the hanging of heavy cloth draperies.

e. Equip all shelter areas with some form of auxiliary lights which will operate entirely independent of the "regular" school power system. Small electric lanterns, or a few flashlights and extra batteries, should be sufficient.

f. A few essential hand tools (pick, shovel, crow bar, saw, etc.) should be kept in each shelter area for possible use in opening up exits blocked by debris.

g. Several small police, or referee's, whistles should be hung in each shelter area. They are ideal for calling rescue workers, if needed.

h. All shelter areas, including entrances and emergency exits, should be clearly marked.

3

4. *Small School Problems*

a. The selection of shelter areas in small school buildings, particularly those consisting of only one, two or three rooms, will often present perplexing problems. For example, there frequently may be no basement or interior corridors. Sometimes it may even appear as if it might be best for the pupils to seek shelter out-of-doors.

b. Most of our smaller schools, fortunately, are situated in the less densely populated areas where likelihood of bomb attacks is comparatively small. In such places, the greatest dangers will probably come from flying glass and from

heat. The thinnest sort of shielding, a plaster wall or even a sheet of paper, will provide protection from the bomb's heat flash.

c. Possibly the safest place for the students is crouched beneath their desks. In that position, the desk tops and sides should provide reasonable protection, not only from broken window glass, but from other flying objects as well.

d. Students should never seek safety near a stove, or directly opposite windows, where broken glass is almost sure to be blown against them.

e. Common sense should be the guiding principle followed in the selection of small school shelter areas.

C. AIR RAID WARNINGS, ALARMS AND DRILLS

1. *School Air Raid Warning*

a. Every school should make arrangements through local civil defense authorities to receive the earliest possible Air Raid Warning. Each school should participate in all civil defense communication tests and practice alerts in its own area.

b. In most communities, the first warning of attack will come to the school by telephone. Some schools, in turn, may be asked to help "fan out" the warning by telephoning to one or more additional schools.

2. *Telephone Warning Chain*

a. Answering the telephone AT ONCE must become a safety habit in every school building. Where children answer the telephone, they must be instructed to call the nearest adult to the telephone AT ONCE for any emergency call.

b. The telephone warning plan should be tested periodically. When it is used for testing purposes, the words "This is a telephone test call" must be the first and last words spoken. The person who answers the telephone must repeat these words before hanging up.

c. A written record of the nature and time of receipt of all communications through the established warning chain should be kept.

3. *School Alarms and Signals*

a. The following signals are suggested:
(1) A series of six short rings repeated at least once. This signal can be given on classroom, hall, basement and yard bells.
(2) The ALL-CLEAR signal is two long rings on the same bells.

b. *The fire alarm signal must not be used to signal air raid alarms.*

4

c. Sufficient practice must be given to make certain that all members of the school promptly recognize the difference between air raid signals and other school signals.

4. Suggestions for Teachers

a. March class promptly to assigned shelter area.

b. Take roll call sheet, or class roster to shelter area.

c. Avoid windows.

d. Provide some form of mental activity for children. (See Part Two, Section C, 3, page 10.)

e. Remain in shelter for further directions or ALL-CLEAR signal.

f. Stay with children until properly relieved.

5. Auxiliary Staff Members

a. Supervisors, medical staff members, attendance officers, and all other school officials should report to stations designated by the administrator.

b. Maintenance workers, custodians, cooks, etc., should also have assigned drill locations and duties.

6. Physically Handicapped Children

a. Adequate provision should be made for physically handicapped children. Special plans for the care of these pupils, as well as those in school infirmaries, should be drawn up immediately.

b. An up-to-date list of handicapped children should be kept. The school medical inspector or the nurse could assist in preparing this list, and in planning for their necessary care.

7. Use of Elevators

a. In all emergencies and drills, elevators should be used only for the immediate carrying of physically handicapped children to the floors where shelter areas are located. Elevators should then be run to the lowest level of the elevator shaft and left there.

b. Operators should then proceed to their assigned shelter areas.

8. Suggestions for Custodians and Building Engineers

a. Air Raid Precautions "Advance Notice"

(1) Stop fuel supply to boilers.

(2) Allow plant to remain in operation under normal conditions except all fires are closed down.

(3) Allow all vacuum pumps to operate and bring back condensate as rapidly as possible.

(4) Turn off all open-flame gas devices (except automatic heaters).

(5) Allow water supply to remain in normal operating condition.

(6) When time has lapsed up to the time of "Short Notice", close down heating plant completely with the exception of operating the return condensate pump. If it is not possible to operate pumps separately, shut them down.

(7) Following an explosion, make thorough inspection of building immediately, both inside and outside.

b. Air Raid Precautions "Short Notice"

(1) Stop fuel supply to boilers.

(2) Pull power switch, or switches, controlling ventilating fans.

(3) Close main header valves and stop all steam engines driving ventilating fans.

(4) Stop air compressor and bleed main air pressure tank.

(5) Keep boiler room watch from safe location nearby.

5

Credits

"Last Testament" by Carol Amen reprinted by permission of *St. Anthony Messenger*, originally published in Vol. 88, Sept. 1980, p. 38.

"The Last of the Deliveries" by Poul Anderson. Published by permission of The Trigonier Trust c/o The Lotts Agency, Ltd.

"Some Pigs in Sailor Suits" by Roger Angell. Used by permission of John Henry Angell.

"To Pay the Piper" by James Blish, copyright © 1956, 1983 by The Estate of James Blish; first appeared in *IF*; reprinted by permission of the author's Estate and the Estate's agents, the Virginia Kidd Agency, Inc.

"There Will Come Soft Rains" by Ray Bradbury. Reprinted by permission of Don Congdon Associates, Inc. Copyright ©1950 by Ray Bradbury; renewed 1977 by Ray Bradbury.

Croutch, Leslie A. Permission to reprint "The Day the Bomb Fell," from *Amazing Stories*, ©November 1950, granted by John Robert Colombo, editor of *Years of Light: A Celebration of Leslie A. Croutch* (1982).

"Foster, You're Dead" ©1955, 1987 by the Estate of Phillip K. Dick from *Philip K. Dick's Electric Dreams*. Collection copyright ©2017 by The Estate of Philip K. Dick. Used by permission of HarperCollins Publishers.

"After the Sirens" by Hugh Hood. Used by permission of the Hugh Hood Estate.

"A Bad Day for Sales" by Fritz Leiber. Reprinted by permission of Richard Curtis Associates.

"That Only a Mother," copyright ©1948, 1976 by Judith Merril; first appeared in *Astounding Science Fiction;* reprinted by permission of the author's Estate and the Estate's agents, the Virginia Kidd Agency, Inc.

Bibliographic Information

Amen, Carol. "Last Testament." *Ellery Queen,* April 1987; 87-97.

Anderson, Poul. "The Last of the Deliveries." *The Magazine of Fantasy and Science Fiction,* February 1958, Vol. 14, No. 2; 85-95.

Angell, Roger. "Some Pigs in Sailor Suits." *The New Yorker,* April 13, 1946, 31-34.

Angus, Douglas. "About Time to Go South." *The Magazine of Fantasy and Science Fiction,* October 1957, Vol. 13, No. 4; 95-101.

Bermel, Albert. "The End of the Race." *Galaxy Magazine.* April 1964, Vol. 22, No. 4; 127-130.

Blish, James. "To Pay the Piper." *IF: Worlds of Science Fiction.* February 1956., Vol. 6, No. 2; 39-51.

Bloch, Robert. "Daybroke." *Star Science Fiction.* Jan. 1958; 68-77.

Bradbury, Ray. "There Will Come Soft Rains," *The Martian Chronicles.* William Morrow, 2011; 248-256.

Cloete, Stuart "The Blast," Part 1. *Collier's.* April 12, 1947; 11-14 & 59-71.

Cloete, Stuart "The Blast," Part 2. *Collier's.* April 19, 1947; 19 & 69-87.

Crouch, Leslie "The Day the Bomb Fell." *Amazing Stories.* Nov. 1950, Vol 24, No.11; 100-107.

Dick, Philip K. "Foster, You're Dead." *Star Science Fiction Stories No. 3.* Ballentine Books, 1954; 64-85.

Hood, Hugh. "After the Sirens." *Esquire.* August 1960.

Leiber, Fritz. "A Bad Day for Sales." *Galaxy Science Fiction.* July 1953, Vol. 6, No. 4; 112-119.

Merril, Judith. "That Only a Mother." *Astounding Science Fiction,* June 1948, Vol. XLI, No. 4; 88-95.

Philips, Rog. "Atom War." *Amazing Stories.* May 1946, Vol 20, No.2; 74-91.

Silverberg, Robert. "Road to Nightfall." *Fantastic Universe.* July 1958, Vol. 10, No. 1.

Tenn William."Generation of Noah," originally published as "The Quick And The Bomb." *Suspense,* Spring 1951; 66-76.

Thomas, Theodore. "Day of Succession." *Astounding Science Fiction,* August 1959, Vol. LXIV, No. 6; 66-76

Venable, Lynn. "Time Enough at Last." *IF: Worlds of Science Fiction.* January 1953, Vol 1, No. 6; 95-99.

Wylie, Philip. "Blunder. " *Collier's.* January 12, 1946; 11-12 & 63-64.

Further Reading Suggestions

Nonfiction:

Bradley, David. *No Place To Hide.* Little, Brown & Company, New York, 1948.

Brians, Paul. *Nuclear Holocausts: Atomic War in Fiction 1895-1984.* Kent State University Press, 1987.

Garrison, Lee. *Bracing for Armageddon.* Oxford University Press, New York, 2006.

Hersey, John. *Hiroshima.* Alfred A. Knopf, Inc., New York, 1946.

Rose, Kenneth D. *One Nation Underground.* New York University Press, New York, 2001.

Scheibach, Michael. *"In Case Atom Bombs Fall": An Anthology of Governmental Explanations, Instructions and Warnings from the 1940s to the 1960s.* McFarland And Co., Jefferson, NC, 2009.

Stonier, Tom. *Nuclear Disaster.* Meridian Books, New York, 1963.

Welsome, Eileen. *The Plutonium Files.* The Dial Press, New York, 1999.

Wendt, Gerald & Geddes, Donald Porter, Eds. *The Atomic Age Opens.* The World Publishing Company, New York, 1945.

Novels:

Burdick, Eugene & Wheeler, Harvey. *Fail Safe.* McGraw-Hill Book Co., Inc., New York, 1962.

Foster, Richard. *The Rest Must Die.* Gold Medal Books, New York, 1959

Frank, Pat. *Alas Babylon.* J.B. Lippincott, New York, 1959.

Merril, Judith. *Shadow on the Hearth.* Doubleday & Company, Inc., New York, 1950.

Roshwald, Mordecai. *Level 7*. McGraw-Hill Book Co., Inc, New York, 1959.

Rein, Harold. *Few Were Left*. The John Day Company, New York, 1955.

Shute, Nevil. *On the Beach*. William Morrow and Co., New York, 1957.

Van Vogt, A.E. *Empire of the Atom*. Macfadden Books, New York, 1966.

Wylie, Philip. *The Smuggled Atom Bomb*. Lancer Books, Inc, New York, 1965.

Wylie, Philip. *Tomorrow!* Rinehart & Co., Inc, New York, 1954.

Wylie, Philip. *Triumph*. Doubleday & Co., Inc, New York, 1963.